Due to illness, Jean Plaidy was unable to go to school regularly and so taught herself to read. Very early on she developed a passion for the 'past'. After doing a shorthand typing course, she spent a couple of years doing various jobs, including sorting gems in Hatton Garden and translating for foreigners in a City café. She began writing in earnest following marriage and now has a large number of historical novels to her name. Inspiration for her books is drawn from odd sources – a picture gallery, a line from a book, Shakespeare's inconsistencies. She lives in London and loves music, second-hand book shops and ancient buildings. Jean Plaidy also writes under the pseudonym of Victoria Holt.

D0280074

Jean Plaidy

The third book in the Georgian Saga

Caroline, the Queen

Pan Books London and Sydney

First published 1968 by Robert Hale and Company
This edition published 1975 by Pan Books Ltd,
Cavaye Place, London SW10 9PG
© Jean Plaidy 1968
Text decorations by B. S. Biro
ISBN 0 330 24550 3

Printed and bound in England by
Hazell Watson & Viney Ltd, Aylesbury, Bucks

Contents

The transformation scene   7

The late King's will   31

Coronation   41

The Queen's secret   59

'You may strut, Dapper George'   67

The marriage plot   74

Frederick's homecoming   92

Regency   105

Statesmen quarrel   121

Lord Fanny   134

The Prince's mistress   165

Musical interlude   185

Sarah Churchill's bargain   197

Walpole in danger   212

A royal marriage   231

The end of a habit   250

Court scandals   261

The Prince and his mistress   293

The King's temper   309

The Prince's bride   323

The King's absence   336

Accouchement at midnight   361

The secret betrayed   374

Bibliography

Lord Hervey's Memoirs Edited by Romney Sedgwick

Caroline the Illustrious, 2 vols. W. H. Wilkins, MA, FSA

Caroline of Ansbach R. L. Arkell

Caroline of England Peter Quennell

George II and his Ministers Reginald Lucas

Sir Robert Walpole J. H. Plumb

Lives of the Queens of England of the House of Hanover, 2 vols.
  Dr Doran, FSA

The Four Georges Sir Charles Petrie, MA

The House of Hanover Alvin Redman

The Dictionary of National Biography Edited by Sir Leslie
  Stephen and Sir Sidney Lee

History of the Four Georges and William IV Justin McCarthy

The Four Georges W. M. Thackeray

British History John Wade

History of England William Hickman Smith Aubrey

England Under the Hanoverians Sir Charles Grant Robertson

Eighteenth-Century London Life Rosamund Baynes Powell

Letters of Lady Mary Wortley Montagu

Notes on British History William Edwards

A History of Everyday Things in England, 1500–1799 Marjorie
  and Peter Quennell

George II

The transformation scene

The Prince of Wales lay on his back, snoring. To sleep after a heavy meal in the middle of the day was a custom he had brought with him from Hanover. This was no light afternoon nap; but like everything the Prince did it was performed with precision. He lived by the clock; there was a time for eating, for sleeping, for doing business, and even for making love. In fact, throughout the court his habits were a joke of which he was ignorant; but his wife, who had made it her first duty to discover as much as she could of what was going on around her, was well aware of this.

Poor George Augustus, although he was more popular than his father, the King, who could not speak a word of English, appealed strongly to the people's ridicule. He was choleric and a lack of inches had made him ready to assert his importance; his quarrels with his father, his habit of walking up and down outside his mistress's apartments, watch in hand, that he might visit her at exactly the appointed time, had provided material for the lampooners who frequented the city's coffee houses and taverns and seemed to be of the opinion that the royal family's chief duty was to amuse its subjects.

But on this hot June afternoon when the bees buzzed busily in the lavender which formed the sweet-scented border in the flower gardens of Richmond Lodge, the Prince slept, unaware that it was to be one of the most important days in his life.

Close by in her apartments Caroline Princess of Wales was knotting, an occupation she favoured because it kept the hands busy while the brain was not in the least concerned with the thread in her hands.

So hot! she thought. And on these hot days she felt fatigued nowadays. It was something she never admitted to others but occasionally in the privacy of her own apartments she faced the fact that her health was not what she would wish it to be. The subject was like a threatening cloud – not overhead at the moment – just perhaps a shadow on the horizon; but it was there, and each week she fancied it was a little bigger.

Of course, she told herself angrily, I'm perfectly healthy.

Women had these troubles. After all she had had seven children, and a few miscarriages. Louisa, the youngest child, was now three, and it had been after her birth that the trouble had started. It frightened her, for an internal rupture could be a dangerous and humiliating affliction, and she was terrified that someone would discover her secret. George Augustus had once been aware of it. He hated illness in those around him. She supposed it reminded him that he too was not immortal.

'It will clear up,' she had told him. 'It is nothing . . . it happens after a difficult childbirth now and then.'

He had accepted that; and she had been fortunate in being able to hide from him the pain she felt. She wondered, though, whether he was later aware of it and preferred to pretend, as she did, that it did not exist.

Henrietta Howard was sitting in the ante-chamber now with Charlotte Clayton, no doubt dozing, but ready to come in at precisely the right moment when they would prepare the Princess for her husband's visit.

Henrietta was George Augustus's mistress, but the affair was certainly not one of tempestuous passion. He had selected her long ago in Hanover whither she had come to seek her fortune, and it was merely because he believed he ought to have a mistress that he had chosen her. At that time he had been very content with his wife. Now of course he had other mistresses, but she always believed it was to prove to these cynical observers his immense virility rather than due to any overriding passion. However, Henrietta remained – a habit. Yet a man who made love with his eye on the clock could not really be seriously involved.

The Princess smiled fondly. She felt affectionate towards her little man; her position was a difficult one, but she knew how to keep it tenable. He was fond of her, for he was a sentimental man; he was proud of her, for she was a good-looking woman; there was one quality which she must not make too obvious and that was her intelligence, for George Augustus was not the man to tolerate a woman who was known to be cleverer than himself. But it was not beyond the wit of a clever woman to hide her cleverness. It had been done in the past and would be done again. She in any case had been successfully doing it for many years.

She dismissed her fears. The King was in Hanover. Long might he stay there. What a pleasure to have the old ogre out of the country. She believed that if he would only stay away for a year, she and George Augustus would wean any affection the people had for the King completely from him. He was a silly old man in many respects. He did not appreciate this country which had fallen into his lap like ripe fruit from a tree. He preferred his little Hanover principality to this great kingdom, Herrenhausen to Hampton, the old Leine Schloss to St James's. He, with his German speech and his German habits, kept his two German mistresses whom he had brought with him thirteen years ago from Hanover; they were the delight of the people because surely they must be the two ugliest women in the country and did such good service to the writers of lampoons. But the King did occasionally show an interest in English women. There was that saucy creature, Anne Brett, who was at this moment giving herself such airs at St James's Palace and would doubtless receive her title and coronet when her lover returned to England. But it was Ermengarda Schulemburg who had accompanied him to Hanover – Ermengarda, now Duchess of Kendal, the mistress who was like a wife to him and with whom, some said, he had even gone through a form of marriage in the last year or so since he had heard of the death of George Augustus's mother in the prison of Ahlden in which he had placed her.

There was such joy in contemplating his absence.

He despised George Augustus, but she happened to know that he had far more respect for the Princess of Wales than he had for the Prince. That meant, though, that he was more watchful of her than of his son; and she had had to be very careful, knowing him for the vindictive man he was. She would never forget what he had done to his wife – the mother-in-law whom she had never met – because she was guilty of one infidelity. He had not only divorced her but sent her to a dreary exile which had lasted thirty years and had such a short while ago ended.

From her first days at Hanover she had realized that she must never put herself in a position similar to that of her unfortunate mother-in-law.

Not that she ever would. Sophia Dorothea must have been a foolish, frivolous creature; Caroline would never be that.

She yawned and looked at the clock. Not yet three. Another hour before the Prince came to her apartment and they took their walk together in the gardens. He was a great walker and so had she been before she had begun to feel this affliction – slight, she insisted, and something many women suffered from. She fancied there was a little gout in her feet. She shuddered, remembering the stories she had heard of the King's predecessor, Queen Anne, who had so often had to be carried in her chair to important functions.

Anne had been the Queen and Caroline, though she might one day bear that proud title, would be but a Queen Consort, and that was very different from a Queen Regnant. Very different indeed. For when a Queen Consort depended on the whims of a choleric little husband she would have to be very careful.

Yet she was recognized for a clever woman. Prime Minister Walpole was more respectful now, although she knew he had once referred to her as 'that fat beast, the Prince's wife'; but he was aware that the day would come when he would wish to be in the good books of *Queen* Caroline, and she herself knew that when that day came she would need his services. They understood each other. He had disappointed her at that time when he had patched up the quarrel between George Augustus and herself on one side and the King on the other, because although he had promised that he would see that the King gave over the guardianship of her elder children to her, he had not done this. Still, she understood he was the shrewdest man in England and he was one whom she would want as her chief minister.

The thread fell from her hands and she dozed.

She awoke startled.

'Henrietta! Charlotte!'

'Your Highness . . .'

'Vot is this?' In spite of all the time she had been in England she still spoke with a German accent and was apt to express herself quaintly. 'Vot is this clatter?'

'Someone has arrived, Your Highness,' said Henrietta.

The Princess yawned.

'It is better to be dressed now,' she said. 'I vill not then keep the Prince vaiting ven he comes. Go to the vindow and see who is coming.'

Henrietta moved to the window. She walked with grace though she was not exactly a beautiful woman; her fine but abundant hair was her greatest beauty; but she was ageing, thought the Princess, and lately she had become so deaf that she could seem almost stupid – which was far from the truth. Caroline was sure that the Prince only performed his precision love-making as a habit.

'It is Sir Robert Walpole, Your Highness,' said Henrietta.

'Vot can bring him here at this hour,' wondered Caroline. 'Come, it is vell I am dressed.'

Sir Robert Walpole had been working in the study of his Chelsea house when the messenger arrived. He knew whence he came and that he could only bring news of the utmost importance.

The King was in Hanover and Walpole's brother-in-law, Lord Townshend, was in attendance there; it was from Townshend that the messenger came.

Walpole lifted his unwieldy body from the chair and went to meet the messenger. Prepared as he was for important news he could not suppress an exclamation of dismay as he read that King George I had died of a seizure on his way to Osnabrück.

He steadied himself, summoned a servant, gave orders that the messenger should be provided with refreshment, but first his coach must be made ready for a journey and brought to his door, and called to his valet that he might be suitably and immediately dressed for a solemn occasion.

As his orders were obeyed he was saying to himself: this could well be the end. But at the very same time he was telling himself that he would not allow it to be. Walpole was not so easily defeated.

So, he mused, the little fellow is now the King. George the First is dead. Long live George the Second.

He must be the first to say so. That was the immediate necessity. Townshend would know that well enough and not have sent the news to anyone else.

By the time he was ready to leave the house his carriage was waiting to take him from Chelsea to Richmond.

'It has to be quick,' he told the coachman. 'Not a minute to be lost.'

The coachman understood.

'Change horses half way,' ordered Walpole, 'but make them work.'

He sat back against the upholstery and pictured the scene at Richmond. It was what many had been waiting for, but no one had suspected it would come just yet. The old King, although he had suffered a couple of seizures, had seemed as if he were going on for a very long time. Walpole wished he had; they had been on good terms.

And not dissimilar in character, mused Walpole. Both gross in habit, crude in speech, and lacking in culture. Walpole laughed aloud, and his laughter reminded him that there was one difference: he was a merry man; the late King had been a dour one.

How, he asked himself, am I going to ingratiate myself with the little fellow? I should have begun to woo him earlier, of course. But his father wouldn't pay his debts and it is the Princess who is important. And the Princess? Well at least we understand each other. She's a clever woman and I've always known it. Not like that fool, Townshend, paying attention to Henrietta Howard and ignoring the Princess . . . beg her pardon, the Queen.

Queen Caroline! She would be the one to cultivate; for as long as she could convince the little man that he ruled her she would be able to do what she wanted with him. Together we will rule England, thought Walpole. And you, little man, will not prevent us . . . providing of course that Madame Caroline will stand with me.

Would she? Ah, there was the point. He had called her a fat beast at one time, and she had heard of it. Politicians should guard their tongues, which was not always easy when a politician's tongue was both his best friend and his worst enemy.

That reminded him – what he said to the new King would be of the utmost importance. His tongue was going to have to be very clever to extricate himself from this delicate situation.

He looked out of the window. He knew every inch of the road to Richmond, for recently he had acquired the Rangership of Richmond Park and had bought the Old Lodge. This he had made into his home . . . his real home where Maria Skerrett waited for him; and every week-end he spent there with her and their two-year-old daughter rejuvenated him. It was strange to him, this feeling he had for Maria. He had never been a sentimental man until he had met her; his marriage had been a failure from the beginning, although when he had married Catherine, daughter of Sir John Shorter, Lord Mayor of London, she had seemed an ideal choice, being both beautiful and wealthy. Long ago he had gone his own way, she had gone hers; she was extravagant in manners and money. Her lovers were numerous and rumour had it – and Walpole had never given himself the trouble of attempting to discover the truth of this – that the Prince of Wales himself had been among them.

Walpole had lived heartily, drinking, hunting the fox and women, seeking power; he had liked to boast of his exploits with women; his conversation at table was coarse in the extreme and his accounts were accompanied by the loud laughter which shook his unwieldy frame. But he never joked about Maria

Skerrett; he never mentioned her; she had shown him a new way of life which never ceased to make him marvel.

Even now as the coach rattled along the rough roads and he was thinking of the interview with the new King which could be so momentous as to mean the end of his career as a politician of importance, he was consoling himself that if he should fail he would be content to live quietly with Maria and little Molly.

The coach had stopped. The horses would have to be changed; they were exhausted.

'Then hurry,' shouted Walpole.

He closed his eyes. No one must be there before him. That would never do. He saw himself arriving late and the Prince already transformed into a king. A minute before he had thought he would be happy living quietly at the Old Lodge or Houghton in Norfolk with Maria. No, he was a politician, an ambitious man, and could not throw aside his main reason for living and expect to find contentment. Maria provided the solace, the respite, the haven – the real flavour of life was power.

They were off again. And in due course they had arrived at Richmond.

He went to the Lodge and shouted to the guard that he wished to be conducted to the Prince without delay, but he did not wait to be conducted, and he made his way to the royal apartments.

The Duchess of Dorset who happened to be in waiting, hearing the commotion of his arrival, came to the door of the royal suite to remind him that the Prince was sleeping, the Princess resting, and that as it was only three o'clock the time had not yet arrived for waking them.

'Nevertheless they must be awakened. I have important news.'

'Sir Robert, the Prince is *undressed*. It is his practice at this hour . . .'

'I know His Highness's practices, but I tell you there must be no delay. Tell him I have come. Tell him I have news of the utmost importance. Tell him I must see him without delay.'

The Duchess looked dubious; but Sir Robert clearly must be obeyed.

She lifted her shoulders slightly and leaving Walpole impatiently in the ante-room called to one of the Prince's attendants and told him to awaken His Highness as Sir Robert Walpole was waiting to give him news which could not be delayed.

George Augustus sat up in bed; his first impulse was to look at the clock.

'Vot is this?' he shouted. 'It is but three o'clock.'

'Your Highness, Sir Robert Walpole is waiting to speak to you. He said it is a matter of the utmost importance.'

'It should vait,' snapped the Prince, always bad tempered to have a habit broken. 'I haf not my sleep finished.'

'Your Highness, Sir Robert was most insistent.'

'Sir Robert!' growled the Prince. He was not very pleased with that man. He had not done what he promised when he had attempted to patch up the quarrel between the Prince and his father. He had made slighting remarks about the Prince's abilities to act as Regent. And such remarks had been carried back to His Highness by Sir Robert's enemies. George Augustus was like his father in the fact that he never forgave a slight. 'That man should take care . . .'

'Your Highness . . .'

'I know . . . I know. I vill to him go. I vill to him tell I must not be disturbed at this hour.'

The Prince rose from his bed, picked up his wig which had been placed on a table nearby and crammed it on his head. His valet sprang forward but he waved him aside.

He stood in his underwear, a little man with a fresh complexion now ruddy from annoyance, his bulbous blue eyes blazing with anger.

His valet would have helped him into his breeches, but the Prince snatched them from him and it was at this moment that Walpole, who had determined to wait no longer, came into the room.

The bulging blue eyes glared at the minister, but Walpole had sunk to his knees, taken the hand which held the breeches and said: 'Sire, your father, King George the First, is dead. You are now the King of England.'

'Vot!' cried George Augustus.

'Your Majesty's father is dead.'

'That is von big lie!'

'Indeed not, Your Majesty. I have a letter here from Lord Townshend. Your father, King George, has had a seizure and died on the way to Osnabrück.'

'Let me see this!' George Augustus snatched the letter and, dropping his breeches, held it with both hands.

'Mein Gott,' he whispered. 'Then it is so!'

'Your Majesty.'

The new King stared at Sir Robert without seeing him. Already there was a new arrogance, Walpole noticed. The transformation from powerless Prince, kept deliberately in the background by a father who despised him, to King of England, was taking place.

This one could be more difficult to handle than his father, thought Walpole.

'As Your Majesty's minister I would have your orders,' said Walpole quietly; and he felt that the very clock on which the King set such store, not because it was a valuable piece, which it undoubtedly was, but because it registered all-important time, had stopped, waiting for what would happen next, for the following seconds could reveal whether the King would keep his father's trusted minister.

The moment dragged on. What was going on behind the prominent blue eyes? Was the new King remembering past discrepancies? What had he, Walpole, said when, as Prince of Wales, George Augustus had sought the Regency during his father's absence from England? 'He doesn't deserve it. We've done enough for him; and if it were to be done again we would not do so much.' Such remarks were apt to be carried back, and these Guelphs were vindictive by nature. They never forgot a slight.

Walpole could see that the King was remembering.

It came: 'My orders?' he said. The blue eyes narrowed. His mind was ranging over his ministers and his choice fell on a favourite of his, Sir Spencer Compton. He shouted: 'You vill go to Chiswick, Sir Robert, and take your orders from Sir Spencer Compton.'

Walpole bowed. This was the end. The verdict had been given. He was dismissed. He had been right to guess that the new King would want to settle old scores. Take his orders from Spencer Compton. It was an insult.

But there was nothing to do but bow himself out.

The new King looked at the clock.

'It is not time yet to rise, I vill finish my sleep,' he said; and as Walpole made his way to Chiswick, the King went back to bed.

Charlotte Clayton, flushed scarlet, came into the Queen's chamber.

'Your Majesty!' she cried.

Caroline was on her feet.

'It's true. I heard every word. The King died on his way to Osnabrück.'

'Dead!' whispered Caroline. Her eyes were brilliant. The tyrant removed. The way clear. 'I must go to the . . . to the King.' She spoke the words triumphantly.

'He has returned to bed, Your Majesty. The time for rising has not yet come.'

Charlotte was laughing at him. Never mind. It *was* ridiculous of him. He was a King and he went to bed to finish his nap!

She walked past the woman and into his bedchamber.

He was certainly not sleeping.

'I have heard.'

'That you are Queen of England?'

'That you are the King.'

He got out of bed. 'Vell,' he said, 'that old rogue has gone at last. I thought never vould he die.'

'And you, George Augustus, are now the King. That is von thing he cannot stop.'

'He can stop nothing now . . . the old scoundrel.'

'Ve should be on our way to Leicester House. There vill be so much to do.'

'I have dismissed that fat ox Valpole. He vill now know he has been von fool.'

Caroline was alarmed. Walpole may have abused her and her

husband at times; he may not have kept his promises; but they needed brilliant men about them if they were to rule wisely and safely; and she believed Walpole to be the most astute politician of his day.

'Dat is von pity,' she declared.

'Vot you say?'

'He vill be your enemy.'

'But I am the King now. It is not for me to fear men, but for them to fear me.'

'He is clever.'

'And I am von fool?'

She had gone too far. She would have to be even more careful now.

'You vill be such a king as the English never have before had. They vill be vishing to see you now.'

He smiled at her. He was very fond of her. She was his good and docile wife. Occasionally he must reprove her for her tendency to instruct. But she was a good woman, a good wife; and she knew who was her master.

'Then,' he said, 'together vill ve go. The King and the Queen.'

'I must not forget,' she said, 'that I must be in mourning . . . just a little. For ven there is a new king an old one must die.'

It was a warning to him. Accept your subjects' homage, yes; but do not show too blatantly how delighted you are by your father's death. It's true that you are, but it might appear unseemly. Even the most cynical people honour the dead for fear there should be some truth in the belief that they sometimes return.

'No,' he said, 'this you must not forget.'

She had made her point; now she would go to her apartments; her woman should dress her. In what? She wondered. Black bombazine. That would be discreet and black was becoming to her fair skin.

She would ride through the streets; the people would be pleased; these English were always pleased at the prospect of revels; and a new king meant a coronation.

And while she rode she would be thinking of how she could

make the new King see that he must not dismiss his most brilliant statesman for the sake of settling old grudges.

The news was spreading quickly through the city. The apprentices scarcely waited for their masters' permission to run into the streets; the merchants were close on their heels; from windows women leaned out shouting to each other.

The new King and Queen were coming this way.

The ballad-singers were at every corner; there was not a sedan-chair to be had for the nobility were all on their way to Leicester House to pay quick homage. They were part of the jostling crowds which filled the streets about Leicester Fields to which it was believed the new rulers would make their way.

The habitually noisy streets were now deafening with shouts and cries; the tin trumpets of the newsmen were heard now and then above the babel; the long brooms of the crossing sweepers had become formidable weapons; the gingerbread woman was doing good business in contrast to the knife and scissors grinder whose services nobody wanted on a day such as this. Old Colly-Molly-Puff the pieman had sold out his trayful and was fighting his way back to his home for more; the pickpockets were busy and the crowd was screaming with laughter at the man whose wig had been stolen, he couldn't tell how; but those in the know understood that the man who was carrying a small boy on his shoulder might know something of its whereabouts, for the small boy carried a basket and it was very likely that the wig had been whipped off its owner's head and placed in that basket and was now being carried fast to the wigmaker who would pay a good price for it. The little shoe-black was almost crushed to death; the even smaller chimney-sweep could see nothing either. But at least they were part of the merry, roistering street scene which had become charged with a new hilarity and excitement because the old King was dead and a new reign was about to begin.

And then there was a shout for silence.

'They're coming. They're coming.'

And there was the carriage with the little King in his tall wig and a touch of mourning, looking solemn yet secretly delighted, as well he might, for everyone knew how his father had hated and humiliated him – and now old George was dead and here was young George to take his place.

He was a German too, but at least he knew how to smile and he could speak English – after a fashion. He was fond of England, which was more than his old father had been; and he had a wife living with him and giving him children. The old one had had a wife too, but he'd treated her badly so it was said, sent her into exile because she took a lover. Who could blame her after taking one look at George! And there was the old man making no secret of his scandalous relationship with his two comic German mistresses, known in the London crowds as the Maypole and the Elephant – one tall and thin, the other short and fat, both old, both ugly – and a few young and pretty ones to make a bit of variety. That was all very well. It gave them something to laugh at; but they'd never liked German George; and they were prepared to like this George, who seemed half English anyway.

And the Queen? Yes, they had an affection for the Queen. She was always affable; she loved the English, she said; she'd rather live on a dunghill in England than return to Hanover. That was what they liked to hear. When she had walked – and she walked often – she would talk to anyone she met and however humble they were, she would show an interest in them and their lives. Moreover, they had been sorry for her when the old King took her children from her and only allowed her to see them when he permitted it.

A cheer for the Queen.

So, on through the streets to Leicester House rode the new King and Queen.

In St James's Palace three girls were impatiently awaiting a summons.

Anne, the eldest, who was eighteen, had always dominated her sisters and now she announced that it could not be long before they were sent for.

'This will make all the difference to us. We shall no longer be kept here like children. We shall live gaily as princesses should.'

Amelia who was two years younger than her sister Anne clasped her hands together and gazed up at the ceiling. 'Husbands will be found for us,' she murmured.

Anne looked at her critically and Caroline, the youngest, being only fourteen, always took her cue from Anne.

'Husbands, of course,' said Anne. 'But I shall only accept a king. Nothing less will do for me.'

'Do you think they will find enough kings for us all?' asked Caroline.

'Of course,' snapped Anne. 'But because of The Quarrel nothing has been done. Now you will see how different everything is going to be.'

'Mamma will be delighted to have us back with her,' said Caroline. 'And how glad I shall be! It'll be wonderful to live under the same roof with them . . . as we always should have – but for Grandfather.'

'I'm not sure that it will be wonderful,' put in Amelia slowly.

The others turned to her. Amelia was the beauty of the family; she had inherited a little of the Stuart features and she had her mother's fine complexion and abundant hair; she lacked Anne's arrogance and was healthier than Caroline.

'But why not?' asked Caroline.

'I am not sure of Papa. The things one has heard . . .'

Anne burst out laughing. 'Oh, Papa is a vain little man. Everyone knows it. But Mamma is well respected.'

'Anne,' cried Caroline, shocked, 'you are talking of the King.'

The two elder girls began to laugh.

'It's true,' said Anne. 'That is what makes life suddenly exciting. Old Grandpapa is dead and Papa is King. *We* are more important because believe me it is better to be the daughters of a king than the granddaughters of one.'

'We shall all be together,' said Caroline. 'The whole family . . .'

'Don't hope for too much,' warned Amelia.

'Well, we shall join our brother and sisters – but young Mary and Louisa are just silly babies,' said Anne.

'They could hardly be much else being four and three,' put in Amelia.

'So very much younger than we are!' sighed Caroline.

'As for William, everyone knows that he is a spoilt little beast.'

'Mamma adores him, I believe.'

'And Papa.'

'Idiot! Papa adores no one but himself. He flies into a temper if his pages don't powder his periwig as he likes it; and he goes round the Palace complaining because the housemaid has put a chair in the wrong place. This, my sisters, is your future King.'

Caroline giggled obediently as she always did when Anne expected it; but Amelia said: 'And you should be careful. We were spied on before . . . how much more so we shall be now.'

'Let them spy. We're the King's daughters now.'

'But Papa would be very angry if he heard you. You know how he always has to be flattered.'

'Never fear, I shall do the flattering when it's needed, but I must have the joy of saying what I really think behind his back.'

Caroline laughed obediently and Anne smiled, acknowledging her appreciation.

'It's natural that Mamma should love William; after all he's a boy,' said Caroline.

'Which reminds me,' put in Anne, 'our eldest brother will soon be here. They're bound to send for Fred.'

'Fred!' mused Amelia. 'I wonder what he's like.'

'A horrid little German, you can be sure.'

'Well, he has spent all his life in Hanover.'

'Poor Fred!' sighed Caroline. 'They call him Fritz over there.'

'I've no doubt he's a regular little Fritz.'

'You must not make yourself hate him before you see him, Anne,' warned Amelia.

'I don't have to make myself. I do already.'

'But why?'

'Imagine him. He was seven years old when Papa and Mamma left Hanover and they haven't seen him since.'

'What would he be now?' asked Caroline.

'Over twenty . . . nearly twenty-one,' said Anne. 'He's two years older than I.'

'Do you remember him, Anne?'

She narrowed her eyes. 'Yes, I think I do . . . a little. He was very spoilt. He had rickets for a long time and couldn't walk . . . but that was before I was born. They called him Fritzchen and it was quite sickening the fuss they all made of him.'

'So you were jealous?' asked Amelia.

'Of course. I wanted to be the eldest . . . and a boy . . . so that in time I could be Prince of Wales. Then Queen Anne died and Grandpapa came to England and after a while Mamma brought us girls, but Grandpapa wouldn't allow Fritzchen to come. He had to stay behind and look after Hanover.'

'What, at seven?' asked Amelia.

'He was a figurehead. Grandpapa was quite fond of Fritzchen, which is saying something, for he wasn't fond of anyone else . . . except the poor old Maypole. I wonder what she is doing now.'

'I'm sorry for her,' said Amelia. 'It must be terrible to be a king's mistress and be important and then suddenly he dies . . . and nobody cares about you any more.'

'Don't worry about *her*. She looked after herself very well, I'm sure.'

'I wasn't thinking about money. It's rather strange that a man like Grandpapa could be faithful to a woman like that – for all those years. And she was terribly ugly too. I heard she was almost bald under that awful red wig.'

'He wasn't exactly faithful. That reminds me. Mistress Anne Brett must be feeling very sorry for herself. Do you know she threatened to speak to Grandpapa about *me* because I wouldn't allow her to alter the arrangement of this palace. What is she thinking now, do you imagine?'

'She's busily packing and preparing to leave, I'll swear,' said Amelia.

Anne threw back her head and laughed. Caroline did the same.

'It's a small matter,' said Amelia. 'Scarcely worth feeling triumphant about. The point is that everything will be different for us. Our parents will come here . . . we shall all be together. Instead of being two separate families, there'll be one. The family will be reunited; we shall be with our little brother and sisters. And Fred will most certainly come home.'

'When?' asked Caroline.

'Very soon. After all he is Prince of Wales now. Fancy that! Fritz who has never set foot in England is Prince of Wales.'

'I know why you hate him,' said Amelia. 'You would like to be Prince of Wales.'

'How could I be?'

'You could be Princess of Wales,' said Caroline. 'And if there were no boys . . .'

Anne stood up and raised her eyes almost ecstatically to the ceiling.

'Do you know,' she said, 'if I could be Queen of England, if only for one day, I'd be willing to die the next.'

'Anne!'

'It's true,' she declared. 'And I'm sure I'd make a better ruler than Fritz . . . or Papa . . . or Grandpapa. There was a Queen Anne of England. I was named after her. They call her good Queen Anne.'

Amelia stood up. 'Listen. You can hear the sound of trumpets. Papa and Mamma are passing through the city.'

The girls were silent, listening.

Sir Spencer Compton came in all haste to Chelsea. He was a worried man. Greatly as he appreciated the honour the King had done him, he was a little uncertain of his ability to hold the high office which was being thrust upon him, and now right at the beginning of his new duties he was confronted by a task which he was incapable of performing, and he feared he was going to show not only the King but the whole court that he could not compare with Walpole.

It was the simple matter of the King's Speech which it was his duty to prepare and he had no idea how to do it.

There was one man who knew exactly what should be said and what left unsaid; that man was Sir Robert Walpole.

Walpole had, when informing him that the King had dismissed him and told him to take his orders from Sir Spencer Compton, assured the latter that he would be willing to help in any way possible. Well, here was a way in which he could help.

'I have come,' said Sir Spencer, 'to ask you to write the King's

Speech, because for the life of me I have no idea how it should be done.'

. 'Leave it to me,' said Walpole. 'I will do it immediately and it shall be in your hands in good time.'

'I am indeed grateful,' Sir Spencer told him.

When he had gone Walpole went to work on the speech, amused and gratified that his services should be so quickly needed; but there was a desolation in his heart, for he was already realizing how much power meant to him and he felt deeply depressed because it seemed that he had lost it for ever.

Even in the streets they would already be talking of his fall. He was not so clever as he had thought he was. He had been so sure of himself that he had neglected to fawn on the Prince of Wales and the Prince of Wales was now King. He was not sure of the new Queen; he had displeased her now and then, but she was too clever a woman to bear long grudges and in the last years they had appreciated each other.

But the King had dismissed him. And even though the new favourite had to ask his help the cry had gone up; it was echoing throughout the court and the city: Walpole is dismissed.

There were so many things to be done, thought the Queen, as she sat before her mirror and Charlotte Clayton with Henrietta Howard loosened her hair and unbuttoned her gown, to give her greater comfort.

The girls must be brought into the family again, and Frederick must come home. She used to think of him as Fritzchen, but that was long ago. It must be years since she ceased to think of him at all. Indeed since young William was growing into such a charmer she had almost wished that her firstborn had never existed. What would he be like after all these years? He would be like a stranger . . . a German stranger.

But that could wait. Even the girls could wait a while. There were more pressing problems.

'How I hate this bombazine!' she sighed.

'It is quite becoming to Your Majesty,' Henrietta told her.

Caroline eyed herself. Yes, Henrietta was right. The black showed up the fairness of her skin and the magnificence of her shoulders and bust – that bosom which George Augustus declared was the most beautiful in the world.

But this was no time to be thinking of what she looked like. There were important matters to be dealt with and the most important was that the King should not act foolishly now that he had ceased to be the Prince who was of no account because it was his father's wish that he should not be.

She could see fearful pits yawning at their feet. The situation in Europe was very tricky; and there was one man who was so well versed in foreign affairs that they would need him; that was Sir Robert Walpole. There was one man who could keep the government steady; and that was Walpole.

In fact, thought Caroline, he is crude and uncultured, his morals are questionable; he is ugly and too fat; he drinks too much; he is not exactly a charming man; but he is the man we need.

She thought of the King's delight when he had come to tell her how he had dismissed Walpole. 'I have said to him: "Your orders you vill take from Spencer Compton." He vas scarcely off his knees ven this I tell him.'

And she was expected to applaud such promptitude, such sly action, such a neat way of paying off old scores, when she wanted to shout: But we need this man. He is the only one clever enough to help us. If he does not work for us he will work against us.

But one did not presume to advise the King; she never had done that to the Prince of Wales. And yet how often had she persuaded him – in such a manner that he was unaware of it, of course – to decide on what she had already decided.

Tonight he would preside over his Accession Council; he must not make it known during the meeting that he had dismissed Walpole. But Henrietta had told her that Sir Spencer Compton was already being treated with homage and that Walpole was being ignored.

Something would have to be done. She wondered how she could do it.

Her women, used to her pensive moods, worked silently; they were doing her hair when the King came in. He was dressed for the Accession Council meeting and he sat down heavily in the chair which Henrietta hurried to place for him.

'Ha, my tear,' he said, looking affectionately at his wife, 'I see you are looking very beautiful ... as beautiful as a queen, eh?'

'And you look like a king.'

'Ve must grow accustomed to looking so.'

He smiled at the two women and his gaze lingered on Henrietta. She is getting old, he thought; now that I am King perhaps I should choose new mistresses. I should not continue with a woman who is no longer young.

He scowled. 'Vy haf you covered the Queen's neck?' he demanded. 'Is it because you haf not a beautiful neck that you must cover the Queen's?'

He snatched the scarf which was about Caroline's shoulders.

'There. That is better. Now ve see this beautiful neck.'

Caroline nodded dismissal to the two women and they went quietly out.

'This is a most important meeting,' said Caroline. 'The Council vill be assembled to hear your speech. You vill have it by now.'

'No, I have it not.'

'But ...'

'It vill come. It vill come. Compton is von good man.'

'I hope he can write as good a speech as Valpole.'

'That fat old fox. I tell you he is von scoundrel. You should have seen his face. It came out so neatly. You vould haf laughed.'

No, thought Caroline. I should have groaned.

'Vell, the speech should be here.'

'You should not vorry, my tear. Ah, I think it comes now.'

The King's page had appeared to say that Sir Spencer Compton was in the King's ante-chamber.

'Bring him here,' commanded George.

Sir Spencer came in with the speech which Walpole had just brought to him.

The King read it aloud.

'It is vith great sorrow that I hear of the death of the King, my dearest father ...'

George grimaced. But of course it was what was expected of him. He must pretend to mourn; although the gaiety of his expression would surely belie that.

'My love and affection is for England and I shall preserve the laws and liberties of this kingdom. I shall uphold the Constitution . . .' Yes, this was what they wanted to hear.

Caroline came and looked over the King's shoulder as he read; Compton watched them with relief. He was very uneasy; he knew he was unfitted for the task; he was no Walpole. It was only due to the latter's help that he had extricated himself from a difficult situation in the first hours of his new office. Suppose Walpole had refused to write the speech !

The King was saying, 'No, this vill not do . . .'

Compton started. 'Your Majesty does not like the speech?'

'It is vell enough. It is vell enough. But this must be changed. Change it now.'

'What . . . what does Your Majesty wish to say?'

'I do not know. It is for you. Do it now. The women vill give you a table and chair . . .'

'Your Majesty, it would be a great mistake to change the speech.'

'Vat is that?'

'Your Majesty, the speech should remain as it is.'

'But I say this is not goot. This paragraph . . . he must be changed.'

'It would be better to leave it as it is.'

'Better. But I say this vill not do.'

Compton was bewildered. How could he change the speech? It was Walpole's work and he could not imagine what might be substituted for the offending paragraph.

'I . . . I will take it away, Your Majesty,' said Compton. 'I will need to do this.'

'Then do not be long. I must haf it . . . soon.'

When he had bowed himself out, the offending speech under his arm, the King looked at the Queen. She was examining the stuff of her gown; she dared not look at the King for fear she betray a certain triumph. It had occurred to her that the King was going to see that he had acted rashly.

It was only a short time later when they heard that Walpole was asking for an audience.

'This I vill not give,' said the King. 'I haf not the time. Vere is this speech. Vat has happen to Compton?'

'It may be that Valpole hav come about the speech . . .' began the Queen, an idea occurring to her.

'How is this?'

'If you thought fit you might permit him to come. There could be no harm.'

The King looked at her in a puzzled fashion and then said he would see Walpole. Caroline was inwardly exultant when she saw that Walpole was carrying the speech.

'Vat the . . .' began the King.

'Your Majesty. Sir Spencer Compton has asked me to adjust the paragraph of which you do not approve.'

'But vy . . . ?'

'Your Majesty, I had written so many speeches. Sir Spencer so few. And so . . .'

'You wrote this von, Sir Robert?' asked the Queen.

Their eyes met. It's not too late, thought Walpole. She is with me.

'I wrote it, Your Majesty. The need for haste . . .'

'Yes, yes,' said the King testily. 'Let us see this paragraph.'

The Queen read it with him. 'I am sure the King vill say that is vat vas needed,' she said.

'It is vat vas needed,' said the King gruffly.

Walpole bowed his head; he stood before the King and said : 'Your Majesty, if I can serve you in any way . . . in or out of office, you may depend upon me.'

'I shall remember,' said the King, and turned away.

Again a look was exchanged between the Queen and the minister. Walpole bowed and went out.

The King was annoyed.

'I do not like this man,' he said.

'He drinks too much,' agreed the Queen.

'He is von big fat ox.'

'His conversation at table is most coarse.'

'It is vell he is dismissed.'

'It is vell if ve can find better men than he.'

'Vat you mean?'

'There is much to be done. Perhaps you vill not vant to hurry to make a new ministry.'

'I am tired of this man. He takes bribes. He is von greedy old rogue.'

'There will be other greedy rogues. He must be rich by now. Perhaps Your Majesty will say that others less rich might be more open to bribes.'

'Vat is this?'

'Old leeches are not so hungry as young ones . . . it is often so.'

The King looked at his wife for a few moments and she said quickly: 'It may be that Your Majesty vill think so. May I look at your speech?'

She read it through and he continued to watch her.

'It is good,' she said. 'That sly old Valpole wrote it. I know his style.'

'He is von fat old leech,' said the King; and the Queen laughed immoderately.

He was pleased; but he was also thoughtful. Perhaps, he was thinking, he should not be too hasty.

The late King's will

The new King, his speech in his hand, entered the council chamber where his ministers were assembled.

George noted with pleasure the new deference they accorded him. They were wary too, a little apprehensive, wondering whether in the past they had sided too openly with his father against him.

I shall not forget! George gleefully told himself. They shall regret their mistakes.

Already Walpole was regretting. He had heard the fellow only had to enter a room and all backs would be turned on him. Now he must be wishing that he had remembered that a Prince of Wales, however out of favour with the reigning monarch, in turn becomes the King.

He acknowledged their homage and read his speech of regret for his father, and if any of them felt like tittering they made no sign but composed their faces into attitudes of respectful melancholy.

He went on to say how he loved England and how he intended to devote himself to the service of his country.

It was a speech of tradition – no better, no worse than its

predecessors, but it had the virtue of being what was expected and was greeted with applause.

The Archbishop of Canterbury, Dr Wake, was a timid man who was a little unsure of his position, having been completely submissive to the previous king, and anyone who had been so must almost inevitably be on bad terms with the new one. But Dr Wake had contrived not to offend the new King while being on good terms with his father. In any case such a man made little trouble and George's feelings for him were neutral.

He now approached the King and put a document into his hands.

'Your Majesty, this is your father's will which he entrusted with me, asking that I would present it to you on the event of his death. This I now do.'

George looked at the document. A will! The old scoundrel had decided to outwit him at the end. Who knew what was in that document. He could be certain, though, that it would be something to cause embarrassment to the son he had hated.

His ministers were watching him expectantly. The Archbishop was holding the will. Clearly he was awaiting the formal command to open it and make its contents known.

Everything was according to the tradition which had been followed through centuries. Now was the moment to read the late King's will.

But his son held out his hand for the document, scarcely glanced at it, and thrust it into his pocket.

'Now,' he said gruffly, 've have some business to discuss.'

The Archbishop was astounded; the members of the council could scarcely believe what they had actually seen; but the King was testily waiting to continue with the meeting, as though the will was of no importance to him.

The King made his way to the Queen's apartment, and as soon as he entered she recognized that he was deeply disturbed, so she dismissed her attendants and waited patiently for the outburst.

He was not as choleric as usual, which might be a bad sign, for it could mean he was too disturbed for an outward display of anger.

He stood for some seconds rocking on his heels, his face, which had been pink when he entered, growing red; his blue eyes seeming to bulge more with every passing moment.

Still she did not speak.

Then slowly he took a document from his pocket and held it before her eyes.

'The old scoundrel's vill,' he said.

He saw her catch her breath; he saw the faint colour touch her face and neck. There was no need to explain to Caroline the importance of this paper.

'Vat does it contain?' she whispered. Wild thoughts were running through her mind. He would pursue them even after death. Did they think that they were rid of him? That document could deprive them of their inheritance. But could it? George Augustus had already become George II; would it be possible for the old man to have his grandson Frederick substituted for his son? Frederick! The son for whom in the past she had so longed and had now almost forgotten – because the old scoundrel had decreed that they should live apart. No, not that. But it was certain there would be something to plague them in that will. Money they needed would be directed elsewhere. The Duchess of Kendal would be given a large part of the wealth which by right belonged to the King and Queen of England.

She was watching her husband anxiously, and he shook his head while a slow smile of triumph spread across his features.

'No one living knows. Let him keep his secret. He is dead now.'

'But . . . surely it was read at the council?'

There was pride in his face. He was the King now; he would know how to rule and no one should be allowed to forget that.

'I did not ask it to be read. I took it when Vake gave it to me and put it into my pocket.'

Now she was smiling – approval, admiration. How he loved her! They would stand together against all their enemies.

'And they said nothing?'

'To the King!'

Then she laughed. 'No, of course, they vould not dare . . . not to the King. And now?'

'You know vat he did to my mother's vill?' demanded the

King. 'Do you think she vould have left all she had to him . . . her enemy? Do you think she vould have forgotten me and my sister? She loved us alvays. Ven my Grandmother Celle visited her the first thing she wanted to know was "How is my son George Augustus? How is my daughter Sophie Dorothea? Are they vell, are they happy?" And she was rich. Vat did he do vith her vill? He destroyed it. Vat did he do vith the vill of my Grandfather Celle which you can depend left much to me and none to him? He destroyed it. And now vat shall I do vith his vill, eh? I tell you this. I shall treat him as he treated others.'

The King went to a lighted candle and held the document in the flame.

For a few seconds it seemed as though it refused to burn; then the thick paper suddenly leaped into flame.

The King smilingly watched it until he could hold it no more; then he threw it into the fireplace and together he and the Queen watched it blacken and writhe until there was nothing left but the charred remains.

The King was peevish. The Queen understood why and was not displeased. Secretly she was determined to set Walpole back in his place for she realized that the imperative need of a king such as her husband was a strong government. There was one man she wanted to see at the head of that government and that was Walpole.

'Valpole, that fat old ox!' cried the King every time his name was mentioned. Then she would laugh and agree that he was a fat old ox; she would admit that he had not fulfilled his promises to either of them; but in her heart she knew that they must not harp on old grievances; they needed the most able statesman in the land to head their government and that man was Walpole.

She came to her husband's apartment and when they were alone she asked him how Compton was acting with regard to some of the important matters which needed prompt settlement.

George scowled. 'It is delay . . . delay . . .'

'The Civil List is the most important. Perhaps he does not delay with that.'

George's face grew red; his hands went to his wig. He did

not snatch it from his head, she noticed, which had been a favourite habit in the days when he was Prince of Wales, stamp on it, and kick it round the room; kingship had given him some dignity.

'He vants me to accept vat my father had. And I have this big family.'

'It vill not do.'

'This I tell him. But he say the Parliament vill not agree.'

'They must be made to see . . .'

'They vill. I shall insist.'

He drew himself up to his full height and inwardly Caroline sighed. The little man must know in his heart that he could not stand against his Parliament.

'They vill give me vat my father had and for Frederick because he is Prince of Vales now, he shall hav the £100,000 which I had.'

'Frederick to have £100,000! But that is a nonsense.'

'It is a nonsense. For vat should he vant so much?'

'Frederick to have £100,000 and you to have just the same as your father who had no big family.'

'I tell him it is a nonsense . . . and he say that he vill a difficulty have in getting the Parliament to agree to anything else.'

Momentarily Caroline thought of Frederick. He would have to come home now. The prospect filled her with some dismay. How strange! Once her dearest wish had been to have her little Fritzchen with her; but that was thirteen years ago. All those years she had not seen her son; he was Frederick now, no longer dear little Fritzchen. A German, she feared, who had never seen England; and she had her little William now and she desired for him the honours which would be Frederick's.

He would have to come home now though because he was Prince of Wales. But certainly he should not have £100,000.

'And Compton is a little slow,' suggested Caroline tentatively, fearful that her husband might remember that the man was his choice.

But George was too angry to remember. 'He does nothing . . . nothing. He says, "The Parliament . . . the Parliament . . ." But

I vill have them remember I am the King.'

'Perhaps another man would be of more help to us. Let us think who there might be ... Pulteney ...'

The King scowled and the Queen nodded to show she agreed with his lack of enthusiasm for that one.

'And who else,' she went on. 'Wyndham ...'

'No,' said the King promptly.

'There is Newcastle ...'

'Newcastle.' The King's anger broke out. 'That ugly baboon. Never! Never.'

The Queen nodded. They were remembering a long ago occasion when the King had forced Newcastle to become sponsor at one of the children's christening, and the quarrel which had broken out between George and Newcastle at the bedside which had resulted in that bigger quarrel between the King and his son. George scowled now to remember the humiliation of being placed under arrest, while Caroline remembered how she had been parted from her children.

Newcastle was the last man. Yet he was an able statesman, and there were not so many of those.

'It leaves only Valpole,' said the Queen, and then feared she had been too bold.

'Valpole ...' grumbled the King.

'He is perhaps the only man who can increase the Civil List ... and it must be increased. Ve have so many children. Valpole can do it. I remember your father's saying that this man could turn stones into gold.'

'For his own benefit he vill do this.'

'But to do it for us vill be to his benefit. The fat ox vill understand this.'

George was thoughtful. It was true.

'It is no harm to send for him,' said the Queen. 'Then Your Majesty can judge him.'

'I vill see him,' said the King.

So Walpole presented himself to the Queen. Caroline was delighted that he should first come to her. George must not know this, but it was how it should be in the future, and it delighted her to know that Walpole understood this.

'The King is not satisfied with the Civil List,' she told him. 'Compton does not seem to be able to make them understand how we are placed. He vill give me only £60,000 a year and it is not enough.'

'Your Majesty should have £100,000 a year,' declared Walpole.

The Queen's eyes gleamed. £40,000 more than Compton had wanted to provide.

'You think this could be arranged?'

'I believe, Your Majesty, that I could arrange it.'

A tacit agreement? wondered the Queen. Give me your support and you shall be well rewarded. £40,000 a year! It was a good sum.

'You can svay the House, Sir Robert,' she said with a smile. 'I know that vell. Perhaps you have some suggestions for the King?'

'The late King had a Civil List of £700,000, and His Majesty, then Prince of Wales, received £100,000.'

'This Compton vants to give our son Frederick, now Prince of Vales, this although he is a young man unmarried and the King, when Prince of Vales, had a family to support.'

'Your Majesty, the £100,000 which was paid to the Prince of Wales should be added to the £700,000 Civil List, and Your Majesties should decide what you will allow the Prince from it.'

'That is von good idea.'

'Then I do not see why a further £130,000 should not be provided. The King's subjects will rejoice to see him keep a more kingly court than his father did.'

'And the Parliament?'

Walpole smiled. 'I think there is one man who can arrange their acceptance of these proposals.'

'Sir Robert Valpole?' asked the Queen.

Walpole bowed. 'At the service of Your Majesties,' he answered.

Walpole was triumphant. The King had implied that he should continue in his old office provided he get the Civil List passed through.

There was no subtlety about George.

'I vant it for life,' he said; 'and remember, it is for your life too.'

It had not been difficult. The government knew that Walpole's future hung on the passing of the Civil List; and it knew too that without Walpole it could not long exist. So there he was, the fat ox of a man, smiling blandly at them, laying the suggestions before them which he knew they could not afford to oppose.

Bribery of a sort – but not unknown in politics.

The King and Queen had their money; and Walpole was returned to power.

He laughed to himself as he rode down to Richmond to tell Maria about it.

'You, my dear,' he said triumphantly, 'are not the only one who can't do without me.'

While the King and Queen were congratulating themselves on the easy way in which they had acquired a large income, a blow struck from an unexpected direction.

Letters were delivered to the King and among them was one from his distant cousin the Duke of Wolfenbüttel.

The Duke had written that he was in a somewhat delicate position, and he hoped the King of England would advise him what should be done.

King George I, His Majesty's father, had left with him a copy of his will in case the original was lost in some way. He did not want to interfere in his cousin's arrangements in any way, but he had heard that the King of Prussia had hoped that his wife, Queen Sophie Dorothea, who was after all the daughter of the late King, would have profited from her father's will. The Duke of Wolfenbüttel was hard pressed at the time and he sent congratulations to his more affluent relative. He was also in a quandary, for on one side was the King of Prussia who, he believed, was ready to pay handsomely for a glimpse of the will, and on the other his friend and cousin George II. He was writing this letter first of all to ascertain the wishes of His Majesty. It gave him great pleasure to have the Duchess of

Kendal as his guest at Wolfenbüttel, for he knew full well in
what great regard the late King had held that lady . . .

When the King received this letter his eyes bulged with fury.
He took it to the Queen who read it and looked very grave.

Who would have thought the sly old man would have made a
copy and deposited it where it was out of the reach of his son's
hands!

And what a stroke of ill luck that the Duchess of Kendal, who
would no doubt profit as much as anyone from the late King's
will, should at this time actually be staying as a guest in the
house of the man who had a copy of the will.

The promptest action was clearly needed.

'At least,' she said, 'Volfenbüttel has not made its contents
known. I suppose Your Majesty will do as he is asking and *buy*
this copy of the vill?'

'Got damn him!' cried George.

'And as soon as possible. He might change his mind. The
Duchess of Kendal is actually under his roof. Who knows what
pressure she might bring to bear.'

'She is vithout power.'

'She is on the spot. And the King of Prussia may vell make a
big offer for the vill.'

'I vill send a trusted man at vonce.'

'And I vill write to the Duchess assuring her of my friendship. It vould be vell if she came back to England . . . and
quickly.'

The King despatched a messenger without delay and the
Queen went to her apartments and immediately wrote to the
Duchess.

'My first thought, my dear Duchess, has been of you in the
misfortune which has befallen us; I know well your devotion
and love for the late King, and I fear for your health; only
the resignation which you have always shown to the divine
will can sustain you under such a loss. I wish I could convey
to you how much I feel for you, and how anxious I am about
your health, but it is impossible for me to do so adequately. I
cannot tell you how greatly this trouble has affected me . . .'

Caroline paused to smile cynically. What joy it had brought! No more to be plagued by that old scoundrel, to have her children with her. Would poor Ermengarda see through this hypocrisy? Not she! She had always been simple – except in money matters. Ah, there was the point. If she knew of the existence of that will, she would guess that she would be one of the main beneficiaries and she would no longer be the King's simple Ermengarda Schulemburg whom he had made Duchess of Kendal. Money had always sharpened Ermengarda's wits.

Caroline continued:

'I had the honour of knowing the late King, and you know that to know him was sufficient to make one love him also ...'

Oh, no! That was too much! But in Ermengarda's present mood she would accept it. George I had been a god to her when he lived; now he would naturally have become a saint. And Ermengarda must come back to England; she must be safely settled in the shadows for ever more.

'I know that you always tried to render good service to the present King. He knows it too and I hope you realize that I am your friend. It is my pleasure and duty to remind you of the fact and to tell you that I and the King will always be glad to do all we can to help you. Write to me, I beg you, and give me an opportunity to show how much I love you.
Caroline.'

Its falseness was apparent in every line. But Ermengarda might not see this. She was almost out of her wits with grief for the King whose constant companion and devoted mistress she had been for so many years.

Caroline despatched the letter that it might arrive at the same time as the Duke of Wolfenbüttel received the handsome sum George was sending in payment for the will.

There were many anxious days before the copy of his father's will was in the King's hands and, once there, immediately given the same treatment as the other copy.

Coronation

Everyone's thoughts were now occupied with the coronation.

The Queen had dismissed the governess of her eldest girls and had decided that she would supervise their education. It was a little late now, Anne being nearly nineteen years old and even Caroline only four years younger. Oh, how angry she could become even now when she thought of the years that old monster George I had kept them from her! Still, that was over now and she must make the best of it.

Here she had all her children under her care now. Even Frederick would have to come soon.

Not yet, she thought. The longer they kept him out of England the better.

She went to the nursery, for she had commanded the elder girls to be there with their little sisters and brother as she wished to talk to them all together.

When she entered the elder girls curtsied, but the young ones rushed at her and Anne looked on with haughty disapproval as young William claimed first attention.

She could never resist him. He was her favourite and she was touched by love and pride every time she saw him. Darling William, already Duke of Cumberland.

'My darling!' said Caroline fondly. 'And you have been goot boy?'

'He is never a good boy, Mamma,' said Anne coldly.

William swung round and ran at his sister preparing to pummel her.

'I am a good boy. I am. I am. I am the best boy in the world, I tell you.'

'Oh, William, William, that vill not do. Come here at vonce to Mamma.'

William stuck out his lower lip and grimaced at Anne before turning to his mother.

'Now, you vill tell me how you are getting on with your lessons.'

'I am very clever, Mamma.'

'So he says,' retorted Amelia.

'No, no. It is Jenkin who says so.'

'And you have been reading Mr Gay's fables.'

William nodded, smiling at the memory of the fables.

Anne interrupted by saying: 'Mamma, what are we to wear for the coronation?'

'Ah, the coronation! That is vy I have to you come. You vill all be taught your part and I know you vill do as you should. It vill be von great experience to see your father and me crowned. And I shall so proud of you be.'

'*I* shall be there!' cried William.

'And that,' retorted Anne sourly, 'will ensure the success of the occasion.'

William nodded gravely, believing this to be so, and his mother laughed.

Anne was so angry she could have slapped the spoilt child. The only thing that gave her satisfaction was that his arrogant little nose would soon be put out of joint, for surely Frederick would have to come home shortly. Then Master William would learn that he was only a young brother. From the way he behaved now one would think he was the heir to the throne.

'Mamma, shall we carry your train?' asked Amelia.

'Yes, my dear, you three eldest shall carry my train.'

'*I* will carry it!' cried William.

The Queen laughed as though he had said something very clever.

'You are too young,' Anne told him. 'And boys don't carry trains.'

'If I want to carry a train . . .' began William ominously.

But Amelia interrupted. 'Can three of us carry the train then, Mamma?'

'Oh, yes. You three will carry it and you will be wearing your purple robes of state, with circlets on your heads.'

'Not coronets?' asked Anne, always anxious that no outward sign of royalty should be omitted.

'No, dear. These vill be borne before you by three peers.'

Anne clasped her hands ecstatically. 'Oh, how I wish that *I* were going to be crowned. Mamma, you must be the happiest woman in the world.'

'I am happiest most to have my children vith me.'

'Shall I be crowned?' asked William.

Anne laughed loudly. 'You are not even Prince of Wales. It is the Prince of Wales who becomes the King. You were born a little too late, dear brother.'

'Mamma, why was I born too late?'

Never was there such an arrogant six-year-old, thought Amelia. It was time brother Frederick came home if only to show Master William that although his mother spoilt him outrageously, he was not the most important member of the household.

'My darling, these things vill be.'

The Queen was regretful. William himself could not have wished more heartily than she that he was the firstborn and therefore Prince of Wales.

'But *I* don't want them to be.'

'And even William, Duke of Cumberland, can't have everything he wants,' replied Anne.

How sharp she is, how acid! thought the Queen. That must be corrected. And there was Amelia, looking almost mannish although so good-looking; and little Caroline stooping too much. Mary and Louisa were such babies, of course, but they seemed to be her very own because they had not been taken from her and she had always had charge of them. She feared that the quarrel with the late King had had a marked effect on her family.

She must correct their faults, but gently because she loved them tenderly and wanted to keep their love.

'Soon,' went on Anne, addressing William, 'your brother will return and you will meet the Prince of Wales who will be the most important of us all.'

William looked questioningly at his mother who said : 'I daresay your brother vill come to England in due course.'

'Should he not be here for the coronation, Mamma?'

'That is impossible. He could not leave Hanover yet.'

'But when, Mamma, when?' insisted Amelia.

'That ve cannot yet say.'

The pleasure was spoilt. It was true he would have to come home. And she, his mother, had to admit that she didn't want him. To her he would be as a stranger, a German stranger !

Perhaps she could get Walpole to help her contrive some scheme for keeping Frederick in Hanover. It was an idea. Frederick to remain as Elector of Hanover and William to be Prince of Wales. Even Walpole could never arrange that. Still, the longer they could keep Frederick in Hanover, the more hope there would be of making young William Prince of Wales.

She could not take her eyes from him – her beloved son. He was already a little man at six years old – very sure of what he wanted; and clever, too, if she could believe his most excellent tutor Jenkin Thomas Philipps who had published for William's use his *Essay Towards a Universal and Rational Grammar* and *Rules in English to Learn Latin*.

'Now,' said the Queen, 'I vant to hear from you all. How are you elder girls spending your time, eh? And you little ones must tell me how you are progressing with your lessons ... Come Louisa, my dear.' She lifted the three-year-old onto her lap. 'And you too, Mary.' Mary, a year older than Louisa, was overawed by the presence of her elder sisters who were almost strangers to her, and came shyly to her mother. But William was of course pushing for the first place.

The older girls remained rather aloof – Anne haughtily, Amelia indifferently, and Caroline diffidently.

Oh dear, thought the Queen, how difficult this welding together of her family was proving! Every day her grudge against the late King seemed to deepen when she considered what his cruelty had done to her family.

If I had always had them under my care ... she thought.

She was determined to be a good mother, and good mothers were supposed to love all their children equally. At least they always swore they did. She could not help it if her gaze rested a little more lovingly on young William. After all he was her son ... There was Frederick, but she couldn't count him.

She had tried calling him Fritzchen in her mind in the hope that it would help her return to the love she had once had for him; but it was no use. She did not know what he looked like, for a young man of twenty must look very different from a boy of seven. And to think he had been only seven when she had left him. Another thing to blame that wicked old monster for. He had parted a mother from her son and during thirteen years the longing for her child had been suppressed until, with the coming of other children, it had been stifled altogether.

What is the use of pretending? Caroline asked herself. I don't care if I never see Frederick again.

But his name was on everyone's lips. Even here in the nursery her children were talking about him.

When is Frederick coming home?

The question came between her and her peace of mind. She did not want Frederick and the reason was that she deeply regretted he was her firstborn; she wanted all the honours that would be his for her adorable, bright, and utterly spoilt six-year-old William.

'At least,' said Anne, 'we shall be properly dressed for the coronation. Papa will not be allowed to be so mean as to stop that.'

'Oh, Anne!' cautioned the Princess Caroline.

'It's the truth,' replied Amelia. 'Papa hates parting with money. That is why we are all kept so poor. It's not fair.'

'He asked to see my accounts,' complained Anne, 'and when Mrs Powis brought them he said that the braid on my top coat was too wide and could have been half the width – thus saving money. Who would think we were princesses? We might be charity girls!'

'Sometimes I think,' said Amelia, 'that it would have been better not to be so highly born. I am sure maids of honour enjoy a freer life than their mistresses. There is our mother, Queen of England, but not daring to speak her mind for fear she offends Papa.'

'But he does all she tells him nevertheless.'

'Without knowing it,' said Amelia. 'I think our father is not half as clever as he thinks himself.'

The elder girls began to laugh and Caroline looked a little shocked. 'He is after all our father and the King.'

'Dear Caroline! You always believe the best of everyone. For me I prefer rather to tell the truth than deceive myself.' That was Amelia. She was kneeling on the window seat in a pose which her mother would have deplored, for it was not femininely graceful. She glanced down to the courtyard below and her manner changed; a smile touched her lips and she waved a greeting.

Anne was quickly beside her.

'So . . . you are flirting with Grafton.'

Amelia was still looking at the man on horseback whose dark, handsome looks and physique made him outstanding.

'I am acknowledging the greeting of Charles, Duke of Grafton,' retorted Amelia tartly.

'You know that is most unwise.'

'I cannot see that it is unwise to give or return a greeting.'

'Greeting! You know it is more than that. You know you have a fancy for him.'

'*You* are inclined to think *you* know too much, sister.'

Caroline moved away to another window and stood there gazing out. She was always seeking to escape from her more forceful sisters who were constantly quarrelling. Quarrels were commonplace in this family. There had been the Great Quarrel between Grandfather and Papa – and now that was over minor ones were continually springing up between members of the family.

'Who is Grafton?' demanded Anne. 'I think you forget that you are royal.'

'It is as well that all of us don't keep reminding everyone on every occasion of the fact,' retorted Amelia. 'And the Duke of Grafton is as royal as you are.'

'His grandfather was a king, I know, since his father was the bastard of Barbara Villiers and Charles II. A very pleasant recommendation.'

'They say he inherited his father's brilliance and charm and his mother's beauty,' said Amelia.

'And doubtless the immorality of both. For shame, Amelia! You know you are all but betrothed to the Crown Prince of Prussia.'

Amelia shivered. 'I hope that I never have to make that marriage.'

Caroline drew farther into her corner, shivering slightly. She had heard stories of the terrible King of Prussia who beat his children, locked them up and starved them and then worked out how much he had saved by keeping them without food. He quarrelled constantly with his wife, their aunt Sophia Dorothea, tried to beat her too, and because that wasn't possible contented himself by spitting into her food when it was a dish she especially fancied.

What a household for poor Amelia to enter! No wonder she thought longingly of staying in England and marrying a man who was as handsome and charming and daring as the Duke of Grafton.

Caroline was terrified of the day when she might have to go away. It wouldn't bear thinking of. But they were growing old now and they were no longer merely the granddaughters of a king; they were the daughters of one; and that made a difference. Matches would be made for them and princesses always had to do what was expected of them.

How sad it was for a princess to grow up! It was better to be young even though their childhood had been overshadowed by the Great Quarrel when Grandfather would not allow them to see their parents. Caroline had suffered then because of dear Mamma who loved them so and whom they loved. Not being allowed to see Papa had been no great hardship, for they could not help being a little ashamed of the way in which he strutted and was so conceited, and anxious to prove he was the master of them all – which he wasn't although he was King, for kings were ruled by their parliaments; and it was becoming well known that the Queen had a bigger influence, and the only one who wasn't aware of this was the King. All this made him a ridiculous figure in spite of his brilliant uniforms and all the pomp with which he liked to surround himself, for although he was mean enough with his daughters, he was not with himself.

Caroline listened to her sisters quarrelling over the Duke of Grafton and let her own thoughts stray pleasantly.

She wouldn't think of the time when she too must go away. Perhaps it would never happen. After all, the King had so many daughters, he couldn't find royal marriages for all of them. Some might be allowed to marry in England.

There was one figure which kept intruding into her mind – that of elegant Lord Hervey of whom her mother was so fond.

He was one of the most brilliantly clever young men of the court – clever in a different way from Sir Robert Walpole. Lord Hervey made amusing verses and witty conversation; he was very very handsome and, she was sure her mother agreed with this, one of the brightest lights of the court.

He had recently married Molly Lepel, one of the court beauties, but she remained in the country and rarely came to court, so it was almost as though Lord Hervey was a bachelor.

So Caroline sat dreaming of Lord Hervey while Anne and Amelia quarrelled over the Duke of Grafton.

The coronation was to take place in October and during September little else was talked of throughout the court and the city.

The King strutted in the park wearing brilliant uniforms, reviewing troops. He was very pleased with himself. The Queen busied herself with state affairs, going carefully through all documents in order to render, as she told the King, the little assistance of which she was capable.

He was pleased, and as long as she never showed that she had a firmer grasp of affairs than he had, as long as she always made a show of waiting for his opinion before passing her own, he was contented.

Caroline was delighted that he showed such a pleasure in pomp and ceremony, for this was what the people enjoyed; they would gather to cheer him in the park and often when she was at Kensington she would watch him from her window.

She too must not give up her habit of sauntering, always remembering to smile and chat affably with the humblest who approached her. She realized the importance of this. It was where George I had failed so wretchedly. In fact, sauntering tired her more than it used to. It might have been due to that unmentionable infirmity of which she refused to think; there was a touch of gout in her legs which was almost as disturbing, for if she could not walk with the King whenever he wished it, he would be irritated and it might be necessary to confess that she was unable to. *That* must never happen.

George was in the highest spirits at this time. He was a new enough king to be a novelty to his subjects and as yet had not had time to do anything of which they could disapprove. All he had to do was parade in splendid uniforms and acknowledge the cheers. He was delighted with the manner in which he believed he had acquired a larger Civil List than his father, for he was immediately able to forget the part Caroline had played in this and she, in accordance with her practice, made no effort to remind him. He was eagerly awaiting the coronation which would be the most dazzling spectacle of all.

He came to the Queen to talk to her about it. She was busy with state papers, her feet resting on a footstool which seemed to ease her legs, but when the King came in she hastily kicked it aside.

'Ha!' He glanced quickly at the papers and then sat down stretching his legs out before him.

'I have been looking at the robes,' he said with a smile. 'They are very fine.'

She smiled at him. 'Crimson velvet edged with ermine vill suit you. You have tried them on?'

He confessed it, and she had a quick picture of him strutting

c.q.—3

before mirrors. She tried not to think of the suppressed smiles of his attendants but she guessed they would have been there.

'The cap of state is very fine,' went on the King.

'I remember seeing your father vearing it.'

The King laughed. 'It did him not much become!' he jeered. 'He looked as if he vere going to his execution rather than his coronation.'

'You vill look so different.'

His expression changed. Rarely was a man so easy to read, thought Caroline; and was thankful for it. It helped her to assess his moods quickly and so avoid pitfalls.

'The jewels in this cap are very goot. They sparkle vell against the crimson velvet.'

'The people vill be delighted.'

'It vill be the best coronation they have ever seen.' The King reluctantly turned his mind from the contemplation of his own splendour to think of the Queen's.

'You too must dazzle them, my dear.'

'It vill be the King on whom every eye vill rest.'

'But they vill not forget the Queen. He had no queen. They remembered she was shut away in prison . . . and he had put her there. No queen . . . only those two mistresses of his. I remember how the people laughed at him. Our coronation vill be different. You vill be there . . . the Queen . . . and the girls vill hold your train. They vill see that we are von big and happy family . . . now that the old scoundrel can no longer plague us. You must sparkle vith jewels.'

'Ah, jewels,' said Caroline. 'Vere shall I find them? Your father gave away all the jewels to those mistresses of his. I vas looking into this only today. There is nothing left but one pearl necklace.'

'The old scoundrel . . .' George's eyes bulged in the familiar way. 'But jewels there must be. They must them give back . . . We must have jewels . . .'

'I vill find a vay of acquiring some.'

He nodded. He was not really interested in *her* jewels. He was seeing himself smiling, bowing, his hand on his heart. He could hear the acclamation of the crowds. Everybody was going to be glad on that day that the old King was dead and a new one was being crowned.

The Queen was at her wits' end to know how to procure jewels for the coronation. The King would be displeased if she did not glitter from head to foot; and how could she, when the royal jewel cases were empty and she could not even trace which of the late King's mistresses were in possession of the gems. Ermengarda Schulemburg, Duchess of Kendal, no doubt possessed many of them, but she was still abroad and certainly could not be asked to return her late lover's gifts . . . not by letter at any rate.

Caroline summoned her two most trusted women, Mrs Clayton, on whom she depended perhaps more than any other, and Henrietta Howard, the King's mistress, who had for many years proved herself a good and discreet servant to the Queen. That these two ladies disliked each other intensely did not disturb Caroline.

'I need jewels,' she said. 'There is only one pearl necklace in the jewel boxes.'

'But, Your Majesty, that is impossible!' cried Mrs Clayton.

'I fear not. The late King vas occasionally a generous man to his mistresses . . . particularly as he grew older.'

'I'll swear that harlot Anne Brett has looked after herself.'

'Ve can scarcely blame her for that. Perhaps ve should all have done the same in her place. But I need jewels. I must have them for the coronation.'

Henrietta Howard said: 'I'm sure every lady in your household would be delighted to lend Your Majesty everything she has.'

'You think so, Henrietta.' The Queen smiled. 'It is a strange position – a coronation and no jewels for the Queen to wear.'

'If Your Majesty will give me permission I will discover discreetly whether I can acquire the jewellery.'

'Yes, Henrietta, you vill be discreet I know.'

Henrietta bowed her head. She was a little weary of discretion. She herself received very little reward for her services. She was a little tired of those regular visits of His Majesty. Sometimes she wanted to laugh aloud when she saw him come into the apartment, watch in hand. 'It is exactly nine o'clock, Henrietta. Time ve made love.' It would be hysterical laughter. She knew that throughout the Palace people would be looking at the time and making ribald remarks about her and the King.

It was said that she had all the disadvantages of being a king's mistress and none of the advantages. It was true.

If she had not a husband from whom she wished to escape; if she were free; she would like nothing better than to retire from court, perhaps marry again, this time using more judgement, retire into private life, perhaps to the country, far away from the court where she must wait on the Queen and be prepared to receive the King at precisely the same hour every evening for the same purpose.

And now she must find jewels for the Queen's coronation.

Mrs Clayton was thinking how shocking it was that the Queen should be without jewels; she was a self-important, self-righteous woman and prided herself on her understanding of religious matters. The fact that Henrietta was the King's mistress disturbed her far more than it did the Queen, and although Henrietta had had no jewels to boast from the King she was linking her now with those rapacious women who had denuded the Queen of her rightful possessions.

'I am sure,' said Mrs Clayton, 'that I can find the jewels Your Majesty will need.'

At a very early hour in the morning Caroline was dressed by her women – and everything she put on had to be new. She then went quietly out of the Palace where a chair, bearing no distinguishing marks, was waiting for her. Mrs Howard, who accompanied her, was carried in a hack sedan, and thus, Mrs Howard preceding her by a very short distance, the Queen was carried across St James's Park to the House of Lords and there in Black Rod's Room she was dressed in her state robes.

This was Coronation Day.

As her robes were being adjusted she looked with pride at the diamonds which decorated her skirts and which had been borrowed from the Jews of London for the occasion because although so many ladies had been eager to provide her with their pearls and jewels she needed more than they could give. She wanted to glitter on this occasion as no Queen had ever glittered before. The King would expect it; so would the people; and she was nothing loath. She enjoyed these ceremonies; and on this day of her coronation she was determined to forget everything but the fact that she was being crowned Queen of England. She refused to think of her painful legs or of that other matter which she kept so secret, or the fact that she must continually placate the King and make sure that she never gave him an inkling of who really reigned, or the fact that Frederick would have to come home and her darling William could never be Prince of Wales.

This was the great day and she intended to enjoy it, decked out as she was in borrowed finery, which was comic really considering she was the Queen.

From the House of Lords she was escorted to Westminster Hall where George was already seated under the canopy – a glorious, glittering figure. He gave her a quick glance of approval, so it was well worth borrowing from her ladies and the Jews. How fine he looked! She was reminded of the day he had come courting her, incognito as Monsieur de Busch; he had attracted her then; and over the years, the often difficult years, she had she supposed, grown used to him. But she was fond of her little man for all his conceit, for all his infidelities; and he was fond of her; she often thought that however many mistresses he took she would always have first place in his affections.

These thoughts made her happy.

The sword and spurs were presented and the Dean and Canons of Westminster had appeared carrying the regalia. For George St Edward's crown, the orb, sceptre, and the staff; and for her, the crown, sceptre, and ivory rod.

On their cushions of cloth of gold these were presented to the King and Queen and then given to those who would carry them in the procession to the Abbey.

Now it was time to make their way from the Hall to the Abbey and the way they would take was canopied in blue cloth and a rail had been fixed on either side of this path.

The people were crowding into the streets so as not to miss a moment of the ceremony and a military band was playing as it led the procession from the Hall to the Abbey. The King's herb woman led a party of the Queen's maids to sprinkle fragrant herbs and flowers along the way the procession should pass. First came the peers and peeresses, magnificent in their robes of state, holding their coronets, and after them the Lord Privy Seal, the Archbishop of York, and the Lord High Chancellor.

Caroline, who followed them, preceded by the Duke of St Albans, who was carrying her crown, was conscious of this being the proudest moment of her life. She had always secretly loved pomp and ceremonies even in the days when she had lived as a girl with the erudite Sophia Charlotte, Queen of Prussia, and had pretended to despise what Sophia Charlotte called empty ceremony because Sophia Charlotte had. But it wasn't true. She loved the glitter of the diamonds she had borrowed, the milky sheen of pearls, the richness of velvet and ermine; and, most significant of all, the crown which St Albans carried with such reverence. If only Sophia Charlotte could see her now, what would she say? Don't mistake the glitter of tinsel for gold; don't attach more importance to power than to understanding. But the old Electress Sophia – through whom the Hanoverian branch of the family had come to the throne – would feel as Caroline did, for what Sophia had longed for beyond everything on Earth was the crown of England.

Oh yes, this is a proud moment. Somewhere among the people who were assembling in the Abbey would be Sir Robert Walpole and Caroline believed that if they were careful – and of course they would be – between them he and she would rule England, for the little man – today such a splendid little man – who was at the very heart of this procession could be manipulated as though he were a puppet doll, provided one pulled the strings so expertly that he was unaware of their existence.

On either side of her were the Bishops of Winchester and London, and the three Princesses were bearing her train. Anne would be a proud girl on this day. As Princess Royal she would make sure that her sisters behaved with decorum. Not that one need fear they wouldn't. Amelia had her own dignity and

Caroline was quite meek. They must look very charming in their purple robes with the gold and jewelled circlets on their heads. She hoped theirs weren't as heavy as hers for it pressed hard on her head and was giving her a headache. Her legs were a little painful too.

She impatiently dismissed such infirmities from her mind, smiled at the crowd, pressing close to the rail, who cheered her wildly. And she guessed the forty barons of the Cinque Ports who carried the canopy made a colourful background for her, with the Sergeants at Arms going ahead and following behind.

The crowd was growing very excited, for behind the Queen came the four principal ladies of the Queen's household and among them was Henrietta Howard, and everyone wanted a glimpse of the King's mistress. They were a little disappointed; she was neither ravishingly beautiful nor comically ugly. There was a mildness about her, yet her gravity was charming and she had very beautiful hair of a striking light brown colour. The King's habits of visiting her were talked of because such gossip quickly became common knowledge and there were titters of amusement in the crowd.

But when the King appeared the ridicule disappeared for he made a very fine figure under the canopy of gold in his crimson velvet furred with ermine and edged with gold lace. On his head was the cap of state – crimson velvet, decorated with enormous jewels and edged with ermine. His ruddy complexion gave him a look of health, and because he was delighted to be the hero of the day, his blue eyes were benign and beamed goodwill on all.

At the west door of the Abbey the Archbishop of Canterbury was waiting with other distinguished members of the Church and the procession began to move slowly up the nave.

As Caroline seated herself on her chair of state facing the altar she glanced at her husband on his. She thought how young he looked – like a boy who has at last grasped a gift for which he had waited a long time. He, of course, was completely unaware of her – unaware of everything, she thought, half affectionately, except himself. Well, no one could deny that this was his triumph more than hers, his day; he was the King of England and she but his consort.

The Archbishop was conducting the communion service and afterwards the Bishop of Oxford preached the sermon.

George then subscribed the Declaration against Transubstantiation and took the Oath of Coronation.

He left his chair to kneel at the altar where he was anointed by the Archbishop, presented with the regalia, and the ring was placed on the fourth finger of his right hand. When the crown was placed on his head the trumpets sounded and all the guns in the Park and at the Tower fired the salute.

It was an impressive moment. Then the Te Deum was sung and the King sat solemnly on his throne while the peers, now wearing their coronets, which they had put on when the salute had rung out, paid homage to the King.

After that it was the turn of Caroline.

After the coronation in the Abbey, Caroline and George, in the centre of the procession, returned on foot to Westminster Hall for the banquet.

Seated on the dais with the King and her daughters, Caroline looked complacently about the hall at the long tables at which sat the dukes and duchesses, earls and countesses, and all the nobility.

George, benign but alert for any slip in etiquette or protocol, was flushed and beaming. Caroline knew that he had only one regret which was that the father he hated could not be here today to see how well he comported himself and how delighted his people were with him, that he might draw comparisons between his own coronation and that of his son. But of course if the old man were here none of this would be taking place. Yet George would be thinking: If only he could see me now!

Caroline was telling herself that this was indeed the most glorious day of her life and wishing her legs would not throb so. They were more swollen than ever before; and there was that dull internal ache which could terrify her.

Not today, she thought. She must not think of it today.

The first course had been served and the moment for the King's Champion to enter and make his traditional challenge had come.

How magnificent he looked on his white horse, very magnificently caparisoned, the red, white, and blue feathers in his helmet waving gracefully as he rode, the all important gauntlet in his hand.

His voice echoed throughout the hall.

'If any person of what degree soever, high or low, shall deny or gainsay our Sovereign Lord King George II of Great Britain, France, and Ireland, Defender of the Faith, son and next heir to our Sovereign Lord King George I, to be the right heir to the Imperial Crown of this Realm of Great Britain or that he ought not to enjoy the same, here is his Champion who says that he lyeth and is a false traitor being ready in person to combat with him and in this quarrel will adventure his life against him on what day soever he shall be appointed.'

Down he flung the glove and there followed a somewhat tense silence for everyone knew that the city abounded with Jacobites who believed that the son of James II was the true King of England and that the Germans should be sent back to Hanover.

Caroline glanced at the King, but George was unperturbed. He had a blind faith in his ability to charm his subjects. He could not believe that they wanted the man across the water who had made a feeble attempt to come back in 1715 when George I had ascended to the throne – a miserable attempt that was no real attempt at all – and then had gone flying back to France as soon as King George's soldiers marched up to the Border.

But no one came forward and twice more the Champion repeated the challenge, and twice more no one came forward to accept it.

The King then called for a gold bowl from which he drank the health of his champion and the bowl was taken to the Champion who drank from it; then bowing to the royal table he left the hall with the bowl as his reward.

That anxious little ceremony over, the Queen felt relaxed and turned her attention back to the table. The two thousand wax candles which lighted the hall were dazzling, but the brightness was tiring and she found herself longing for her bed. Not so

George; he was eager for this day to go on. So were the Princesses, particularly Anne, who was giving herself, her mother noticed, the airs of a queen.

It was eight o'clock before the banquet was over and the royal party left the Hall for St James's Palace.

Through the crowded streets to the sound of cheers. At every few yards, it seemed, there was a bonfire and the faces of loyal subjects reflected in the ruddy glow were joyfully bent on pleasure.

'Long live King George. Long live Queen Caroline.'

Here was George, bowing, hand on heart, yet watchful lest there should be more applause for the Queen than the King.

Caroline was thankful that there was not.

And there was the palace dark against the sky, lit by the glow of bonfires.

To the sound of singing and cheers and the ringing of bells, Queen Caroline sat down heavily in her chair and called to her ladies to disrobe her.

Thoughtful Henrietta slipped a footstool under her feet to rest her aching legs.

The coronation had caught the public imagination. The management of the Drury Lane theatre had the idea of playing a coronation of its own and they staged it to take place at the end of Shakespeare's Henry VIII in which Anne Oldfield played Anne Boleyn. The pageant of Anne's coronation which ended the play drew crowds to the theatre; and it was said that Queen Caroline herself was not as splendidly clad in Westminster Abbey as Anne Boleyn was on the stage of Drury Lane. Everyone was delighted with the show except Colly Cibber who was playing Wolsey, and in this new presentation his role was naturally reduced. No one cared for that; crowds went to see the coronation on the stage and night after night the theatre played to full houses.

When the King and Queen went the people stood on their seats and cheered them.

Those were the days of triumph.

Caroline of Ansbach

The Queen's secret

It had always been clear to Caroline that a king and queen who did not show themselves frequently would not be popular with the English people. The money paid to the present King far exceeded that which had been given to his father and the people wanted something in exchange.

They wanted a court – a gay court; they wanted to be amused; they wanted to see their King and to enjoy a little gossip at the expense of the royal family.

Walpole visited the Queen in her closet as he always did before an audience with the King; it was a tacit agreement. They would talk almost casually about matters which Walpole considered important, and between them decide on a line of action. Caroline's task would be to bring the King to their point of view in such a manner that he would think that the project they wished to put into action was entirely his idea. This was not always an easy matter. But Caroline had grown in tact and skill and she was greatly aided by the conceit and blindness of the King.

Caroline would as if by chance be in the King's closet when Walpole called; they would even make silent signs to each other – when to stress a point, when to speak, when to be silent.

It was a wonderful game of power and politics and Caroline delighted in it. Everything that she had been forced to suffer was of no consequence if only she could keep the position she now held. She and Walpole between them would make England great; and the only concession they must make was to let the King imagine he was the prime mover in all their schemes. Even this difficulty added zest to the game.

'There should be a tour of the royal palaces,' Walpole suggested. 'The people expect it. It is a long time since royalty have used Windsor Castle.'

'Neither the King nor his father ever liked the place,' declared Caroline.

'Even so, it would be wise if Your Majesties visited it for a while.'

It was not easy to persuade the King.

'I believe the people of other parts of the country must be jealous of those who see you so frequently,' Caroline told her husband.

He was sitting down and, crossing his legs, he smiled with pleasure.

'Ah, but I cannot in all places be at vonce.'

'That is true, but they forget it. I'll swear they vish much to see their King.'

She saw the expression in his eyes; he was imagining himself riding through towns and villages and the people running out to cheer him, perhaps throwing flowers in his path – buxom women, comely girls. Perhaps he should have a new mistress. He was weary of Henrietta. She was getting deafer every day.

'Perhaps you vould decide you might visit some of your palaces.'

'I might this do,' he said.

'The people of Vindsor never see you.'

'I do not like the place. It is too big . . . too much a castle. The forest is goot ... for the hunt. That I like. But no more.'

'Then you do not wish to go to Vindsor.'

'I do not vish it. You look disappointed.'

'No. I was thinking of the people of Vindsor.'

He did not speak any more but later when Walpole called and Caroline was in the King's closet with him, the King said: 'I have come to a decision. My people vish to see me and I believe it is time I visited them all. I shall go to all the palaces ... and this vill include Vindsor. I do not like the place but the people vill expect it.'

'I am glad Your Majesty has had the idea of paying these visits,' said Walpole. 'It is a brilliant notion and I am sure it will do much good.'

The King was smiling complacently. Neither Walpole nor the Queen looked each other's way.

It was exactly as they planned. And what did it matter if the King thought the plan was his? What did anything matter as long as he did what they desired?

'In the past,' said Walpole, 'the royal family dined every Sunday in public. It was an occasion to which the people looked forward eagerly. It should be revived.'

'Is it necessary?' asked the Queen.

'Your Majesty, it is very necessary to retain the popularity you and the King have won during the coronation.'

'But to dine in public ... !'

'A small concession, Madam, for popularity. His Majesty should be made to conceive the idea.'

The Queen looked at him sharply. Was it wise to allow him to speak slightingly of the King, even to her? He read her thoughts and answered them with a look. If they were to work together they must dispense with subterfuge. She was the Queen, but he was a great statesman and her adviser; without him she could not expect to hold her position; and although he needed her, perhaps she was not quite so necessary to him as he was to her.

She decided that she would ask only absolute frankness from Walpole. He recognized this and was satisfied. They understood each other so well that often there was no need of verbal explanation.

She said : 'I vill speak to the King. I doubt not that ere long you vill hear him say that ve must dine in public on Sundays.'

'And, Madam, there is one other matter. The Prince of Wales cannot stay indefinitely in Hanover.'

'Oh . . . he has much to do there.'

'He is the Prince of Wales. His place is here. The people will not wish him to remain abroad.'

'The people vill say he is von German. Perhaps it is better he does not come.'

'Your Majesty cannot mean you would keep him in Hanover for ever !'

'He could be the Elector . . . vy not?'

'Elector of Hanover when he is Prince of Wales ! I fear, Madam, that would not please the people.'

'I have another son.'

Walpole looked shocked.

'Madam, the Prince of Wales is the Prince of Wales . . . and nothing can alter that.'

'Because it vonce vas, must it alvays be?'

'Always, Madam. Perhaps Your Majesty would speak to the King . . .'

'Oh . . . sometime. The King vill not vish to have Frederick here.'

'Madam, the people will wish it. Only today on the way to the Palace I heard the question: "Where is Fred?" Your Majesty, the people are apt to be disrespectful when they think themselves unheard.'

'And often ven they are heard.'

He smiled deprecatingly. 'It is well to remember, Madam, that the will of the people should be the first consideration of us all.'

He was right; she acknowledged it; but although she soon persuaded the King to return to the habit of dining in public on Sundays, Walpole heard no more about the return of Frederick.

In the state chamber at St James's Palace the table was laid for dinner.

Those who were privileged to see the royal family eat were already in their places. The officials in the royal livery had collected their tickets and they now stood expectantly behind the rail gaping with wonder at the magnificent plate that decorated the table, waiting for that ceremonial moment when the trumpets would announce the arrival of the King, the Queen, and their daughters.

At last they came – splendid glittering figures – smiling, bowing while the watchers cheered. They seated themselves at the table and the food was brought in. The band played softly while the meal progressed and the people stared in wonder to see the King and Queen served by kneeling ladies and gentlemen. It was a wondrous sight and people pointed out the Princess Royal as the haughty one who was not nearly so good looking as her sister Amelia who might have been called pretty even if she were not a royal princess; and the small pale one was Caroline.

The other children were too young to come to the table, but the people saw them on certain occasions and they were very interested in them.

Now they pressed about the rail which divided them from the diners, longing to be nearer, to hear what was said.

And then suddenly a voice from the back of the crowd shouted: 'Where's Fred?'

The King grew a shade pinker and the Queen pretended not to hear.

One of the officials was looking for the man who had spoken and there was silence in the crowd, for no one wanted to be thrown out.

The royal family went on eating as though nothing had happened.

The Queen retired early that night. She was very tired and her legs were swollen. What distressed her most was that voice she had heard at dinner.

Walpole was right, of course. He almost always was. The people were asking when Frederick was coming home. How much longer would they be able to keep him away? The King had been in a bad mood for he hated the thought of Frederick's coming home. It seemed to be a foregone conclusion that

Frederick would hate his father as George had hated his.

Perhaps, thought the Queen, we shall grow to love him. But how could she love anyone who displaced her darling William? She was being foolish. Frederick would not displace William for William had never been in a position to be displaced. Yet she was as resentful as the King.

Why did they have to talk continually of Frederick? Why could they not let him stay in Hanover where he was apparently enjoying life?

She was tired suddenly. She had felt quite ill at dinner.

She would retire early. They could say she had letters to write.

As she rose her legs seemed quite numb; she stumbled and fell.

Charlotte Clayton was at her side.

'Your Majesty.'

The Queen smiled faintly. 'I slipped. I am a little tired. I think I vill go to bed.'

Charlotte Clayton had been watching the growing friendship between the Queen and Sir Robert Walpole. It seemed to her that whenever she wished for a little *tête-à-tête* with Her Majesty, Sir Robert was either with her or on the point of calling.

Charlotte did not approve of Walpole. The man was a notorious lecher; he drank to excess; his conversation was crude; he was, in Charlotte's eyes, not worthy of the Queen's friendship.

In the past she and the Queen had been very close. They agreed about so many matters. They had had many interesting theological discussions; but since the coronation and the closer friendship between the Queen and Walpole, Charlotte felt shut out.

Moreover, she had always guessed that Walpole did not like her. There would come a day when he would poison the Queen's mind against her and the Queen would become so besotted by the man that she would be ready to believe all he told her.

That must not happen. But how prevent it? Was she, Charlotte Clayton, going to stand out against the chief minister?

Something would have to be done.

It was definitely wrong for the Queen to be closely attended by the King's mistress – and for all the woman's soft ways and meekness Charlotte would never like Henrietta Howard – and a lecher like Walpole. One good godfearing companion had to be close at hand.

She was growing really alarmed. Only a few days ago she had heard Walpole speak of her disparagingly. He had called her 'that old viper'. He never guarded his tongue but there was something in the tone of his voice which made her realize his dislike of her.

She was not going to be pushed aside at Walpole's decree. The Queen needed her . . . and she needed the Queen.

The Queen was lying on her bed. Charlotte stood at the foot looking at her, her eyes were round with horror, her face pale.

'Your Majesty . . .'

'It is nothing . . . nothing . . .' said the Queen.

'But madam, I saw . . .'

'Nothing at all . . . nothing . . .'

'Madam . . . I should call your physician.'

'Please say nothing about it.'

'But . . .'

The Queen was almost pleading. 'You know, Charlotte, what is wrong.'

'I can only guess, Your Majesty.'

'It is something which many women suffer from.'

'But the physician . . .'

'Do not speak to me of physicians. Listen Charlotte. I have had this . . . affliction since the birth of Louisa.'

'But Your Majesty should have treatment.'

'No. No one must know. Do you understand that? It will pass, I tell you. It will pass. Charlotte I ask you . . . I *command* you . . .'

'Your Majesty!' Charlotte bowed her head.

'No one must know. I should feel so . . . ashamed. It is such an unfortunate affliction. The King . . .'

'Oh, Madam!'

'Listen to me, Charlotte, I command you.'

'Your Majesty, I would never disobey your command. This shall be our secret.'

Our secret. Sorry as she was for the Queen, Charlotte felt a thrill of triumph. She shared a secret with the Queen; always Caroline would remember it.

A secret, thought Charlotte, which she would share with no one . . . not even Robert Walpole.

'You may strut, Dapper George'

To Windsor went their Majesties; they walked in the Park; they dined in public; they hunted in the forest – the King, young William, Anne, and Amelia on horseback, and the Queen in her chaise and Caroline in another. The Queen did not care for the hunt and she made Lord Hervey ride beside her and entertain her with his witty talk, for that young man was becoming a greater favourite with her every day.

They were pleasant days at Windsor, but the King was a little sullen because he hated the place and was longing to be back at Hampton or his beloved Kensington. Still, the cheers of the people delighted him and there was no doubt that they had been wise to make the tour.

Caroline made sure that they spoke to the people whenever possible; moreover, she gave a sum of money towards paying the creditors of many who had been for years in the debtors' prison there and thus secured their release.

Caroline could have been very gratified apart from the nagging pain she suffered now and then, apart from wondering whether Anne should be reprimanded for showing too much haughtiness, Amelia for flirting with the Duke of Grafton, Caroline for not sitting up straight, William for his forwardness. The one of whom she must be most watchful was of course the King. Never must she betray by a look that she believed herself to be his intellectual equal.

There were so many things to remember.

Everything was going well. At the last general election Walpole had emerged triumphant; his government had been returned with a big majority, having secured this by bribery; he laughed at the ease with which it had been accomplished, explaining to Maria Skerrett during brief respites from public life at Richmond that every man had his price. He was ruling with a cynical ease which proved to be the best possible thing for the country. He wanted a successful England and that meant an England at peace both at home and abroad. The Jacobite menace was always with them but under Walpole it grew more remote. Unscrupulous he might be, but he was a strong man and he wanted to see the country strong. In this Caroline was immediately beside him. Their alliance was becoming friendship. They were both fully aware of each other's qualities and the greatest bond between them was their need of each other.

Choleric, conceited little George, although he was no absolute monarch, was not without power. The government needed the support of the King and Walpole knew that Caroline could slip those invisible reins on her little man and lead him where she would. Her dexterity, her tact, her cool intelligence and her ability to play the humble wife filled Walpole with admiration. They were ideal partners; and it was not long before the results of their rule began to be seen. Trade increased at home; the price of wheat fell; credit abroad rose. Politicians were aware of this; and the people knew that life was more comfortable than it had been for a long time. For this they would reject romantic dreams of a handsome King across the water, of the stories of the charming King Charles II and his lovely court. The Hanoverians might be dull and ugly, but if they brought prosperity to England the English preferred them to the more glamorous branch of the family.

The reign was becoming popular thanks to Caroline and Sir Robert Walpole.

But they were surrounded by astute politicians and enemies. William Pulteney was one, Viscount Bolingbroke another. Both these men were intensely ambitious and coveted Walpole's position. That he owed much to the Queen was apparent to them and they and their friends believed that the best way to disrupt this alliance was to bring it to the notice of the King.

George himself was of the impression that the country's growing prosperity was due to him. He liked to compare his reign with the previous ones, himself with other Kings of England to his own glorification.

On one occasion he said: 'These Kings of England . . . they have not known how to rule . . . they have not ruled. Others have ruled for them.'

Bolingbroke, always ready for mischief, pointed out that the constitutional monarchs of the day lacked the power of the kings of the past. Such a remark was bound to anger George.

'Pooh and stuff!' This inelegant expression was a favourite of his. 'I vill show you. Charles I was ruled by his vife, Charles II by his mistresses, James II by his priests, Villiam III by his men-favourites, and Anne by her vomen-favourites.'

'And Your Majesty's father?' asked Bolingbroke.

George's blue eyes bulged. 'By anyvon who could get at him!' he sneered. The sneer was replaced by a delighted smile. 'And who do they say governs now?'

Bolingbroke bowed to hide the mockery in his eyes.

'Who but his august Majesty, King George II.'

George was satisfied; but Bolingbroke saw what mischief could be made by the mere suggestion that the King was led by the Queen.

Bolingbroke had always been a frequenter of taverns and coffee houses where writers congregated, for he had long realized the power of the pen and he made full use of it. Consequently, shortly afterwards a verse was being quoted and laughed over, not only in the coffee and chocolate houses but throughout the court:

You may strut, dapper George, but 'twill all be in vain,
We know 'tis Queen Caroline, not you, that reigns.
You govern no more than Don Philip of Spain.
Then if you would have us fall down and adore you,
Lock up your fat spouse as your dad did before you.

Bolingbroke's next task was to see that this verse was brought to the King's notice.

It was not difficult for one of Walpole's enemies to arrange this; and the place in which it should be done appeared to be in the apartments of the King's mistress. Henrietta was not taken into the scheme; she would never have agreed to that. All she wanted was to live in peace. But Bolingbroke, Pulteney, and members of the Opposition were soon able to arrange it and a young lady in whom the King was displaying a fleeting interest was soon found to show him the lampoon.

'Such lies these scribblers write, Your Majesty. Why this latest verse which has caught everyone's fancy . . .'

George was not inclined to show interest in what he called 'boetry' which he said was for little men like Mr Pope not for kings and the nobility. However, the matter was pressed and eventually he asked to see the rhyme. By what seemed to be an odd chance the lady had one in the pocket of her gown, torn in halves to show her contempt for it.

But it was not difficult to put the two pieces together and when he read them George was overcome by such a rage that those who had planned the scheme could not have been more delighted.

He turned to the unfortunate gentleman nearest him who happened to be Lord Scarborough, and cried: 'Have you seen this . . . this scandal!'

Scarborough, a little pink, took the paper and frowned at it.

'Have you?' cried the King. 'Have you?'

'Yes, Your Majesty.'

'Then vere have you it seen? Who showed it to you?'

'I . . . I could not in honour tell Your Majesty.'

'You stand there and tell me . . .'

The whole of the room was watching, some with alarm, but some with amusement – secret amusement – and others in delight.

'Your Majesty . . . it was a lady.'

The King's face was tinged with purple; the veins stood out at his temples.

'It is von lie!' he screamed.

'Your Majesty, the whole Court knows this . . .'

'Then vy such lies are they written?'

There was silence and as the King's rage increased he turned to Scarborough and for a moment everyone thought he was going to strike the noble lord.

Instead he said in a low voice which betrayed sorrow, disappointment, and a fury which could break into a frenzy at any moment: 'Had I been you, Scarborough, I should have shot the man who showed me such insolent lies.'

'I . . . understand, Your Majesty, and this I should have done . . . but it was a lady . . .'

The King did not answer. He strode from the room.

The matter rankled in his mind. He had been forced to look at the truth and he did not like it. The people were hinting that he was a man who was governed by his wife! It was the very conclusion he was determined to avoid.

He did not tell Caroline of the incident. He was determined that he would not be the one to bring that scurrilous verse to her notice; but his manner towards her changed.

It appeared that he disliked her. She could never offer the simplest opinion but he could deride it. He began by doing so in front of her women.

He would call for her in her apartments so they could do their walk together in the park.

'I do not care for that cloak. You vill another vear.'

'Oh, that one is a little heavy for this time of the year.'

'I say you vill this von vear.'

The women were startled, but Caroline meekly put on the cloak.

Something has happened, she thought. Why should there be so much drama about a cloak?

They sauntered in the gardens. If she made a comment to anyone he would immediately contradict it.

'Pooh and stuff. That is von nonsense.'

The Queen was humiliated, but smilingly she agreed with all he said.

He strutted ahead of her. Let her keep her distance. His voice was strident, arrogant. He was implying to everyone that he was the master and the Queen was entirely subservient to him.

She dared not offer an opinion, for if she did he would certainly contradict it. Yet he did not change his habits in one way. He always visited her at precisely the same time as before; they walked at the same hour; the state papers were still delivered to her for perusal. The King's great obsession was to show the court that the Queen was his slave.

His greatest pleasure seemed to be to snub her in public, and he never lost an opportunity of doing this.

'The position,' Caroline told Walpole, 'is becoming intolerable.'

'You will overcome the difficulty,' soothed Walpole. 'A plague on these scribblers.'

So it became a new challenge to lead the King even more skilfully than ever before; and gradually she made a little headway. Her method must be to express an adverse opinion of something she sought to bring about. The King would immediately see its advantages; and once he had committed himself she could agree with him and strengthen his views.

But she did not enjoy being constantly humiliated before the court. Yet although Walpole's enemies rejoiced, their exultation was only temporary, because it soon became obvious that the Queen was ready to endure the snubs for the sake of power.

Walpole came to the Queen.

'I must speak to you about the Prince of Wales,' he said.

Caroline's spirits sank. 'Is that necessary?'

'Very necessary. We cannot keep him out of the country much longer. The Opposition are attacking us for allowing him to remain so long away. They will have the people behind them. The King must be made to see that action should be taken at once.'

'The King vill never agree.'

'We must make him agree.'

'You know the difficulties vich have arisen.'

'I know Your Majesty always to make light of difficulties.'

She did not answer; and he knew that in this matter she was in complete agreement with the King. She, as much as he, did not want Frederick to come home.

But Walpole was going to insist.

'It is unthinkable,' he said, 'that the Prince of Wales should have reached the age of twenty-one and never have visited the country he will one day rule. Your Majesty will, I know, realize that there can no longer be any delay.'

The Queen sighed. Life was very difficult. She had had to endure the King's public slights; and now her friend and ally was going against her wishes.

She wondered how long she and the King could hold out against Walpole and the Parliament. In such a country where the Parliament ruled, it would not be easy; yet she could not reconcile herself to receiving her son.

The marriage plot

In the old Leine Schloss Frederick, Prince of Wales, was wondering why his parents did not send for him. He could not understand the position. When his grandfather was alive it had been reasonable enough. Grandfather had been King of England and Frederick's father Prince of Wales. As his grandfather was also Elector of Hanover it had seemed natural enough – at least not incomprehensible – that he, Frederick, should remain at Hanover to represent the family. That was his grandfather's explanation on his visits. But now, his father had been King for over a year and still he was not invited to go to England.

'I don't understand it,' he said to his friend Lamotte, who was an officer in the Hanoverian army. 'Surely I should be in England by this time.'

'Doubtless Your Highness will be recalled soon now.'

'Soon! I've been waiting for more than a year for that summons.'

Frederick stood up and paced up and down the apartment. He was a good-looking young man, but short like his father; he had the heavy, rather sullen Hanoverian jaw and the rather protuberant blue eyes; but because of his youth these had not become accentuated as in the case of grandfather and father –

and the good skin and bright hair gave him a pleasing appearance.

'Well, Your Highness enjoys life in Hanover.'

Frederick considered it. It was true. He had his position and everyone wished to be in his good graces. He had his mistresses and his men friends, and both pleased him equally. It was not that he had anything to complain of in Hanover. But he was the Prince of Wales; he had never seen England; and he had not seen his parents since he was seven. Therefore he was piqued because although they had been at liberty to send for him for more than a year they had not yet done so.

Did they think he was a child still?

If they did, he would soon disillusion them.

'I have no intention of waiting another year, Lamotte,' he said.

'What will Your Highness do?'

'I'll think of something. It's time I was married for one thing. I should be producing a family . . . a *legitimate* family. After all it will be for me to provide England with a future king. I want to try my skill on the battlefield. In fact I want them to understand I am no longer a boy. If they don't act soon, Lamotte, I promise you I shall. There is my cousin, Wilhelmina. We should be married by now.'

'You think your father will agree to the match?'

'But it was arranged by my grandfather. Wilhelmina and I would be married by now if he hadn't died. My Aunt Sophia Dorothea wants it.'

'It will depend, of course, Your Highness, on your uncle the King of Prussia and your father the King of England.'

'Everyone knows that my uncle of Prussia is a madman.'

Lamotte was silent and Frederick burst out laughing.

'Oh come, Lamotte, you don't have to be cautious with me. You know how he treats his family. I should imagine Wilhelmina will be glad to escape. She will look upon me as her rescuer and she'll love me for that alone.'

The Prince was gazing dreamily ahead. The boy had very romantic notions, Lamotte thought.

'Why should I wait!' cried Frederick suddenly. 'Poor Wilhelmina! What will she think of me? Doubtless she is waiting for me to come and rescue her and take her away from Berlin . . . for what a hell that must be. My uncle is brutal to them both . . . I don't know how they endure it. They say he thrashes them with his own hands – my cousin Fritz *and* Wilhelmina. I'll swear she is waiting for me to come and take her away.'

'She will know, Your Highness, that everything depends on the whim of her father . . . and yours.'

'Oh, these parents! Why should they rule our lives when we are of age? I tell you this, Lamotte: I am going to marry my cousin Wilhelmina and there shall be no more delay.'

'I don't see how, Your Highness . . .'

'Of course you don't. But I've thought of a plan. I am going to Berlin and if necessary I shall carry off my cousin. I shall bring her back to Hanover and together she will come with me to England.'

'You think she would agree?'

'Have you forgotten that in the first place she will escape from that hell on earth and in the second by marrying me she will become Princess of Wales. And you ask if she will agree!'

'So Your Highness plans to go to Berlin.'

'Not just at first. First I shall send an ambassador . . . a secret ambassador. How does that strike you, Lamotte? He shall travel to Berlin and find a way of sounding the Princess Wilhelmina, and the Queen. . . . The ambassador will tell them that I intend travelling to Berlin and that if the King of Prussia and the King of England won't give their consent we shall do without it.'

'And how do you think the Queen will respond to that?'

'My dear Lamotte, she wants this marriage more than anything in the world. It was her idea in the first place that there should be a double marriage plan. Wilhelmina for me and my sister Amelia for her son Fritz. Her daughter to be Queen of England in due course and her niece, my sister Amelia, to be Queen of Prussia. It will keep the two crowns in the family. That is her plan and she longs to see it put into practice. There will be no opposition from that quarter.'

'And you think your ambassador will succeed in this mission?'

'I am sure he will. He has never failed me before.'

'So you have chosen him.'

Frederick smiled. 'Certainly. You will begin making your preparations to leave at once, my dear Lamotte.'

Lamotte was uneasy as he came into Berlin.

It was all very well for Frederick to assure him that he had been given this mission because he was a trusted friend. There were times when it was safer not to be on too intimate terms with princes. This was a delicate mission and it could so easily go wrong; and those who had been commanded to help carry out such missions were often blamed.

Would it be possible for Frederick to marry without the consent of his father? He supposed so if the King of Prussia gave that consent; and if the King of Prussia knew that it was against the wishes of the King of England that his son should marry Wilhelmina he would most certainly approve of the match; for nothing could give the King of Prussia more pleasure than the discomfiture of the King of England.

Yes, it was indeed a delicate mission. And how best discharge it?

Frederick had sworn that he would give Lamotte three weeks to prepare the way before he himself left Hanover for Berlin; by the end of that time he expected Lamotte to have found out what his reception would be – but, he had pointed out emphatically, he intended to come in any case. If they were prepared to welcome him, all well and good; he would come and marry Wilhelmina. If not, he would come in secret and elope with her.

The Prince must be welcomed to Berlin, thought Lamotte. An elopement would be disastrous; in any case Wilhelmina might decide against such a measure. Lamotte was not as certain that she was as eager for the marriage as Frederick was.

Lamotte had a friend who was a chamberlain to the Queen of Prussia and to this young man, whose name was Sastot, he decided to present himself. If Sastot could arrange a meeting with the Queen that would be the best move because of one thing Lamotte was certain: the Queen of Prussia was as eager for this marriage as Frederick himself.

But the affair must be kept an absolute secret, for it could be disastrous if a hint of what was happening reached the ears of the King of England.

He presented himself at Sastot's residence telling the servants that he was a nobleman travelling for pleasure and had just arrived in Berlin so thought he would call on an old friend.

Sastot was delighted to see him and when they were alone together Lamotte asked him if it would be possible for him to obtain an interview with the Queen.

'A gentleman travelling for pleasure wishes to be presented to the Queen! What are you thinking of, Lamotte. You know that's not possible.'

Lamotte sighed. 'I feared not. I shall have to disclose the nature of my business for I have no doubt that that will secure me an interview.'

'Your business? What business is this?'

'You must keep this secret. If it became known why I am here the whole plan would founder.'

'I can't wait to hear.'

'Now, Sastot, you swear secrecy?'

Sastot swore.

'I come from Frederick, Prince of Wales.'

'I guessed it.'

'He is impatient for marriage with the Princess Wilhelmina and as his father seems to have forgotten his existence he has decided to take steps on his own.'

'I don't think there will be any difficulty in my obtaining an interview for you with the Queen if *that* is your mission.'

'But remember, Sastot, the most absolute secrecy. If this became known the King of England would certainly take action and heaven alone knows what the King of Prussia would do.'

'Lock his daughter away and starve her to death most likely. On the other hand I heard him shout at her only last week that it was time she married and stopped being a burden to him.'

'Poor Princess! She will be devoted to the Prince if he rescues her from that. So you will go to the Queen without delay, tell her I am here, and impress on her the need for speed.'

'I will. She will be delighted.'

Guessing his mission, Queen Sophia Dorothea could scarcely wait to receive the ambassador from Hanover.

If this marriage could come about it would be wonderful. It

had always been her most cherished ambition; and once it was completed she would have Fritz married to his cousin Amelia and Amelia would come here in Wilhelmina's place when Wilhelmina went to England. What better arrangement could there be?

Poor Wilhelmina, she had suffered a great deal from her father's violence. Her shoulders were still black and blue from the blows he had given her only a few days ago. She always wanted to cry out: Don't stand there, Wilhelmina, looking indifferent. It only makes him worse. If you'd only whimper and cry he'd stop. He wants to subjugate everyone ... including me, and when he has done so he loses interest.

Fritz suffered most from the King. Why the boy didn't turn on his father astonished her. He could have put up a good fight, but he meekly accepted abuse and violence and longed for escape. Perhaps it was because this fearsome husband of hers was the King that they were afraid of him – all, of course, except Sophia Dorothea.

She smiled, remembering those occasions when he had come at her, arms uplifted, eyes ablaze with rage; and she would defy him, or perhaps pick up whatever object was nearest preparing to throw it at him – on one occasion there had been a knife. He had laughed at her, spat at her, kicked her stool across the room, and shouted: 'You ... you with your puny strength! So you would fight me!' Then he would laugh as though the idea was too ludicrous to be treated seriously, and stride out of the room.

One thing she knew; he would never harm her. She was too important to him. In his way he loved her, odd as that might seem. And she – well at least she would find life dull without him.

He supplied the excitement in her life; but to her children she was tender and loving; and because they had such a father, they turned to her and were devoted to her.

She was contented; she had her wild, mad husband who, she knew, could no more do without her than she could without him; and her two beloved children. There was no fear of the King's encroaching on the affection they gave her. They loathed him. As for him, he didn't want love from them, only fear. He spoke of them to their mother with contempt. 'Your daughter,

Madam. Your Fritz.' As though he had had no part in producing them.

Dear to her heart was her double marriage plan and she believed this would have come to fruition by now if her father had lived. But when George I died, the plan had been shelved, although he had promised that when he next came to Britain his grandson Frederick should be betrothed to Wilhelmina and Fritz to Amelia. It would have been perfect. The cousins would have been well matched. She would have welcomed Amelia to Berlin; and she was sure that Caroline and George would have welcomed Wilhelmina to England.

And then, unexpectedly, her father had died, and of course the King of Prussia and the King of England hated each other.

Her brother – strange to think of George Augustus as the King of England – had always been a conceited little popinjay; and he could have his violent moments too. She laughed, remembering how he used to kick his wig round the room in moments of rage. But she did not remember his ever attacking anyone, so perhaps Caroline and his children were safe in that respect. And by all accounts Caroline knew how to manage him. She had always known Caroline was a clever woman from the days when she had first come to Hanover as her brother's bride. They had liked each other then, but their acquaintance had been brief because very soon after the marriage of George Augustus and Caroline, she herself had married and come to Berlin.

In England Wilhelmina would be happier than in Berlin, for she could trust her daughter with Caroline, and Frederick by all accounts was a young man rather like his father had been. If Wilhelmina was clever she would manage Frederick as Caroline managed George Augustus.

Therefore the Queen gave immediate audience to Lamotte and when he stated his case she told him that nothing could please her more than to further this match; she would see her daughter at once and point out to her her good fortune.

'Wilhelmina, my child.'

The Queen came quietly into her daughter's apartment.

'Oh, Mother!' Wilhelmina rose and embraced the Queen. She was a tall girl, not beautiful, yet by no means plain; she had a bright, intelligent face and at the moment it was softened by the tenderness she always showed towards her mother.

'You are excited,' said Wilhelmina, looking into her mother's face. 'What has happened?'

'Such news! I am delighted. Oh, my poor sweet child, how it has grieved me to see you suffer.'

'Oh . . . father?' said Wilhelmina with a shrug. 'That is nothing new.'

'I am always afraid that one day he will kill either you or Fritz.'

'I don't think so, Mother. We are after all good bargaining counters. I think he would remember that in time.'

The Queen shuddered. 'His rages are terrible. It would not surprise me if you are longing for the day you will escape from them.'

'Escape?'

'Well, my darling, you will marry one day.'

'I suppose so.'

The Queen smiled. 'And perhaps that day is not far distant. There is one young man who is most impatient.'

'Who, Mother?'

'Your cousin Frederick, of course.'

'I . . . I was afraid you were going to say that.'

'Afraid?'

'I know there was once a plan and that when my grandfather came here it was discussed.'

'If he hadn't died you would be married by now. I'll swear.'

'I don't know, Mother. Sometimes I think even grandfather wasn't eager for the marriages.'

'My dear, he was just bargaining with your father. He wanted a bigger dowry for you.'

Wilhelmina looked relieved. 'That is something he will never get from father.'

'Your father will have to do his duty.'

'I didn't know that he ever did that. He does what he wants, not what is his duty.'

'Your father!' Sophia Dorothea raised her hands in an expression of incomprehension.

'Since he grudges me my food it is scarcely likely that he will provide me with a dowry. And if I shall not be accepted without . . .'

'You despair too easily, my dear.'

'I don't know that I would call it despair. I do not wish to leave *you*, Mother.'

'My dearest! But princesses cannot stay forever with their mothers. You will have to marry in time and your cousin Frederick is a very impatient young man. He declares he is in love with you and refuses to wait any longer.'

'Since he has never seen me, the first seems unlikely; and as he is not in a position to decide whether or not he will marry the second seems equally so.'

'I have not explained. He has sent a messenger to tell me he proposes to come to Berlin and if your father will not consent, to carry you off.'

'It sounds as though he is a very foolish young man.'

'He is a romantic young man who is in love.'

'With a woman he has never seen?'

'With his cousin of whom he will have heard a great deal. Wilhelmina, this is your chance. You will one day be Queen of England. Think of that.'

'And never see you again?'

'I shall visit you there.'

'Papa will never allow the expense.'

'And you shall visit us here.'

'That would cost money too.'

'Don't be so glum, child. This is a wonderful opportunity. You will marry. You will leave this place. Oh, my dear, when I see the way your father treats you I could long for the day . . . much as I shall hate parting with you. But you will have a good life. You will manage Frederick as Caroline manages your uncle. All you have to allow him to do is have his mistresses. He'll ask nothing more. And you will go to your Aunt Caroline who is a sensible woman. I know that. I liked her when we were at Hanover together. She will tell you how to manage Frederick as she manages your uncle.'

'It is not my idea of marriage, Mother.'

'Oh, romantic notions! I should have thought life here would have long stifled those.'

'Rather they have encouraged them. All marriages can't be like yours and father's.'

'And you want one which is not like ours?'

'As unlike as possible.'

The Queen sighed. 'My darling, you are wise in so many ways; it is only experience you lack. I tell you this : I am delighted with the prospect. And the fact that Frederick is impatient for the marriage pleases me more than anything else. Wilhelmina, I am so delighted. I shall at last see you settled and happy and at the same time see all my wishes realized. What greater joy could I ask? Why, you are crying.'

'It is the thought of leaving you, Mother.'

They embraced and Wilhelmina tried to hide the misgivings she felt. She tried to set aside her doubts as she listened to her mother's explanations of what a glorious prospect lay before her.

This was such a cherished dream of Sophia Dorothea's, and Wilhelmina longed to please her mother.

The King came in while they were talking together.

He looked at them through his little bloodshot eyes and cried out : 'What plot's this, eh? You look sly. Out with it. Your girl had better tell me what she has been up to, woman, or by God I'll flay her till there's no breath left in that slothful body of hers.'

'We were merely discussing a little project,' retorted Sophia Dorothea, always pert with him because to have showed fear would have put her into the position her son and daughter were in. 'And I fancy even your high and mightiness might not be displeased with this one.'

'Do you think she would ever please me? She sits about this place eating my food, drinking my wine. By God when I think of what she costs me I wonder I keep her. Come here, girl.'

Wilhelmina stood up. She was defiant, her mother noticed and that was better than cringing.

Her father seized her by her hair and shook her to and fro. Wilhelmina's face was scarlet but she kept her eyes lowered.

'Don't be impudent you slut, you whore, you lily-livered spawn of a . . .'

He looked at his wife.

'Of a madman,' said Sophia Dorothea to turn his attention from her daughter to herself.

It succeeded; he released Wilhelmina, throwing her from him so that she fell to the floor. Sophia Dorothea saw that she was unharmed. She and her brother had had long practice in falling where their father threw them. Sophia Dorothea said quickly: 'Go to your own apartments.' The girl hesitated. Why would both Wilhelmina and Fritz think they had to protect *her* from their father. Didn't they know yet that she could manage him?

'Go,' she repeated imperiously; and picking herself up, Wilhelmina obeyed.

'Well?' The King advanced scowling.

The Queen picked up a heavy book which was lying on a table and laughed at him. She saw the mad mischief leap into his eyes as he approached.

'So you think to fight me with that book. Where will you aim for?'

'At your mad eyes,' she answered.

'Well, I'm waiting.'

'It would be more sensible to talk.'

'Sensible. *You* . . . sensible!'

'A little more than you, I hope, or heaven alone knows what would happen to us all.'

'Don't show your concern for me, Madam. I should get along very well without you and your children.'

'Who happen to be yours.'

'Can I be sure of that?'

'It's true they seem sane reasonable beings . . .'

'You are going too far, Madam.'

'*You* have already gone too far. But I will talk to you. Save your quarrels for another time. The Prince of Wales wants to marry Wilhelmina without delay.'

'I always thought he was half-witted.'

'I happen to think him a most sensible young man. He is tired of being neglected by his family.'

'Huh! That fool of a brother of yours. Of all the conceited young idiots . . .'

'He's not so young now. He's a father . . . a little older than you are in truth. And he has a son and a daughter . . . as you have. Yes, you may call them mine, but they are yours also and it is time you remembered your duties as a father. Frederick is coming here and he wants to marry Wilhelmina.'

'He'd have to take her without a dowry.'

'Don't be a fool. Of course she'll have a dowry.'

'By God, I'll take my riding whip to you if you don't control your tongue.'

'All in good time, but before you try your stable manners on me I'd like you to think of this plan. It's the best thing that can happen for Wilhelmina and imagine – you won't have to feed her in future. That will be for her husband to do.'

'I suppose in return they'll want us to have that girl of theirs here.'

'Amelia for Fritz. It is part of the plan.'

His eyes narrowed. 'I'll not have her here. I've heard something of her. I want no haughty young woman walking about my Court with her nose in the air, making trouble. No, I don't want George Augustus's girl here and I won't have her.'

'Fritz will have to marry at some time. Why not a daughter of the King of England?'

'I tell you I won't have that girl here. If I ever hear you or Fritz mention her name again I'll flog you both. Fritz will marry when I say so and I'll choose the bride.'

'Well, at least you will not say no to Wilhelmina's taking Frederick.'

He took her by the shoulders and shook her; she knocked his hands away. He could have struck her and sent her falling to the floor but he didn't. He didn't want to hurt her physically. He only wanted to enjoy verbal battles with her. He'd save the floggings for his children.

'I'll be glad to be rid of the girl,' he growled.

So, thought Sophia Dorothea, half of the marriage plan would be fulfilled. And when Wilhelmina was safely married the time would come for Fritz to marry the Princess Amelia. She had no doubt that she could bring that about.

She was receiving guests in her apartments and everyone noticed what good spirits she was in. Bourguait, the Envoy from the Court of St James's, was especially graciously received, and he complimented her on her healthy looks.

'I am in very good spirits,' she told him. 'And it is because of a very special piece of news.'

'Then I am delighted.'

'And a little curious?'

'While not presuming to inquire the nature of Your Majesty's good fortune, I should naturally be delighted to congratulate you.'

'Which you could do much better if you knew what it was about.' She laughed. Sophia Dorothea was not noted for her discretion. She decided then that as the Prince of Wales was so determined and the King of Prussia would clearly put nothing in the way of the project there was no need to keep silent about it. 'Then I shall tell you,' she said. 'My daughter is going to marry the Prince of Wales.'

'Your Majesty!'

'Oh, yes. It's true. Frederick the Prince is so impatient he has decided to come here and claim his bride. Of course we shall welcome him. And the King will raise no objections. Between ourselves, he is as eager for this marriage as I am ... and as our dear young people are. You look startled?'

'I ... I have to remind Your Majesty that I am the Envoy of His Majesty the King of England who is as deeply concerned in this matter as Your Majesties of Prussia. It is my duty to inform him without delay.'

'That is surely not necessary. The Prince has made up his mind.'

'Your Majesty, I must humbly point out that the marriage of the Prince of Wales is most decidedly the concern of his father the King, and that I should be failing in my duty if I neglected to tell him of this plan.'

'But to do so could spoil everything!'

'If the Prince is so determined it may be that the King will be pleased to give his consent. The Princess Wilhelmina and the Prince of Wales have been considered almost formally betrothed for some time.'

'Of course. The King of England will be delighted that his son has shown that he can act like a man.'

'It may well be so.'

Bourguait said no more; but as soon as he left the Queen he despatched a messenger to St James's with the news that the Prince of Wales was planning to visit Berlin, his intention being not to wait for his father's consent to his marriage.

George came hurrying into Caroline's apartments, his wig askew, his eyes bulging.

'Something is disturbing Your Majesty,' said the Queen, rising from the table where she sat reading some of the state documents which she made a habit of perusing each day.

'Dismiss these people. Vat a fool you are! Can't you see that I vish to talk to you.'

That was the manner in which he addressed her since the appearance of that unfortunate verse – and always in the presence of others.

Caroline flushed slightly, but showed no resentment at his rudeness; she merely nodded to her attendants who quickly retired.

As soon as they had gone the King sat down and testily waved a paper.

Caroline came to him, took it, and read it.

She caught her breath in dismay. How could Frederick be so disobedient? The idea of taking matters into his own hands, and trying to arrange his own marriage! He must be mad.

'Vell?' growled George.

He was looking at her almost appealingly. She must say what must be best done and then he would tell her that he had made up his mind what action to take.

'That he could dare!' she whispered.

'My Got, ve shall trouble have vith this young man.'

'Perhaps Your Majesty vill decide there is only von thing you can do now.'

He nodded, waiting.

'They are saying he should come here. Perhaps you vill think there is no alternative but to bring him to England now, since it is clearly not safe for him to be out of Your Majesty's control.'

'To bring him here!' the King said dismally.

'Perhaps I am wrong . . .' said Caroline hastily.

'Do ve vant him here? He vill von big trouble be.' The King's English always suffered when he grew agitated, and he was agitated now.

'He vill be trouble there ... more trouble perhaps than here. Here he vill have to obey Your Majesty.'

They looked at each other dolefully.

'I hav my mind made up,' said the King. 'I vill him teach to make a marriage vithout my consent.'

'I am sure you are right,' said the Queen. She smiled. 'As you alvays are.'

He leaned towards her and patted her shoulder. It was only when others were present that he remembered he was displeased with her.

Lamotte had returned to Hanover and Frederick was delighted with what he heard.

'Tell me about Wilhelmina,' he insisted.

'She is a handsome girl, very tall and good-looking.'

'And meek? Is she meek?'

'Her father has seen to that.'

'That is good. I always wanted a meek wife. And is she delighted that she is soon to have a husband?'

'She is not a girl to betray her feelings. The Queen is overjoyed. The King is not displeased. There will be no difficulty. They will now be preparing a great welcome for you.'

'I wish I could see my parents' faces when they receive the news. They'll be furious. They'll regret leaving me alone all this time in Hanover. They'll see too that I don't need them. I shall take Wilhelmina to England ... without delay. What do you think of that, Lamotte?'

'I am not sure what kind of reception you would have.'

'They would have to welcome the Prince and Princess of Wales.'

'Perhaps, Your Highness. But the King is of greater importance than a Prince and I remember how your grandfather treated your father when he was Prince of Wales.'

'It seems to be a habit in this family to quarrel. But I was on the side of my grandfather in that dispute, you know.'

'That was because you never saw your parents and heard only his side, perhaps.'

'I didn't dislike Grandfather. He was always good to me. I wonder how I shall feel about my father and mother. I wonder if my mother wants to see me. By all accounts she is the one who rules, so had *she* wanted me, presumably I should have been recalled.'

'I think you should act very carefully, Your Highness.'

'I intend to. But I am determined to leave within the next few days for Berlin. I think I shall give a farewell ball to all my friends in Hanover ... all those who cannot accompany me to Berlin. Don't you think that's an excellent idea?'

Lamotte agreed that it was.

Frederick chose Herrenhausen – that favourite of palaces – largely because it was more intimate than the Alte Palais or the Leine Schloss.

The great hall was ablaze with the lights of thousands of candles and all the nobility of Hanover were present. Frederick presided, in high spirits. It was a long time since he had been so pleased with himself.

He led the dance with his favourite mistress and comforted her, telling her that once he was in England he would send for her. She must not grieve because he would have a wife. Wives were necessities but mistresses were for pleasure.

She understood, remembering stories she had heard of Frederick's grandfather who had been faithful to his two old mistresses until the end and had shut his wife away, keeping her a prisoner for thirty years.

Frederick was gayer than any remembered his being before. He was merry with his male friends and assured them that he would send for them too.

During the evening when visitors arrived at Herrenhausen, the Prince was surprised that they should come at such a time, but he declared that on this occasion all were welcome.

The visitors proved to be from England and they were led by a man who announced himself as Colonel Lorne.

'I must speak privately to Your Highness without delay,' he

said; and the Prince took him into a small chamber close to the ballroom.

'You have letters for me?' he asked.

'From Your Highness's father. I have them here. I have orders from His Majesty to return to England tomorrow and it is my duty to tell Your Highness that you must accompany me.'

'Accompany you . . . to England.'

'On the orders of His Majesty your father.'

'But . . . I am going to Berlin.'

Colonel Lorne coughed deprecatingly. 'I am sorry to have to inform Your Highness that His Majesty's orders are that you leave Hanover with me tomorrow, for England.'

Sophia Dorothea spent a great deal of time at the topmost tower of the palace watching the road for visitors. He would come with a small party of friends and followers. She had given orders that he must be entertained royally, and even the King had not objected.

He might pretend that it was because he wished to be rid of his daughter, but he was pleased at the prospect of this marriage. If Wilhelmina married the Prince of Wales and became Queen of England and he no longer had to feed and clothe her, he would be delighted.

Sophia Dorothea laughed. The first half of the plan satisfactorily completed. Then she would busy herself with the second.

Soon she would be welcoming the Princess Amelia to Prussia and when Fritz had a wife he would be happier – and his father would not dare flog a married man.

She had thought Frederick would come before this. She had heard such stories of his eagerness.

And then one day she saw the rider. A solitary rider – that was strange. But of course he would come to announce the arrival of his master.

She would tell them they would not have to wait much longer. In the kitchens they could start preparing for the wedding feast – for wedding feast there would be in spite of the King's objections.

Yes, the rider was in the Hanoverian livery.

She went down to greet him. She wanted to be the first to receive the announcement of the Prince's arrival.

She took the letter he gave her. She read it. She would not believe it. She could not take it in. Not at this stage. It would be too heartbreaking.

But there were the words staring at her: The Prince of Wales had left Hanover for England on the orders of his father. He would not be coming to Berlin.

So . . . there would be no marriage.

The King of Prussia stormed through the Palace. Now it seemed the one thing he had wanted was the marriage of his daughter to the Prince of Wales and it had failed.

He summoned his son and daughter with his wife to his presence.

'You fools!' he shouted. 'You have ruined this between you! By God, I'll kill the lot of you.'

He had a whip with him and he began flogging his son and daughter.

The Queen shrieked at him to stop; but he shouted back at her to take care he did not use the whip on her. Sick with rage and disappointment she fell fainting to the ground and her women carried her to her bed where she lay in a state of collapse.

The King contented himself with beating his son and daughter in such a manner that they too had to be carried to their beds and their wounds attended to by the court physician.

He then shut himself in his room and swore at everyone who approached him; the Queen lay sick with disappointment; the Crown Prince stoically thought of the time when his father would be dead and he would be King Frederick of Prussia; and Wilhelmina thought: at least I'm still unmarried.

Meanwhile Frederick Prince of Wales was on his way to England.

Frederick, Prince of Wales

Frederick's homecoming

It was about seven o'clock in the evening of a dark December day when Frederick arrived by hackney coach like any private visitor at the Palace of St James's.

He did not look in the least like a frustrated bridegroom. Indeed he was secretly pleased at the way everything had turned out. He had not wanted marriage so much as to bring home to his parents that he would no longer endure their neglect. After all, what had a young man of twenty-one, who was after all Prince of Wales, to fear from his parents?

Riding from Whitechapel he had seen a little of the city, and dark as it was, it had excited him. As he rode he was telling himself, 'One day I shall rule this land. What have I to fear?'

The coach had drawn up and Colonel Lorne was saying: 'This is the Friary, Your Highness. I shall now conduct you to the Queen's backstairs and you can present yourself to her without delay.'

To his mother, he noticed, not to his father. It was true, he supposed, that his mother was the important member of the family.

Colonel Lorne preceded him up the stairs and scratched on a door which was opened by a middle-aged woman whose appearance was charming, if not striking.

'Mrs Howard, the Queen should be informed without delay that the Prince of Wales is here.'

Mrs Howard looked startled; then she saw the Prince and swept him a deep curtsy which Frederick acknowledged with a gracious bow.

Mrs Howard disappeared and came back in a few seconds.

'If Your Highness will come this way . . .'

He followed her into the apartment and there, waiting for him, was his mother.

For some seconds they looked at each other, neither speaking. It was after all an important moment in their lives. This was the mother who had said such a tearful farewell to him fourteen years ago and had fought so desperately to have him brought to England for a few years – and then appeared to have become resigned to his absence, and after that, indifferent. This was the son whom she had lost so long ago that she had forgotten him and whom she now saw only as an impostor come to take what she would prefer her darling William to have.

The emotion they felt was smothered in a resentment on both sides.

'Welcome home, Frederick,' said Caroline, extending her hand.

'Thank you . . . Mother.' Frederick took it and kissed it.

There was nothing she could think of to say to him. She felt cold; it was scarcely possible to believe that this was the child she had borne and cherished with such love and devotion. There was no sign of her little Fritzchen in this young man. He was elegant, she noticed; he had gracious manners; and he was very like his father – at least what George Augustus had been at his age. There were the same full, pouting lips, the blue eyes that were too prominent, the neat figure, shapely but too small for manliness. She wondered if he was as conscious of his low stature as his father was of his. She hoped not, for that awareness had helped to make George the difficult man he was.

'You have had a good journey?'

'Well, scarcely that, Madam. The crossing was bad. I thought we should all be drowned.'

'It is bad at this time of year.'

She noticed that he spoke English better than she or the King did. His English tutors had done their work well. That would help him to popularity with the people here. He must not, of course, be too popular.

'You vill vish to meet your brothers and sisters. And the King vill vish to know that you are here. I vill have him told.'

She gave the order to one of her women.

A strange welcome after all these years! thought Frederick. His mother did not altogether surprise him, for he had heard a great deal about her. She was a tall, buxom woman who was still not without beauty and only slightly marked by smallpox. Her hands were beautiful and her neck and shoulders magnificent. She was stately and had an air of queenliness. He wished that she had shown more pleasure in his arrival.

But he was determined to enjoy life in England. He was, after all, Prince of Wales; there would be many to remember that and it was certain to be more exciting here than it had been in Hanover.

The King came into the apartment. Frederick was looking at what could well be himself in twenty or thirty years' time.

The blue eyes were less clear, the complexion more ruddy, but there was the Hanoverian jaw, the Hanoverian eyes.

The King noticed that his son was of his own height and was gratified; he did not like men to be taller than he was and he was continually being annoyed to find they were.

Apart from that he was irritated. He did not want his son here – sons meant trouble. He seemed eager to please, though. All the more reason to be watchful, he warned himself.

'So you've come home,' he said gruffly.

'Yes, Your Majesty.'

'We had to stop that Berlin nonsense.'

The Prince flushed. 'I felt I was of a marriageable age, sir.'

The King turned away and said to the Queen: 'So he's come home then.'

The Queen smiled as though he had said something very wise.

'As Your Majesty says, the people vill be interested to see him.'

'And I to see them . . . and this country. I have often thought of it.'

'You speak good English,' said the Queen.

The King scowled. Although he was unaware how bad his own accent was, he knew that the Prince's was superior.

'Not like a German at all,' went on the Queen with a smile.

'It is not a bad thing to be a German,' said the King.

'It is a good thing,' answered the Queen quickly.

'It is von very good thing.'

The Prince was bewildered, reading something beneath the surface of the conversation. It seemed as though the Queen were very much in awe of his father, which was contrary to the reports he had heard. He had expected to find her in command. Perhaps the rumours which had come to Hanover were not true. His mother seemed afraid of his father; and his father was a testy little man who was not going to pretend he was glad to see his firstborn.

A strange homecoming!

Frederick was glad when the rest of the family arrived in his mother's apartments to meet him.

It was rather exciting suddenly to find oneself a member of a large family.

They were presented to him in order of age. Anne first, haughty, not very attractive, being short like her father and plump like her mother. She looked with disdain at this new brother when she was presented, as though she would have preferred him to stay in Hanover.

'I remember you well,' he told her pleasantly.

'I don't remember you.'

'You were, after all, two years younger.'

She resented that; if he had not been born, if she had had no brothers, she would have been the heir to the throne. A second Queen Anne! She could never forget it; it rankled and festered because what she longed to be more than anything was a queen. And this young man – as well as spoilt William – stood in her way.

'Well, you're here now. I was in the middle of a singing lesson when I was summoned.'

'I'm sorry.'

'Mr Handel is my professor. I believe him to be possessed of genius.'

'That must be very pleasant.'

She looked at him scornfully, but Amelia was now waiting to be presented.

Amelia was decidedly prettier than Anne, and more pleasant. She whispered to her brother that she had been very interested in his plans to marry their cousin, particularly as, he knew, she might well be betrothed to Wilhelmina's brother. Poor Amelia! he thought. How would she fare at the Court of Prussia? Would the madman of a king dare to treat her as he treated poor Wilhelmina and Fritz?

'I should not care too much that the marriage is delayed,' he told her. 'One day I will have a great deal to tell you of the Court of Berlin.'

Then there was Caroline – delicate and gentle, eager to make up by her welcome for the lack of warmth in that of the others. He thought Caroline might be his favourite sister.

The other little girls were too young to impress him much; but they seemed pretty little creatures. His only brother, William, Duke of Cumberland, took an immediate dislike to him, and he to William.

'So you're our German brother,' said the arrogant boy.

'I'm as English as you are,' Frederick reminded him.

'What! You have lived all your life in Germany. I have never been there.'

'It is an omission you will probably rectify when you are old enough.'

Frederick turned away from the boy and spoke to Caroline.

He was thinking what a strange homecoming this was. This gentle girl seemed the only member of the family who was glad he had come.

The King and Queen decided that the Prince of Wales should slip quietly into his place at court. There should be no fanfares of welcome, no *fêtes* to celebrate his arrival.

George somewhat grudgingly admitted him to the Privy Council where he was formally created Prince of Wales. It disturbed him to see that his son was an immediate success. His youth, his good manners, and his ability to speak the language with scarcely a trace of German accent was applauded. It was his own family who behaved ungraciously to him.

The two chief offenders were Anne and William. Anne was his enemy from the first largely because she resented his sex and his being her senior. The older she grew, the more fearful she was of not finding a suitable husband and nothing less than a prince would satisfy her; if she could become a queen she would be slightly reconciled to being excluded from the crown of England. Therefore the return of this elder brother was particularly galling to her. William sulkily showed his resentment. He had been treated as the only son; all the privileges which came to the male of the family had been his; and now to have a brother thrust upon him, and an elder brother, was insupportable. He made no effort to hide his resentment.

It flared up on the first occasion the whole family went to church and William, according to his custom since he had been able to walk, prepared to lead his mother to her place.

'My dear William,' she whispered, 'this will be your brother's duty now.'

William's face was purple with rage.

'Why should it be?' he demanded. 'He's a German. I am an Englishman. I won't stand aside for this German.'

'You will stand aside for the Prince of Wales,' his mother told him.

So Frederick led her to her place and his younger brother William hated him fiercely and wished he had stayed in Hanover.

Anne, watching the incident, shared her brother's hatred.

It's not fair, she thought. He's weak. That's obvious. He'll be led anywhere. And he is the Prince of Wales whereas I, because I'm a year or so younger, and a woman, can never be Queen of England because of him! I'll have to go away from home to marry some prince.

c.q.—5

She shivered; not at the fear of leaving home, but that a prince might not be found for her.

Frederick did not brood on his lukewarm reception. He found his new country exceedingly exciting. It was entirely different from Hanover. The streets were full of gaiety, noise, and colour; he liked to ride through them, for sometimes he would be recognized and a shout would go up of 'Long Live the Prince of Wales!'

Those garrulous, inquisitive people had already sensed the royal family's resentment towards the eldest son and immediately ranged themselves on the Prince's side. Ever since the old King had died, and before that, they had been asking why the Prince was not in England; now they were delighted to see him; he was a pleasant-looking, pleasant-mannered young man, fresh-skinned and charmingly affable, speaking their language with scarcely any trace of a German accent.

London seemed full of adventure and excitement. Gay's *Beggar's Opera* was drawing crowds to the theatre and there was a great deal of controversy over this piece because many declared that MacHeath the highwayman was meant to be a sly portrait of Walpole and Peacham of Townshend. That this could happen was enlightening to the Prince. It never could have been so in Hanover where the Elector was all-powerful. It was amusing to see how the English treated their kings, how they made ballads about them, did not hesitate to shout abuse at them, expressing their disapproval of any act which offended them.

Therefore their welcome to him was doubly appreciated. The cheers which came his way were genuine. No one cheered in London unless he or she wanted to, so when he went sightseeing and his carriage was brought to a standstill by the crowds who wanted to have a look at him, he no longer felt neglected.

It would be well, the Queen hinted to the King, if the Prince was seen more in public with his family. Walpole had pointed out to her that rumours were going round that the Prince was not being fairly treated and if they were not careful there would be a split in the family as there had been in the previous reign. She would well remember how disastrous that had been.

A visit to the theatre was arranged and the entire family, with the exception of Mary and Louisa, went to see *Henry VIII*.

It was a glittering occasion with the King and Queen, their three daughters and two sons; and the theatre was crowded, not so much for the sake of the play, but because so many wanted to see them.

George had Frederick on his right hand, in between himself and the Queen – much to the chagrin of William who had been accustomed to take that place; and as the party came into the royal box everyone in the theatre rose to cheer them.

But the name which they shouted louder than the rest and more repeatedly was that of the Prince.

And there was Frederick bowing, smiling, acknowledging the greeting, taking it all as a tribute to himself – which it was.

The Queen was uneasily watching the King, whose jaw grew more sullen with every passing cheer.

The question of Frederick's allowance came up for discussion. When he was Prince of Wales, George had had an income of £100,000 a year and had found it inadequate, but it was absurd he said, that Frederick should have the same. When he, George, had been Prince of Wales he had had a family. £34,000 was ample for Frederick. It was true that that extra hundred thousand had been added to the Civil List, but he could use what was left over after paying Frederick.

'I have much to do vith my money,' declared the King. 'It shall not be vasted by frivolous puppies.'

The Prince should have his own household officers, but no establishment of his own. He could share his sisters' table.

'He is von young man,' said the King, 'and new to England. Later ve shall see.'

The Prince was as yet too much engaged with discovering the pleasure of his new country to worry much about such details.

He enjoyed his popularity; he was seeking friends from those who flocked about him; he gave a ball on the island in St James's Park and it was a great success. People found him charming and – unlike his father – good tempered. He arranged that a play should be acted in the gardens at Richmond. This was called

Hob in the Gardens and was yet another triumph. Everyone congratulated the Prince on arranging it, and even his mother and sister Anne enjoyed it.

He revelled in such entertainments and seemed very pleased with his new life; but the enemies of the Queen and Walpole were watching him closely. They thought that in time he might be a willing tool in their hands; and since his family made no great effort to hide the fact that they resented his coming to England, the novelty would soon begin to fade. Then it might be possible to start another Hanoverian family feud – always so useful to the enemies of the German line.

The King had been thinking more and more of Hanover. It was nearly fifteen years since he had left, and looking back over those years Herrenhausen, the Leine Schloss, and the Alte Palais seemed enchanting fairy palaces compared with St James's, and even Richmond and Kensington. Not so grand of course, but grandeur was not everything.

He did not like governing through a parliament. In Hanover his father had been the supreme ruler. Here the elected members of their Parliament could prevent a King's having his own way.

Pooh and stuff! thought the King. That's no way to rule. Better to be a real king of a small state than a titular one of a big country.

When it rained or the wind blew he would complain of the English climate.

'Do you remember those varm, sunny days in the gardens of Herrenhausen?' he would ask the Queen.

She did remember. She also remembered delightful sunny days at Richmond, Hampton, and Kensington; and she doubted that there would be much sun in Hanover at this time of the year. But always being one step ahead of the King she guessed that he was thinking of paying a visit to Hanover.

This would not displease her, unless of course he wanted her to accompany him. That was hardly likely. Her duty would be to stay at home. Someone would have to govern in his absence. The Prince of Wales? It should be so traditionally, but how could a young man so recently come to England take over the task?

She was excited at the prospect of herself being appointed Regent. It would be comforting not to have to work on the King in order to force her – and Walpole's – ideas upon him and let them simmer in his mind until he thought they were his own.

And surely she would be appointed Regent? The King would never consent to allowing the Prince of Wales to take on that important role.

She encouraged him in his love of Hanover; she would recall to him pleasant occasions. The days, for instance, when she had first come there; their marriage; how he had shown her the beauties of the place.

He would sit listening with the tears in his eyes.

When Walpole visited her in her closet the Queen whispered to him that the King was talking more and more fondly of Hanover.

Walpole smiled slyly. 'I have often heard him say that England was his country, that he never wanted to leave England, that if any man wanted to find favour with him he must call him an Englishman.'

The Queen smiled almost fondly. 'That was in the days ven his father was alive. He loved England because his father hated it. If his father had loved England he vould have hated it.'

Walpole nodded. 'And now he is falling in love with Hanover. England displeases him. He has to keep in step with his Parliament. His son is becoming very popular with the people. I can see why he is falling out of love with England.'

'I think he is planning a visit to Hanover.'

'And why not? He should visit his Electorate now and again. He could appoint a Regency.'

'A . . . a Regency. And that would be . . .'

'Madam, there is only one Regent under whom I could serve.'

'The Prince of Wales is too young, too inexperienced, too recently come to this country.'

'I should certainly not serve under His Highness. I was referring to Your Majesty. The only possible Regent.'

'You think the King vould agree?'

'The King must be made to agree, Madam.'

After that there was every incentive to persuade the King how enjoyable – and necessary – a visit to Hanover would be.

The Parliament was not pleased; the people were not pleased. It was hoped that the new King was not going to follow the old one's example of taking frequent trips to Hanover. It was for the King of England to forget his minor possessions and concentrate on English affairs.

'The devil take England,' said George to Caroline. 'The devil take Parliament. I to Hanover vill go.'

She agreed with him that he should go. Hanover needed him. It was long since he had been there and he would not want to forget that he was the Elector as well as King of England.

He let himself be persuaded.

'And Frederick?' he asked. 'Vot of that boy? I vill not take him vith me.'

'You may safely leave him here. You know you can trust me to keep an eye on him.'

'They vill say he vill be Regent.'

'Valpole vill not agree to that.'

The King smiled. In the last year he had become reconciled to that fat ox. He thought that the minister always agreed with him and never saw that between them Walpole and the Queen arranged that he should agree with them. Yet George was shrewd enough to see that the country was steadier than it had been for some time; and although he thought this was due to his wise rule, he admitted to himself that he could not have managed so successfully without a reasonable chief minister. So he, like the Queen, was growing fonder of Walpole.

'There is von only who shall be the Regent,' said the King. He took Caroline's hand and kissed it. 'Who vould I trust but my dear Caroline?' His eyes filled with tears so he did not see the triumph in hers. 'You have been von goot vife to me, Caroline. I shall never forget.'

'I think I am the luckiest voman in the vorld,' she answered.

Such conversations were a delight to him; he often indulged in them when they were alone, but in company he still snubbed her and ridiculed her, because he continued to smart under the implications in that unfortunate rhyme.

A respite, the Queen was thinking. She would not have to placate him, not have to be humiliated before people; she would be able to rest now and then when she was fatigued; she would not have to walk in the park with him when her legs were swollen. She would enjoy many a delightful *tête-à-tête* with Walpole. They would decide policy together and not have to spend so much time planning how they should deal with the King.

But she must not show her pleasure; she must be resigned to his departure while at the same time assuring him that he could trust her to do exactly as he would during his absence.

The weather was clement, for May had come; and George set sail for Hanover.

In Kensington Palace Caroline held her first council meeting.

The Commission of Regency was read and all present came to her for the honour of kissing her hand and swearing loyalty.

The first was the Prince of Wales.

His manner several noticed was a little sullen. Was he at last beginning to be a little resentful? Was he asking himself why he, being of age and being the Prince of Wales, was denied the office of Regency during his father's absence?

There were three men who were aware of the effect the Queen's Regency was having on the Prince of Wales. These were Viscount Bolingbroke, William Pulteney, and William Wyndham. They were the most formidable members of the Opposition and Walpole had long considered them his greatest menace.

They met soon after the King's departure from England and Bolingbroke, the leader of the group, talked freely of the Prince of Wales.

'He is beginning to be piqued,' he said. 'Soon he will be angry. Then will come our chance.'

'Do you think,' asked Wyndham, 'that we might attempt to whip up his anger a little? After all he is Prince of Wales, and it is natural for a Prince of Wales to be Regent in the absence of his father.'

'Wait a while,' said Pulteney. 'It may be that the time is not yet ripe. He has been here such a short while and he may believe that just now he is not in a position to be the Regent.'

Bolingbroke put in: 'Yes, I think perhaps we should wait a while.'

His companions were a little startled, for Bolingbroke was by nature an impulsive man.

'In a short time,' continued Bolingbroke, 'he will become very exasperated. Then he will be of more use to us. It is worth while to wait for a time ... But we will continue to keep a close watch.'

The others agreed and during the months that followed they watched everything that happened to the Prince of Wales; they were biding their time until they would approach him, let him know how badly he was being treated, and so make him the figurehead of the Opposition – not only to Walpole's Ministry but to the King and Queen.

Regency

The Queen was busily reading letters from Hanover. The King and Townshend, who was with him, must be kept in touch with foreign affairs, although domestic matters were left to Caroline and her council. Townshend was growing jealous of Walpole's alliance with the Queen; the two men were brothers-in-law for Townshend had married Walpole's sister Dorothy who had been devoted to her brother and to her husband; she it was who had been in fact responsible for the great accord between the two men and had brought them to a partnership which had been profitable to them both. But with the death of Dorothy, which had brought a great grief to both men, the alliance had weakened. Townshend, a man of almost puritanical views, began to look with distaste on the life Walpole led : his drinking with his friends down at Houghton, his coarse conversation, and his living openly with Maria Skerrett while his wife was alive. Moreover, they were thinking along different lines politically.

Walpole had been glad to have Townshend out of the country, but there was a disadvantage to that, for being in close company with the King he might attempt to influence him; and without

Caroline there to guide George, this could have disturbing results.

Caroline, as usual, was in complete accord with Walpole and agreed that Townshend must be carefully watched as it would not be difficult for him to drive a wedge between herself and the King.

George was writing long letters to her from Hanover. He was a good letter writer and, in fact, was more fluent with the pen than orally. He wrote either in French or German, both of which he spoke and wrote easily.

All was going well in Hanover. He had one regret which was that his dear Caroline was not with him. He wanted her to know that there would never be another woman who meant so much to him as his dear wife, and he often thought of the day when he had come courting her and fallen in love on sight – a state which had never changed with him.

He would not say that he had not a mistress. The German women were different from the English. They were more docile. He had come to the conclusion that he was more honoured as an Elector than as a King. In England there was always the Parliament; in Hanover there was only the Elector. The English did not deserve to have a King. They wanted to govern themselves. So they set up a Parliament. He was heartily sick of parliaments. Here in Hanover he had his council meetings, yes; he had his ministers; but he was the Elector and he would have his dear Caroline know that the Elector in Hanover was a far more *respected* person than the King of England.

Caroline paused, for the letter was long; and she was thinking that the rhymes of the lampooners still rankled. In Hanover none would dare mock the Elector. It was a pity they had in England.

He went on to describe his latest mistress and all the intimate details of his love affair. How she wished he would have the tact to keep that to himself.

He was a man of great needs, as she knew. He must, like most men, have his mistresses, and now that he was a bachelor for a time, that was necessary. She would understand that, for was there not complete understanding between his dear Caroline and himself? He had found a warm-blooded creature – 'Plenty of flesh on her, my dear Caroline – you know our German woman –

and she is so delighted to be noticed by the Elector. She trembles with joy every time I approach.'

Caroline sighed. This was too much. Let him at least keep the details to himself. She read on, wondering what other revelations were to come.

The next communication was more startling. 'Townshend thought we had given you too much power and wanted to curtail it. He was working out some scheme whereby the smallest matters should be sent for our approval before you could put them into action. I pointed out to him that I trusted my dear wife as I trusted no other. I told him he did not know how I had always taken you into my confidence, how I had kept you informed of all state matters and even discussed them with you. "No," I said to Townshend, "if there is one person in England whom we can safely trust, that is the Queen." '

There was no doubt that Townshend must be watched.

Walpole was a constant visitor, and when she disclosed the information that Townshend had tried to curtail her power, he became very thoughtful.

'I think,' was his comment, 'that something must be done about my brother-in-law. He is becoming a nuisance.'

'You would have to be very careful.'

'Your Majesty should have no fear.'

'I am sure I can leave him in your capable hands.'

'We must see what can be done when he returns from Hanover. In the meantime there is the Treaty of Seville with which to concern ourselves. And one matter of less importance, but one which we cannot ignore: this affair with the Portuguese government.'

Caroline nodded. She had been disturbed when she had heard that the Portuguese had put an embargo on a British ship which was lying in the Tagus. The whole world must know that Britain would not allow her ships in foreign ports to be so treated.

'Let us deal with this matter immediately,' she said. 'Then we can give our attention to the Spanish Treaty.'

'Your Majesty is right as usual. If we show ourselves firm with the Portuguese that will be to our credit in the other matter. We must take a firm line.'

'Firm,' agreed the Queen, 'but friendly. I will send for the Portuguese envoy and together we will put the matter before him.'

The Queen's handling of the Portuguese incident was effective. The Portuguese agreed to raise the embargo without delay and Townshend wrote that the King liked extremely what Her Majesty said to the Portuguese envoy.

Caroline was delighted, but she knew that the Spanish treaty was a far more delicate matter.

This treaty was calculated to end the conflict between Spain and England which had long had an adverse effect on English trade with America. Peace between the two countries would be an excellent prospect and desired by both sides, but there was one point in the treaty which required very careful handling. This concerned the Rock of Gibraltar. The English had captured this in 1704 and it was a matter of some dismay to the Spaniards that the English should own this little portion of the Spanish mainland. However, it was a very important spot and Caroline and Walpole were most eager not to relinquish it.

It might, Walpole pointed out to her, be the one clause in the treaty which would cause the Spaniards to hesitate.

'Townshend,' he said, 'is advising we give it up for the sake of other concessions we shall receive.'

'And your advice?'

He smiled: 'I imagine that Your Majesty and I are in accord on this matter. I would say that we should do our utmost to retain it.'

'Unless of course . . .'

Walpole nodded slowly.

'You have raised it with the Spaniards?' asked the Queen.

'No.'

They smiled. 'Then we will say nothing . . . we will pretend the thought of Gibraltar has never entered our heads. It is just possible that we may conclude this treaty without its being mentioned.'

'The Spaniards are most eager to conclude it.'

'And so are we, but we will hide the fact.'

They were as usual in complete accord.

The Queen decided that all her family should accompany her to the house of Sir Robert Walpole in Chelsea to dine with her favourite minister.

It was the greatest honour in the world, Walpole had told her; and he had made all the arrangements himself.

These were pleasant days. If only George would stay in Hanover, if only the Queen reigned alone, how much simpler state affairs could be!

Between them – he and the Queen – they had successfully concluded the Treaty of Seville. William Stanhope, England's Ambassador and Plenipotentiary in Madrid, had worked in close cooperation with Walpole and the Queen and as a result the treaty had been completed without the loss of Gibraltar. In fact – as Walpole and the Queen had hoped – it was not mentioned by the Spaniards. This Caroline and Walpole regarded as their triumph and it was when this matter had been successfully concluded that the invitation to dine at Chelsea had been humbly tendered and graciously accepted.

Princess Anne was a little shocked. 'Why,' she said to Amelia and young Caroline, 'our mother seems to forget that we are royal princesses. To dine at Chelsea . . . in the home of Robert Walpole . . . a commoner!'

'Our mother thinks more highly of this commoner than she does of some princes,' pointed out Amelia.

'Oh . . . Fred! Well, who would think anything of him? I wish he would go back to Germany where he belongs.'

'He belongs there no more than the rest of us.'

'Amelia, you're a fool!'

Caroline moved away, as she always did when her sisters quarrelled. It was so disturbing; and in fact she found nothing to dislike in Frederick. She was sure that if they had been affable to him he would have been very ready to be so with them. But she never attempted to argue with her sisters.

Now they were all assembled for the journey to Chelsea. The

whole court knew they were going and it was slyly said that if
the King decided to stay in Hanover the Queen might invite Sir
Robert Walpole to live permanently at the Palace. Why not – he
ruled England – he and the Queen together.

Frederick said little, but he was less contented than he had
been. Several of his friends had pointed out that they had never
heard of a Prince of Wales being passed over for the sake of his
mother. If his father died tomorrow he would be King, but he
wasn't considered worthy to be Regent in his absence!

It was a little strange, thought Frederick. And although he
would have hated to be closeted for hours with that crude creature Walpole, poring over dull state papers, he was beginning to
believe that he should have been offered the Regency.

It was rather pleasant to have a grievance. People were so
sorry for him; they seemed to like him better for it. Moreover, his
mother and father showed rather obviously that they didn't
greatly care for him, so why shouldn't he gain a little popularity
at their expense?

He glanced at his sister Anne, who immediately scowled.
Amelia was indifferent. Caroline might have been more pleasant
but he thought her a dull little creature; as for his brother William, he wanted to box his ears every time he saw him; and the
little girls were nonentities.

He was not really very satisfied with his family.

When they reached Chelsea, Walpole was waiting to greet
them.

He behaved as though this was the greatest honour that could
befall him, but all his deference was directed towards the Queen;
the rest of them were greeted very perfunctorily.

He had invited many guests for this glorious occasion, but the
royal family were to dine in a room alone.

This pleased Anne, who remarked to Amelia that it was no
more than was right. Frederick was less pleased; he could think
of much brighter company than that supplied by his own family;
in fact he could think of few people more dull.

The Queen however was delighted, for Sir Robert himself
waited on them. He said it was not only the greatest of honours
but the greatest of pleasures.

'What a respecter of ceremony you are, Sir Robert!' said the

Queen with a laugh. 'I had not expected to stand on such ceremony here in your home.'

'Madam,' he said, 'no matter where, the Queen's royalty must
be maintained.'

How he delighted to serve her; and she delighted to be
served!

Afterwards the candles were lighted and there was dancing.
The Queen was pleased to look on. It was so comforting to rest
her legs. None of the Princesses danced at first. Anne declined
for them all for she considered it beneath their dignity; but the
Queen implored Sir Robert to dance as she liked to watch the
quadrille.

Frederick joined in and Anne scowled at him. How like him
to curry favour! Everyone would now be saying that the Prince
was more affable than his sisters.

The Queen was smiling and very gay. 'Dancing becomes Sir
Robert,' she said. 'How easily he moves! I should not have believed it possible. Ah, and there is Lord Hervey. Lord Hervey,'
she called, and he came and bowed to her.

'I see you are not dancing, my lord.' She turned to her daughters. 'Now there is an excellent dancer. My lord, you should join
the dancers.'

'With Your Majesty's permission it would give me greater
pleasure to remain at your side.'

The Queen looked well pleased. Anne thought: this young
man, who can at times look more like a woman than a man, is
almost as great a favourite with her as Walpole himself.

'I shall not give you permission,' said the Queen. 'Perhaps one
of the Princesses will dance with you.'

Anne turned haughtily away. Amelia had caught sight of the
Duke of Grafton. But Caroline had half risen. So Lord Hervey
could do no more than beg for the honour.

The Queen sat back in her chair. Such a pleasant day! She
was still glowing with pleasure over the successful conclusion of
the Spanish Treaty.

Fleetingly she thought of George in Hanover. She had a picture of him caressing some plump beauty, and hoped her charms
would be enchanting enough to keep him there a little longer.

A strange thought for a wife to have of her husband, she reminded herself; and then laughed for why should she practise self-deception? No good ever came of that.

Meanwhile George was very happy in Hanover. Here he was supreme ruler; and after all this was his native land. He was more of a German than an Englishman – a fact which, because the case had been the same with his father, he had preferred to forget. But now his father was dead and he could be himself.

Herrenhausen! Home of a hundred delights, with its glorious gardens, its linden avenue, its hornbeam hedges, its lawns and fountains. Here he instituted the same rules as he insisted on in England, but no one laughed at him here. The Germans were so much more serious than the English. One could not imagine them sitting in taverns composing so-called witty verses. No one would laugh if they did. No sly remarks, no disturbing lampoons; only deep respect for their Elector and eagerness to show their pleasure on his return.

Hanover was delightful.

The English in his retinue were a little restive, but much he cared for that! Let them be. They did not like a life that was governed by the clock. They did not appreciate the importance of time.

Another thing: here he spoke German and there could be no tittering about some quaint turn of phrase or the inability to pronounce certain words. It was he who would have the laugh of the English here, if he could be amused by such a triviality, which he could not. It was the English who were always finding something to laugh at and in particular the opportunity to ridicule others.

He never wanted to leave Hanover.

He had two mistresses, because one, in his opinion, was not enough for his prestige, and they were plump, flaxen-haired German women, docile, honoured to be selected, and with a proper understanding of their position in life. He was contented.

Every morning at precisely eleven-thirty he would stand waiting for the arrival of those of his retinue who were lodged at the Leine Schloss. His watch in hand, he would smile when they arrived exactly on the minute.

They would return to the Leine Schloss later in the day and

the process would be repeated at six o'clock. After that there would be the banquet, at which sausages and sauerkraut dominated, to the disgust of the English, and this was followed by cards. But the King would rise at exactly the same minute each night no matter whether the game was finished or not.

Because he had grown very interested in the theatre during his life in England, plays were performed twice a week at Herrenhausen. The performance began at the time decided on by the King and must end exactly on the minute – otherwise he would rise and leave and the show would therefore end in any case.

The English sneered and grumbled among themselves. It was like living in a monastery, they said. They wondered he didn't set up a system of bells. But there was one advantage; everyone in the court would know exactly where the King was at a certain time.

But these habits which had caused such mirth in England were placidly accepted in Germany.

The days were, however, enlivened by the controversy with the King of Prussia, who was not only his cousin but his brother-in-law. George had hated Frederick William when they were boys and he had seen no reason to change his mind. As for Frederick William, he liked nothing better than trouble, so he plunged into the argument with all the violence of his nature.

Townshend tried to persuade the King not to take Frederick William's insults too seriously.

'We know, Your Majesty, the nature of the King of Prussia. The stories we hear of the way in which he treats his family are so shocking that they are almost incredible.'

'Nothing is incredible with that man. He may browbeat his family but he must remember that I am the King of England.'

'We shall not allow him to forget that, Your Majesty.'

'See that he does not.' George's eyes bulged with fury. 'Do you remember when the Prince of Wales planned to leave Hanover for Prussia without my consent, when he thought to go there and marry the King of Prussia's daughter? Well . . . then he encouraged it. Without consulting me, this man encouraged my son to go to Prussia and marry his daughter. That is not all. There was a time when he kidnapped Hanoverian guards for one of his regiments. I tell you, Townshend, this man is a menace to the world.'

'Your Majesty, with your permission I will write and tell him of your displeasure, but both these matters happened some time ago and have perhaps been forgotten by His Majesty of Prussia.'

'Leave it to me,' commanded the King. He was not going to have Townshend nip this quarrel in the bud with one of his bits of diplomacy.

When the King of Prusssia received the letter of complaint from his cousin he was delighted.

He stormed into his wife's apartment where she was taking a little refreshment and, roaring with rage, cuffed one of the Queen's pages and sent him to bring his son and daughter to his presence.

'Your brother!' he shouted, throwing the letter he had received from George into the bowl of soup.

Sophia Dorothea picked it out daintily and read it.

'George Augustus is like you,' she said. 'He longs for a fight.'

'Don't compare me with that popinjay, or I'll kill you.'

She put her head on one side. 'That would be a rather strong action to take,' she said. 'Surely I have often done much more to offend you than make such a comparison.'

He approached her, his hand raised; she smiled at him; so he contented himself with spitting into her soup.

'That,' she added, placidly, 'will not, I fear, improve the flavour.' She began to read her brother's letter, and laughed. 'George is such a fool,' she said.

'So you have sense enough to see that!'

'And you,' she added, 'are a brute. Between you, you should manage to enjoy your correspondence.'

'Enjoy! I tell you that if I had that little brother of yours here I'd take his neck in my hands and choke the life out of him.'

'Don't be too sure he'd let you do it. He's something of a soldier, you know. And what he lacks in sense he makes up for in courage.'

'Then he has to have a lot of courage.'

'He has.'

The Crown Prince and Princess Wilhelmina entered. Their

mother glanced at them anxiously; in spite of the ill-treatment they received from their father they did not appear to be unduly afraid. Blows had become commonplace to them. She wondered when Fritz would turn on his father; as for Wilhelmina, whatever marriage she made she could not find a husband who would ill-treat her more than her father had.

'Come here, you devil's brood,' he cried.

'Aptly named,' put in the Queen.

'I was referring to you, Madam.'

'You are unusually modest. It is your custom to exaggerate your own performance.' Sophia Dorothea always attempted to turn his attention on herself and away from her children; they were aware of it and loved her for it; but they were so accustomed to the wild life led in their father's palace that they were prepared for violence.

'And what are you grinning at?' he demanded of his daughter.

'I assure you, Father, that I find very little to smile at.'

He lifted his hand and struck her, but it was a mild blow compared with those he was accustomed to deliver.

'This fool of an uncle, your mother's brother, has been writing to me again. It seems he's annoyed because we won't have his daughter here. You're not going to marry this girl, I tell you. I'll not have her walking about my Court with her nose in the air making trouble. I don't hear very good accounts of your cousins in England.'

'At least,' said the Queen, 'my brother was against the match between Frederick and Wilhelmina.'

'If you hadn't been such a prattling fool, woman, we'd have that girl of yours off our hands and your brother would be paying the cost of feeding her instead of me.'

'The fact is,' put in the Queen, 'that George Augustus wants us to take *his* daughter but won't take ours.'

'Well, he has some sense after all. He wants to get a girl off his hands and so do we.'

Wilhelmina flinched and the Queen said: 'Although it would be a good match for Wilhelmina to marry the Prince of Wales, I should be desolate at losing her.'

The King threw back his head and laughed. 'You fool!' he

shouted. Then he turned to his daughter. 'Do you think *I* should be desolate too? Do you?'

'No, Father,' answered Wilhelmina. 'I know you would be glad to be rid of me. It would save you working out so often how much it costs to feed me.'

He caught her by the ear. She stood very still because the more she moved the more painful it would be.

'Well,' said the King, releasing her, 'it would save me time as well as money. But they won't have you, daughter. The King of England won't have you, and the Prince of Wales does not want you either.'

Wilhelmina said with some spirit: 'He has written to say that he is eager to marry me. He has even said that he is foolishly in love.'

The King laughed again. 'Foolishly. He admits that. The young man has never seen you.'

'Perhaps accounts of my life here make him feel he would like to rescue me.'

The King was bewildered. Wilhelmina was growing like her mother. She was showing some spirit. She would have to be married soon. He did not want to have to contend with another woman's sharp tongue.

This thought made him less violent than usual. He turned to his son. 'And you . . . when are you going to marry, eh? You'll take the wife I find and say thank you.'

The Queen looked anxiously at her son. He was always calm, in contrast to his father; it was as though he was only half aware of him as something that must be endured for a while, but not for ever. The Queen believed that in her son were seeds of greatness and that the King was aware of this, and was sometimes overawed by it and sometimes goaded to even greater violence.

Fritz listened impassively.

'Well, well,' cried his father. 'Don't stand there like a dummy.'

'I shall be pleased to marry when a suitable bride is found for me,' said Fritz.

The King looked frustrated. This family of his would give him no cause to chastise them. Only his wife provoked him, and he did not care to harm her.

'This fool of a King of England!' he shouted. 'Where's the letter?'

'A little the worse for a dip in the soup,' said the Queen, throwing it at him.

It fluttered at his feet; and Fritz picked it up and handed it to his father who proceeded to read it in loud derisive tones.

'Do you know what I am going to answer this popinjay?' He glared at them all and went on: 'I am going to tell him to go back to England where perhaps they are foolish enough to put up with him. I'm going to tell him that if he stays here . . . in Germany . . . if he writes such letters to me I will take my sword to him and cut off his head and send it back to his dear wife in England who, I understand, is fool enough to let rule him. I'll tell him what I think of him. What a family!'

'Your own,' murmured the Queen.

But the King was too intent on composing an insulting answer to hear her.

George paced up and down his apartment, eyes blazing. Townshend was doing his best to placate him.

'This madman!' spluttered George. 'This cousin of mine! How my sister lives with him, I can't imagine. He's mad, I tell you. But mad or not he shall not insult me in this manner.'

'Your Majesty, a note couched in such undiplomatic language should perhaps be ignored.'

'Ignored. Let him insult me and and I ignore him! I tell you this, Townshend, I shall not allow this to pass. Do you know what I am going to do? I am going to challenge the King of Prussia to a duel.'

'Your Majesty, that would not be possible.'

'And why, pray?'

'Two Kings cannot fight a duel. It has never been. It could not be.'

'Then we will be the first, for I tell you this, Townshend: I will not be insulted by this man.'

'Your Majesty . . .'

'My mind is made up. I shall challenge the King of Prussia and tell him to choose his weapons.'

Townshend looked at his master helplessly; but he could not

control him as the Queen and Walpole managed to do.

The King of Prussia was delighted to receive his cousin's challenge. His family had never seen him in such a good mood. A choice of weapons. He could not decide, he told his wife, whether it should be swords or pistols. He would enjoy firing a shot through his silly heart; on the other hand it would give him even greater satisfaction to slice off his even sillier head.

The Queen shrugged her shoulders; she did not believe for a moment that the two foolish men would ever be allowed to fight in single combat; their ministers would find some way of putting a stop to such antics.

She was right. The King of Prussia's ministers conferred with those of the King of England and between them they worked out a compromise whereby the two Kings could abandon their foolish project without loss of face on either side.

Townshend, when he did not have to placate the King, was a past master at this art; and so well did he work with the Prussian ministers that in a short time they were trying to bring the two Kings to an agreement about the marriage of the Crown Prince and the Princess Amelia.

This brought satisfaction to George, but less so to the King of Prussia. After all, pointed out the latter, George would have one less mouth to feed, he one more, by such an arrangement.

The Queen replied that then they must marry Wilhelmina to the Prince of Wales and although they gained one mouth they would lose one so the feeding bills would not have increased.

The letters went back and forth between Hanover and Prussia. But the situation did not change; each had a daughter of whom he wished to be rid and neither wished to take the other's daughter off her father's hands. But at least the plan for a duel was dropped and the two Kings were writing to each other, with the help of their ministers, in civil terms.

George wrote that he would like to see this matter of the marriages settled before he left Hanover; Sophia Dorothea was eager for the completion of what she called the Double Marriage Plan; but the Kings could not agree.

The King of Prussia finally wrote that he would only agree to his son's marriage to the Princess Amelia if, on that marriage, the Crown Prince of Prussia became the Regent of Hanover.

This George blankly refused; and, to the dismay of Sophia Dorothea, once more the negotiations came to an end.

There was no longer any excuse for remaining in Hanover. George regretfully had to admit this and Townshend was at his side, urging a return.

'It grieves me,' said the King. 'How beautiful everything is in Hanover!'

'Her Majesty the Queen will be eager to have you back,' Townshend pointed out.

The King's eyes filled with tears. 'The dear Queen,' he said. 'There is no one who will ever take her place with me, Townshend.'

Townshend bowed his head and knew he had made his point. They would make preparations to return to England without delay.

George presided over his last levée. He wished, he said, that these levées should be held at precisely the same hour every Saturday as they had been during his stay in Hanover. He would not be there, but he would look at his watch and remember that they were assembled in this room. His chair would be empty and they would bow to it as though he occupied it. Only thus could he bear to leave Hanover.

Caroline was at Kensington Palace awaiting news of the King's arrival.

She was sorry that he had not stayed a little longer in Hanover. Life had been so peaceful; and she and Walpole had achieved so much. Now the King was on his way home and they would have to be so careful. How easily they had dealt with the tricky Portuguese affair and the even more important Treaty of Seville!

Walpole, who was growing more and more frank, expressed his misgivings because the happy days of the Regency were coming to an end.

She was at the window when she saw the outriders approaching the palace. This must mean that the King could not be far off.

She summoned her family – every one of them, even little Mary and Louisa.

'Your father is home,' she said, 'we are going to meet him.'

'On foot!' cried Anne.

'Certainly. It is what he would wish.'

She took Frederick's arm and on the other side walked Anne, her head high so that all would recognize her as the Princess Royal. William, always a little sullen when an occasion such as this one thrust him into second place, walked with his sisters. Through Kensington to Hyde Park, with the people falling in behind them and the cry going up: 'The King is back.'

When they reached St James's Park the royal coach was visible and when they reached it, this came to a stop and the King alighted.

He was beaming with joy.

Caroline was thinking how well she knew him. Nothing could have pleased him more than to see his family come on foot to greet him.

He took the Queen in his arms and embraced her warmly, the tears in his eyes. The people cheered wildly.

'I am happy to be back,' said the King, 'because I have missed *you* so much.'

He spoke in French and Caroline answered unthinkingly in the same language. It was some time later before she realized the significance of this.

Then he kissed all the children in turn and the cheers of the watchers grew more ecstatic.

When the greeting was over, the King took the Queen by the hand and helped her into his coach; the rest of the family used the coaches immediately behind the King's and so the royal party came to St James's.

Statesmen quarrel

The King had changed since his visit to Hanover. He no longer
attempted to speak English on all occasions. He slipped easily
into French or German and everyone else had to follow him.
This did not inconvenience Caroline, who had always been
aware that she spoke English with a German accent, and because
Frederick spoke the language so much better than his parents it
gave him an advantage. Most of the courtiers spoke French if
not German, so the former was the language chiefly used.

But the change was significant. The King, who had once never
let an opportunity pass without declaring his love for England,
now never let one pass without expressing his dislike.

'This is the worst climate in the world,' he would say whenever the wind blew or the rain fell. 'How different it is in Hanover !'

Or : 'These English do not know how to cook. The food in
Hanover was delicious. We shall have to bring cooks over to
teach them how to cook.'

The gardens of Hampton and Kensington could not compare
with those of Herrenhausen; the people in the streets of London
were unruly, those in Hanover were well disciplined; in Hanover

he had been supreme ruler, here there was always that miserable Parliament.

'Soon,' he said, 'I shall have to pay another visit to Hanover.'

The Queen said that although that would sadden everyone in England she was sure it would please everyone in Hanover.

'You seem pleased that I should go?'

How careful one had to be! Had her voice carried a lilt because she was thinking of being Regent once more?

'Your Majesty must surely be joking.'

He grunted, for he could not imagine that she was not delighted to have him back.

He was a good husband. He had spent every night with her since his return. She was a beautiful woman, his Caroline; there were times when he almost wished that a man need not have mistresses to prove his virility. In fact, Caroline pleased him as well as any woman. She always had; she always would, he assured himself. He liked a woman to be plump and Caroline was that. Her bosom was the best in the world – so soft, so ample. Oh, yes, he would be well content to retire to bed with her at precisely the same time every night if he had not felt that his courtiers expected something else of him.

He called on Henrietta Howard as usual – every evening on the stroke of the hour; but he did not go to bed with her. That was a habit he had changed since returning from Hanover. She was getting old and she was deaf, which he found irritating; in fact if she were not such a habit he would cast her off.

But Caroline was so much more to his taste.

As for Caroline, she dreaded the King's regular habits, for that secret illness of which she believed none knew except Mrs Clayton was becoming more and more painful, and each night she feared that the King might discover it. That would drive him away from her, she knew. He could never tolerate illness – and such an illness would be an end to all desire on his part.

Strangely enough, for all his infidelities, he still desired her; and she believed that in this was her strength. All the mistresses he had had – and they had been numerous – had never given him the pleasure she had. He had told her this, for there was nothing he enjoyed so much as discussing with her his love passages with other women. She knew a great deal about the sexual habits of many women of the court – solely because the King had taken her into his confidence. That he did this was meant as a compliment. They were his mistresses; she was his wife. He would have her know that *he* never forgot the difference.

Subconsciously Caroline knew that while she held this supremacy she could rule the King, and while she ruled the King, Walpole must take her into his confidence. But if she lost her physical hold on George, which she would do if he were embarrassed by her affliction, then she would also lose her power to lead him,

It was of the utmost importance that she keep her secret.

She wished that it were entirely her own secret and that Mrs Clayton had not discovered it. Sometimes, by an expression, Mrs Clayton betrayed the fact that she was thinking of it; since she had revealed her knowledge there had been an air of closer intimacy in her manner. She ruled the household under the Queen and even though Caroline did not always approve of her manners she felt herself unable to protest. It was slight, it was subtle, but it was there. Another woman held the secret which Caroline must at all costs keep from the world.

Henrietta Howard was very much aware of the change in the King since he had come back from Hanover. It was time she left, she knew. She would not be sorry to go and when she looked back over the years since she had become the King's mistress she realized that they had been singularly unprofitable. The fact was, George was a mean man where others were concerned. He liked to spend money, but on himself. Theirs had been unlike the usual relationship between a King and his mistress. She had no grand titles to show for her years of service, no rich lands which brought in good revenues. All she had had was a place at court as a bedchamber woman – not even a Lady of the Bedchamber, but a bedchamber woman.

She had served the Queen well too, and in fact it was Caroline who wished her to stay at court and hold her place in the King's life. Why? Because she was reliable, because she was insignificant, because if she went the King would think it necessary to replace her by a woman who might lack her quality of amiable placidity.

A sad end to a life of service, thought Henrietta.

She would like to retire and live in peace. She never wanted to go back to her husband; and that of course he would not want either, for he had no interest in her apart from the £1,200 paid to him by the King for his permission to allow her to stay in the Queen's household.

If she returned to him he would lose that, and he much preferred it to her.

Well, he must do what he would about that; Henrietta was tired of servitude. Moreover, she believed that very soon the King would break the habit of visiting her and then her sole duty would be to act as bedchamber woman to the Queen.

She would miss court life in a way. The little parties she gave in her apartments were always well attended by those people who mistakenly believed that the way to the King's favour was through his mistress. Lord Townshend had been one of these, and still clung to the belief; Henrietta knew that this was one of the reasons why the Queen disliked him so.

She was in a melancholy mood. The King had been particularly unpleasant; he had snapped at her and called her a fool, and then been annoyed because she had not quite caught what he said, and had asked him to repeat it. It was true he had stayed the appointed time, but he had kept looking at his watch as though he found it hard to believe that time could pass so slowly.

Oh yes, it was certainly time she left court and found solace elsewhere.

In such a mood she went to assist at the Queen's dressing. The Queen had, since she came to the throne, been very eager to follow the old traditions of royal behaviour which her father-in-law had abandoned. For him it had been enough to have his two Turkish servants, Mahomet and Mustapha, to dress and undress him; this had caused a great deal of resentment throughout the court, for it dispensed with so many remunerative posts in the bedchamber. Caroline, however, had reverted to the old customs, and her rising and retiring were conducted with traditional ceremony.

As bedchamber woman it was Henrietta's duty to bring the basin and ewer, kneeling to present them to the Queen. This Henrietta felt too much of an indignity for a woman who had for so many years been the King's mistress. Who ever heard of a King's mistress remaining a bedchamber *woman* all her life!

She brought the basin and ewer for the Queen but did not kneel, and the Queen immediately noticed the omission.

'My dear Howard,' said Caroline, 'what does this mean? You know you should kneel when you present the basin and ewer.'

'Madam,' answered Henrietta, the colour leaping to her cheeks, 'it is something I cannot do.'

Oh dear, thought Caroline, she is suddenly going to give herself airs because of her relationship with the King . . . after all these years!

'Have you pains in your knees?' asked the Queen.

'No, Madam. That is not the reason.'

'So it is not pain but . . . dignity.'

'I will not do it, Madam.'

Caroline sighed. 'But my dear Howard, I am sure you will. Fie for shame. But go now. Go away and we will talk of this another time.'

The Queen summoned another of the bedchamber women to perform the duty which Henrietta had refused, but she was thinking, the matter must not rest here. Henrietta must either be made to do her duty to the Queen irrespective of her relationship with the King or go. And if she went and another younger, more attractive woman replaced her . . .

The Queen shuddered; and in her own apartment, Henrietta, wondering what she had done, was less disturbed than the Queen.

Sir Robert Walpole came to the Queen's closet and Caroline immediately informed him of the incident.

He looked grave, for like Caroline he realized the importance of keeping Henrietta in her position. 'The King must not form a new and more attractive habit,' he said.

'It's true,' replied the Queen, 'but I vill not have insolence from the King's *guenips*.'

Walpole laughed. 'I will speak to Mrs Howard,' he said. 'I will tell her that she should inquire of Lady Masham who served Queen Anne for so long and held a position with that Queen far more intimate and affectionate than Mrs Howard holds with the

King, yet remained bedchamber woman and I believe observed every rule of etiquette. I am sure Lady Masham will tell Mrs Howard that the kneeling position is a necessary one. Then she will be satisfied and so will you.'

'That is von goot idea,' said the Queen.

'There is another of your ladies who deserves a little attention,' went on Walpole. 'I am referring to Mrs Clayton. I think that good lady has too high an opinion of herself.'

The Queen was silent, but her lips tightened and a wary expression came into her eyes. Walpole was conscious of this and was immediately alert.

'I fancied she was a little insolent to me,' he went on, 'as though she almost resented my visits to Your Majesty.'

'Clayton is a good woman,' said the Queen rapidly. 'She has been vith me for a long time. I find her an excellent servant.'

'Ah, these women, they work well for a while and then it occurs to them that they are indispensable. It seems to me that Mrs Clayton at times almost believes she is Your Majesty.'

The Queen laughed uneasily.

'I certainly think that she believed herself to be of greater importance than Your Majesty's ministers.'

'I vill speak to her,' the Queen promised.

Sir Robert turned the conversation to his brother-in-law Townshend. 'It would seem, Madam, that we are surrounded by those who would flout us. Townshend is becoming intolerable.'

'Then,' replied the Queen almost blithely, 'vile ve vork to keep Mrs Howard, ve must plan to rid ourselves of Lord Townshend.'

Walpole plunged into an animated account of his relative's shortcomings, but all the time he was wondering what had happened between the Queen and Mrs Clayton to make the Queen so uneasy when she was criticized. Had the woman some hold over the Queen? That seemed impossible, but naturally Walpole must make it his business to find out.

Lady Masham, from her retirement in the country, was very ready to help Mrs Howard with her little problem. The bedchamber woman, it seemed, must always remember that she was in an inferior position to the Lady of the Bedchamber. When the Queen put on her shift, although the bedchamber *woman* brought it to the chamber, she must hand it to the *lady* to put on. As for the basin and ewer, this must be brought in by the bedchamber woman who should put it onto a table before the Queen. Then the woman must *kneel* beside the table while the lady looked on. When the Queen began to wash her hands the woman then rose and poured the water over Her Majesty's hands. The bedchamber woman must not forget that she was not a Lady of the Bedchamber.

In view of such corroboration from one who had long served a Queen and was acquainted with every rule of court etiquette, Henrietta could only humbly admit her fault and when she next presented the basin and ewer remained on her knees in the required manner.

Caroline showed that she bore no resentment, and only felt relief that there were now no difficulties between her and her good Howard.

Now Caroline and Walpole could devote their attention to Townshend. He was a man Caroline had never liked. He was quick-tempered, domineering and jealous; and at the same time puritanical. His dislike of his brother-in-law had been growing since his wife Dorothy – Walpole's sister – had died, and was now more like hatred. There was nothing to keep the two men together; and there was a great deal to separate them.

Townshend deplored Walpole's way of life, which he considered highly immoral. He was irritated, too, because Walpole had built Houghton, a magnificent country mansion in Norfolk not far from Townshend's own splendid house at Raynham. They were both proud of their estates and sought to rival each other; and whereas the Raynham house had at one time been the finest in the neighbourhood, Houghton, under Walpole's extravagant care, began to rival it and then outshine it.

At Houghton Walpole had one of the finest collections of pictures in the country. He had made a fortune out of the South Seas Company and had stocked his house with treasures. Raynham was decidedly put into the shade.

Moreover, to Houghton came those who were seeking places at court; it was an honour to be invited; Walpole kept an open house and spent vast sums on entertaining. The wine flowed liberally and there were many of what Townshend called 'drunken orgies' taking place at Houghton. These parties were the talk of the countryside. They were extremely costly but Walpole did not care. He was a man who liked to surround himself with drinking companions and he found plenty ready to enjoy his lavish hospitality. To Houghton he often brought Maria Skerrett who presided over the parties with him; and the sounds of singing and laughter so disturbed the peace of the countryside – so said Lord Townshend – that when Walpole was at Houghton he found it necessary to leave Raynham.

The brothers-in-law had quarrelled over the Treaty of Seville which Walpole had carried through in a manner which was not in accord with Townshend's wishes. While Townshend was shocked by Walpole's profligacy, Walpole sneered at what he called Townshend's hypocrisy.

The antagonism was at its height when one day, at the Queen's levée, Caroline asked Townshend where he had dined.

Townshend replied: 'With Lord and Lady Trevor, Your Majesty.'

At this remark Walpole who was standing by the Queen's chair became very alert. Lord Trevor had succeeded the Duke of Kingston as the Lord Privy Seal a few years previously, although Walpole had thought him scarcely the man for such an office; and as the rift between Walpole and Townshend widened so had Townshend drawn closer to Trevor. Lady Trevor, his second wife, to whom he had been married for nearly thirty years, was an old and actually a very ugly woman and noted as much for her virtue as for her lack of beauty.

Walpole laughed and said in a voice which could be heard by all surrounding the Queen: 'Madam, I think Lord Townshend is growing *coquet*. After all he has had a long widowhood. He has called so frequently at Lord Trevor's house recently that I suspect he has designs on Lady Trevor's virtue. That is the only reason I can think of to account for it.'

Townshend's temper flared up and he regarded his brother-in-law with hatred. 'I am not one of those fine gentlemen, sir,' he cried, 'who indulge in folly and immorality even though they are of an age when one would have hoped they might have been past such manners. Youth and idleness would not, in my opinion, excuse such conduct, but often this deplorable way of life is adopted by those who should know better. There are liberties, sir, which I am as far from taking as I am from approving. I have not the constitution that requires such practices, a purse that can support them nor a conscience that can digest them.'

Walpole smiled cynically and said quietly: 'Why, my lord, all this for Lady Trevor!'

Caroline was annoyed with Townshend because he had so far forgotten his respect for her as to attack Walpole in her presence. He should have made some light response as Walpole had to him; and if he wished, taken the matter up with his brother-in-law at some later date.

Townshend had turned to Walpole, his fists clenched, but Caroline said: 'I think it is time for cards.'

And even Townshend knew that that was an order for him to say no more.

Townshend must go. That was what the Queen said to Walpole. She had no intention of upholding a man in a high position who had sought to curtail her powers when she was Regent. Townshend must go, said Walpole to the Queen. He was developing a hatred for his one-time friend and ally which could only bring disaster.

'All went well enough,' Walpole confided to the Queen, 'when the firm was Townshend and Walpole. Now it is Walpole and Townshend, he does not like it.'

'There is only one thing to be done, my good Sir Robert,' replied Caroline. 'It must be Walpole alone.'

'There is the King,' Walpole warned her.

She knew that well enough. George had to be made to believe that Townshend should be asked to resign and that was not easy, for George liked Townshend, who had accompanied him on his journey to Hanover. Townshend was a good man, but not as important as Walpole certainly.

They would have to be very careful in condemning Townshend to the King.

*   *   *

Every time the brothers-in-law met there was trouble, and this came to a head at the house of a Colonel and Mrs Selwyn who had invited them to dine at their house opposite St James's Palace.

Townshend arrived ready to take offence and expecting it. Walpole was nonchalant, seeming at ease, but determined not to let a chance of plaguing Townshend pass by.

Dinner began and Walpole drank with his usual abandon while Townshend was his abstemious self. They were soon engaged in a disagreement which threatened every minute to turn into an open quarrel. The host and hostess were uneasy; the rest of the guests expectant.

And when Walpole cried: 'Sincerity? What is sincerity? There is no man's sincerity I doubt so much as yours, my lord!' Townshend lost his temper. He leaped from his seat, spilling wine over the table, and took his brother-in-law by the throat.

Walpole threw off Townshend and the two men stood for a few seconds glaring at each other malignantly; then Walpole clapped his hand on his sword and Townshend did the same. The hostess shrieked and there was clamour throughout the dining room.

'I must stop this,' cried Mrs Selwyn. 'You shall not fight in my house.'

But Walpole had drawn his sword and Townshend had done the same.

'No!' screamed Mrs Selwyn, and ran towards the door with the intention of calling the palace guard.

One of the guests stopped her.

'There'll be such a scandal. It will be all over the town if you call the guards. Sir Robert! My Lord Townshend . . . for God's sake put your swords away.'

Even Townshend's temper had cooled a little and he was thinking how ridiculous it was for two middle-aged men – one the premier statesman of the land – to be facing each other, swords drawn, at a dinner party.

Neither would be the first to put his sword away although neither had any wish to continue with the farce.

'There will be such a scandal,' wailed Mrs Selwyn. 'Oh, Sir Robert, I beg of you . . .'

Sir Robert turned to her and, sighing, replaced his sword in its scabbard. Townshend did the same.

'It is impossible for us two to work together,' said Walpole firmly.

'That is one matter on which I am in complete agreement with you,' replied Townshend. 'I shall retire from any ministry in which you serve.'

Walpole bowed his head.

He excused himself to his hostess. After such a scene he believed it was for one of the offenders to retire, and he would do so with his apologies.

He went immediately to the Queen.

'Townshend has resigned,' he said.

She was delighted and he explained exactly what had happened at the Selwyns.'

'Can you call this a resignation?' she asked. 'He was not speaking officially.'

'Madam, we must take it that he *was* speaking officially.'

Walpole then asked for an audience with the King; the Queen was present, but she said nothing while Walpole explained that Townshend had tendered his resignation.

Would His Majesty agree to Lord Harrington's taking Townshend's place?

The King had nothing against Harrington. He looked at the Queen who lowered her eyes. She did not want him to know that she and Walpole had long ago decided that as soon as they could rid themselves of Townshend they would set Harrington up in his place.

'Harrington . . .' The King put his head on one side.

'I am of the opinion that he would serve Your Majesty well,' said Walpole.

Yes, Harrington would be a good man – a lazy, easy-going man; just the type who would suit Walpole for he would not attempt to frustrate him as Townshend had done.

'Does the Queen think Harrington would be a good man?' asked the King.

'I know nothing of politics. Your Majesty knows all.'

Oh, dear, thought Walpole. Was that going a little too far? But no! The conceited little man was swallowing the flattery and savouring it. He really believed it was so.

'Harrington, I think,' said the King.

To his surprise, Townshend realized that he had retired from the Ministry.

Well, he was weary of conflict in any case and that there would always be while Walpole was the chief minister. Chief minister! thought Townshend. He had made himself the sole minister. The Queen had helped him in this for he was the Queen's man. If Townshend had had the foresight to seek his fortune through the Queen instead of through Mrs Howard he might not find himself outside politics now.

But it was over and done with. And he had a charming estate in Norfolk. It could be more rewarding, perhaps, developing that than fighting against an old ruffian like his brother-in-law, for any man who engaged in conflict with Walpole must fight a losing battle.

So to Norfolk went Townshend, and the field was clear for Walpole and the Queen.

Lord Hervey returned to England from a stay abroad where he had gone to recuperate from his almost perpetual ill health; and the Queen was delighted to welcome back her handsome Chamberlain, who sparkled with the wit she failed to find in the Prince of Wales.

Mrs Howard kept her place; Townshend was dismissed. And this was very comforting.

But while the Queen played cards and enjoyed the witticisms of her Chamberlain, while she knotted in the King's company and led him the way she wanted him to go, Walpole continued to wonder what hold Mrs Clayton could possibly have over the Queen.

There was one whom both Walpole and the Queen seemed to have forgotten. This was the Prince of Wales. Since he had been denied the Regency he had been growing more and more dissatisfied. He himself would have been perfectly content to go on as he had been; he was lazy and good-tempered generally, but there were many who resented Walpole's power and who knew that such power could never be theirs while there was such a strong alliance between Walpole and the Queen. All astute observers of the scene knew that the Queen led the King and that only the King was unaware of this; so therefore if they wished to set up in rivalry against this powerful triumvirate, they must look beyond their Majesties.

And here was a Prince of Wales – not only neglected by his parents but disliked by them.

Bolingbroke, Pulteney, Wyndham, and such men were watching the Prince of Wales and dropping casual hints now and then to remind him of his ill-treatment.

There was another who was deeply aware of the Prince, but his methods of using that young man would be different from the ambitious politicians. This was Lord Hervey, court beau and wit.

So while the Queen and Walpole concerned themselves with the waywardness of Mrs Howard, the secretiveness of Mrs Clayton, and the intolerable conduct of Lord Townshend, Lord Hervey was seeking to become the intimate friend of the Prince of Wales.

Lord Fanny

Lord Hervey lay back languidly as the carriage rattled along the road to Ickworth. He had been long away from home and was pleased to be back; he would not, of course, stay long at Ickworth. A few weeks would suffice with his wife and children; then he and Stephen Fox would go to court. That was where the excitement lay nowadays.

He gazed across at Stephen – his beautiful, beloved companion. All the Fox family were noted for their beauty, but Stephen was surely the most beautiful of them all. Stephen caught his eyes and gave him a look of adoration. Theirs was a relationship on which some might frown. Let them! thought Hervey. What did he care? He was glad to provide gossip, for when a man ceased to be gossiped about, that man might as well be dead. That was his philosophy.

He studied the tips of his elegant shoes with the diamond-studded buckles. Everything about Hervey was elegant. The frilly front of his muslin shirt rippled over his brocade waistcoat; his almost – though not quite – knee-length velvet coat with the turn-back embroidered cuffs, his exquisite lace cravat were all in the latest fashion and his three-cornered hat perched on top of his flowing wig was a masterpiece of millinery. From his person there rose a delicate but none the less pronounced scent and his cheeks were delicately touched with rouge. Stephen said he was as beautiful as he had been in those days ten years ago when he had first appeared to dazzle the court of the Prince and Princess of Wales who had now become the King and Queen.

Those days seemed far back in time. Much had happened since. Hervey had fallen in love with beautiful Molly Lepel and married her, for he was proud to be both a lover of men and women. He imagined it gave him a two-edged personality which was interesting.

Molly had suited him. For one thing she had been the most beautiful, most written about, woman of the court. At least she had shared that honour with Mary Bellenden, and there had been a constant controversy in those days as to which of the girls was the more beautiful. Molly had beauty and charm. Moreover, her personality fitted his. She was a strange woman, his Molly. She had shared his life for those first years without intruding on it. It had appeared to be a perfect marriage – and a fruitful one. Sons and daughters had been born to them and there would doubtless be more, for they were both young. He was in his early thirties and Molly was four years younger than he was. She stayed with the children at Ickworth and had no desire to return to court. She had lived her early life in courts and had had enough of them. In the country she entertained a great deal, looked after her children, and her life was complete in the world she had made for herself. Hervey visited her now and then as a close friend might; she never questioned the scandals which surrounded him; she never criticized his friends. The fact was that Molly did not care.

Molly was a cold woman without jealousy. Hervey could have his lovers – male and female – and Molly implied it was no concern of hers. When he came to Ickworth he was welcome. It was his home; she bore his name and his children. His preference for others was no slur on her because she had been recognized as one of the most beautiful and attractive women of her day; she could have had lovers by the score; but Molly did not want lovers. She wanted her life to go on as she had arranged that it should; that did not include any emotional disturbance, for Molly had no time in her life for emotion.

A strange *ménage*, some people thought. But it satisfied Molly and John Hervey. What man, he was asking himself now as the carriage was coming into Ickworth, could have gone off travelling abroad with a beloved friend, and return with that friend to his wife and be received with a cool cordiality which was more comforting in the circumstances than any warmth could have been.

His thoughts were going on ahead of Ickworth, for he had decided that it should be a short stay. And then . . . to court. It would be amusing to renew his acquaintance with the Prince of Wales. He and Frederick had become good friends when he had visited Hanover before the Prince had come to England; in fact Frederick had been quite overwhelmed by the polished manners and elegant charm of Lord Hervey. Later they had resumed that friendship and if Hervey had not had to travel abroad for the sake of his health, it would have progressed still farther.

The thought of his health made Hervey feel a little wan and Stephen immediately noticed this.

'You are feeling ill?'

'A little faint.'

'My dear soul, lie back and close your eyes. I fear the jolting of the coach . . .'

'The jolting of the coach,' said Hervey quietly, enjoying his friend's concern. 'Nothing more.'

'Did you take your spa water before we set out?'

'I did, I swear.'

'It should raise your spirits.'

'My spirits are high enough, dear boy. It is the flesh that is weak. I think I will try that mixture of crabs' eyes, asses' milk, and oyster shells. I have reports that it sweetens the blood.'

'I will see that you have it.'

'My *dear* Stephen!'

Such devotion was pleasant; it was for its sake that he had taken Stephen with him on his travels. Dear Stephen! Quite his favourite person at the moment. Stephen had cosseted him, remembered his medicines, listened to his poetry, adored everything he did. He was so much warmer than Molly. Not that he would criticize Molly one little bit. Molly was just the wife for a man such as he was.

'Close your eyes,' commanded Stephen. The only time the dear boy commanded was when he was acting the nurse. 'You should rest for the remainder of the journey.'

Hervey obeyed, and allowed himself to drift into a pleasant state of semi-consciousness when the impressions of Venice and Florence became slightly jumbled together and he was not sure whether he was walking beside the Arno or the Grand Canal. The sun had been so welcome, and he had written a great deal of poetry which he so enjoyed reading to the appreciative Stephen. Sometimes he felt he would ask nothing more but to stay at Ickworth with his family – and Stephen – and spend his days writing.

That would never suit him for long, though. He was a mischievous sprite; he must be at the core of life; he must be at court, stirring up trouble, seeking a high place in the confidence of people through whom he could make himself important – important in politics which played their part in history.

He was too egotistical, too vain, too mischievous to spend his days in retirement.

There would be fun to be had at court now. Walpole was supreme, some said, and Pulteney was determined to pull him down. It would be fun to live close to such a battle, to work in the shadows, to use his pen as some men used their swords. Oh, yes, there was a great deal of amusement to be had at court.

Therefore it would be just a short respite at Ickworth and then away to adventure.

He himself was no politician of fixed ideas. He had been returned as a Member of the House of Commons for Bury St Edmunds some years before and since he had in those days belonged to the court of the Prince and Princess of Wales and Walpole had at that time been the King's minister – and that King was George I – he had joined Pulteney's Opposition.

But George I had died and the Prince of Wales had become George II, and although George II had at first rejected Walpole he had afterwards reinstated him. This meant that Walpole was the confidant of the Queen; and as Pulteney was still in opposition against Walpole, there was only one thing Hervey could do and that was change sides. He had become a Walpole man.

He was evidently not a man to be despised. His pen could be vitriolic, his tongue sharp; and Walpole was so pleased to have him on his side that he had asked the Queen to receive him in her household as Chamberlain. This was a source of great pleasure to Hervey; it meant he could be constantly near the Queen, and as he had his duties at court, he could also keep in close touch with the Prince of Wales.

Very satisfactory, he was telling himself now. So, after a little respite, to court he would go.

The carriage was approaching the Ickworth mansion. Hervey opened his eyes. Stephen looked at him anxiously to make sure he was not going to faint and with a little sigh Hervey sat up straight, adjusted his cravat, and smiled at his friend.

'I feel better,' he said, 'but I should like to try the blood sweetener.'

They left the carriage and went into the big hall. Lady Hervey, looking very cool and outstandingly beautiful, was calmly waiting to greet him, her children about her. Beside her, to Lord Hervey's astonishment, and some chagrin, was William Pulteney.

Hervey patted the heads of his eldest son, George William, and his eldest daughter whom they had named Lepel. The children had been well trained by their mother, and received him as coolly as she did. He was pleased with his family.

'William guessed that you would be arriving today, and he and Anna Maria are staying here. William is anxious to have talks with you.'

'Is that so?' replied Hervey languidly. 'Stephen will be staying until I return to court.'

Mary gave Stephen her beautiful smile, which meant that she allowed her lips to curl a little and her eyes to open wider.

'That will indeed be a pleasure,' she said.

'Stephen will unpack for me,' murmured Hervey. 'I do not trust the servants with some of my precious things.'

'Of course,' replied Molly.

As he went to his rooms, Hervey was wondering what proposition Pulteney had to put before him. He no longer felt as friendly towards Pulteney as he once had; his friendships did wane quickly. And Pulteney could scarcely feel so kindly towards him now that he had made it clear that he was a Walpole man. Still, it was gratifying that Pulteney should seek to bring him back to the fold. And Molly was evidently eager to help in the change.

Oh no, thought Hervey. If I am going to court I must be a Walpole man, for Walpole has managed to become the friend of the King *and* the Queen.

He turned to smile at Stephen.

'I do wonder why Pulteney has come here,' he said. 'And, oh dear, he has that vixen of his with him! She's a good-looking woman but has nothing to recommend her but her looks. I should like to know the purpose of his visit.'

'You will soon discover, however he tries to hide it from you.'

Hervey sat down on the bed as though exhausted.

'You are feeling ill?'

'A touch of the vertigo; I think I may have to go back to the seed and vegetable diet.'

'Oh dear, it has *such* a weakening effect. Perhaps you should rest here at Ickworth for a while.'

'The diet works wonders,' replied Hervey. 'I shall be well in a few days. Put out my pomade and my powder, dear boy. Then you can help me repair the ravages of the journey.'

Dinner was over and they sat in the drawing room – an intimate family party. There was Molly in flowered silk gathered up at the sides to show her very elaborate blue satin petticoat, the sleeves of her gown billowing at the elbows and ending in frills of soft lace; a patch near her eyes called attention to their beauty; she was now sitting with that utmost grace with which she performed every duty of the hostess. Anna Maria Pulteney was less elaborately dressed. She and Pulteney were very wealthy but Anna Maria did not like spending money and not only was very careful in her own expenditure but saw that her husband was too.

Pulteney was soberly dressed, but Lord Hervey looked like a

gorgeous dragonfly in lavender lace and satin; and Stephen, more simply dressed but very handsome, sat back in the shadows ready to show his devotion whenever his dearest friend demanded it.

Pulteney was wondering how far he could trust Hervey. He would have to trust him because he needed him. A man with a pen like Hervey's should be on one's side; and the fact that Walpole had been so eager to welcome him into his fold and had secured him the post of Chamberlain to the Queen was an indication of how his services were regarded.

During Hervey's absence abroad, Pulteney had been bringing Lady Hervey to his point of view and as she disliked Sir Robert Walpole intensely, she was delighted to help him.

Together, thought Pulteney, we will persuade him.

Conversation was desultory – all knew, except perhaps Stephen, that they were skirting about the subject they wished to discuss. They talked of Venice and Florence. Pulteney was a great talker, one of the most eloquent of men; and he liked to air his knowledge of the classics and throw in a Latin tag here and there. Hervey was not surprised that he could not endure coarse Sir Robert. He was highly amused, waiting for Pulteney to come into the attack while he skilfully hedged him off with the beauties of the sunset on the Grand Canal and a discussion of the merits of Michelangelo and Tintoretto.

Pulteney represented Heydon, a borough in Yorkshire, and was one of the leading Whigs. When he had married Anna Maria Gumley, of low birth and high fortune, he became one of the richest men in the country; but Anna Maria had turned out to be a vixen who kept a tight hold on their income and invested it in such a manner that it increased rapidly. At the beginning of his career he had worked with Walpole until Sir Robert had offended him in the year 1721 by not offering him a post in his Ministry. He refused the peerage which was offered him and very soon afterwards became one of Walpole's deadly enemies. He joined forces with Bolingbroke and that was indeed a formidable alliance, for between them they set up a journal which they called the *Craftsman*, and with this they began their attack. In it they wrote of a certain Robin (Sir Robert) and the object of the journal was to discredit him and to expose his sly ways to readers. Pulteney was a brilliant writer and Bolingbroke had years before discovered the power of the written word.

Sir William Wyndham, a firm Jacobite, joined with them and the three formed a new party which was made up of discontented Whigs and Jacobites; they called themselves the Patriots and their aim was, they declared, to work for the good of the country and expose the evil doings of those in high places.

And now, thought Hervey, Pulteney is here to attempt to lure me away from Walpole to his Patriots, perhaps to add my literary skill to his in the *Craftsman*.

Oh, no, certainly not. I have no intention of working under Pulteney and Bolingbroke. I am going to work alone and go my own way; and I shall begin through my friendship with Frederick, the Prince of Wales.

'William has been a frequent visitor during your absence,' said Molly at length when there was a pause in the description of European scenic grandeur.

'How kind of him to relieve the tedium of Ickworth.'

'How could there ever be tedium where Molly is?' asked Pulteney, smiling at his hostess.

Hervey saw the familiar lift of the lips, the opening of the eyes which remained cold and serene.

'We discussed your talents,' she said. 'They are too great to be wasted.'

'How kind.'

'If you could persuade Lord Hervey to read his latest poem to you . . .' began Stephen.

But Hervey silenced him with a loving smile.

'Let us discuss my talents,' said Hervey. 'I thrive on flattery.'

'This is no flattery,' said Pulteney.

Anna Maria, who hated prevarication, said bluntly: 'They want you to join the Patriots.'

Hervey took a kerchief from his sleeve and waved it before his face. Stephen half rose in alarm; Molly sat smiling and Pulteney was very alert.

'That would be far from simple,' murmured Hervey.

'Why so?' asked Pulteney sharply.

'I have my appointment to serve the Queen.'

'Why should you not continue in it?'

'Do you think Walpole would allow one who was no longer a friend to hold a post so close to the Queen?'

'That would be for the Queen to decide,' said Anna Maria.

'The Queen and Walpole share each other's views, Madam. What Walpole thinks today, the Queen thinks tomorrow.'

There was silence.

'I should be the loser by one thousand pounds a year,' declared Hervey languidly.

'Your father would be delighted to give you a thousand a year,' suggested Molly.

He smiled at his wife tenderly.

'My dearest, you think all have as high an opinion of me as you have.'

'I dislike Walpole,' said Molly. 'He is a coarse creature. He tried to seduce me once when I was at court.'

'Unsuccessfully?' inquired Hervey.

'Certainly unsuccessfully.'

'The fool!' said Pulteney. 'He is a disgrace to the country.'

'A disgrace who has brought peace,' suggested Hervey.

'It was time for peace. There is always a time for peace after wars.'

'He is credited for the peaceful times and the new prosperity.'

Molly said: 'If your father would make up the loss of the stipend you receive as the Queen's Chamberlain would you consider leaving Walpole?'

There was silence in the room.

Hervey looked at them; Pulteney, so flatteringly eager; Anna Maria suspicious, the vixen; and Molly, cool, seeming impartial. She wanted him to say yes. She did not care that her husband should be the crony of the man who had tried to seduce her. Fastidious Molly, how she must have hated the coarse old man! Was she capable of feeling elated at the thought of his fury when he knew he had lost such an important adherent as Hervey? It would be interesting to see.

'My father would not do so,' he said.

'But if he did . . .'

Hervey lifted his shoulders; the assumption was that his loyalty to Walpole hung on his stipend he received as the Queen's Chamberlain.

Stephen was alarmed, for he knew more of the secret plans of his dear friend than anyone.

'If you gave up your post you would hardly be received *intimately* at the court.'

'That's so, dear Stephen.'

'But . . . it is necessary . . . that you are at court.'

'Entirely necessary.'

'And yet . . .'

'Dear boy, you disturb yourself unnecessarily. There is no question of my giving up my post. My father will never agree to pay me the thousand a year.'

'And if he had . . .'

'He never will. My dear boy, do you imagine that I would give up this brilliant chance of being in close court circles? Never! But if I say to my wife I wish to be on friendly terms with your would-be-seducer, she will be displeased. And if I say to William Pulteney : "You are a clever fellow but I prefer to stand in the good graces of one whom I think is more clever," he will be offended. But if I say I do what I do for the sake of one thousand pounds a year, they are only disappointed; they understand and in a way they approve. Madam Vixen also. She has always such respect for money. It's the line of least resistance. I shall go back to court, sighing because I must smile at the man who would have seduced my wife, I must call my friend the enemy of one who believes himself to be my true friend. Oh, blessed thousand a year.'

Stephen smiled.

'How clever you are !'

Hervey nodded. 'And growing a little tired of the country life. This intrigue here in Ickworth has made me eager to plunge into others. Our stay will be shorter than I had at first planned.'

Lord Hervey had miscalculated. His father, Lord Bristol, who disliked Walpole intensely, was pleased that his son was considering severing his connection with him.

Molly had written to him explaining that her husband would have allied himself with Pulteney but for the fact that he had to consider the thousand pounds he received each year in payment for his duties as Chamberlain to the Queen. It went without saying that to turn from Walpole would be to lose the post, and it was for this reason only that dear John did not raise his voice against Sir Robert.

The Earl replied to his dearest daughter-in-law that he understood the predicament and was ready to do anything that would help his dear Jack. Therefore he need have no fear of relinquishing his post for his father would make up for all that he lost.

When Molly received the letter she did not run out to the gardens where Hervey was walking in deep conversation with Pulteney; that would have been showing an eagerness, and Molly never did that.

She was as serene as ever and it was only after they had dined and were seated together in the retiring chamber that she produced the letter from Lord Bristol.

Hervey listened in dismay. Stephen's large eyes were fixed fearfully on his friend's face.

'So,' said Pulteney, 'this matter is settled.'

'No, that is not so,' answered Hervey.

'But you can have no objection now. You will lose nothing. Your father is willing to reimburse you.'

'I do not recollect saying that my decision depended on this thousand a year.'

'But you distinctly . . .'

'I do not believe I passed an opinion. You assumed. *I* said nothing.'

Pulteney was furious. Hervey had never seen him so angry.

'You said . . . you implied . . .'

'I implied nothing. As I remarked, and I pray you forgive the repetition, you assumed. And wrongly as it has turned out. I have no intention of relinquishing the post.'

With that Hervey rose and bowing to his wife and Anna Maria, declared his intention to retire. He had a great deal to do for he intended to set out for St James's without delay.

He left the next day, leaving a furious Pulteney who refused to speak to him.

Molly paid him a placid farewell and went back to her social life, giving parties, looking after the poor of the district, caring for her children, as though she had never attempted to persuade him to leave the Walpole party in favour of the Patriots.

Hervey smiled as the carriage rattled through the Suffolk lanes on its way to London. He was singularly blessed in his marriage. As for Pulteney – a plague on him!

As soon as Hervey returned to court he began to ingratiate himself with Frederick. This was not difficult, for Frederick was always looking for new friends, flattery, and excitement; and Hervey, with his wit and elegance, his knowledge of the world and of politics seemed to the Prince a most engaging companion.

Frederick was restive. There were plenty to tell him that he was not treated fairly by his parents. He was kept short of money, which was a bore and a humiliation. His sisters, with the exception of Caroline, openly disliked him; so did his parents. Whenever he could plague them, he would. And there were plenty to help him do it.

But he was not serious by nature. He did not want to be seriously involved in politics; he liked to surround himself with merry companions and drink together, play cards, or perhaps wander incognito through the town to see what adventures came their way.

After the manner of his father, he believed that it was due to his dignity to take a mistress or two, although the company of his own sex delighted him and it seemed to him that Lord Hervey was the ideal companion.

Very soon they were firm friends.

Stephen Fox was a little jealous of Hervey's devotion to the Prince, but Hervey wrote comfortingly to Stephen that the Prince was a fool and that it was not through friendship that they were so much together. While he was forced to spend his time with Frederick his thoughts were with Stephen, and when he was at a banquet at Lord Harrington's and Stephen's name was proposed as a toast, he had felt himself blushing as a man's favourite mistress would have done on the same occasion. Stephen was the person whom he adored more than all the others in the world bundled together. Stephen should remember this – no matter what gossip he heard of Hervey and his new friend.

Like his father, Frederick enjoyed discussing his love affairs. They were numerous, he told Hervey. And what of his?

'Numerous also,' replied Hervey languidly.

This delighted Frederick, who went on to explain the charms of the daughter of one of the court musicians.

'The hautboy player. She is very charming . . . and so humble. Yet it cost me all of fifteen hundred pounds to set her up in her own establishment.'

'Generous of Your Royal Highness. The honour should have sufficed.'

That delighted Frederick. 'Oh, I like to be generous with those who please me.'

Over-generous, thought Hervey. There'll be debts.

'She is very different from Madame Bartholdi. You know Madame Bartholdi?'

'An excellent singer. I have heard her at the opera.'

'A passionate woman.'

'My dear Fred, most women in England would feel passion for the Prince of Wales.'

How easy it was to please. He liked Hervey to call him Fred. He prided himself on his democratic attitude. That was why he liked to roam the streets at night incognito.

His latest acquisition was the daughter of an apothecary at Kingston and he was constantly taking boat there to see her.

So tiresome! thought Hervey.

He himself had his duties in the Queen's apartments. Caroline had always liked him; she reminded him of how he used to ride along beside her chaise when the hunt was on and amuse her with his conversation.

'Are you still as witty as you were then, Lord Hervey?' she asked.

'I trust Your Majesty will give me opportunities of assuring you that I am more so.'

She laughed. 'I hope it is not venomous wit like little Mr Pope's and so many of his sort. It is so much more clever to be witty and kind, Lord Hervey, than witty and cruel.'

'Your Majesty, being both witty and kind, is the cleverest of us all.'

'There is no need for flattery. You should save that for the Prince of Wales. Ah, how different everything is now! I remember when you were a very young man and were courting Molly Lepel. How is dear Molly?'

'Very well and very fruitful.'

'Somehow I did not think you would be father to so many.'

'I am delighted to be able to surprise Your Majesty.'

'And I am delighted to see your friendship with the Prince of Wales. If you can teach him to be a little more serious . . .'

He smiled. 'When I am scarcely serious myself?'

'A little more—' she was going to say 'like yourself', but perhaps that would be too strong. There were always people within earshot and she did not want to start a scandal about herself and Lord Hervey. He was, after all, about fourteen years younger than she was, but she had always had a fondness for him and she knew she brightened when he stood beside her chair and enlivened her with his conversation. George would be furious if there was so much as a breath of scandal about her. And he was difficult enough to handle as it was.

'A little more princely,' she said. 'I fear he wastes his time in the company of—'

'Men like myself?'

'No, you will be good for him. I am sure of it.' She turned away. She would have to be careful.

Hervey was well aware of her caution and was amused by it. There was nothing he liked so much as to exert his charm, and to have made the Queen aware of it delighted him.

Perhaps he should spend more time near to her.

He noticed one of her maids regarding him with some interest, and when he left the Queen's presence he found her at his side. She was very handsome and very voluptuous. He knew of her. She was Anne Vane, at present mistress of Lord Harrington, although Harrington was by no means the first man to have been her lover.

'My lord,' she said, 'it is good to see you back at court. I trust you will stay.'

There was invitation there. Hervey considered it. She interested him, partly because she must be as different from his wife as a woman could be. Molly was as cool as April; this woman was hot as August.

Her gaze was flattering: 'You bring out the male in me,' he said.

She laughed understanding. Hervey was an interesting character. Two-sided, it was said. There was the feminine side and the masculine. He liked this to be said. It made him seem so interesting. Although he preferred perhaps the company of his men friends, he was, he wanted people to know, not without interest in women.

'We must talk together sometime.'

Anne Vane opened her mouth and let her tongue appear between her white teeth.

'Some say there is no time like the present,' she said.

'And do you say it?'

'On this occasion most emphatically? And my lord?'

'Slightly less emphatically.'

'I am sure I should know how to make you more emphatic.'

'And my Lord Harrington?'

'Is spending a few days in the country.'

'That must make you very sad.'

She smiled and laid her hand on his arm.

Hervey found Anne Vane an interesting mistress; and the liaison became more intriguing when Harrington returned. Hervey had no wish to make it known that he was Anne's lover. Stephen was so jealous and there was always someone to carry such news.

He did not know what Frederick's reaction would be either, for he and Frederick were drawing closer together every day, and the Prince was beginning to tire of the apothecary's daughter.

To please the Prince he suggested they should write a play together, and this delighted Frederick. Of course, thought Hervey, I shall do all the work; but it was worth it to have people saying that he and the Prince were becoming inseparable.

The play was difficult to write, for he had never tried his hand at playwriting before. It required a more sustained effort than the writing of verses or the notes he was accustomed to make in his journal. He had his doubts as to the virtue of the play, but Frederick was enthusiastic about it. Poor Fred! He had no literary taste!

When the play was finished Frederick insisted on sending it to Wilks, the actor-manager at Drury Lane.

'He must put it on the stage,' cried Frederick. 'No one shall know who wrote it. The King and the Queen will come and admire it and then and only then shall they know that the son whom they despise has some talents.'

Hervey regarded the Prince tolerantly. Did he really think Wilks would put on their little piece if he didn't know the Prince had had a hand in it? Didn't he see that the only hope of its ever being on a stage was because his name went with it?

But one must placate royalty, which often meant deceiving it.

'You, my lord, will know exactly how to manage this. I want to go to the theatre and see our play.'

'Leave it with me,' said Hervey.

This Frederick was pleased to do, being certain that in a short time he and his dear friend would be sitting in a box incognito watching the audience delight in their work.

'This is not a play,' cried Wilks scornfully.

'I think you should put it on nevertheless,' Hervey told him.

'The audience wouldn't sit through it.'

'I still think you should put it on.'

'There's court interest in this?'

Hervey nodded.

'Well, I must let the audience know. They'll not take it otherwise.'

'Orders are secrecy. Put on the play first. Revelations will come after.'

'I don't like it,' said Wilks. 'Nor will the audience.'

*　　*　　*

Frederick and Hervey sat back in their box. The Prince's eyes were shining with delighted anticipation as he surveyed the audience who had no notion who he was. Even Hervey had disguised his elegance with a big cloak.

'I love the opening when the players come on to the stage one by one . . .' burbled Frederick.

'Let us hope the audience do.'

The play began. Frederick watched enchanted, which was more than the audience did. Hervey was aware of their restiveness before Frederick was. They coughed; they shuffled their feet; they talked together and in less than ten minutes they were shouting for Wilks.

'Take this off and put on a proper play,' shouted someone from the pit.

Frederick sat back in his seat, his face white.

'They . . . they don't like it . . .'

'They don't know it was our work,' replied Hervey cynically. 'They're judging it by Gay's standards . . . not by those of royalty.'

'They . . . don't . . . like it!' repeated Frederick stupidly.

The audience was more than restive; it was angry. Had they paid good money to see nonsense like this? When they compared this with the *Beggar's Opera* or *Henry VIII* there was only one thing they could do.

Someone stood on his seat and shouted it.

'Give us a play or our money back.'

'Our money back! Our money back!' screeched the audience.

Someone threw a mouldy orange on to the stage. It was a signal. Missiles were falling thick and fast until Wilks came to stand by the footlights. He held up his hand; there were jeers and catcalls, but Wilks was enough of a man of the theatre to know how to handle an audience.

'Good people,' he said, 'I agree with you. This should never have been offered. You shall all have your money back and come tomorrow when we will have a good play to offer you.'

'Hurrah!' shouted someone.

Wilks was relieved; he had averted a riot and he had thought at one moment that his theatre was going to be destroyed.

Frederick and Hervey left the theatre crestfallen. Hervey had had a good opinion of his own work; as for Frederick he could not understand how what had seemed a work of genius in the privacy of his apartments could become banal verbose dialogues on a stage.

Although he would have been ready to claim his share of the credit had the play been a success, he now assured himself that the main work had been Hervey's.

Hervey did not know it, but Frederick, that night, began to look at his friend a little critically.

Hervey could not endure failure and during the next day had an attack of vertigo while he was waiting on the Queen.

He explained afterwards to Frederick that he had successfully hidden this from Her Majesty by gripping a table to steady himself until the attack had passed.

The fact was however brought home to him that he needed a rest. His medical adviser, Dr Cheyne, had suggested he retire to the country for a few weeks and there exist on a strict milk, seed, and vegetable diet. He was going to ask Stephen Fox to accompany him because his family were so healthy they did not understand illness; and Stephen was such a good nurse.

He trusted to be back with His Highness feeling well again in the shortest possible time.

Frederick said that his dear friend must of course go to the country; his health must be their first concern.

So to Ickworth went Hervey, and when he had gone the Prince realized how much he missed him and wondered what he could do to pass the time.

Anne Vane was wondering too. Strangely enough Hervey excited her more than any of her lovers and she was piqued because he had not even bothered to let her know he was going to the country. This was not the treatment she expected and she wondered how she could pay him for his neglect.

She had an idea when she saw Frederick disconsolately sitting by one of the fountains in the palace gardens . . . alone.

She walked past him and dropped her kerchief, letting it

flutter close to his feet. He did not see it, so she approached with a show of timidity and sweeping a curtsy asked if she had His Highness's permission to retrieve her kerchief.

Frederick was always charming and gracious to his father's subjects. In fact, in public he was charming and gracious to his family. This won him much popularity which the King was fast forfeiting now that he never failed, when the opportunity arose, to praise Hanover to the detriment of England.

He took the kerchief, and rising and bowing he presented it to Anne Vane.

She took it and let it drop again.

'How careless of me! I . . . I am overwhelmed by Your Highness's graciousness.'

'Oh . . . it is nothing.'

'But Your Highness is always so kind.' She had raised her eyes to gaze at him with adoration.

'I have seen you often . . . and admired you.'

'Not as often as I've seen you . . . and I'll swear you didn't bestow as much admiration on me as I did on you.'

'You are very kind.'

She giggled slightly. It was an invitation. Anne Vane had never believed in delay. Once she had made up her mind she was ready. One of the advantages of losing one's virtue, she often said, was that one was so often spared the anguish of decision : Should one? Shouldn't one? Why not? was always the answer. What was one more among so many?

'It is Your Highness who is kind.'

'Would you care to sit a while?'

She would esteem it the greatest honour.

So she sat and they talked. She did not mention Hervey. She was the most sensuously inviting woman he had ever met, her great virtue being that she always believed the love affair of the moment was going to be the best she had ever known, and was able to get her partner to share that belief.

Frederick was delighted. He ceased to miss Hervey.

He had a companion very much to his taste and that very day Anne Vane became his mistress.

How pleasant to be in Ickworth! Hervey wondered why he did

not come more often. Molly was as coolly aloof as ever, never reproaching him, the perfect wife for a man such as he was.

It was amusing to write his poems and pieces. Pulteney had never forgiven him for that last little difference between them when he had thought he could persuade Hervey to give up his allegiance to Walpole and thus his post as Chamberlain to the Queen.

There had been sly little digs at him in the *Craftsman* and that venomous little Mr Pope had referred to him under a thin veil of disguise which didn't deceive any as 'Lord Fanny'. A slur of course on the feminine side of his nature. Fools! They didn't realize that to be both masculine and feminine was to have the best of both worlds and was a matter for congratulation rather than ridicule. And when with it went a title, money, leisure, and a pretty wit, the possessor of all these was to be envied.

He was very pleased with the manner in which he arranged his life, and he meant it to be more and more entertaining. In time Frederick would be the King, and his closest friend and adviser was going to be John, Lord Hervey.

At the moment he was busy writing the dedication to a pamphlet which was entitled *Sedition and Defamation Displayed*. The dedication was to his enemies, the promoters of the *Craftsman*, headed by Pulteney. This would teach the man to be more careful when he set his writers to work on Lord Fanny, who might paint his cheeks, who might suffer vertigo at levées, but who none the less was a man who could face the wiliest politicians on an equal footing.

Stephen Fox came into the room, quietly, reverently.

'I disturb you . . .'

'Never, dear boy. Come here and read this.'

Stephen read with absorption, now and then chuckling aloud.

'It's sheer genius,' he said.

'I trust it will make Pulteney writhe.'

'I'm not surprised Walpole is eager to keep you on his side.'

'Ah, the power of the pen, Stephen boy. Never forget it.'

'You have made that plain to me. But . . . I have news from the court.' Stephen looked anxious. 'Anne Vane has become the Prince's mistress.'

Hervey was silent for a while; then he burst out laughing.

'Fred will always follow me. Really, I don't think the poor fool has an original idea in his head.'

'You . . . you have no objections?'

'My dear boy, what is Anne Vane to me? Nothing. What is Fred to me? As little. No, that's not true. I respect the title Prince of Wales even when it's attached to poor fool Fred. As for Anne Vane, the creature adores me. This is pique, Stephen, pure pique. But it offers opportunities. I shall use her to keep her eye on our little Prince for me. She shall report all his doings. Then I shall not have to return to the court so soon. This is good news. I will write to the woman and you must send a messenger to deliver the letter to her. She shall tell us all that is in his mind. I will write to her without delay.'

At Ickworth Hervey continued to enjoy his days. He was writing a good deal; he was pleased to be with his wife and family; and Stephen was with him.

'I do declare,' he said, 'that Frederick is a great trial to me. He is false, silly, and plagues me. My dearest Stephen, there was never a man less like your dear self than our silly Prince.'

That delighted Stephen and Hervey enjoyed pleasing him. Molly liked him to stay with the family now and then. It looked well; and in view of the fact that he did attract a certain amount of scandal when he was at court, it was necessary to become a respectable married man now and then. It showed everyone that Molly was not concerned in these scandals and that her marriage was as firm now as it had been in those early days when she and her husband had been content to live at Ickworth together and the children had begun to appear.

But peace was suddenly shattered.

Hervey, like everyone else, avidly read the *Craftsman* when it made its appearance and since his *Dedication to the Patrons of The Craftsman* in that pamphlet *Sedition and Defamation Displayed*, he had been expecting some reaction.

Yet when he saw it he knew that it was so damaging that he would have to take some action.

He called Stephen to him. He was trembling with rage – as

he held out the paper to his friend.

It was written by Pulteney and was titled *A Proper Reply to a Late Scurrilous Libel*.

'At first [wrote Pulteney], I was at a loss to imagine who could have composed this little work, but the little quaint antitheses, the laboured jingle of the periods, the great variety of rhetorical flourishes, affected metaphors and puerile witticisms proclaim this to be the production of pretty Mr Fainlove.'

He had, he wrote, made efforts to discover the author and had been told the secret by someone who had asked him not to treat the gentleman too harshly. 'He is young and innocent. What would the ladies say? Ah, but you know he is a Lady himself, or at least such a nice composition of the two sexes that it is difficult to distinguish which is most predominant.'

Stephen winced. He could not bear to read any more. But there was more. There was a hint of the practices in which Mr Fainlove indulged; and these were such which he could not allow to go unchallenged.

He said : 'You will write a reply.'

'It needs more than a written reply, Stephen.'

'What do you mean?'

'There is only one answer to this. I must call him out. This is death . . . to one of us.'

'No !'

'My dear boy, that is what Pulteney intends, and I should be called a coward if I did not meet the challenge. I could not face the court again if I allowed this to pass.'

'But he does not mention you by name.'

'My dear Stephen, you are wilfully blind. There is no one at court who will read this . . . and you can be sure everyone is reading it at this moment . . . who will not know that Mr Fainlove is John Hervey.'

'But . . . a duel ! You cannot . . . You must not !'

'You seem to think that I shall be the loser.'

'This is not a battle of words.'

'No . . . of swords. Have no fear. I shall give a good account of myself. And it is the only answer, for the girlish creature he makes me out to be would not be capable of crossing swords with such an opponent.'

'I am . . . *terrified*.'

'You shall be my second. Now do not try to persuade me from this. It is inevitable. The battle has gone beyond words, and only the sword will defend me now.'

In the Park, behind Arlington Street, on a bitterly cold morning, Pulteney and Hervey faced each other.

In an agony of fear Stephen Fox looked on, too disturbed to feel the cold, cutting January wind which whistled across the park.

Lord Hervey had been very cool and had declared that nothing would make him give in now although all the way to the scene Stephen had been urging him to turn back.

Pulteney looked equally grim. The fact that they had once been friends made them both the more bitter.

They approached each other; they drew their swords; the signal was given and for the first seconds no sound was heard but the clash of weapons on the still morning air.

Stephen felt himself ready to swoon as Pulteney's sword caught Hervey's arm and a dark stain was visible on his friend's sleeve.

But now Pulteney was showing blood. Hervey's sword had touched his neck. There was grim determination in their faces. On this cold and snowy morning one of them was going to die.

Pulteney was the better swordsman; that became evident to the watchers. Stephen was almost fainting with fear; but Hervey seemed unconcerned. At least if this were the end, it would be a dramatic exit – the sort that would be expected of Lord Hervey.

Pulteney believed the victory was his. At any moment he would run his adversary through the heart. He thought of Molly of whom he was fond. What would her reaction be to the man who had murdered her husband? And what happened to a man who killed another in a duel? Would he be obliged to flee the country?

This was folly, madness! How had they allowed this matter to come to this point?

He was ready now, the advantage was his. His sword was poised. In a few seconds Lord Hervey would be a dying man.

Pulteney's foot slipped on the snow. Was it by accident? None of the watchers could be absolutely sure. But the moment of decision had come . . . and passed.

Pulteney's sword had gone wide of the mark. Hervey gave a little shout of triumphant relief. And then Stephen had run out and placed himself between the two opponents.

'This has gone far enough,' he said. 'You have both proved your courage. No good can come of proceeding further.'

Pulteney's second joined his voice to Stephen's. This was the best way in which to end a duel. Each had been wounded; none was the victor. But they had both shown that they were ready to die to defend their honour. Wise men ended at this point. No good could come of continuing.

Pulteney was only too glad to end the affair. He had no wish to kill Hervey, nor to be killed by him.

He held out his hand. Hervey was secretly exultant too. Who wanted to die in one's prime when life offered so much that was exciting? But Pulteney had made wounding . . . and damaging comments.

He ignored the extended hand, bowed stiffly and leaning on Stephen's arm walked away.

Stephen took him to his house and there dressed the wound in his arm; and all the time he was congratulating his friend on his escape from a situation which must never be allowed to arise again and yet had defended Hervey's honour.

His courage vindicated, Hervey stayed briefly at court. He saw a little of Frederick but Anne Vane kept out of his way. The Queen was courteous and kind; and quite clearly showed that she was glad he had had the courage to face his adversary; and she was even more glad that he had come through that dangerous affair unscathed.

He went back to Ickworth where Molly greeted him as usual. She had heard of the duel, but since he had returned safely and suffered no ill she saw no reason to dwell on the matter, and it was forgotten.

Molly was pregnant and in due course a son was born. Hervey decided that he should be called Frederick after the Prince of Wales and asked Frederick to come down to Ickworth for the christening. This Frederick declared himself delighted to do and the christening was performed to Molly's satisfaction and the great joy of the neighbourhood.

Frederick gave no sign of his changed feelings for Hervey. In fact when he was with his old friend he easily slipped into the old habit of friendship and the Herveys had no idea that anything had changed.

When Anne Vane had received Hervey's letter she had been furious. If he thought she was sitting in her apartments waiting to hear from him he was mistaken. In some respects she preferred Frederick. He was less *du monde* perhaps; but he was the better for that.

She re-read the note.

To act as his spy! This was a joke, and she would teach Mr Hervey a lesson.

Should she show the letter to the Prince? It might not be a bad idea when she had prepared him. But the impertinence of Lord Fanny!

In her apartments she was preparing herself to receive the Prince. He came without ceremony, for that was how he liked it. They had a great deal of fun together, riding out in the streets in hack sedans, being carried side by side and pretending to be on the fringe of the court. It was much more gratifying to be the Prince's mistress than any other man's at court – not excepting the King. Ugh! Fancy being George's mistress! Not much fun in that. Poor Henrietta Howard, who had held the post for so long and got all the scandal with none of the glory!

Oh, yes, it was very different to be the beloved of the Prince of Wales.

There was a little trouble looming in the not very distant future. She was certain now, but this of course wasn't the time to mention it. However, she had made up her mind that the infant was going to be the son ... or daughter ... of a Prince. Neither Harrington nor Hervey were good enough to be named as the father of her child.

She was setting a tiny black patch close to her eyes when the Prince entered. She leaped from her stool and embraced him.

'My Prince!'

He was delighted with her. A simple young man really; and she had such experience of young men, so she knew exactly how to treat him.

Later, when they lay side by side in her bed, she talked of Hervey.

'I have a confession to make. I feel that I can no longer keep this to myself. You mean so much to me that I can't bear to have a secret from you. You are not my first lover.'

Even inexperienced Frederick had not thought this for one moment. He told her that everything that had gone before in their lives was nothing. The past was over; it was only the present and the future which mattered.

'I was seduced by a man of whom I believe you have rather a high opinion. That is what has made it so difficult for me to tell you.'

'You should not disturb yourself, dear Anne.'

'But I do, my Prince. I think only of you. And I must tell you what is in my mind. I must *warn* you ...'

'Warn me?'

'Yes, because this man who pretends to be your friend is only using you.'

'Using *me*!'

'He hopes to. But I shall not allow it. Let me explain. I was seduced by Lord Hervey.'

The Prince coloured slightly. He was quite clearly devoted to the man. He said: 'Well ... you are very pretty, Anne, so I suppose we must try to understand ...'

'That is not all. He cared for me no more than he cares for you. He merely wanted to use me. He wants me to act as his spy.'

'On whom would you spy? What can you know of the court more than he does?'

'My dearest, this is hard to say. But he wants me to spy on *you*. He wants me to lead you the way he wants you to go.'

'But he is my friend. He can talk to me himself.'

She rose from the bed and put a flimsy robe over her naked body. She looked frail and very provocative. Opening a drawer she drew out a letter and began to read it to him.

He could not believe that Hervey had written so about him. But she insisted on his reading it himself.

Then she snatched it from him and tore it into bits. She flung it up so that it was scattered over the bed; then she threw herself upon him.

'Does he think I should ever be disloyal to my dearest Prince? Never . . . never . . . never !'

The Prince was overcome by such devotion, and at the moment could think of nothing but making love.

But later he began to brood on Hervey's duplicity.

In the next few weeks the main point of discussion between Anne and Frederick was Lord Hervey, and Frederick was beginning to believe that he had been very mistaken in the man he had made his friend.

Hervey continued to write to him amusing doggerel which always made him laugh because it was directed against members of the court. When Anne saw one of these she said: 'It's very funny, but I wonder how he writes about *you* to *others* !' And that made Frederick stop to think.

All the same, as soon as he received a note from Hervey he would begin to feel the old fascination and Anne was aware of this.

Frederick needed a friend of his own sex to replace Hervey and she knew the very man.

George Bubb Dodington was one of the richest young men at court; he was not really of very good family and would be very grateful to her if she introduced him to the Prince of Wales.

His real name was Bubb, his father being Jeremiah Bubb who had been an Irish apothecary on the look-out for a fortune, when he had discovered the daughter of George Dodington, a member of a rich and ancient family of Somerset. George Bubb was sent to Oxford and in time became Member of Parliament for Win-

chelsea. He added Dodington to his name and called attention
to himself by his lavish spending, mostly on houses. His country
mansion in Dorset, said to be as magnificent as a Palace, had
been designed by Vanbrugh and contained a James Thornhill
ceiling. He had also acquired two houses near London, one at
Hammersmith and another in Pall Mall. He had the means at
his disposal to entertain a Prince.

He was not without wit; he wielded some influence; but the
nobility were inclined to despise him. It was for this reason that
Anne Vane selected him to take the place with the Prince which
had been Lord Hervey's, for he was just the man Hervey would
despise most, and to be replaced by him would be an additional
insult.

Frederick liked George Bubb Dodington as soon as he met
him in Anne's apartments. He called him affectionately Bubb
and proceeded to win money from him. Bubb seemed to be
delighted to lose to the Prince; money spent in this way seemed a
good investment; and as the Prince was always short of it this
seemed a basis on which to build the friendship between them.

Frederick was entertained at the Hammersmith villa and was
deeply impressed by the magnificence of it. Bubb, large, fleshy,
vulgar, not without wit, and humble to his Prince, was the
right antidote to languid Hervey.

On his first visit to La Trappe, Bubb made sure that the
occasion should be impressive. He himself greeted the Prince
and led him up the marble staircase to the marble and lapis lazuli
gallery, and presented to His Royal Highness Mrs Behan, his
mistress, who was as sumptuously gowned in rich brocade and
jewels as the Queen might have been for a state occasion and
even the Prince was dazzled.

Anything that could have been crowded into the mansion had
been brought here, except good taste. All Bubb wanted to say to
the world was: See how rich I am. Anything I want I can buy.

With Mrs Behan twittering her delight and the sweat gleam-
ing on Bubb's fleshy face, Frederick was delighted to give such
pleasure.

How different from Hervey who always pretended that he
was bestowing a favour.

The banquet was served on gold plate with Bubb and Mrs

Behan insisting on waiting on the Prince themselves, for, as Bubb said, if it were possible to pay someone enough to do the honour he would willingly, but he reckoned that only the host and hostess should wait on the Prince of Wales.

With Anne beside him Frederick enjoyed the banquet and all the sycophantic laughter every time he made a joke.

It was a most successful evening and when he won several hundred pounds from his host at cards, it grew even more so.

'I hope,' declared Bubb when he escorted the Prince through the gallery studded with lapis lazuli and semi-precious stones to his carriage, 'that Your Highness will continue to honour La Trappe.'

'You may ask me again,' Frederick told him. 'I shall be happy to come.'

And he and Anne, embracing in the carriage which took them back to St James's, agreed that it had been a delightful evening.

'I think Bubb is a much more pleasant friend than Lord Fanny,' whispered Anne.

And they laughed together at the antics of Lord Fanny; and Frederick said that he would spend his winnings in buying a piece of jewellery for his dearest Anne.

At La Trappe, Bubb was sprawling in a chair almost bursting out of his brocade jacket.

'All went well,' he said.

'It couldn't have been better,' agreed Mrs Behan, perching on his knee.

'It's only the beginning.'

'Don't lose too much to him at cards.'

'It'll be worth every penny I lose. When did you know me not to get value for money?'

'The best of us can be caught.'

She was very specially privileged and very determined to see that he was not robbed. In fact she was really his wife although the world thought she was his mistress. That was a necessary subterfuge because he had once become deeply involved with a woman named Strawbridge to whom he had promised marriage. He had been foolish enough to give her a bond for ten thousand pounds which she could turn into cash if he ever betrayed her by marrying another woman.

Mrs Behan was a sensible woman. She didn't consider the standing of wife to be worth ten thousand pounds, particularly when she had attained that position in fact.

So she was known as his mistress and would be until Mrs Strawbridge no longer existed to plague them.

Therefore with her, Bubb could discuss his future plans with the utmost freedom.

When Hervey came back to London and called on the Prince of Wales it was a great shock to be met with the statement that the Prince was unable to see him. And the shock grew greater when he was informed that if he cared to wait in the ante-room with others who wished an audience it might be that his Royal Highness would favour him.

Hervey went white with rage.

'Does His Highness know that it is Lord Hervey who waits on him?'

His Royal Highness did know, but it made no difference.

He saw the Prince come out of his apartment in the company of Miss Vane and a vulgar person of immense bulk, dressed – or rather overdressed – in brocade and embroidery, with jewels, someone whose name he did not know and, except for the fact that he was in the company of the Prince of Wales, would not have wished to know.

'Who is the tradesman with the Prince?' he asked. 'A merchant in rich materials obviously.'

'No, my lord,' was the answer. 'It is the Prince's friend, Mr George Bubb Dodington.'

'Bubb Dodington!' cried Hervey, looking as though he were going to faint. 'I never heard of the creature.'

Then he walked soberly away. What had happened during his absence? He knew that he had been a fool to stay away so long.

The situation became clearer to him every day. He was no more than an acquaintance to the Prince, who greeted him civilly when they met but showed no desire to be alone with him.

It was intolerable. That he, the elegant wit, could be replaced by that . . . buffoon! It was unendurable. He knew who was behind this. He had seen the malice in her eyes. She had arranged this out of pique. Because he had ceased to become her lover, because he had shown no resentment that Frederick was, she had sought to take her petty revenge.

Well, she should see what happened to those who dared behave so to Lord Hervey.

The Prince's mistress

In the Queen's apartment the company were playing quadrille. Caroline had no wish to join. She was a little tired, though determined that none should guess it. Mrs Clayton was hovering, but the Queen could not bring herself to look at her attendant – and friend.

The relationship between them had changed subtly since Charlotte Clayton's discovery of what ailed the Queen. Charlotte never referred to this as she knew well that it was the Queen's wish that she should not; but it was there between them. Charlotte had a great many humble relatives and it was one of her hobbies to find places for them.

The Queen sighed. It seemed that since the discovery Charlotte *had* brought forward a greater number of indigent relatives. 'Your Majesty, my niece . . . my nephew . . . my cousin . . . would like this or that . . .'

There was no threat. How could there have been? How could Charlotte blackmail the Queen? Besides, there was great devotion between them. But Caroline always saw that Charlotte's wishes were gratified; and Charlotte enjoyed playing the benefactress in her impecunious family, for that must have been very pleasant to a woman who craved for power. Craved for power? Did she? As any would. She was regarded, through her place at court, as the head of her family; and clearly she enjoyed it.

And in her heart Caroline knew that what Charlotte asked – in reason – would be hers because of the secret they shared.

Henrietta Howard was restive. She was always restive nowadays. She had no longer any desire to stay at court. It was true her position was growing more and more humiliating. The King still called at her apartments precisely at the hour he always had. But he spent the time in abusing her, telling her of his dissatisfaction with her. Poor Henrietta! She was longing to escape. Where to? That scoundrel of a husband of hers who was being paid by the King to allow his wife to stay in the Queen's employ? A very uneasy position for everyone. And the King was casting covetous eyes on silly little Lady Deloraine who was governess to Mary and Louisa. She was an extremely pretty woman and had a connection with royalty because her husband's father had been Charles II's illegitimate son, the Duke of Monmouth. A sad position for Henrietta, who was no longer even the King's mistress; and who should have left court long ago and would have done so if the King had been helped to break a habit of years standing.

And how can I help him, sighed Caroline, when in Henrietta's place there might be some charming, scheming, *clever* woman.

Life, it seemed, would never run smoothly. Frederick was a constant anxiety. Charming and affectionate towards his parents as he was in public, in private he showed his dissatisfaction with what they did for him. He wanted more money; he wanted more prestige; he wanted to marry.

He must have none of these . . . yet. She and Walpole could not afford to have such a rival, and rival he would quickly become with those wolves of the Opposition ready to pounce on him and make him the centre of a Party which, with Frederick at its head, might well win public support. She remembered the old days of strife between the previous King and his son. History had a way of repeating itself.

Young William was looking handsome and bright tonight; but as soon as he set eyes on his brother he would appear sullen, for he refused to hide his feelings and he deeply resented Frederick. The girls were present. Amelia looked by far the handsomest of the three, but how she favoured masculine styles! She was far too fond of outdoor sports and, Caroline knew, excelled at them. She was bold, perhaps a little brazen. One might think so now to see her openly flirting with Grafton. What a bold and handsome fellow Grafton was! Another result of the promiscuous life of that indefatigable lover, Charles II. Grafton was the son of Barbara Castlemaine's son and claimed to be the grandson of Charles Stuart. These people gave themselves airs and secretly, Caroline guessed, believed themselves to be more royal than the present German branch of the family. Grafton doubtless thought he had a chance with Amelia and Amelia would be nothing loth.

Where are we going to find husbands for the girls? sighed Caroline. It was so difficult being firmly Protestant, which they must be since it was the reason why the English had accepted them, when almost every eligible Prince in Europe was Catholic. It restricted choice so; and now that Sophia Dorothea's double marriage scheme had come to nothing, what of a husband for Amelia, what of a wife for Frederick?

She and Walpole were not anxious to provide a wife for the Prince of course, for marriage would add to his importance. But it was certainly time Anne was married. And she was getting bitter too.

And there was Grafton trying to compromise Amelia so that marriage might be *necessary*.

Life was full of difficulties.

And Caroline was stooping a little, which was worrying because she was so delicate, learning to dislike her elder brother because all the others did, particularly William who would have been the Prince of Wales but for Frederick – and how she wished he had been!

She disliked her eldest son. She might as well face it, for to say anything else would have been hypocrisy. If only he had never been born, there would be much less strife in the family, because it was only since his coming that the trouble had been so pronounced. If she could only find suitable husbands for the girls! If William could be Prince of Wales; he would not be of age for many years, which would give her and Walpole – and of course the King – years of freedom to rule as they thought fit, without interference from an Opposition which each day was seeking to draw Frederick into its net.

Troubles swirling around, conflict within the family circle! It seemed what they must always expect.

Frederick had come in and had created the usual stir. They were bowing and curtsying which was only right, of course, as he was the Prince of Wales. He came to her and she tried to see him dispassionately – a little man, like his father, neat as George was, and elegant too; he paid attention to the minutest detail of dress, as George did. He was so like his father that this should have endeared them to each other. It had the reverse effect. Frederick lacked his father's quick temper. One could never imagine Frederick's taking off his wig and kicking it round the room – a trick of George's in the old days. Frederick was too careless; all he wanted was to enjoy life in the company of his chosen friends. And his chosen friend now was that impossibly vulgar Mr Dodington.

Frederick kissed his mother's hand charmingly – always so charming in public. In private he would be sullen, always ready to talk of his debts, wondering why he could not have more money.

She complimented him on his healthy looks and after a short conversation he left her to wander among the guests and say a few words to each.

She watched him and saw that he had joined Anne Vane, one of her attendants, and that he stayed at her side. She knew the girl was his mistress. That was of no great importance, except of course that the girl had not the best of reputations. She would have preferred him to have chosen a mistress as discreet and as modest as Henrietta.

She noticed that her daughter Caroline had suddenly become animated, almost pretty, a faint flush in her cheeks, her eyes brightening.

The reason was clear. Lord Hervey was presenting himself to the Queen.

Caroline's own spirits lifted. Lord Hervey was always so amusing. She enjoyed his company more than anyone else's – more than Walpole's, although, of course, she and the great statesman had so much of importance to discuss together.

'My lord, it is a pleasure . . .'

'Your Majesty is gracious.'

He was very handsome and most magnificently dressed. His cheeks were only faintly touched with rouge. Poor man, thought the Queen, he suffers and must disguise his pallor for he doesn't want everyone asking after his health.

She shuddered at the thought of such a distasteful subject.

'Pray be seated beside me,' she said. 'Now amuse me with the latest gossip.'

Hervey did this so effectively that now and then the Queen's laughter rang out. The Princess Caroline came to sit on the other side of Hervey and joined in the merriment, although not in the conversation, preferring to sit quietly listening.

'Lord Hervey,' chided the Queen, 'I fear you have a wicked tongue.'

'Alas, so much more entertaining than a discreet one. Is it not sad that the discreet and the virtuous are invariably bores?'

'One could never call you that, Lord Hervey.'

'I have always thought that I would be wicked while I was young giving myself time in which to repent and spend my last years . . . no, months . . . in being virtuous, a plague to myself and a bore to my friends.'

'I should not listen to such talk.'

'You see, I even tempt Your Majesty to forget your habitual virtue.'

'Are you suggesting that I am a bore since I am virtuous?'

'It is the privilege of royalty, Madam, never to bore.'

'What do you think of this man, Caroline?' the Queen asked her daughter. 'Do you not think that we should dismiss him from the court?'

The Princess Caroline blushed and murmured that the court would be a dull place if Lord Hervey were banished from it.

'There's a nice piece of flattery for you,' laughed the Queen.

Hervey looked intently at the Princess and said: 'I hope with all my heart that it is not flattery.'

c.q.—8

The Princess looked uncomfortable and turned her gaze on the company. Hervey was completely assured. Why was he fretting about lost favour with the Prince when he had the undisguised approval of the Princess and – what was more important – the Queen?

But this very approval made him more angry with the Prince who had treated him so churlishly as to thrust him aside for the sake of the vulgar Bubb. And Anne Vane too! How dared they!

They were whispering together now. Could it be about him? He had made a discovery about Anne Vane. He had his friends about the court and her secret was one which she could not expect to hide for long.

Anne Vane was pregnant.

What an interesting situation! It was just possible that he himself might be the father. Harrington might be too, but of course the young woman would almost certainly bestow paternity on the Prince of Wales.

It would discountenance Mistress Vane considerably if she were dismissed from court because of her condition.

Hervey could never resist maliciously attacking his enemies and with a sudden feeling of spite he leaned closer to the Queen and whispered: 'I'll swear Your Majesty is disturbed about the condition of that young woman.'

'What young woman is this?'

'Anne Vane. She is *enceinte*.'

'*Enceinte!*' Caroline began to fan herself rapidly. 'How inconsiderate of her!'

'Very inconsiderate, Your Majesty. Well brought up young ladies should know it is an unpardonable offence. To err is natural, but to make public that which should be private is such vulgarity. Still, I am not surprised considering the company the young woman keeps.'

The Queen looked astonished for even from Hervey she would not take insults to the Prince of Wales.

'I mean that mountain of flesh, that vulgar tradesman, that adorner of his vile and unwieldy person . . . Bubb Dodington. Any man who gets himself born with such a name has no right to enter polite society.'

The Queen looked relieved. 'I believe Mr Bubb Dodington to be a Member of Parliament and a respected citizen.'

'He is respected by sellers of brocade, jewels, and building materials, Madam. They wrest a good living from his extravagances. Miss Vane is a close friend of his . . . and I repeat that it is small wonder that she has behaved in this indecorous vulgar way.'

'You think Mr Dodington is the father?'

'I think, Madam, that there are a number who could claim that not very creditable role, but I do not think that gentleman's mistress would allow him the opportunities which would be necessary if he were to share Miss Vane's ubiquitous favours.'

The Queen smiled, but she was almost immediately serious.

'I want no scandal at the court.'

'Then in that case Your Majesty will want no Miss Vane.'

'You are right, Lord Hervey. I shall consider her case immediately.'

Caroline meant what she said. Frederick was mistaken if he thought she was going to have his mistress growing obviously more and more pregnant in evidence at her court.

She considered very carefully how she would rid herself of Anne Vane.

She was at Kensington, which was her favourite palace, because it seemed to her more homely than St James's or Hampton Court.

In her rooms on the first floor on the eastern side of the palace she lay in bed and thought that she would lose no time. She would act this very day.

She often thought this was one of the most enjoyable times of the day. She would lie in bed and rest her limbs – and she always felt better when she was lying down – and very often she would give audience from her bed. If her visitor were a man he would stand outside the door and talk to her from there, for she was determined that no scandal should touch her name. That would alienate the King immediately, for the one thing that would be unforgivable to him would be to besmirch his supremacy in any way.

Then there would be the ceremony of dressing which took place all too soon, presided over by Charlotte Clayton who on some mornings seemed to give herself such airs of authority that the others resented it, particularly Henrietta Howard who, the Queen often noticed with relief, now made no objections about kneeling with the basin and ewer.

When she was dressed she stood at one of the six great windows looking down on the gardens. Such a pleasant sight and how she loved those gardens! She delighted to walk in them; she was sorry she could not walk more often, but her legs did swell so much and there was that other unmentionable trouble. Whenever she thought of it she would give Charlotte a quick look. Sometimes Charlotte intercepted that look and an expression of reassurance would come over her face. Or did the Queen imagine that? Your secret is safe with me.

The children were waiting to join her at breakfast in Queen Mary's gallery.

They greeted her formally and she sat down and Mrs Purcell, her retiring woman, hovered to adjust the kerchief about her neck. Charlotte's sharp eyes were on Mrs Purcell, always watchful that none of the women should take too much upon themselves.

William was lounging by the window; young Caroline sat hunched over the table; Anne looked sullen; Amelia was already dressed for riding. The little girls were in their nursery presided over by Lady Deloraine. Oh dear, she hoped the King was not paying too much attention in that quarter. She believed that lady might become a little difficult . . . not on her own account, of course; she was far too stupid. But she had heard that the Prince and Mr Dodington visited her apartments frequently. That might mean trouble. Still, that was for the future. The immediate problem was the dismissal of her son's mistress.

The sight of Amelia made her uneasy. How far, she wondered, had her daughter's flirtation with Grafton gone. Amelia was so arrogant, almost as arrogant as Anne, although in a less sour manner. Anne was a great trial to her. Poor girl, she should be married. She needed to be married. But whom could she marry? Only a prince would suit Anne and where was that prince?

Some kings and queens had longed for children; she and George, it seemed, had too many.

Not that she did not care for them as a mother. If only they had not been royal, how easy it would have been to have made suitable matches for them. She was sure Amelia would have willingly married Grafton.

She felt impelled to speak to her daughter and that delay might be dangerous.

'I noticed,' she said, 'that you spent last evening at the side of the Duke of Grafton and scarcely spoke to anyone else.'

'His conversation was more interesting than that of others, Madam.'

Arrogant, almost insolent. If I had had the care of them when they were young it would have been different. Resentment flared within her against the late King who had taken her children from her and refused to let them meet their parents without his permission. Therein lay the root of all the trouble. If Frederick had been allowed to live with them instead of being kept away in Hanover all those years, might there not have been a better understanding between him and his parents? Most assuredly. The troubles of the family lay within its own circle. An alarming thought.

'I think you should be careful not to give a wrong impression with that young man,' said the Queen.

'Scarcely young,' mocked Anne. 'He's old enough to be your father, Amelia.'

'He is certainly more attractive than my own.'

'Amelia!' The Queen was horrified. If such remarks should reach the ears of the King they would never be forgotten, nor forgiven.

'Oh, Mamma, we don't have to flatter him when he's not here, surely.'

Caroline glanced at the women. 'The King does not need flattery,' she said. 'One only has to speak the truth.'

That made them titter. They saw their father too clearly, and they were too rebellious to pretend otherwise. One had to remember that with the exception of William – and he was precocious – and Louisa and Mary in the nursery, they were no longer children.

The Queen, anxious to change the subject from this dangerous criticism of their father, turned on Amelia. 'Your conduct with that man is causing comment. I find it disgraceful.'

'Nothing to what it was at Windsor,' commented William, making a face at his sister.

'Be silent, you spoilt little beast.'

'Mamma, did you hear what she called me?'

Anne said: 'I endorse it. The Duke of Cumberland is a spoilt little beast.'

The Princess Caroline looked anxiously at her mother. Dear child! thought the Queen. She hates this family bickering as much as I do, and it is chiefly because she fears the effect on me.

William lunged towards his sister as though he would strike her. Caroline called him sharply to order and he thrust out his lip sullenly.

'Now you *do* look beautiful,' commented Amelia. 'The handsome Duke of Cumberland!'

'I will not have this,' said the Queen. 'Purcell, bring breakfast. I am hungry today.'

'What would Your Majesty like?'

'Chocolate, of course, and some fruit with sour cream.'

Purcell retired to bring the food and the Queen turned once more to Amelia.

'I shall speak to Grafton,' she said. 'He shall come to my first drawing room.'

She was already rehearsing what she would say to that arrogant man who tried to remind her every time he met her that he was a direct descendant of King Charles II and she was merely married to a member of an odd sprig of the royal tree. Insufferable man. And now he was trying to – or possibly had – seduced Amelia.

Amelia was looking smug, certain of the manner in which her lover would discomfit her mother. It was intolerable that the Queen should submit to such humiliation. Nor would she from any but her own rebellious brood.

'Mamma,' said William, 'when Amelia and Grafton were hunting in Windsor Forest they left the hunt and went into a private house in the forest. They stayed there for some hours. Everyone wondered where they were and thought it so odd that they had both disappeared . . . and without attendants.'

'How dare you say such things, William,' said his mother.

'You have always told us that we should speak the truth, Mamma.'

'This is . . . gossip.'

'It is also the truth, Mamma.'

'Amelia, I am sure you will wish to deny this.'

'No,' said Amelia pertly. 'I don't, Mamma, because you have taught me also to speak the truth.'

'This is . . . outrageous.'

'Oh . . . what are we to do?' cried Amelia petulantly. 'Are we to remain virgins all our lives because no one finds husbands for us?'

'I do not think it will be possible to find a husband for *you*, Amelia, if you behave in this way.'

'And what of Anne? She is interested in no one because there is no one at court whom she considers worthy of her. But does she fare any better? She is husbandless too.'

'This is a most unsuitable conversation,' said the Queen, 'and I forbid you to continue with it. I shall speak to Grafton and ask him for an explanation of this Windsor incident.'

'Pray do, Mamma, if you consider it wise. But he will not care, you know; and if others hear of it they will exaggerate it and I believe you will not be pleased with the outcome.'

'I have not asked your opinion, Amelia. And now, no more of this most distasteful subject. Ah, here comes Purcell.'

Food was always comforting and the Queen greatly enjoyed a cup of chocolate. So did the rest of the family.

The Queen sent for more chocolate and when she was drinking this the King came in to take the Queen for a walk. The Queen, hearing his voice outside, looked at her watch. As she might have imagined he had come exactly at the expected time but she had been so disturbed by the conversation that she had not noticed that they had delayed too long over breakfast.

The King looked with distaste on his family. The breakfast should have been over. He was never in a very good mood in the morning and this was the most trying time of the day for the Queen.

He took out his watch and regarded it. The Queen saw

Amelia and Anne exchange glances. They must be careful, she thought. He must never know that they laughed at him.

'Late!' he said. 'You people have no idea of time.'

He spoke in German. He had long given up speaking English to children who spoke it better than he did.

'We have been talking,' said the Queen with a quick smile. 'It made us forget the time.'

'Time should never be forgotten. Only fools forget time.'

He looked at her as though she fitted into that category and her spirits sank. This was going to be a difficult morning, and before her lay not only the task of placating the King but of dismissing her son's mistress.

'That is so,' admitted the Queen.

'Of course it is so. William, don't stand there like that . . . slouching like some stable boy. Stand up. Hold your back straight. Look animated when I come into the room.'

William tried to do all these things and looked rather comical, but the King was already glaring at Amelia. 'More like a man than a woman. I don't like those clothes of yours. Do you hear me?'

'I beg Your Majesty's pardon but I didn't quite catch . . .'

'Pray listen when I speak to you. Pay attention, my girl, or you will be in trouble.' He turned to the Queen on whom he liked to bestow the full force of his irritation when he was in one of his morning moods. 'And stop stuffing. No wonder you're so fat. How can you expect otherwise when you sit about swilling chocolate like some fat pig at the trough.' The King was not noted for the elegance of his expressions especially when he was irritated; and he undoubtedly was now. It was all due to their being late finishing breakfast; they had violated one of his sacred rules; they had ignored Time.

'Well, come along,' he said. 'It's time for our walk.'

So the Queen had to rise, leaving her chocolate and the fruit and sour cream unfinished, to go and walk in the garden.

The guards and the gardeners, the courtiers who accompanied them heard his voice raised in anger as he criticized her. She walked too slowly because she was too fat. She guzzled like a pig and that was *why* she was too fat. He did not like the colour of the gown she was wearing. She had dozed over cards last night. He had seen her nodding and pretending to be awake. He had heard her snore. Yes, she had snored. And when he had come to take her for a walk she had not been ready. She had kept the King waiting. He was angry; he was irritated; but he enjoyed her company more than that of any other person and there was a note of fierce pleasure in the voice that went on upbraiding her.

Oh dear, life was very difficult. Her legs had been more swollen than usual last night and the pain . . . it had been impossible to ignore it. Now he was walking too fast and she found it difficult to keep up with him, but to ask him to slacken his pace would be to call down further abuse.

So she puffed along beside him and she thought that life would be intolerable if she did not know – and all wise people at court knew – that for all his shrill abuse and for all her outward meekness she, with Walpole at her side, was the real ruler of the country.

As for George, as the walk progressed he gradually grew better tempered. Even though he did abuse her for her fatness, secretly he liked her fat. He thought her the most beautiful woman at court; he would rather be walking in the garden with her than with anyone else. The abuse was really for those who looked on, not for her; he had never forgotten that nasty little rhyme about her being the real ruler. He had to sneer at her in public; he had to show that he was the master and she dared not answer back. It was the only way he could convince himself. So he strutted a little ahead of her like some cocky little bantam, while she puffed along those few paces behind him; and his show of irritation was the sign of inner contentment.

Back in the Palace the Queen lay on her bed to rest her legs.

Charlotte Clayton put cold compresses on them; she said she had heard of this from Lady Masham who used to do it for Queen Anne.

'If it weren't for these swollen legs I should feel very well,' said the Queen almost defiantly.

Charlotte deliberately lowered her eyes to show she understood.

'Of course, Your Majesty.'

Caroline sighed and at that moment Anne Vane came in to perform some duty and the Queen remembered the unpleasant task which lay before her.

'Oh . . . I have something to say to Miss Vane.'

'Miss Vane,' called Charlotte, a little officiously, 'Her Majesty wishes to speak to you.'

Anne Vane came forward and curtsied. Oh yes, thought the Queen, she is clearly pregnant.

The Queen waited, expecting Charlotte to retire as would have been natural in the circumstances, but Charlotte busied herself at one of the cupboards and made no attempt to leave.

Caroline hesitated and then decided that it could not matter if Charlotte remained, for soon everyone would know that Anne Vane had been dismissed.

'I think,' said the Queen coolly, 'that you may have something to tell me.'

'I . . . Your Majesty?'

She was feigning innocence, but she knew very well what the Queen was hinting.

'It would have been better if you had told me yourself,' said the Queen. 'When do you expect your confinement?'

Anne gave a little gasp, but she was not really frightened. This was no ordinary indiscretion. She had the honour of being mistress to the Prince of Wales.

'Oh . . . Madam!'

Charlotte Clayton was frankly listening now, her lips pursed in disgust.

'It is no use attempting to disguise the truth,' said the Queen. 'I cannot allow you to remain at court. I asked you when your child is expected to be born?',

'There are . . . another three months, Your Majesty.'

'Well, it's time you were going.'

'His Highness . . .'

'You may make your preparations immediately.'

'Madam, if His . . .'

'Pray go at once to your apartment and prepare to leave. You must return to your home without delay.' The Queen turned to Charlotte. She might as well make use of her since she was here. 'Mrs Clayton will see that you obey my orders without delay.'

'Madam . . .' began Anne Vane.

But Charlotte had taken the girl by the arm and was leading her very forcibly from the apartment.

Anne ordered the carriage to go to La Trappe at Hammersmith.

There she was welcomed by Mrs Behan to whom she told the story of her dismissal.

'Wait till George comes,' advised Mrs Behan. 'He will know what to do.'

He did. He went himself to the Prince of Wales to tell him what had happened and as a result Frederick came riding to La Trappe.

Anne threw herself weeping into his arms. She had been ignobly turned out of the court. They were all against him and so against her for they knew how she adored him.

Frederick, who was growing more and more resentful as he grew more and more in debt, agreed with her that the way she had been treated was a slight on him. But they must think what they were going to do.

'I can't go home,' cried Anne. 'What can I do? And I can't stay here. Oh, my Prince, what have we done?'

Frederick consoled her. He was delighted that they were going to have a child. She must not have any fears. He would look after her.

'But where can I go?' she asked.

Dodington suggested that the Prince might like to set her up in a house of her own. No one could prevent that; and there she could live in peace and comfort with her child.

'That's the answer!' said Frederick; and Anne agreed with him.

'I know of a house in Soho Square which would be ideal,' Mrs Behan told them. 'Anne can stay here until she is settled in, and she and I will go and look at it tomorrow.'

The Prince was very grateful to his kind friends; and the next day Anne Vane and Mrs Behan went to see the house which enchanted them both.

The Prince liked it too. It was expensive, but he never worried about money until the bills were presented to him; and who was going to worry about supplying the needs of the Prince of Wales?

The house was fitted out with the finest furniture and plate until it was almost as grande as La Trappe.

Frederick was delighted and promised Anne £1,600 a year. So the entire matter was settled to the satisfaction of Anne and the Prince, for Dodington allowed him to win £5,000 from him at the gaming table to pay for the initial costs.

This was most convenient and everyone concerned was delighted; except Lord Hervey, who realized that Anne Vane's position was slightly more secure than it had been before.

Anne Vane began to give herself airs. She was now the acknowledged mistress of the Prince of Wales; she went about proudly proclaiming her condition and making no attempt to hide it.

It was useless for Hervey to make wry jokes about the mystery surrounding her condition. We all know what, he commented, but only Miss Vane can tell us who.

Anne resented this deeply, for secretly she had admired him more than any of her lovers and she had worked against him by bringing Dodington to Frederick's notice because she had been wounded at his desertion.

She was at great pains however to hide her feelings for Hervey and show her affection to the Prince whom she must, at all costs, keep her devoted lover.

And when, at a reception in the Prince's apartments, Hervey happened to be present and they came face to face, he bowed ironically with a mischievous look in his eyes. Dearly she would have liked to stop and talk to him, but instead she affected not to see him and by sweeping past him with the air of a very great lady, she managed to humiliate him.

Hervey was a man who could not bear humiliation. It called forth all the spite and malice in him.

He went to Stephen to tell him about his fury.

'If that silly little slut thinks she can snub me she is mistaken.'

'She is not worth a thought from you.'

'I was aware of the titters.'

'People like to titter.'

'Particularly when they see others ridiculed.'

'Oh come, my dear, it could not have been as bad as that.'

'I shall not allow it, and I know how to frighten her.'

'Leave her alone, John, my dear. No good can come of wasting time on such a silly creature.'

'If foolish Fred knew that that child she so proudly carries could have been fathered by at least three of us he might not be so eager to accept it as his.'

'Leave well alone, dear John.'

Hervey smiled at his friend, but he was not going to leave well alone.

No one should insult him with impunity.

He wrote a letter addressed to Anne Vane which he asked a friend to deliver to her apartments.

The young man was a little reluctant, knowing of the discord between Hervey and the Prince's mistress, and told Hervey that he had no wish to be caught up in a quarrel between them.

'Nonsense,' said Hervey. 'We are not really bad friends. That was a bit of play-acting for the sake of the Prince. He's a jealous young man, you know. I have heard of an excellent midwife and I want her to know of this. My dear fellow, you'll earn her gratitude if you take this note along to her.'

He smiled ruefully as his friend went off with the note. He always felt relieved when he put his emotions on paper.

Anne Vane took the letter and as she read it let out a gasp of horror. No one could write as colourfully as Hervey when he had a mind to it and he had set down, with all the invective and venom of his nature and literary skill, what he would tell the Prince of his mistress. He would open Frederick's eyes to the woman who had deceived him. He would let him know that the child he so fondly fathered might well be the child of a triumvirate. Anne Vane had deceived him cleverly and Hervey was going to let him know.

Anne grew pale; she was terrified; the letter fluttered from her hand; she fell to the ground and lay there as though dead.

The young messenger wondered why the friendly note from Hervey telling her the name of a good midwife should have upset her, so he knelt beside her and seeing that she was in a faint read the letter. He was horrified. Anne Vane was in a precarious condition, if anything happened to her he might be blamed.

He called to Anne's maids and they soon revived her. She lay moaning on a sofa and he knelt beside her imploring her forgiveness, telling her that he had been misled by Hervey, that he had no idea what the note contained.

'Lies!' moaned Anne. 'All lies.'

'I'll call him out for this. He swore to me that it was a friendly note recommending a midwife.'

'You must not fight with him.'

'But I shall,' declared the young man. 'He deceived me.'

Anne Vane entreated the young man but his mind was made up, and while they were talking one of her servants had sent a message to the Prince telling him that his mistress had been taken very ill. So Frederick came riding to Soho Square with all speed to find Anne reclining on the sofa with a young man pacing up and down the room swearing revenge on Hervey.

Anne held out her arms to the Prince who embraced her.

'It is terrible ... terrible!' she cried. 'Lord Hervey nearly brought about my death.'

The Prince was very angry and demanded to know exactly what had happened.

Anne told how the young man had been sent with the note.

'I swear, your Highness,' interjected the young man, 'that Lord Hervey told me the note merely recommended a midwife.'

'And where is the note?'

'Oh, it is dreadful ... dreadful!' cried Anne, but she had become alert and she called to one of her old servants who had been with her for many years. 'Where is that wicked letter?' she asked.

The woman looked as confused as Anne could have wished and declared that she had destroyed it because she had thought it unfit to be looked at by anyone ... such a pack of cruel wicked lies it was, that anyone who knew Mistress Vane would have thought it only proper to do what she had done – and that was burn it.

Anne was relieved and fell fainting into her lover's arms, but she quickly revived and then implored Frederick to prevent the young man from challenging Hervey to a duel.

Frederick was glad to comply and the young man, now that he knew that he could not be blamed for what had happened, was also relieved.

Frederick said: 'I will never again have the slightest regard for that monster.'

He meant it; and as it was impossible to keep such an event secret, soon the whole court knew of it. It was not considered a very creditable action on Hervey's part and as a result he found himself coldly received everywhere, even in the Queen's apartments.

The only one who tried to make excuses for him was the Princess Caroline.

Hervey was still under a cloud of disapproval when Anne's son was born. The Prince proudly acknowledged him and he was named FitzFrederick. Anne held delighted court in Soho Square and many people of standing flocked to her receptions.

Being a father gave Frederick prestige, and men who were dissatisfied with the Walpole regime and despaired of ever receiving honours under it, were looking more and more to Frederick.

Bolingbroke, that inveterate mischief maker, believed that this was the time to come forward and he asked a friend to arrange a meeting at his house between himself and the Prince. He wanted this to be done secretly, for he did not want Walpole to be warned that his intentions towards the Prince were beginning to take a more definite form.

The meeting was arranged. Frederick was excited. He knew what it portended. He was growing more and more restless. How could he live in the style that was expected of a prince on the pittance his father allowed him? Why should he be continually snubbed by the King who seemed determined to treat his son as shabbily as his own father had treated him?

Bolingbroke arrived at the house in good time and was shown into the library to await Frederick's coming.

He was standing up turning over the pages of a large book

when Frederick entered and as he turned sharply the book fell to the floor. The Prince advanced, and as he attempted to kneel, Bolingbroke fell over the book.

Frederick helped him to rise and smiling said : 'I trust this is an omen of my succeeding in raising your fortunes.'

A great exultation filled the adventurer at those words. It was clear to him, not only that Frederick understood the purpose of their meetings, but that he was willing and ready to allow himself to be used.

Musical interlude

Frederick was now in opposition to Walpole and the King and Queen, with George Bubb Dodington advising him, and Pulteney, Wyndham, and Bolingbroke to support him.

Walpole came to see the Queen privately that he might discuss this new menace with her.

'The trouble is,' said the minister, 'that besides being personable and affable, he has a grievance. The people are always ready to support those whom they think are ill done by. You will remember His Majesty's popularity when he was in opposition to his father.'

Caroline remembered it well.

'The King is most displeased with the Prince's conduct,' she said.

'Perhaps,' suggested Walpole, 'the Prince should be paid a higher income.'

'The King would never hear of it. We should never be able to persuade him.'

Walpole understood. There were more important matters for which the Queen must save her persuasive powers.

'Then we must be very watchful,' Walpole went on. 'Particularly of Bolingbroke, who is out for trouble.'

'At least if he is supporting the Prince he is not with the Jacobites.'

'Your Majesty has, as usual, pointed out the important factor. While he is trying to stir up rebellion within the family circle he is not making trouble overseas – which could be more disastrous.'

'I am beginning to think,' said the Queen, 'that my dear first-born is the greatest ass and the greatest liar and the greatest *canaille* and the greatest beast in the whole world, and I heartily wish him out of it.'

Walpole was taken aback. It was unlike the Queen to be un-just, and although he agreed that Frederick was an ass and had not a great respect for the truth, this was a harsh pronounce-ment.

'He has caused nothing but trouble since he came to England,' went on Caroline. 'Oh, how I wish we could send him back to Hanover!'

'Alas, if he were but a daughter we could marry him out of England. Now when he marries he will remain and demand an even greater status.'

'He must not marry . . . yet.'

'We cannot allow him to remain a bachelor for ever, Madam. Remember he *is* the Prince of Wales.'

'And he has discovered this. His teachers must have been working hard to instil a little sense into his addled pate.'

'He has shrewd teachers, Madam. I would that we could have taken their place.'

'Oh, he would never listen to me.'

Walpole regarded the Queen a little sadly and wondered why it was that she who was such a shrewd woman in so many respects should have this obsessive hatred for her son. He believed that Lord Hervey was to blame, for he was constantly at the Queen's side, pouring venom into her ear; and how strange that she should listen to him to the detriment of her own son.

The Princess Caroline was besotted about the fellow; was the Queen too?

Fortunately Hervey was a Walpole man, otherwise the

Queen's fondness for him might be a cause for alarm.

'Our brother Frederick is the biggest fool alive,' declared the Princess Anne to her sister Amelia. 'Do you know, I dislike him even more than I do William.'

'William is an arrogant little beast but I agree with you that Fred is a fool. I'd rather have William's conceit than Fred's folly. He is a disgrace to the family.'

'I wish he'd die,' said Anne vehemently.

Amelia regarded her cynically. 'What a *happy* family we are! One of us is always wishing the other dead. Grandfather hated Papa and Papa hated Grandfather even more. I wonder how many times Papa wished *his* father dead. A hundred times a day, I'll wager.'

'*I* didn't dislike Grandfather. He was not stupid like Papa. He was determined to be obeyed and so he should have been, for he was King; and he had his own way. The reason he didn't take on more of the government himself was because he never really cared for England and wanted to go back and rule Hanover. Perhaps he was a fool after all. England is so much more important. Oh . . . if only Fred and William were dead.'

'Then,' pointed out Amelia, 'you would have to kill off Papa before you could be Queen.'

'It would come in due course. Something to look forward to. Then I shouldn't have to wait for a husband.'

'Who is so long appearing.'

'I know. Amelia, do you think we are going to remain single all our lives?'

'It seems very probable.'

'But it can't be. Imagine when Fred is King. What will become of us?'

'We shall be given a household between us and be known as the three virgins of England.'

'I won't endure it. I'd rather marry . . . a baboon . . . providing he were a King.'

'Alas, it seems no suitors are available . . . not even royal baboons. Oh, Anne, I should love to see you swinging on a tree, a crown on your head. Of one thing I'm sure, you'd swing *regally*.'

'Don't talk nonsense. I tell you I would willingly die to-morrow if I could be Queen of England today. And to think by a little accident I could be.'

'Two little accidents. Accident Fred and Accident William.'

'You don't care like I do, Amelia.'

'Well, I should have to wish for three deaths – yours included, my dear sister. But I agree with all you say about Fred. I grudge him every hour he continues to live. I wish he'd have an accident in the hunting field or fight a duel to the death for his silly Anne Vane.'

'At least you console yourself flirting with Grafton.'

'You could take similar consolation. Oh, no, it would be beneath your dignity. It is a comfort. Grafton is amusing and fun to be with and we both enjoy shocking Mamma.'

'Poor Mamma!'

'Oh, she enjoys her conferences with Walpole and her light entertainment with Hervey. Life is not all being Papa's docile wife who is all the time deceiving him!'

'Deceiving him!'

'Oh, only into believing he is the Deity in person, whose will is law. Only making him believe that *he* really thought first of what she has planted in his mind.'

'You say the boldest things, Amelia.'

'At least let us be bold with words if we are restricted in actions. Sometimes I wish I were not a Princess. It must be far more fun to be a lady in waiting . . . like Anne Vane for instance.'

'Having to put up with Fred?'

'She has other consolations so I've heard. In any case, fancy being Queen and having to put up with Papa!'

'You are right. Why should we not at least *say* what we think. And I say with you, Poor Mamma! Papa must be the greatest trial. Particularly when he is in his worst humours, for then he is a devil to everyone. What surprises me is how angry he gets about small things. Have you noticed that? It is the little things that bother him. Perhaps his page has not powdered his periwig to his satisfaction. I heard him complain the other day because a housemaid put a chair in an unaccustomed place. Then of course there is this obsession with time. It is because he has such a *little* mind that he is so concerned with little things.'

'Now you are speaking frankly and it makes sense. As I said, poor Mamma! Who wants marriage, which might bring a husband like she has. And *he* is a king.'

'I repeat,' said Anne firmly, 'I would marry anyone who could give me a crown.'

Amelia shrugged. It was nearly time to go hunting and she was certain that Grafton would be of the party. She was a Princess; and they would not – or could not – find her a husband. Well they could not complain if she indulged in an occasional flirtation. She might so easily by now have been married to the Crown Prince of Prussia. She wondered what would have happened to her if she had. The King of Prussia was a madman and a brute. At least the King of England was only a fool. And she was sure flirtation with Grafton was far more exciting than marriage with Frederick of Prussia would have been. By all acccounts he was more interested in military affairs than marriage; and the idea of living under the same roof with such a father-in-law! The thing to do was enjoy life as it came and that was what Anne should learn to do.

'It's time for my music lesson,' said Anne. The hardness of her expression softened a little. 'I must not keep Mr Handel waiting.'

'What is it today?' asked Amelia. 'A lesson on the harpischord or singing?'

'Both.'

'You used to perform well, sister.'

'It is such a pleasure to play for Mr Handel. He is a genius.'

'Fred never plays now.'

'Not with Mr Handel. I suppose he didn't care for criticism.'

'He was not bad at the fiddle.'

'No. Nor the cello. I used to enjoy it when we three played together. Frederick seems less ... offensive then.'

'Oh, he has become too important. A mistress in Soho Square

and so many influential men ready to tell him how they admire him.'

'Well, at least we agree on one thing : Fred. Now I must leave you, sister. And, as you say, Mr Handel is waiting for me.'

In the music room Georg Friedrich Händel, who was known as George Frederick Handel, was waiting for his pupil. This was a lesson to which he always looked forward. The Princess was an apt pupil with the right respect for the most important matter in the world : music. Moreover, she, who was so haughty to everyone else, had the grace to be humble before a man of his talent.

The post of music master to the King's daughters was an enviable one. Not that he cared for money. He cared only for music. But money was necessary to live.

As the Princess entered he lifted his unwieldy frame from the stool on which he was seated and, bowing, kissed her hand.

'I am a little late, dear master,' said Anne. 'The Princess Amelia detained me.'

Handel smiled and when he smiled his heavy, rather bad-tempered face became almost attractive. The smile rarely appeared for anything that was not concerned with music, but the Princess Royal was a very special friend of his.

As she sat at the harpsichord and played the piece he set for her, her expression softened and she became almost pretty. When she had finished, Handel complimented her and said that her touch was sure; after that he made a few criticisms to which she listened attentively. The most endearing characteristic of the royal family was their love of music, thought Handel, watching her. They all had good ears and a strong appreciation. He was extremely grateful for this because to it he owed his comfortable living, and he was a man who liked comfort.

It was the same with the late King who, for all his lack of appreciation for beauty in any other form, was blessed with this love of music. George I had forgiven Handel, who had fallen into disfavour for having come to England during the reign of Queen Anne and deserting Hanover by remaining there. But when George came to England Handel was restored to favour and in the year 1715 had composed his Water Music which was played when the royal family took barge from Whitehall to Limehouse. George had been delighted with this music and had completely forgiven the composer his neglect of the past. Handel was received at court and in due course entrusted with the musical education of George II's daughters. George II had been merely a Prince of Wales at that time although, after the famous quarrel between the father and son, George I had had the charge of the young Princesses.

That was long ago, thought Handel, and that Prince of Wales had now become King. There was, unfortunately, a new Prince of Wales.

'You are looking troubled, master,' said the Princess. 'I trust my playing did not displease you.'

'It was good,' Handel told her, 'apart from the faults I mentioned. But I have been disturbed lately.'

'You disturbed, master! But that should not be. You have your music to think of. Now running in my head is the exquisite music of *Acis and Galatea*. I am taking a party to the Haymarket tomorrow night to hear *Rinaldo*.'

'Your Highness has a rare love for music.'

'But you have not told me why you are disturbed.'

'People do not come to hear opera as they once did and it is very difficult to make the Haymarket pay. Alas, artistes have to be paid; they won't sing without it. And ever since Gay's *Beggar's Opera* found such popularity, that light music seems to be the kind people look for.'

'How foolish of them!' Anne's eyes flashed. 'If I were Queen I would make a law forcing people to go to the opera . . . *your* operas, master.'

He gave his rather beautiful smile.

'You would be a good friend, I know. Ah, it was different in the old days. You will not remember the trouble I had with those two women. They were two of the best singers in the world, I am sure. But each thought she should be the Queen of Music and could not abide the other one.'

'Master, of course I remember. It was not so long ago . . . only a few years and I have always been interested in musical matters. You are referring to the sopranos Cuzzoni and Faustina.'

He nodded, his eyes under his very bushy black brows suddenly twinkling.

'You told me yourself,' she reminded him, 'how they would not sing together and how you picked up Cuzzoni . . . was it?'

'Yes, Cuzzoni.'

'You picked her up, carried her to the window and threatened to throw her out if she would not sing in your opera.'

'And she did.'

'Poor woman!' laughed the Princess, 'she had to save her life.'

'And very beautifully she sang. She and Faustina together. The opera was *Alessandro* . . . But we are wasting time; let me hear the harpsichord suite which I wrote for you.'

She played it with skill and he was pleased with her.

'You did not tell me, why you were disturbed,' she said afterwards.

'Oh, it is nothing. Only that Italian Buononcini. People are comparing his music with mine and I tell you his is worthless . . . worthless.'

'Indeed it is worthless,' said Anne.

'But people are foolish. They who have no true musical appreciation begin to believe what they are constantly told. They go to the opera because it is fashionable . . . not to hear music.'

'I will ask the King and Queen to come with me to the Haymarket to hear your new opera. They will be delighted to. And I will see that the whole court attend. Then you will not have any fear of not being able to pay the artistes.'

'Your Highness is gracious.'

'As a reward for my graciousness I demand to know what you are working on now.'

Handel sat down at the harpsichord and began to play; Anne listened. He was a genius; he was a master of music; and if she could command everyone to listen to his operas she would do her best to persuade those who would do him most good to attend the Haymarket.

Soho Square was filled with the carriages and sedans of the great. Anne Vane was holding a soirée.

Anne was in her element. She lived in luxury; whenever she

went out in her carriage people pointed out the mistress of the Prince of Wales; people in high places sought her company. She had never been so important in her life.

She had her nursery where little FitzFrederick flourished with his nurses and attendants. The Prince of Wales visited the child frequently and delighted in attempting to discover a likeness to himself. Anne was constantly discovering resemblances and George Bubb Dodington and Mrs Behan bore her out that the child was the living image of the Prince.

The friendship between Frederick and Bubb was not quite so firm as it had been. The Prince continued to win large sums of money from his friend, but Frederick's character had changed after contact with men such as Bolingbroke and Wyndham. He was less simple than he had been. Bubb, he believed, was a bit of a buffoon with his vulgar displays of lapis lazuli in his house and his brocades and velvets on his scarcely prepossessing figure.

Behind Bubb's back Frederick was apt to laugh at the easy manner in which he had been allowed to take his winnings. The fool was really paying for the privilege of calling the Prince of Wales his friend.

Frederick was important. Bolingbroke said so. He was ill-treated by his father, but it would not always be so. Soon he would be found a wife; his debts would be paid and his father would be forced to give him an income commensurate with his position.

Frederick was beginning to realize his own importance and changing subtly from the young man who had come to England eager to make himself pleasant and popular.

Townshend had asked for a place in his household and got it. That, thought Frederick, would be a blow to his father and old Walpole. Occasional meetings with Bolingbroke, listening to commiseration on his ill-treatment, planning for better days – all this was changing Frederick.

Now his greatest pleasure was to bring discomfort and embarrassment to his parents.

So, on these occasions when Anne entertained in Soho Square, he made it clear that he liked as many Members of Parliament as possible to call on his mistress. They were received with flattering pleasure and more and more were flocking to these gatherings.

The fact that Walpole was uneasy was a great delight to his enemies, who said that it was the same story all over again. Once the present King had held a second court in Leicester House in defiance of his father's at St James's.

Now here was Frederick Prince of Wales defying *his* father.

Anne, the Prince beside her, was telling Bubb what a pleasant gathering it was and how pleased she was to see so many of the *King's* court with them.

'There might have been more,' said Bubb, 'but half the court is at the Haymarket.'

'Oh, Handel!' cried Anne. 'That is the Princess. She says he is the finest musician in the world. But some seem to like the Italian. I myself for one.'

'Buononcini is a fine musician,' said Bubb. 'How does he compare with Handel? His Highness will tell us, doubtless.'

'They are different,' said Frederick. 'Handel is so German and Buononcini typically Italian.'

'I suppose I am very stupid with *no* taste,' sighed Anne. 'Am I, my love? I find Handel a bore.'

'You could never be stupid,' said Frederick, kissing her hand.

'No,' pouted Anne. 'Look how I produced my adorable Fitz-Frederick.'

'And,' whispered some malicious voice, 'deluded Fred into thinking he was his.'

But no one heard or even cared to listen, for so many of those present believed it would be profitable to support the Prince's party, as no one had a chance of breaking into Walpole's.

'Buononcini is a fine musician,' said the Prince.

Then everyone began comparing him with Handel and declaring that Handel was heavy, obsessed with religious subjects, and above all dull. Buononcini's was gay, as music should be. It was a mistake to delude oneself into thinking that because music was dull it was good.

And the King and the Queen and Princess Anne doted on Handel.

'Buononcini should set up in opposition,' said Bubb. 'I'd wager Handel would still command the biggest audience.'

'What will you wager?' asked Frederick.

'Two thousand.'

'Make it five and I'll take you on.'

Dodington agreed and the bet was made. When the Prince betted others must too and that evening nothing else was talked of but the Italian and German musicians – not so much their merits but who could draw the bigger crowds, for that was to be the test.'

Buononcini must have his rival theatre, but it was not difficult to obtain backers for a proposition so favoured by the Prince.

Soon at the theatre in Lincoln's Inn Fields Buononcini's operas were being performed in rivalry with Handel's at the Haymarket.

The Princess Royal was furious, seeing in this her brother's hatred of herself and his parents; and that he should direct this against her beloved music master was more than she could bear.

'It will be useless,' she stormed to Amelia and Caroline. 'Lincoln's Inn will never rival the Haymarket. And how can anyone in his senses compare the Italian with great Handel?'

But music had little to do with the affair. The King's court was dull; the Prince's was becoming more lively. To it went all the rebels, all the young who wanted a change; and the way in which they could show their willingness to follow the Prince was to go to the theatre in Lincoln's Inn Fields.

Anne was desperate; she implored her parents to come with her to the opera.

'Frederick is deliberately flouting us all,' she declared; and the Queen agreed with her.

As for the King, he had hated his son from the first and he was ready to make a state occasion of a visit to the Haymarket.

And each week it became more and more obvious that the audience at the Haymarket was growing less and less and that at Lincoln's Inn Fields greater.

There came a night when the King, the Queen, with the Princesses and young William, all seated in the royal box, were the only audience for the Handel opera.

To make this more humiliating the roads were jammed on

the way to Lincoln's Inn Fields, and as the theatre was filled to its capacity, people stood outside to wait for the Prince and his friends to leave that they might give them a cheer and shout 'Long Live the Prince of Wales . . . and Buononcini.'

The Prince had won his wager. The King was mightily discomfited; Handel and the Haymarket were in financial difficulties; and Walpole and the Queen were worried.

This was the full cycle.

The Prince of Wales had now come into the open as the enemy of the King and Queen.

Sarah Churchill's bargain

There was a woman who watched the antics of the court with
malicious pleasure. She was one of the richest women in England
and had at one time been the most powerful. This was Sarah, the
widowed Duchess of Marlborough.

Her husband had died in 1722, and since then she had lost
the zest for life except when she was quarrelling. Consequently
she gave herself up to this, which was to her an exciting pastime.

She had had a glorious quarrel with John Vanbrugh over the
building of Blenheim; she had others with all the members of
her family in turn and especially her two living daughters. She
had turned her attention to her grandchildren and the story was
current that she had blacked the face on a painting of Anne
Egerton, her granddaughter, and scrawled beneath it: 'She is
blacker within.' She had quarrelled with Lord Sunderland, her
son-in-law, because he had remarried; she had indulged in
several lawsuits, but these were minor matters and Sarah could
not forget the days when, as chief adviser to Queen Anne, she
had been at the centre of the nation's affairs. That was where she
longed to be and only that could give her something to live for
now that her husband, her dear Marl, was no more.

Therefore she must quarrel with the most important man in the country; and no quarrel meant quite so much to Sarah as her quarrel with Sir Robert Walpole.

It was galling for her, who had been the wife of the greatest general of his age, who had ruled him and ruled Queen Anne, to find that Walpole dismissed her as a silly old woman of no importance to him. Gone were the days when she could have marched into action against him, could have undermined his power, could have set her own men around him to pull him down. Now she was just a feeble old woman, or so they thought.

Marlborough was dead and she had to be doing something all the time to forget that depressing fact. The only time when her face softened, when she felt lonely and defenceless, was when she thought of him in the days of his prime – the handsomest man alive, she had thought, and a genius among his fellows – and remembered then that he was gone for ever.

But she never allowed such moods to continue. She would stamp through her house – either at Windsor or Marlborough House next to St James's – harry her servants, summon whatever members of her family were at hand, berate them, scorn them, and tell them they were unworthy to be the offspring of the great Duke.

Only when she was angry could she find a reason for living.

There were a few people who did not irritate her. Of her grandchildren, most of whom she had quarrelled with, as they grew older, she cared most for Diana Spencer, her dear Lady Di as she called her. Lady Di was young, handsome and intelligent. Her family thought her extremely clever to be able to keep on good terms with the old lady, but Di seemed to manage it without much effort. She had always seemed to be able to please her grandmother, even in the days when as a child she had been so much in her household, for Diana's mother, Anne Churchill, had died at the age of twenty-eight and had left her children to her mother's care.

Di was spirited and yet tactful; she was beautiful, and Sarah was reminded of her own youth through the charms of this lovely young girl.

Sarah liked a woman to have spirit (as long as it did not clash with her own); such a woman of course was a rare find, but she had managed to keep on good terms with Lady Mary Wortley Montagu, as much a character in her way as Sarah was in hers.

Lady Mary had almost as many enemies as Sarah had, for while Sarah blundered through with her frankness Lady Mary could not resist displaying her satirical wit. Lady Mary was a traveller and eccentric and, like Sarah, cared little for opinion and went her own way.

When she was in London she occasionally saw the Duchess; she had a fellow-feeling for a woman who had once been in the thick of affairs and now found herself living on the perimeter. 'Poor Sarah Churchill!' she would say. 'I must go and call on her.'

It was always interesting to hear Sarah's views of the latest scandal, particularly when one had been away. Sarah would put forward her forceful views and, of course, believed that she knew everything.

So Lady Mary called on Sarah and the old lady was delighted to see her.

It was very pleasant to hear Lady Mary's accounts of her notorious quarrel with Pope, who had hated her since she had laughed at his declaration of love for her. Now of course the little man was using his pen to attack her and that unpleasant Irishman Dean Swift was helping him. There was always a controversy going on around Lady Mary.

They discussed Lord Hervey, with whom Lady Mary was on friendly terms, although she disliked Hervey's wife.

'I never could endure Mary Lepel,' she said. 'The woman seems only half alive to me.'

Sarah agreed with her. She could not endure people who were only half alive.

'Wherever we look there are always quarrels,' said Mary. 'Everyone seems to indulge in them.'

'Ah, that's true. Do you know my dear Marl and I never quarrelled.'

Lady Mary forced herself not to show a little impatience, for once Sarah started on her favourite subject she was inclined to indulge herself to the boredom of her listeners.

· 'Only rarely,' she amended. 'Oh, yes, there were rare occasions when even we quarrelled. He was jealous of me . . . and I admit, I of him.' She looked fiercely at Lady Mary. 'Although of course there was no need. I remember once I cut off my hair to annoy him. He loved my hair. Oh, it was very fine in those days. Such a lot of it, and golden colour. Lady Di's hair reminds me of what mine was when I was her age. Mind you hers hasn't the colour . . . nor do I believe the fine texture . . . but it reminds me.' The Duchess's old face lost a little of its grimness. 'He said nothing at the time and I thought he did not notice, but on his death, my dear, I opened the drawer of his cabinet and there I found . . . my curls. He had kept them all those years. That was devotion for you.'

'Very touching,' agreed Lady Mary. 'There must be very few women who were loved as you were.'

'There is no one on earth like him. As I told Coningsby and Somerset when they asked for my hand after his death. The heart and hand which once belonged to the Duke of Marlborough shall never be given to anyone else, I said . . .'

'I know. I know. You have heard, of course, the latest scandal from court. The Prince is now in open defiance. Who can blame him? They have treated him very badly.'

'They are an impossible lot . . . these Germans. Would to God we had never let them in. I used to say to Marl what'll happen when the Germans come, and we both thought that James across the water might have served the country better.'

'Well, we let them in and here they are. They are dull and stupid . . . except, of course, the Queen.'

'That woman!' spat out Sarah. 'I took a dislike to her as soon as I saw her. Jumped-up piece! Who is she? Where is Ansbach? And tell me, what would she have been if George hadn't married her? Some petty count or other would have taken her up perhaps. And the airs! And the graces! And she goes around with that coarse, crude humbug. Don't talk to me about Robert Walpole. I could tell you something of that man. I could tell you what sort of parties he gives at that place of his . . . what is it, Houghton? And filled with valued treasures which a man of crudeness couldn't appreciate apart from the fact that they cost good money. And where did he get his money? Out of the South Sea Bubble. His fortune represents the losses of others . . .'

Sarah paused. She and Marl had done very well out of the South Sea Company. But she never allowed such considerations to bother her.

'And that woman he lives with. Moll Skerrett. Queening it there at Houghton at his table. And where is my Lady Walpole all this time? Oh, she is consoling herself with Tom, Dick, and Harry, and George. For they say our gracious King was one of them. And this is the man, if you'll believe it, who governs all our lives. If Marl had lived . . .'

Lady Mary nodded sadly, but she was thinking that Marl-borough had been out of favour before the arrival of the first German George and there had been rumours of certain shady deals which did not enhance his reputation. But she refrained from mentioning these matters; it was such restraint which enabled her to keep on moderately good terms with the old war-horse.

'Oh, they have their troubles,' she said. 'The Prince is a real thorn in their sides.'

'Poor boy!' Sarah was always temporarily on the side of her enemies' enemy.

'They say his debts are enormous.'

'And do you wonder at that! Those misers bribed Walpole to see that the Civil List benefited them . . . and they kept the Prince's share for themselves. Robbers! Harpies! I wonder the people don't send them packing. Let them go back to Hanover. I hear they think so much of the place.'

'The King praises it, but the Queen, I think, does not share his opinion.'

'She knows what side her bread is buttered. Madam Ansbach is fond of England. Of course she is! She was a pauper before she married so well. And then she comes here and she takes her place on the throne and she and that old fox Walpole put their heads together and between them they rule. Of course she is satisfied! And the little bantam struts about thinking he is a king. Bah! Send the whole boiling back to Hanover, I say.'

'The Prince is ready to rebel, I heard. He wants his debts paid, a place in the government of affairs, and a wife.'

'He's entitled to them.'

'At the moment he is seen often at the house of his mistress. They say the child could take his pick of several fathers.'

'The young man should be married.'

'The difficulty is to find a princess. She has to be Protestant, remember. She would have to have a big dowry. But where is she?'

'She's to be found . . . if they look. The truth is that bantam cock and that fat elephant don't want him married. No, they want to keep him down. The last thing in the world they want is to see him married. It would give him too much power. *They* want it all. Madam Caroline and Master Walpole . . . they are the ones who are holding that young man back from his natural rights.'

She would have gone on had not Lady Di been announced.

She forgot her indignation at the sight of this beloved grand-child.

'Come here, my dear,' she said. 'Lady Mary Wortley Montague has been enlivening me with the latest court scandals. You can join us.'

The Duchess of Marlborough had an idea. She kept it to herself as yet. She knew very well that if she mentioned it to anyone . . . just anyone . . . they would think she was mad. Well, she was accustomed to being thought mad. And she herself did not think she was mad in the least. She merely thought that everyone else was stupid, timid, and deserved nothing.

She smiled to think what Marl would have said of this idea. He would have remonstrated with her and told her she was too bold. How many times had he told her that? They had quarrelled . . . oh, no, not quarrelled. No one could call it that. They had argued, discussed, disagreed on so many things.

If he had followed me, she told herself fiercely, he would have ruled England, which was what he should have done.

Others said that she had ruined his career, and that but for her he would never have had to face disaster and disgrace.

'It isn't true! It isn't true!' she cried; and put her hands to her face, for there were tears on her cheeks.

They had lost favour with Anne through that sly and wicked Abigail Hill. How was Sarah to have known that she was nursing a viper in her bosom? How was she to guess that the slut she had raised up would in time succeed in driving her from court? That was the cruelty of life. Everyone had blamed her . . . except Marl. Dearest Marl, he had never blamed her. He did not share the general view. He had seen her to the end as Sarah Jennings, the girl whom he had married although she was without fortune.

But that was past and life would be tolerable for a while if she could bring off this plan. It was a great plan. She smiled to think of it. Only she, Sarah Churchill, could think of such a plan and dare to put it into practice.

Secrecy was everything . . . just everything. Let this seep out and they would do everything in their considerable power to stop her. She could imagine the wrath of Madam Ansbach. As for *dear* Sir Robert, the man would lose his calmness for which he so prided himself, and go . . . *mad!*

It was such a wild and glorious plan that no one would believe it was possible. She would show them. And when it succeeded they would have to admit that Sarah Churchill was as redoubtable in her old age as she had been in the days of the great Duke's glory.

So much depended on the success of small details. She had waited in an agony of impatience for an answer to the message she had sent to the Prince of Wales. It was possible that he would refuse her invitation. After all, what respect had these young people for the great ones of the past?

All she had said was that she had a matter which she believed His Royal Highness would find of the utmost importance if he would do her the honour of giving her an interview at Marlborough House. She regretted that she could not come to him but he, who she knew had the kindest heart in the world, would understand that as a very old woman she was often confined to her house. If he would do her the great honour of calling on her, she was sure the Great Duke would look down from Heaven and bless him. The matter was one of secrecy, and if the Prince would humour her he would bring great happiness to an old woman who had once served her country with great zeal, and hoped to do so again.

The Prince was mystified; he was also chivalrous. Sarah Churchill was an old menace, he knew; she spent her time inventing grievances and quarrelling with people, going to law whenever possible. But it was hardly likely that she would quarrel with the Prince of Wales. In any case, if she attempted to, he only had to take his leave.

So, the Prince of Wales called on the Duchess at Marlborough House.

She was filled with emotion to see him.

'It is so good of you to come. How can I thank you ! And how handsome you are ! You must forgive an old woman who always speaks her mind. But I had not thought your parents capable of producing such a son.'

The Prince was amused. Any slight to his parents nowadays gave him the greatest pleasure and Sarah had wasted no time in telling him that she felt the same as he did about them.

'My limbs are stiff these days, Your Highness. I'm an old woman now, and since the dear Duke went I have felt little inclination to leave my home. Would you be seated, and I will tell you why I have taken this liberty . . . if liberty you think it.'

The Prince replied courteously that it could only be a pleasure to call on the Duchess of Marlborough. He had always loved to hear of the great Duke's victories and one of his greatest regrets was that he had been too young to serve with him.

'You missed a great experience, Your Highness. There was never a general like him. But you know that well. I must remember not to waste your time for which I am sure you have many more uses than waiting on an old woman. I have always been noted for speaking my mind. I say out boldly what I mean. I was never one to hum and hah and take thousands of words to get to a point.'

'An excellent quality !' murmured the Prince.

'My plan is this : I have heard that you are in need of money . . . large sums of money. I have also heard that you wish to marry. I'll say this – that I understand both. You have been treated with miserly contempt by those who sit on our throne. And you have not had that which as Prince of Wales should be yours. Now are you going to stand aside and let them do what they will with you??'

'I do not as yet understand Your Grace's proposition.'

'This is it: I've a granddaughter, Lady Diana Spencer. She is beautiful, intelligent, fit to be a Queen of England . . . in fact a great deal more fit than any I've seen wear this crown. It is my wish that she *be* Queen of England. You could marry her.'

The Prince looked astounded and Sarah hurried on slyly: 'I am a very rich woman, Your Highness, I would give my granddaughter a dowry of one hundred thousand pounds when she became your wife.'

The Prince was too astonished for speech. He looked at the old woman who was watching him expectantly. Marriage to her granddaughter! Secret marriage!

Then he thought of all his debts, and the words which kept going on in his brain were: one hundred thousand pounds.

'Well, well,' said Sarah impatiently, 'what does Your Highness think?'

She herself was thinking that he was a foolish young man, after all; once he was her son-in-law she would have to make him wake up. She relished the task. She saw herself once more a figure of power. The future Queen's grandmother. She would have to go on living to see that. It would be an incentive. She would. Not even God could drag her away before she wanted to go.

This was what she needed to give her life a spice. Only if she could be in the centre of power again could she endure this earth without dear Marl. She pictured him now up in Heaven looking down on her, smiling, applauding, thinking: if I had always listened to your bold schemes for me, Sarah my love, it would have been different.

Well, now there was no one to stop her and she was offering her lovely Lady Di to this inane young fool who had the stamp of Hanover all over his silly face. All the better. All the easier to be led!

'I . . . I had not realized that you would put such a proposition to me,' said the Prince. 'I . . . I must have time . . . time to think.'

This was not refusal then. Time to think? What did that mean? Time to talk it over with ninnies as stupid as himself. Time for Walpole and Madam Ansbach to get wind of the great scheme!

'There are many enemies of Your Highness who would seek to stop such a solution to your problems.'

'I know that well.'

'I can tell you how angry it has made me to hear the talk. Led by the nose . . . that's His Majesty . . . led by Master Walpole. And he does not know it. I hope Your Highness will not allow these people to treat *you* as scurvily.'

'I shall not,' cried the Prince, very bold now that he was not facing them, Sarah noticed. Oh, he would be as easy to lead as a pig with a ring through his nose.

'Oh, yes, they will do everything to prevent this. They do not want to see you married . . . although they know full well it is time you were. They are afraid that married status will give you greater power, that they will have to increase your allowance. I know them. I can tell you this that in the Duke's day I had to deal with . . . vipers.'

'I know of your great experience and . . .'

'It is for you to decide. I assure Your Highness that the Lady Diana has many suitors. I could make an admirable match for her tomorrow, so I shall want a speedy answer. I'll tell you this: shortly she will be here. You will have an opportunity of observing her, talking to her, realizing her worth. I would not want you to take a pig in a poke. Then you can give me your answer tomorrow. Remember it must be our secret. You can depend upon it everything would be done to prevent your seizing this advantage. Meet my granddaughter. Think of what I have said. I will send for her now.'

Lady Diana Spencer, who had been summoned to Marlborough House and ordered to come to her grandmother as soon as she was sent for, came into the room.

She was young and lovely; she walked with grace and her eyes sparkled with intelligence.

'I have a surprise for you,' said Sarah. 'His Highness the Prince of Wales has done me the honour to call on me.'

Lady Di curtsied charmingly and the Prince took her hand.

'Take His Highness and show him the gardens,' said Sarah. 'I know he is very interested in them.'

When they had gone she sat back in her chair and laughed aloud. She hoped Marl really was watching.

She had not felt to alive, so in love with life, since he had gone.

The Prince of Wales stood before the Duchess of Marlborough.

'Well?' asked the Duchess. 'What is Your Highness's answer?'

'I find Lady Diana delightful.'

'Ha! Good enough for a prince, eh?'

'Far too good,' he said falsely.

Sarah did not deny this.

'And so you want to marry her?'

He hesitated. 'Have you considered how angry the King will be?'

'*I* have never been afraid of Kings . . . or Queens,' she said fiercely.

He looked at her with admiration. It was true. Everyone knew how she had bullied Queen Anne.

'Then . . . I will ask you for the hand of Lady Diana Spencer.'

Sarah chuckled. 'Your Highness will not regret this. Now . . . we must act with the greatest caution, for if this project reached the ears of the King or that dog Walpole they would do everything in their power to prevent it, and we might as well face the fact that they have more power than we have.'

The Prince nodded; the more he thought of the proposal, the better he liked it. Lady Di was charming; a hundred thousand pounds was an irresistible bait; and in addition he would have the joy of infuriating his parents.

'The wedding shall take place at my lodge in Windsor Great Park. I shall be staying there with Lady Di and you must ride out there on some pretext. It will not be difficult. My chaplain will marry you.'

'Will he agree, do you think?'

'My chaplain will do as *I* tell him.'

'He might be held responsible by my parents.'

'He is responsible to no one but me.'

'It seems as though you have thought of everything.'

'Naturally I have planned this in detail. I want to see you and my granddaughter happily settled. Now, let us make sure that we have thought of every detail; and we must all make sure that we speak of this to no one. Until the ceremony is over, not a soul must know it is to take place.'

'I understand,' said the Prince; and he went blithely away.

But it was not to be supposed that he was going to keep this secret.

Anne Vane noticed there was something different about him. He was excited, but he resisted all her efforts to worm the secret out of him.

He did take Bubb into his confidence. Bubb was amused and whispered it to Mrs Behan.

'What will happen to Anne when he marries?' she wanted to know.

'Oh, princes keep mistresses you know, even though they may have a wife as well.'

Mrs Behan was thoughtful. She did not believe that Sarah Churchill would allow her grandson-in-law to keep a mistress when he was married to Lady Diana Spencer. If the Prince no longer cherished Anne Vane it would not be so amusing to be Anne's great friend. They would not spend so much time in exalted company.

Mrs Behan thought it was her duty to call on Anne and when they were alone together she said: 'My dear, how do *you* feel about the Prince's plans.'

'Plans,' cried Anne. 'What plans?'

'Don't tell me you don't know.' Mrs Behan clapped her hand over her mouth while she watched Anne covertly.

Anne was growing angry. 'I knew there was *something*. I asked him and he would tell me nothing. What do *you* know . . . that I don't?'

'Perhaps I shouldn't tell.'

'You'll tell me,' declared Anne.

'He mentioned it to George. The Duchess of Marlborough has offered him Lady Diana Spencer.'

'*Offered* him?'

Mrs Behan laughed. 'Did you think as his mistress? Not old Sarah. He's to marry her and get one hundred thousand pounds for it.'

'And he's . . . going to?'

Mrs Behan lifted her shoulders.

'He'd do anything for a hundred thousand pounds,' said Anne blankly. Then she was triumphant. 'They'll not allow it.'

'But they won't know until it's too late.'

'You mean it's to be . . . in secret.'

'Yes, tomorrow . . . at Windsor in the Duchess's private chapel. The Duchess's own chaplain will perform the ceremony.'

'No!'

Anne's future was suddenly bleak. She knew as well as Mrs Behan did that the Duchess of Marlborough would see to it that she was soon dismissed.

She tottered, and was about to fall into a heap when Mrs Behan said : 'Fainting won't help. Some things might, though.'

That was enough to stop the faint.

'What?' demanded Anne.

'Well, if Sir Robert Walpole knew what was going to happen . . . it wouldn't happen, would it?'

'But how . . .'

'A note . . . warning him. That could stop it. He might get such a note. I mean . . . there's no reason why he shouldn't, is there?'

The Prince was preparing to leave for Windsor. He was humming to himself the latest Buononcini melody. When they heard, they were going to be furious.

He pictured himself presenting Lady Diana to them.

'Your Majesties, I want you to meet my wife, the Princess of Wales.'

Nothing he could possibly do would infuriate them as much as this.

His horse was waiting. He would gallop all the way to Windsor and there waiting for him would be the fiery old Duchess and her lovely granddaughter. In the forest lodge he would be married.

Diana was beautiful, but it was not her beauty which he found so delightful to contemplate as the anger he would see on the faces of his parents.

Serve them right! They deserved all the trouble he could bring to them. They had never treated him fairly.

He called to his man . . . the one he was taking with him to Windsor. A trusted servant. He would take no one else.

The door opened. The Prince stared, then he stammered: 'W . . . what do you want?'

'To save Your Highness from disaster,' said Sir Robert Walpole.

They sat facing each other and there was no longer need for speech.

He could not go. He was a prisoner, although discreetly guarded.

'It would be unwise,' said Sir Robert, 'for this to be publicly known. We will keep it as quiet as possible.'

He had argued at first. He would make his own decisions. But the marriage of the Prince of Wales was a decision for the King and his council, not for the Prince himself.

'I shall choose when and whom I marry,' the Prince had said defiantly.

But Walpole had only smiled benevolently. One did not take any notice of childish observations.

The Prince was a prisoner. He would not go to Windsor. And now Walpole was on his guard and would take precautions against such a contingency ever arising again.

Frederick felt defeated and his hatred was doubled. Not so much for Walpole as for his parents.

In Windsor Lodge the Duchess waited. Lady Di waited with her.

'Grandmother,' said Lady Di at length, 'I don't believe he is coming.'

'Spineless idiot,' cried the Duchess. 'He is his cockerel of a father all over again.'

'He may have been prevented.'

'He's been talking too much, I'll warrant. God damn these Germans.'

In spite of her fury the Duchess was a pathetic sight as she sat slumped forward in her chair.

If only Marl were here, she was thinking. We'd send the guards. We'd bring him here by force. We'd make him marry her.

But that was nonsense. Even Marl couldn't do that if he were here and at the height of his glory.

And he is gone, gone, she thought, gone with the glory, and taken with him my only reason for being alive.

Sir Robert Walpole

Walpole in danger

The King was happy because he was going to Hanover.

There had been opposition to the visit. It was, pointed out his ministers, an unpopular move. The people of England could not understand why their King should want to leave his country for the sake of some little German state. It was noticed that he was more affable, that he did not snub his wife so humiliatingly in public, that he was tolerant to his children and now and then even affable to the Prince of Wales. No one could doubt that the King was looking forward to going to Hanover.

Walpole's feelings were mixed. It was easier to deal with business when the King was away; on the other hand the popularity of the Royal House was important and so cleverly had the Queen worked on the King that George was almost as devoted to his first minister as Caroline was.

Still, George was determined to go.

When he was dressed after his afternoon sleep he came into the Queen's apartments to take her for their walk and he was smiling pleasantly.

This time next week he would be on his way.

'You are ready, my dear?'

Of course she was ready. She knew better than to keep him waiting.

He led her out to the garden and he walked by her side to the Upper Paddock to look at the deer. Caroline was very proud of the gardens of Kensington because when her father-in-law had died she had taken an immense interest in them and had even had a hand in the planning. Often she thought that if there were not so many state duties, if she felt as well as she once did, she would be happy to devote a great deal of time to gardening.

She had had the parterres removed and it had been a great pleasure to plan the gardens. The Broad Walk was becoming one of her favourite sauntering grounds; and she was glad that she had had the Round Pond set in the middle of the lawns.

'The gardens are beginning to look so beautiful now,' she said.

The King replied. 'We have nothing here to compare with the statues and linden avenues at Herrenhausen.'

She did not agree, but of course one did not question any statement of the King's.

'I hope all will be well there.'

'You are concerned for me, my dear. All will be well, I tell you. You must not be sad because I leave you.'

'You would not expect me to be happy?'

He smiled complacently. 'Oh, no, no. But you shall be Regent while I am gone. That is good for you and I feel everything is safe in your hands. I said to Walpole, I leave everything safe in your hands and those of the Queen.'

'I shall do my best,' said the Queen.

'Ah, it is good for you. You like to be the Regent. Confess it. You like it, my dear, and for me, I am a man you know . . . and I must be a bachelor now and then. It is the way of the world. But rest assured, my dear, that no mistress will ever be to me as you are.'

She looked at the winding stream which they called the Serpentine and sighed.

'No,' he went on, 'there are some very attractive women at the court and I have honoured them . . . but always I say: they are not the Queen. For me there is only one woman although I may have – as is natural to a man, my dear – many mistresses. So for me the bachelor existence and for you the Regency, eh?'

She smiled at him wanly. Her legs were beginning to ache. If only she could reduce the swelling.

'I shall write to you,' he said.

Oh, yes, he would write long letters telling her intimate details of his love affairs. She could well do without such letters.

'And I shall expect you to write to me,' he went on.

'You may be sure that you will be informed of all that happens.'

'I trust my Regent. So . . . for you the Regency . . . for me the bachelor's life.'

When he was gone she found her health improving. When there was no longer the need to hide all signs of fatigue, that fatigue lessened considerably. She walked at a slower pace, stopping to examine the flowers or comment on the growth of the trees she had planted and which she hoped posterity would be grateful for. There was no need now to keep up with the King.

She now had time to learn more about the nation.

She told Walpole that Kings and Queens were often sheltered from the truth. When her carriage was driven through the city she had seen beggars and stallholders and had wondered how they lived.

Walpole smiled benignly. 'Everyone knows what a good heart Your Majesty has.'

She knew of course that he wanted her to remember that their task was to rule the state; they were surrounded by enemies and they could not take their minds from the matter in hand.

'Yet it seems to me the way the people live is our concern,' said the Queen.

Walpole nodded gravely, waited a few seconds, and then began to explain that a need would soon arise to take action about the Land Tax, which needed revision. He was working out a scheme and as soon at is was ready he would put it to the Queen, who could then acquaint the King of whatever decision they should come to.

The Queen nodded; but her thoughts were with the poor people whom she had seen on her drive.

She was in her apartments reading the documents which had

been laid before her, and suddenly she paused. She held in her hand a death warrant.

She stared at it and wondered whose life she would be signing away. She put down her pen and went to the window. Away in the Upper Paddock she caught sight of the deer; it all seemed so beautiful, but she could not get out of her mind the picture of a cell in Newgate Jail where a man whose name was on that death warrant was waiting for her to sign away his life.

What had he done? she wondered. And why? That was the question. Why?

She thought of the child she had seen, barefoot, wrapped in a tattered shawl through which the flesh showed blue and mottled. Those people stole. Why? Because they were hungry. They killed, because they had never been taught, because life was so hard that they had to fight and perhaps kill to live.

She decided that she would not sign the death warrant until she knew more of that man.

She felt curiously alive and almost exalted. There were several poor men whose lives she had saved. She had refused to put her signature blithely on those death warrants. She had declared that before she did she wanted to know the nature of the crimes of which they were accused.

When Walpole came to her and wanted to talk about the Land Tax she insisted on discussing the state of the prisons.

'I want an inquiry set up,' she said. 'I want to know what goes on there. I want to discover if there is anything we can do to make the lot of these poor people more bearable.'

'They are criminals, Madam,' Walpole reminded her.

'Yes, but *why*? That is what I want to know. I want to discover more about these people. Why do they go to prison in the first place? And I'll begin by knowing what happens to them when they get there.'

She was horrified with what the inquiry disclosed. Poor prisoners were treated with the utmost cruelty, whereas on those occasions when a rich man found himself in jail he could live in comfort by bribing his jailors and even escapes were connived at if the rewards were high enough.

She discovered that there were no beds for the sick prisoners, that there was often no food, that many of them died from cold and starvation; she was deeply distressed and sought a means of reforming the system.

Walpole was impatient. Charitable works were all very well, but there were a great many more important matters on hand. He believed that the best way to reform was through prosperity, and even his enemies would have to admit that, through his peaceful policy, he had brought that to England.

He sought to lure the Queen back to more practical matters.

The King was writing long letters to her which arrived almost daily. He was a better writer than speaker and he went into the most minute details of whatever he did. This included his love affairs which, the Queen noticed with some alarm, were becoming more and more frequent. He would describe the charms of his mistresses down to the most intimate detail; and if he was unable to arouse the passions of any of them he would ask the Queen to give the matter her consideration. As a woman she should understand her own sex.

She would read them through with irritation and exasperation and a little fear. Was he becoming more interested in other women than he had been before?

He had previously felt that he should have a mistress and it used to be said by some of the wits of the court that he was a man who found pleasure with his wife and took his mistresses for the sake of duty. Would they say that of him now?

When he was with her he was an uxorious husband, one might say. He did not seem to tire of her physically; and even when he snubbed her so humiliatingly in public it was the snub of a husband who is interested in his wife; there had never been any question of his being indifferent to her.

Sometimes the thought of her internal disorder would catch her unawares and send the panic running through her. Was he aware of it? Would it turn him away from her? Would it send him more and more in search of other women?

No, she was a habit with him. More than that, he was a sentimental man, and she was enshrined in his heart. His wife, the woman he had chosen; the woman he declared he loved beyond all others. Hadn't she fought all these years to retain that hold on him? Hadn't she suppressed her superior knowledge, at least keeping it hidden from him? Hadn't she upheld him always in private as well as in public? Had she not always outwardly bowed to his will – and it was only when she had brought him round to her opinion that she would admit that that opinion was hers. Yes, she was a habit. But so had Henrietta Howard been; and he only visited her now to grumble at her, to show that he was heartily sick of her and that, if she had not become involved with a certain time of his day, he would have discarded her. In fact, in spite of time, he would have discarded her if his wife would let her go.

Henrietta must stay, thought the Queen; for in her mind Henrietta was linked with the old days.

Let a new mistress take her place – someone young, someone gay, someone less discreet, some power-hungry female? No! Henrietta must remain even though she was restive and wanting to go, even though the King was tired of her.

She put aside his letter and picked up the document on her table.

'Thomas Ricketts,' she read. 'Fourteen years' transportation for stealing a silver-hilted sword . . .'

Fourteen years . . . away from home and family . . . fourteen years to a strange land.

'John Pritchard . . . fourteen years' transportation for house-breaking . . .'

What happened to a home when a man was away from it for fourteen years? And how did he return?

She wrote across the documents. 'The Queen wishes to know more of these cases.'

During those summer months when the King was away in Hanover, Caroline instituted an inspection of prisons and dismissed several jailors who had been caught acting cruelly towards poor prisoners.

She would have liked to reform the prisons, but this, Walpole assured her, was impossible. It would mean raising taxes which would be an unpopular move at the moment.

She must be content with setting up a regular inspection. Then certain evils could be put right, provided it was not too costly to do so.

So she had to be satisfied with pardoning several poor wretches who were condemned to the gallows and saving others from transportation. She raised money to pay the debts of certain people who had been languishing for years in the debtors' prisons.

She would have liked to go on with this work for she was sure there was a great deal to do.

But in September, after a four months' sojourn in Hanover, the King returned.

The King left Hanover reluctantly. When the people came out to see him pass on his journey to the Palace he was sullen, and scarcely returned their greeting.

'How hot it is here,' he said. 'In Hanover there is a cool breeze.'

Oh dear, thought the Queen, the people are noticing. 'The dust from the ground makes you cough. In Hanover there is no dust. What a noisy crowd! They could learn manners from us Germans.'

It was incredible that this was the man who had, when his father was alive, declared himself enamoured of England and all things English. It was not the English he had loved, but his father whom he had hated.

As soon as they sat down to a meal which was taken ceremoniously in public, he complained that the food was ill-cooked. It was tasteless. It was not like the food he had had in Hanover.

And when he and the Queen were alone for the night he declared that in Hanover a man was a King even though he was an Elector. But in England though he was called a King, he was a slave to his Parliament.

She agreed with him docilely enough and wondered whether he would now tell her that the women of Hanover were far more attentive than the women of England; but this he refrained from doing; and appeared to be satisfied with her.

Walpole took an early opportunity of laying his new scheme

before the King. Caroline had already heard of it, but neither she nor Walpole anticipated any obstacle from George.

'It is necessary as Your Majesty has often pointed out,' said Walpole, 'to raise taxes, and certain ideas Your Majesty put into my mind before your visit to Hanover have enabled me to come forward with a plan.'

The King did not question the fact that the ideas were his. Whenever Walpole told him this he believed it.

So he nodded agreeably and waited.

'The largest proportion of taxation comes from the Land Tax, as Your Majesty is well aware,' went on Walpole. 'The landowners are restive. They remind us that during the war they were paying four shillings in the pound. Since we have had peace and cut the army costs we have been able to reduce this to two shillings in the pound. But the landowners say this is too much. I agree with Your Majesty that this tax should be spread and perhaps by so doing we could increase the revenue. I suggest that we bring wine and tobacco duties under the law of excise. This does not make a great deal of difference to the tax imposed. It is rather a different way of collecting. But of course in the wine and tobacco business there is a great deal of smuggling, and this I hope to prevent and so increase revenue considerably.'

'His Majesty is going to say that he approves of this wholeheartedly,' said the Queen with a smile, 'for I see he is thinking that the Civil List depends partly on these duties and if they are increased so will the Civil List be.'

'I was going to say that,' said the King with an approving nod.

'It is true, of course,' said Walpole with a smile. 'I should now like to lay before Your Majesty my plan of the scheme.'

This he began to do while the Queen listened, taking her cue when to speak from the minister; and in any case they had already decided how they would set the matter before the King. Not that George needed any persuasion on this occasion.

The new excise laws would increase the Civil List and that was good enough for him.

Bolingbroke, Pulteney and Wyndham called a meeting of their friends in the Opposition.

'Walpole is going to bring in his excise scheme,' announced

Bolingbroke. 'He can fall on this, and we must see that he does.'

Pulteney pointed out that he would have the landowners with him because of the reduction of the Land Tax.

'We must see that he has no one with him,' retorted Bolingbroke. 'This is an opportunity for which we have all been waiting. This is going to see the end of Walpole.'

'What!' cried Wyndham. 'For a tax on wine and tobacco.'

'We'll call it a beginning.' Bolingbroke's eyes were aflame. 'We'll tell the country what it means. He will start on wine and tobacco and then it will be food . . . everything the people want to buy will be taxed. That will be our cry: "Down with the excise!" ' He turned to Pulteney. 'We'll start at once in the *Craftsman*. "What is Robin the trickster doing now? He is tricking you of your hard earned wages. He is telling you it is only wine and tobacco. Wine and tobacco today. Bread tomorrow. It is only a matter of collecting the tax we will change? Yes, collect it so that more goes out of your pocket and more into Robin's!" '

'You think it will be a big issue?' asked Wyndham.

'My friend, we are going to *see* that it is a big issue.'

Everyone was discussing the new excise proposals. In the coffee and chocolate houses they talked of nothing else. The *Craftsman* was handed from one to another. 'Read this. Read what the *Craftsman* says.'

This was the end of freedom in England, the *Craftsman* told its readers. This was what Robin had been trying to bring about for years. He wanted to make the King an absolute monarch. Did the people remember that certain monarchs had believed in their Divine Right? They had a King who was more German than English, who preferred the little electorate of Hanover to the mighty country which was England. Between them he, his fat queen, and their henchman Walpole would ruin England; they would destroy the liberties of the people; it would be as though Magna Carta had never been signed. Robin was going to introduce his Excise Bill and lead them back to the dark ages.

'To hell with these Germans!' cried the people. 'What are they doing here anyway!'

It was not only the Opposition who saw opportunities in the

excise scheme. Many of Walpole's own ministry were dissatisfied. Why had they not been given this or that job? Why were they in minor ministerial positions when their talents were so much greater than the men who had the jobs? Jealousy always walked side by side with ambition, and this was an opportunity to destroy the most successful minister of his day, the man who had brought peace and prosperity to England, the most powerful of all politicians, the man who had courted the Queen and won her approval so successfully that between them they had the King in leading strings.

These men called a meeting and selected one of themselves to go to the Queen and point out to her that she was being misled in this excise scheme by Walpole, of whom she had too high an opinion; they were to ask her to dissociate herself and the King from the scheme and to let Walpole stand alone in its defence if he wanted to.

For this they chose a Scottish peer, John Dalrymple, Lord Stair.

Lord Stair had a great deal to recommend him for the task. He was a forthright man; he had been slighted and, he believed, treated very badly by Walpole, and he was one of his greatest enemies. He was fearless, and since he felt strongly would put the case well. He was no young fool, being nearly sixty; he was no respecter of persons, and as a Scotsman he had even less love for the Germans than the English had.

Stair had had an adventurous life. When he was only eight years old he had accidentally shot his elder brother, and although he had been pardoned for this, his parents could not endure to have him near them constantly to remind them of what he had done, so he was put in the care of a tutor for three years and after that sent to his grandfather in Holland. His youth had been overshadowed by this event and as he had been entirely innocent it had set up a certain resentment in him. He had, however, become the friend of another strange and withdrawn man, William of Orange, and distinguished himself in battle, serving very successfully under Marlborough. Queen Anne had respected him and made him her ambassador to France, but when Marlborough fell, Stair fell with him.

He then went back to Edinburgh and became the leader of the Scottish Whigs; and there he fell in love with Eleanor, Viscountess Primrose. She was a widow who had been unhappy in her first marriage and vowed she would never marry again. But Lord Stair also made a vow which was that she should be his wife. He achieved this by finding a way into her house, where he hid himself and then at a certain moment appeared at her bedroom window. Such a scandal ensued, for the Viscountess was reckoned to be one of the most virtuous women of her time, that all she could do was to marry him.

He had always been in favour of the Hanoverian succession and with the coming of George I he was appointed a Lord of the Bedchamber, a Privy Councillor, Colonel of the Inniskilling Guards, and sent as Ambassador to Paris. Walpole had earned his dislike by recalling him from this appointment. Then, realizing that Stair was a forceful man, Walpole had tried to placate him by making him Vice-Admiral of Scotland. This Stair accepted, but the Paris affair rankled; and ever since he had been prepared to act against Walpole.

Because he was a man of strong views and not afraid to voice them, because of his resentment against Walpole, he was chosen to present the case against the excise to the Queen, who, on his request, received him in her apartments at Kensington Palace.

He came straight to the point and began by attacking Walpole.

'Your Majesty knows nothing of this man,' he cried, 'but what he tells you himself. But let me tell Your Majesty this: in no age was any minister so universally detested as this man whom you support. Nobody doubts that he absolutely governs Your Majesty. You may have the semblance of power but this man Walpole is the true ruler.'

The Queen was astonished and for the moment could find nothing to say.

'Who are *his* closest friends? Who are those whom he keeps in the highest places – next his own? Argyle and Islay! Is this your choice, Madam? And if so, have you forgotten that these two men tried to set up the power of the King's mistress so that it should be greater than yours?'

Caroline flinched. She hated any reference to Henrietta Howard. And the idea that there should have been any question of her having power was very repugnant to her.

'Mrs Howard . . .' began Stair, but Caroline cut him short.

'Pray remember that you are speaking of the King's servant and to the King's wife,' she said coldly.

Stair then began on the matter which had brought him to her: the Excise Bill. 'Madam, it will be impossible to force this obnoxious Bill through the Lords. It may be that *your* minister will get it through the Commons by corruption . . .'

'Lord Stair, I think you should retire until you are a little calmer.'

'I'm calm enough, Madam. This scheme is so wicked and dishonest that my conscience would no more permit me to vote for it than Walpole's should have permitted him to promote it.'

'Don't talk to me of your conscience, my lord. You make me faint!'

Lord Stair, who resented this remark, went on to storm against Walpole and his nefarious methods.

'You learn your politics, sir, from the *Craftsman* I do believe,' said the Queen sarcastically. 'And as Lord Bolingbroke is your teacher I am not surprised at your ideas and your manners. That man is one of the greatest liars and knaves in any country. This I have found, not from what I have read in scurrilous papers such as you glean your ideas from, but from my own observation and experiences. And now, my Lord Stair, I must ask you to take your leave as I have other matters to which I must attend.'

There was nothing Stair could do but return to his friends and tell them that it was no use talking to the Queen about the Excise Bill, for she stood firmly beside Walpole.

Rarely had there been such excitement throughout the country as there was over the proposed Excise Bill. Meetings were called in every town hall, at every village inn. In London crowds gathered at street corners; banners were held high bearing the words 'No Excise. No Slavery'. And as the weeks passed the tumult grew louder.

Even Walpole's supporters wondered whether it was wise to continue.

The purpose of the scheme had been distorted out of all proportion. All Walpole had suggested was a revision of the wine and tobacco tax, but the whole country was convinced that every need of life would so rise in price that they would be unable to obtain it.

The people did not know that in opposing Walpole's excise scheme his enemies planned to rid the country of Walpole. No matter how his writers sought to counteract the effect of papers like the *Craftsman*, they could not do it. The people wanted a grievance; they liked nothing better than to see the mighty fallen, and Walpole had enjoyed too much power too long. Even those who did not know him wanted his downfall.

As for men like Bolingbroke, Pulteney and Wyndham, they saw in this a chance such as rarely came their way and they were not going to miss it.

Walking through the streets of London, a cloak concealing him for he was a well-known figure, Walpole saw the humour of the people. He heard the shouts of 'No Excise!' He listened to oratory and felt a bitter despair because it was clear that they did not know what the excise was. What did this shouting mob know of government, of the need for taxation? Did they thank him for the years of peace they had enjoyed? Not they! They wanted excitement; they wanted to taunt a politician as they taunted a bull; they were setting him to fight with his enemies as they did their fighting cocks.

He could fall on this . . . down to disgrace, to the end of power.

Maria wanted him to give up, to go to Houghton and forget politics. But how could a man who had once tasted power live without it?

There was Houghton with its treasures; there was riotous living in the country: drink, a heavy table, congenial companions . . . and Maria.

But in London there was power and he had known great power.

'Give up the Excise Scheme,' said his few friends. But were they friends? They were those who if he fell, would fall with him. So perhaps he must call them his friends.

Give up the Excise Bill! Admit defeat! No. That would be the end. He would betray a weakness. That supreme confidence which had carried him through all his troubles would be lost.

'I shall not give up the Excise Bill,' said Walpole.

'And this,' said the Prime Minister addressing a hostile House, 'is the scheme which has been represented in so terrible a light! This is the monster which was to devour the people and commit such ravages on the whole nation.'

The Opposition was waiting to pounce. The Prime Minister's own men were looking on with anxiety. He had explained that he had never had any intention to impose a general excise. The only commodities in question had been wine and tobacco. This he wished to introduce because a great deal of taxes were being lost to the nation through smuggling. This he wished to curtail. The House must understand that he had been wickedly . . . no . . . criminally misrepresented.

Wyndham was on his feet. The Opposition were against any form of excise. The Opposition did not believe in the Prime Minister's protestations. It denounced the entire measure. It regarded excise in any form as the badge of slavery. 'At this moment,' he went on, 'the people of this City are at the gates of the House. They are waiting eagerly to hear the result of this session. They want to know whether we, the Opposition, have prevailed on the Prime Minister's indifference to their poverty and want . . . whether we have thrown out this wicked measure – which we intend to do.'

Cheers drowned this speech and the sounds of voices could be heard without.

The mob must be thousands strong, thought Walpole.

He did not show his alarm. 'These sufferers from poverty and want,' he cried, 'would seem to be very sturdy beggars.'

Pulteney was on his feet. 'It moves me to wrath,' he cried, 'that the Prime Minister should have such indifference to the plight of the poor as to refer to them as sturdy beggars.'

Sturdy beggars! The phrase was referred to again and again during the debate. It was an unfortunate phrase. Walpole knew that it would be seized, used in the wrong context; that he would never escape from it.

The debate continued; and after thirteen hours no conclusion was reached.

One or two of his supporters suggested that Walpole slip out of the House quietly and cautiously, so that he might not be recognized. The mob was in an ugly mood.

The last complaint that could be made about the King was that he was a coward. George had never been that. Caroline and he talked continuously of the excise and what this measure was doing to Walpole. His friends were deserting him after imploring him to drop the unpopular measure. Walpole would have liked to do this, but he could only see that to drop it would so lower his prestige that he would lose his place forever. He would be playing straight into his enemies' hands, which was of course exactly what they wanted.

It astonished him, he told Maria, that the two who should be his most faithful friends in this crisis were the King and the Queen.

George's eyes would fill with tears when he spoke of his Prime Minister. 'That man has more spirit than any other man I ever knew,' he said. 'He is a brave man.'

And bravery was something which George understood and respected.

'We will stand by him,' he told the Queen. 'No matter what happens we will not desert him.'

The Queen was anxious, and when Lord Scarborough requested an interview and she had heard what he had to say she was very alarmed. Richard Lumley, Lord Scarborough, was Lieutenant General of the Army and because he had always been a good friend to her and the King, Caroline knew she could trust him.

His immediate request was to be allowed to resign from his post.

Caroline was horrified. 'But I couldn't allow it.'

'Madam,' he told her, 'there will soon be a revolt in the army.'

'Oh, no, no,' cried Caroline. 'It cannot be as bad as this.'

'There will be mutiny, Madam, if the Bill is not dropped.'

'But you will answer to the King for the army.'

'I will answer for the army against the Pretender,' said Scarborough, 'but not against the excise.'

'Then,' said the Queen soberly, 'in your opinion the only course open to us is to drop the Bill.'

'It is the only way, Madam.'

'Yes,' replied Caroline. 'It is the only way.'

She went to the King and told him what Scarborough had said. Like her, George trusted Scarborough. If Scarborough said the army was on the edge of mutiny, then that was so.

'Your Majesty will say that there is no alternative but to drop the Bill,' said the Queen.

The King nodded. 'We must send for Sir Robert.'

Walpole came first to the Queen.

'We shall drop the Bill,' he said. 'There is no other alternative.'

'I am sorry,' said the Queen. 'You have been grossly misrepresented.'

'I should have foreseen this.'

'Nonsense! How could you!'

'It is a minister's task, Madam, to predict the future . . . correctly. This Bill in itself would have presented no difficulties had it been allowed to pass through without all the lies and malice which my enemies have attached to it. The Prince's attitude towards it has inflamed the public the more.'

'You mean he has set himself on the side of the Opposition?'

'This is Bolingbroke's doing. We have constantly heard that the Prince denounces the Bill. Your Majesties and myself have been fearfully maligned. They call this our Bill. I agree with Your Majesty that the Bill must be dropped, but our enemies will not be satisfied with that. They want a scapegoat and I must be that man.'

'You mean . . . resign!'

'It is the only way.'

'There must be another way and we must find it.'

'Madam, all know that you and I have worked together. Unless I resign and you dissociate yourself from me and my policies they will attack you too.'

'The Queen !' cried Caroline almost regally.

'Madam, the King's grievance against England is that it is the Parliament who rules . . . not him.'

'And you would resign?'

'That Your Majesty's name might not be coupled with mine in this dispute.'

The Queen's expression was very gentle as she said: 'I am surprised, Sir Robert Walpole, that you could think me so mean and so cowardly as to allow this to happen. The Bill must be set aside. I see that. But you will remain in your office. This is not the time – indeed is any time the time? . . . for running away.'

Sir Robert kissed her hand.

'Then, Madam, we fight this together?'

'We fight,' she said. 'And, Sir Robert, the King stands with us.'

London was on the edge of revolt. Never, it was said, in the 1715 revolt did the throne tremble so violently. The Lord Mayor of London, supported by all the officials of the City, rode through the streets on his way to the Houses of Parliament with a petition against the Bill.

This procession was cheered on its way.

In St James's the King and Queen talked together. The Queen had asked Lord Hervey, who as well as being her Chamberlain was also a Member of Parliament, to return to the Palace and report to them as soon as a vote against the petition was taken.

She sat in her chair trying to knot to soothe her mind, while the King paced up and down declaring that if this meant they must return to Hanover he would not think that such a bad idea.

They could hear the shouts in the city.

The Queen could not keep her fingers from trembling. She understood more than the King how near London was to revolution.

It seemed hours before Lord Hervey returned to them. He came quietly by means of the private staircase and as soon as Caroline looked at his face she knew how things had gone. Indeed how could she have expected them to go otherwise?

'So the Opposition was victorious!' shouted the King.

'That is true, Your Majesty.'

The King demanded to know how members of the government had voted and when Hervey told him he shouted abuse after each name.

'Blockhead! Fool! Madman! Puppy! I shall remember them all.'

The Queen shook her head sadly.

'This,' she said, 'is the end of the matter. The Excise Bill will be withdrawn.'

Defeat, she thought. Nothing will be the same again.

Meanwhile the few friends Walpole had were persuading him not to go out into the streets where the mob was waiting for him because in their mood they would tear him to pieces. No matter that they had misinterpreted his Bill; no matter that he in view of public opinion had withdrawn it; his enemies had whipped up public rage against him and they wanted his blood.

It was true that he had more spirit than most men. Instead of depressing him, the situation exhilarated him.

He thought, I'll beat them yet; I'll be more powerful than ever before. For that reason he had no intention of risking his life, so he wrapped himself up in a red cloak and went among the crowd.

'No excise!' he shouted with the rest. 'Where's Walpole? Find Walpole! We'll show what we will do to that fellow.'

And so he passed unmolested and, reaching his carriage, was taken home.

But that night, effigies were burned all over London. There were two figures, both grossly fat. One a man; the other a woman.

They represented Walpole and the Queen.

'We are out of favour,' said Walpole that night to his mistress. 'But we shall not remain so. The thing to do now is to make the people forget all about the excise.'

'And how will you do that?' asked Maria.

'I shall have to think about this. It will have to be a grand occasion. We'll have a royal occasion this time. A wedding would do. That's it – a royal wedding. We must find a husband for the Princess Anne. She's getting restive and she's no longer a very young girl.'

'Where will you find the husband?'

'I must give some thought to that but depend upon it, he must be found.'

A royal marriage

The King paced up and down his wife's apartments, his wig a little awry, his eyes bright with emotion.

'But Orange!' he said. 'Not what I should have chosen for her.'

The Queen nodded sadly. 'What a pity that there is no one else, and it is either him or no husband at all.'

'But she is the Princess Royal. Perhaps Orange would do for Amelia . . . or Caroline.'

'But where should we find a husband for Anne? I daresay Your Majesty is thinking that it would be unwise to marry off the younger daughters before the eldest.'

'That's so. And I fear if Anne does not take Orange, it will be no husband at all.'

'She is twenty-four. She should have been married long ago. Ah, if only we had married her to Louis XV!'

'I never liked the French . . . and a Catholic!'

The Queen nodded. 'At least Orange is a Protestant.'

'The only Protestant in Europe available for marriage.'

'A sad thought,' sighed the Queen, 'when we have Amelia and Caroline to consider.'

'At least we shall get the Princess Royal married.'

'I know Your Majesty's love for our daughter,' said the Queen hesitantly, 'and I know that you would not wish to force her into this against her will. And as it is such a poor match . . . perhaps . . .'

Tears filled the King's eyes. 'She shall choose,' he promised. 'If she does not like this match there will be no marriage.'

The Queen sighed with relief. 'How good you are !'

George was beaming. 'My dear, I have always tried to be a good father. I have not wanted to romp with them . . . nor to have them under my feet, but I think I have been a good father.'

'The best,' murmured the Queen, thinking of Orange and wondering whether he was as ugly as some reports made him out to be.

'Your Majesty will wish to speak to Anne first?'

'Yes, I will speak to her. I will tell her everything. I will hold nothing back. I shall say this : "Your mother, the Queen, and I, your father, will force you to nothing. If you do not like this marriage, my dear daughter, you have but to say, and there shall be no marriage." '

The Queen took the King's hand and kissed it.

Once again the tears glazed his eyes. 'You are the best wife in the world. I want you to know I think that. However many mistresses I take . . .'

'I know, I know,' said the Queen quickly, hiding her irritation under a show of emotion.

The King spoke briskly. 'Now I will send for our daughter. I will take her for a walk and then put this proposal before her.'

Of all his children, although he had never shown any great fondness for any of them, Anne was the favourite.

She was scarcely good-looking, her figure being clumsy and ungraceful, and she was inclined to be too fat; her complexion would have been lovely but for the fact that it was rather heavily pitted by the smallpox she had suffered as a child. But she had a lively mind and had applied herself to languages and spoke English, French, German, and Italian as though she belonged to each of those four countries. She was artistic; she played the harpsichord with real talent, and it was one of her greatest delights to surround herself with musicians. Handel was one of her greatest friends. She also had an excellent singing voice and would invite people from the opera to the Palace to sing with her. She could paint very well and also excelled at fine needlework. She was apt to rise before the Palace was astir and she was never bored because there was always something she had to work on. She was an interesting young woman, but just as her lovely skin was marred by the smallpox, so was her character spoilt by her arrogance and her overwhelming desire to occupy an exalted position. Many times she had been heard to curse her brothers simply because they were boys; had they not been she would have been Queen of England. If that could have been possible she would have been perfectly happy; as it was, she had become embittered; and having been denied the crown of England had had to look elsewhere for a crown. It added to her resentment that there was no eligible suitor available who could give her what she wanted.

She had heard the rumours and knew why her father had summoned her to walk with him in the gardens at Richmond.

'My dear daughter,' said the King, 'I have much to say to you.'

'I know,' she said quietly.

He took her hand and they walked away from the Lodge past the alleys with their clipped hedges to the river terraces.

'You have heard that there is a proposed match between yourself and the Prince of Orange.'

'Yes, Papa.'

'I have told the Queen that I will have you forced to nothing. And she agrees with me. So, my dear daughter, if this match is abhorrent to you, you must say so and we will not have this Orange man. What do you say? But let me talk to you first. Let me tell you what Walpole has said of this marriage. He is a sly old fox, but he is a brave man and he has more spirit than any man I know, and I would trust him as no other to manage the Parliament.'

'Yes, Papa. Pray tell me what Walpole has said of the match.'

'He has said it is not a good match . . . it is not a worthy match. His estate not being a clear £12,000 a year.'

The Princess shuddered.

'But you will have a dowry, my dear. Walpole has talked of £80,000.'

'That will make up for the Prince's lack,' said Anne. 'Do you think Walpole will be able to get them to agree to it?'

'He has not failed yet, my dear.'

'Except with the Excise Bill.'

'That . . .' The King's eyes bulged with remembered fury. 'That was a monstrous affair. That was his enemies . . .'

'And if his enemies decide that I shall not have my dowry?'

The King frowned. He did not like these direct statements. The Queen never spoke to him like this. But this was a sentimental occasion and he did not want to spoil it. If she married Orange she would be leaving England and he wanted to think of her as his dear daughter, not a virago whom he was glad to see out of the way.

'You shall have your dowry,' he said pettishly. 'Walpole has promised me this.' His mood changed. 'The people will be pleased. It is necessary to please the people. They are not very happy with us at the moment.'

'The excise again.'

'Our enemies have lied about us. It is these lampoons and writings. If this were Hanover there would be none of that, I can tell you.'

'But there is, Papa. And we need this marriage. Is that so? We need to have a splendid show for the people to see. We need their cheers. And there is nothing like a royal wedding to please the people. Is that it?'

'A wedding would please them. But you are not bound to it. The English will be pleased with Orange because he is a Protestant, and you know how they dislike the Catholics. Another point is that they are very fond of the Dutch. They took a Prince of Orange for the King in place of Catholic James, and although they disliked him when he was living they've forgotten it now and he brought them, so they think, many benefits. Therefore a Dutch marriage will be popular.'

'Your Majesty is telling me all the reasons why I should marry and at the same time implying that I need not if the project is abhorrent to me. Please tell me now why you think I might not like the match.'

'It is not worthy of you. His fortune is not good enough for the Princess Royal of England and the man . . .'

'And the man?' she said quickly.

'I have heard that he is not handsome.'

'Oh!'

The King pressed his daughter's hand. 'In fact . . . he is deformed.'

'He is . . .'

'Oh, no! He can beget children. But I believe he is hunchbacked and not . . . handsome.'

'I see.'

The King drew his daughter gently to him and held his arm about her.

'My dear, it is for you to decide. I have been fortunate in my marriage. I chose your mother. I went to court her and she did not know who I was. We fell in love with each other, and we have been very happy.'

He released her and stood looking at the river, not seeing it but sentimentally gazing back over the years.

Anne thought: *you* may have been happy with your mistresses and your tremendous conceit so that you think you rule this country, but has my mother? She has had to accept your mistress; she has had to subdue her intelligence, she has had to pretend that she scarcely thinks a thought that is not in complete agreement with yours. Is that marriage?

At least he was not a hunchback. And he was a King . . . a King of England. She would have been like her mother perhaps, ready to accept anything for the sake of a crown. A petty Prince of Orange, she was thinking. £12,000 a year. And a hunchback!

But the alternative? To go on unmarried; and when Frederick became King how would he treat his sisters who, because husbands had not been found them, would be such an encumbrance to him? The position would be intolerable.

What a choice!

And after all the glorious dreams she had indulged in. To

think she might have been Queen of France! What an unkind fate which had denied her great Louis and instead offered her this deformed petty prince; she had lost France for Holland.

I am the most unfortunate princess in the world, she thought; and then: no,, Amelia and Caroline are more so for they will have no choice at all, since if Orange is the only Protestant Prince available where can husbands be found for them?

The King went on: 'And because your mother and I have had such a happy marriage, we could never force you into one which is repugnant to you. So we have decided that if you did not wish for this match, in spite of all the good Walpole thinks it would bring, there shall be no match.'

He was smiling at her benignly and she saw what he was waiting for. 'Papa, you are very good to me.'

Then he took her into his arms and embraced her, so that all those watching from the Lodge saw; and as they knew what the interview was about, they wondered whether that meant that the Princess Anne had accepted or refused the Prince of Orange.

That was Anne's last concession to sentimentality. She decided there and then that she had no room for it in her life.

'Papa,' she said, 'it is a question of marrying this hunchback . . . or not marrying at all. I do not care to remain a spinster. Therefore I say that if he were a baboon I would marry him.'

The King was not noted for his tact. He nodded his head sadly and said: 'Baboon it may well be, daughter.'

And they returned to the Lodge, the decision made.

Bolingbroke came to La Trappe to talk to the Prince and with Dodington discussed the proposed marriage.

'This is a further insult,' said Bolingbroke. 'If there is to be a royal marriage, it should be that of the Prince of Wales. Who ever heard of a prince . . . almost thirty years of age and unmarried. It is a plot to keep you from what is your due.'

Frederick was very ready to be inflamed. He could no longer mildly accept the neglect he received from his parents. It was true that his father had been treated similarly by *his* father, but there was no reason why it should become a family tradition.

'Your Highness is too good natured,' said Bolingbroke. 'But you will not allow this to pass?'

Frederick looked expectant; he wanted to be told what should be done.

'You should have an allowance of £100,000. It was what your father had as Prince of Wales.'

'My debts . . .' wailed the Prince. 'I cannot begin to calculate.' He was regretting his failure to have married Lady Di which would have brought him the £100,000 he so desperately needed.

'Could someone be found to raise the question in the House?' asked Dodington.

Bolingbroke looked uneasy. Frederick was too unreliable to be a good leader; Walpole, even after the excise fiasco, was as strong as ever; and the King was not out of favour so much as he had been because the public were looking forward to the marriage of his daughter.

Any suggestion that the marriage portion should be diverted to Frederick at this time would not be popular.

'I think just at the moment it would be unwise to raise the question in the House, but that is no reason why everyone should not know that the Prince is very dissatisfied with his father's treatment.'

'They already know it,' said the Prince.

'We must see that they never forget,' replied Bolingbroke.

And during that summer when there was so much talk about the coming marriage of the Princess Royal, it was noticed that relations between the Prince and his parents grew more and more strained.

The King never addressed him in public; and someone remarked that the Prince must know what it felt like to be a ghost because when he stood near the King, His Majesty looked through him as though he were invisible to him.

As for the Queen, she spoke to him now and then, but only when it was necessary, and the coldness of her manner was obvious.

So on one side there was the bustle of preparation for the royal wedding and on the other the uncertainty as to how long the present situation between the Prince and his parents could go on.

Lord Hervey was constantly at court. The fact that he had quar-

relled with the Prince of Wales endeared him to the King and
Queen, and the latter in particular had grown very fond of him.

As her Chamberlain he was constantly in her company; she
liked his lively conversation which was spiced with malice and
she allowed him a licence she would have given to no one else.
Often he would sit beside her, beguiling her and the Princess
Caroline with scandal about the people of the court.

For the Queen this was a great release from the company of
the King, and Hervey's favour grew. As for the Princess Caroline, she thought him the most handsome, witty, and amusing
man at court. The fact that he was constantly suffering from
some mysterious ailment endeared him to her, for the Princess
herself did not enjoy good health and Hervey could beguile her
with details of the latest cure for this and that. He would on
occasion arrive at the Queen's apartments looking wan beneath
his rouge and explain to the Princess that he was back on his
diet of asses' milk with powdered crabs' eyes and oyster shells,
but he felt it was sapping his strength and he should go back to
seed and vegetable.

His physical frailty did not impair the agility of his mind,
however, and the Queen's eyes would brighten at the sight of
him, and if he did not put in an appearance she would inquire
tenderly after his health.

All during that summer the court hunted in Windsor forest
on Wednesdays and Saturdays which, with his usual precision,
the King had decided should be hunting time. The Queen,
though she did not care for the hunt, was nevertheless obliged
to attend, for the King would have been most displeased if she
did not. She followed the hunt in her chaise; Lord Hervey, who
confessed to her that he found no pleasure in hearing dogs bark
and seeing crowds gallop, rode beside her, and they continued
their interesting discussions.

With the coming of autumn, news of the arrival of the Prince
of Orange was brought to the Palace.

The King had decided that he should be lodged in Somerset
House and then seemed to lose interest in him, and although the
people were seething with excitement and longing for a glimpse
of the bridegroom, George gave no orders for his reception.

So Orange came to Somerset House without much fuss and ceremony; but he would soon, of course, come to wait on the King.

The Queen sent for Lord Hervey.

He came, delicately handsome, and she gave him her hand, smiling warmly. Hervey kissed it with a flourish.

'As always at Your Majesty's service,' he murmured.

'Go along to Somerset House. I wish to know what sort of animal has come to England to marry my daughter. I hear he is most unprepossessing and I want to know the worst so that I don't show too much shock when I am brought face to face with him.'

Hervey said that Her Majesty could trust him to bring her a truthful account.

Amelia came into her sister's apartments prepared to commiserate.

'He is here,' she said. 'He is at Somerset House.'

'Is that so?' replied Anne calmly. She was seated at her mirror studying her face, for her women had just left her after dressing her hair. Her complexion would really have been dazzling but for the ravages of the smallpox. But then, Anne consoled herself, who did not show signs of the smallpox? And it was in a way an asset, because having passed successfully through the scourge, though scathed, one was for ever immune.

'You do not seem in the least concerned,' said Amelia.

'Should I?'

Amelia threw herself into a chair and folded her arms in a rather masculine gesture. 'My God!' she said. 'Your bridegroom has arrived. He is in London. And you wonder whether you should be concerned!'

'It is all settled. I have made up my mind.'

'And you feel as calm as you look?'

'I have accepted the fact that it must be this one or no one. Him I can tolerate; but no one would be . . . unbearable.'

Amelia laughed. 'You are ruled by your royal dignity, sister. You accept Orange only because he is a husband.'

'He is a Prince too.'

'That's well enough but have you heard the rumours?'

'I have known all the time that he was not . . . handsome.'

'They say he is one of the most ugly men in the world . . . in fact so ugly as to be scarcely a man.'

'I have told Papa that I would marry him if he were a baboon, so I am prepared for the worst.'

'You will not be forced, you know.'

'I know that well.'

'And you can face marriage with a . . . baboon?'

'I have no intention of remaining unmarried, Amelia.'

Anne rose and, in spite of her rather dumpy figure which already showed signs that she had inherited their mother's tendency to fat, she looked very regal.

'It's your choice,' said Amelia, shrugging. 'He will be coming here soon. Then we shall see if the rumours have lied.'

'At least we are prepared for the worst,' said Anne.

'You will want to be alone, I dare say, to compose yourself.'

'Nonsense. I have asked some of my friends from the Opera House to come here. We are going to sing together.'

Amelia stared in astonishment at her sister. It was really true that she was unperturbed.

'My Lord Hervey,' said the Queen, her eyes aglow, 'come and tell me what you found at Somerset House.'

'Your Majesty should not be too downhearted.'

'But a little you mean?'

'Well, your son-in-law is not beautiful.'

'Pray, Lord Hervey, tell me the worst.'

'He is hunchbacked.'

'Slightly or . . .'

'More than slightly, Your Majesty. He stoops so much that seen from behind he would appear to have no head.'

'My God!'

'But his manners are pleasing.'

'And *you* are seeking to please *me*.'

'As always, Madam.'

'But I asked you for the truth and you do not please me by withholding it.'

'Then I will say this. He is hideous, as hideous as he is rumoured to be, but he has princely manners and his conduct is such that, knowing oneself to be in the presence of a Prince, one's mind is taken off his appearance.'

'My poor Anne!'

'Your Majesty has been goodness itself and the Princess has freely chosen this marriage.'

'It is true, but I suffer for her, my lord. You bring me very small comfort, but I'd rather that than lies.'

Hervey replied that beauty, ugliness, sorrow, all these were the greater or the smaller according to the manner in which they were observed. The Princess Anne wanted a husband and she was to have one. He was not beautiful, but he was at least a husband and the Princess had made it clear that she wanted any royal husband rather than none or one who could claim no royalty. In view of this the Queen should not grieve and she would see that the bridegroom was not half as black as he had been painted.

Such comfort, thought the Queen, talking to dear Lord Hervey.

But she was filled with apprehension, even when, passing to her drawing room, she heard the sounds of singing coming from her daughter's apartments.

When the Prince of Orange left Somerset House for St James's the streets were crowded with people who had come out to cheer him.

Dressed in robes of state his deformity was partly concealed; and although he was extremely ill-favoured he showed his approval of the people who cheered him wildly. They were sorry for him. They knew that the King had treated him without respect. This was obvious, for the only equipage the King had sent for him was one coach with a pair of horses and two footmen – a very poor display for a royal bridegroom.

The King was irritable every time the marriage was mentioned because he hated the thought of his daughter marrying what he called a baboon. He had been hoping that Anne would refuse the match; but since she had set her heart upon it and Walpole wished her to marry and so did the nation, what could he do but show his lack of liking for the bridegroom.

However, this neglect endeared the people to Orange. Their King was a German without manners; they hated him; and they were going to make up with their cheers what the King had denied him.

All about the Palace people had thronged to get a sight of the bridegroom and having heard such rumours of his terrible appearance they were pleasantly surprised. 'He is like a monkey,' had been said. 'He has a tail. An offensive odour comes from his person. He is an animal really . . . a monster from birth. He stoops double. He crawls on all fours . . .' Nothing had been too wild to say about the Prince of Orange. Now here he was, extremely deformed, with a face which could only be called ugly, but he walked on two legs; his stoop was not so obvious when he was seated; his robes of state concealed his hump.

And his manners were courteous and even modest.

'Well,' said the onlookers, 'he is not a monkey. He is at least a man.'

Moreover, he was the Prince of Orange and a Protestant. And a royal marriage meant feasting and revelry and it was time they had a royal marriage in the family.

So: Hurrah for the Prince of Orange!

When the Queen saw him her heart sank with dismay.

Oh, my God, she thought, my daughter to marry this . . . monster!

The King received him coldly, thinking it beneath his dignity to show cordiality to a minor Prince who should be extremely grateful to be allowed to marry the Princess Royal.

And he was thinking: if Anne takes one look at him and decides against him, back to Holland he shall go.

But Anne was smiling graciously, accepting him cheerfully – and of course regally.

One would have thought that he was the most handsome Prince on Earth.

Now there was no talk of anything but the royal marriage, which was to take place immediately.

It was true that some of Orange's supporters were disgruntled and expressed dismay at the lack of respect which was accorded their Prince, but Orange himself gave no sign that he noticed any lack of cordiality.

In fact his manners were the one thing about him which endeared him to the Queen.

'At least,' she said to Hervey, 'he acts like a Prince if he doesn't look like one.'

'There have been ugly Princes, Madam, in the history of the world, and ill-mannered ones.'

She laughed at him. 'You do well to remind me.'

He then began to divert her with the story of a Prince who was under a spell which made him appear as a gross monster and by the love of a good Princess cast off the spell and was turned into a beautiful Prince. This told in Hervey's inimitable way, so malicious and yet so amusing, made the Queen laugh.

'Who knows, Madam, the love of our Princess for a husband at all costs may turn our Dutch baboon into a Prince as charming as our own Prince of Wales, which might – or might not – bring delight to his bride! Perhaps in the circumstances it is better to leave him under the spell.'

'You are very wicked, Lord Hervey, and I wonder I listen to you. But, my God, I suffer for my daughter.'

The wedding did not take place on the appointed day because the Prince of Orange was taken suddenly ill with pneumonia.

He was not expected to live; and it was almost as though a breath of relief went through St James's.

'This will make the decision which Anne was not able to make for herself,' said the Queen.

'It is an act of God,' replied the King. 'I did not want to see our daughter married to that man. Why, when I think of our marriage, my dear . . . The excitement! The happiness! Do you remember?'

'I remember well.'

The King's eyes were glazed with sentiment. 'And when I came to you as Monsieur de Busch, you remember that? And you were a little taken with Monsieur de Busch were you not?'

'Greatly taken.'

'And delighted when he turned out to be George Augustus in disguise?'

She laughed. 'Yes, we were happy and ours was a good marriage. That is why we suffer so much to think of Anne's.'

'Oh, if only we could find a nice Protestant worthy Prince for our daughter!'

'Alas, there was only Orange.'

'And he will soon have the life squeezed out of him.' The King laughed at his little joke and the Queen laughed with him.

'But I am afraid,' said the Queen, 'that Anne will be very distressed to lose him, since we can find no one else to take his place.'

They were wrong. Anne showed no signs of distress. She continued to play the harpsichord and to sing with her friends from the opera as though nothing had happened.

The Prince of Orange was in a dangerous state for a week and then began to recover slowly; and it was still believed that he might not live.

The King shrugged his shoulders and said that he would not visit the Prince as if he did not recover he could not marry his daughter and therefore would be nothing to him. He didn't like the man, anyway. He was scarcely a man, being so ugly and deformed. He must look after himself and think himself lucky that he was allowed to stay at Somerset House for his illness.

The Queen suggested that members of the family should perhaps visit the invalid to cheer him up in his convalescence.

'No,' thundered the King. 'I forbid it.'

So through the long winter the Prince of Orange tried to throw off the effects of his illness, ignored by the royal family. His retinue of servants grumbled incessantly about this treatment and would have liked to have left for Holland, but the Prince was diplomatic. He knew that marriage with the daughter of the King of England was the best possible match he could make, and for this he was ready to sink his dignity.

He grew better and went to Kensington and later to Bath to complete his recovery. He was determined that the marriage should take place and he knew that while he remained in England it had a good chance of doing so.

With the coming of March he returned to London and sent a messenger to the King with the news that he was now well enough to marry, and expressed his wish that the long-delayed ceremony should now take place.

Anne, who when he had been ill had behaved as though he did not exist, now showed some interest in her marriage. Once more the King asked her if she was sure that she wanted to go on with it.

'You cannot find me another husband,' was her answer, 'so I have no choice but to take this one.'

'That or allow everything to remain as it was,' the Queen reminded her.

'I choose marriage,' said Anne coldly.

The marriage was fixed for 14 March and was to be performed in the little French chapel adjoining St James's. During the days preceding the 14th there was a great deal of activity not only in the Palace but throughout the court. Velvets, gold and silver tissue were used in the chapel drapings. The lustres and sconces were gilded; and never had the chapel looked so gay. The procession would have to pass from the Palace to the chapel so a covered gallery was set up and covered with orange-coloured cloth.

The Queen, relying absolutely on the good taste of Lord Hervey, commanded him to be in charge of operations and he arranged the decorations not only for the chapel but for the gallery which he determined should look magnificent when it was illuminated; and which he calculated would hold four thousand people.

An air of excitement was everywhere. The only disgruntled comment was that of the old Duchess of Marlborough who could see the gallery from the windows of Marlborough House and grumbled incessantly about it.

'I'm longing for the day when neighbour George takes his orange chest away,' she cried. 'It spoils my view.'

But nobody cared about the old Duchess's complaints; and that was her greatest complaint of all: nobody cared.

And all those who had tickets for a place in the gallery to see the procession pass laughed at her and said she was an old fool who didn't know that her day was over.

But Sarah could laugh as she stood at the windows of Marlborough House and looked out at the gaping crowds. But for a stroke of ill luck she might have shown them that she was still to be reckoned with. What if she had succeeded in marrying Lady Di to the Prince of Wales!

They made a big mistake if they thought they could jeer at Sarah Churchill while there was breath in her body.

It was seven o'clock at night when the ceremony began. Orange, with his attendants, was waiting in the Great Council Chamber for the moment when he must sally forth. The Prince was magnificently attired in gold and silver brocade and his peruke had been very cleverly contrived so that the curls cascaded over his back and hid the worst of his deformity. His attendants glittered beside him and, apart from his low stature, for he appeared to be bent double, he looked less grotesque than on any other occasion.

In the great drawing room Anne, with her ladies, was also waiting for the signal. She looked almost beautiful; there was about her an air of rapt resignation; her gown was of silver tissue and her necklace was made up of twenty-two huge diamonds; she glittered splendidly; and so did the ten girls who were her bridesmaids and whose duty it was to carry the six-yard-long train of silver tissue.

In the King's lesser drawing room George and Caroline waited with their children.

George gave way to one or two mild displays of bad temper. He was thinking that he didn't like the marriage; it was going to cost a great deal; and what had they got for it? Orange! A minor Prince who had nothing much to offer their daughter, and was there simply because he was the only Protestant Prince available.

'Stand up straight!' he shouted to the Duke of Cumberland. 'And don't look so sullen. I suppose you're wishing it was your wedding!'

'That would hardly be possible, Papa, at my age.'

'You don't like anyone to have anything but yourself. And

you could look a little more pleasant, Emily.' Emily was a name the family sometimes used for Amelia.

'It is not really such a pleasant occasion, is it, Papa?'

Oh dear, thought the Queen, her family were becoming difficult. Very soon Frederick would not be the only one who was quarrelling with his father.

'It was a wonderful necklace he gave her,' said William. 'Twenty-two diamonds. I should like to know the cost of them.'

'One would not have thought a poor Prince could give his bride such a gift,' put in Amelia.

'This is not the time to be talking about diamonds,' the King reproved them. 'You ought to be thinking of your sister.'

'I am so sorry for her,' put in young Caroline.

'Be silent,' commanded the King, 'or you'll upset your mother.'

He smiled at his wife. This was one of the occasions when he felt sentimental towards her.

He took her hand gently, for it was time to leave for the chapel.

The watchers in the gallery said that it was more like a funeral than a wedding procession. The Queen was so obviously deeply affected and this was not the emotion of a mother seeing her daughter married; it was clear that the Queen was the most anxious because of the bridegroom.

In his gold and silver brocade he certainly looked like a performing animal dressed up to resemble a man; but his manners were good and he seemed affable; and he was a Prince. Only the bride seemed unaffected. She made her responses in a clear, audible voice and she showed no sign of the repugnance she must have felt.

How can she! thought the Queen. My poor dear child!

But the ceremony was carried out without a hitch and in time the banquet, which was eaten in public, took place. The Princess sat beside the Prince and they were seen smiling and talking together, neither in the least disturbed.

But, thought the Queen, the worst is to come.

She wished that they had not brought this old French custom

to England whereby the married pair were put to bed by their courtiers – always an embarrassment to the couple but in circumstances like this a most trying ordeal.

There was a look of avid curiosity on the faces of all the people assembled in the bedchamber to see the arrival of the bride and groom who were in their separate apartments being undressed and prepared for bed by their servants.

Anne came in in her nightgown, looking shorn of her dignity and, to her mother, extremely pathetic. Caroline was thinking of her own mother whose second marriage had been so disastrous and she felt ready to weep for all Princesses who were given in marriage to men almost strangers to them.

But Anne looked as serene as ever as she was helped to the bed and sat in it awaiting the arrival of the bridegroom.

Then he came.

Oh, God, thought the Queen, it is as bad as I thought. For with his nightcap replacing his flowing periwig he was revealed in all his deformity. From the back he appeared to have no head, so stooped was he, and from the front no neck nor legs.

There was a deep silence as he was led to the bed and took his place beside the Princess.

He did indeed look inhuman.

The Queen believed she was going to faint. Amelia and Caroline were on either side of her and she caught a quick glimpse of the horror on their faces.

Through the room passed all those whose duty it was to pay their respects and wish the marriage fruitful.

And through all this Anne sat up in bed smiling calmly as though, thought the Queen, it were a normal man who was beside her and not this . . . monster.

The Queen had little sleep that night.

She kept waking and thinking of her daughter. My poor child, how is she surviving this terrible ordeal? Does she understand what marriage means?

She was silent while she was dressed and at breakfast she was joined by her daughters who could not refrain from talking of this terrible thing which had happened to their sister.

'I would rather die than marry such a monster,' declared Amelia.

'How she must have suffered!' sighed Caroline.

Lord Hervey joined the party; he was full of chat about what the people were saying.

The Queen sighed and said: 'My lord, I have been weeping bitterly. When I saw that monster come into the room to go to bed with my daughter I thought I should faint. You must be sorry for my poor daughter.'

'Madam,' answered Lord Hervey, 'the Princess Anne seemed satisfied with her lot and I have never been one to pity those who don't pity themselves.'

'My poor, poor Anne. It is all very well for you to talk, my lord. You married one of the most beautiful women at the court.'

Lord Hervey lifted his shoulders and was aware that the Princess Caroline was regarding him intently. Poor child, he thought. How she adores me . . . madly and hopelessly! What does she think will ever come of her passion for me? Still, it was pleasant to be so adored, particularly by one of the Princesses.

'Madam,' he said, 'in half a year all persons are alike. The figure of a body one is married to, like the prospect of the place one lives at, grows so familiar to one's eye that one looks at it mechanically without regarding either the beauties or deformities which strike a stranger.'

As usual Lord Hervey had the power to comfort the Queen.

Yet Caroline and her daughters continued to mourn the terrible fate which had befallen the Princess Anne; but Anne herself showed no sign of mourning; and when she and the Prince appeared together, although he took little notice of her, she was very eager to please him and Lord Hervey said he was sure that in the eyes of his wife the Prince of Orange was Adonis.

The end of a habit

Henrietta Howard was seeking a way out of an intolerable position. The King still visited her, but everything she said he disagreed with, and did not hesitate to tell her so in the most abusive terms. He hated his visits, but because he had been making them for years he could not stop them. He would sit at a table setting his watch before him, waiting for the time to pass.

She had suggested to the Queen that she retire but the Queen would not hear of it. Henrietta knew why. She was known as the King's mistress, and although the relationship between them was now platonic, while she held the post the King set up no one else. His affairs about the court were necessarily brief. He could only have one first mistress and while Henrietta held that post no one else could take it. And, thought Henrietta desperately, the Queen insists that I hold that post because she is afraid of who might take it from me, and there might be someone bold and ambitious who would seek to influence the King.

But it was an intolerable state of affairs.

She had now become Lady Suffolk, for the husband whom she loathed had inherited the title a few years previously and he himself had now died. This had brought home to Henrietta that for the first time in her life she was free. If she could leave court she could retire to her own house, be her own mistress, not be obliged to wait on the Queen or be ready to receive the King; she would not receive faint praise from her and abuse from His Majesty. Oh, what peace, what joy!

She had perhaps not been a clever woman; most in her position would have collected certain prizes. Although she had in the first instance sought honours at court when she had gone to Hanover, it had been, she supposed, to find a place where she could live in some degree of comfort, for she and her husband had been in desperate straits then. Well, she was not a calculating woman and George was not a generous lover; and consequently if she left court now she would not be a rich woman.

But there was one comfort. She had had the foresight to build a house for herself and it was true that George had helped her to do this. The house had been a great comfort to her in moments of humiliation and despair. She had called it Marble Hill; it was plain, white, and Augustan – in perfect taste. It had the most peaceful of outlooks, being set on a slight hill which sloped down to the river. This house had been her joy all during the years of servitude; she herself had planned the apartments with their high ceilings and had designed the frescoes on gold and sepia; she had often sat by the large windows and looked out on the river and dreamed of entertaining her friends there – friends such as Alexander Pope who had always been devoted to her and whose company she found so stimulating. The King had little time, of course, for the man he called rather slightingly 'little Mr Pope' who spent his time writing 'boetry' to which the King always referred with a laugh, as an occupation not for gentlemen nor to be taken seriously. How little he understood. And how astonished he would be if he knew how she longed for the society of such people which would provide her with relief from the boredom of the royal conversation which was so often about soldiering, his prowess in past battles, his regrets that there were no wars now in which he could excel, the number of buttons on a lackey's tunic, or the length of time it took to walk from the Palace to Great Paddock.

Lady Suffolk was so eager to escape that she decided to approach the Queen and beg her to allow her to leave.

The Queen had shut herself in her apartments and mourned for three days after the departure of the Princess Anne for Holland.

It was true that Caroline was anxious for her daughter, but Henrietta guessed that she was in fact taking advantage of her grief to enjoy the comforts of her bedchamber. All those who had served the Queen intimately knew that her health was not all that she pretended it to be; and that she was continually putting up a brave front because the King disliked illness of any sort.

Henrietta herself had grown quite deaf, and this was a further reason why she wished to go. The King was irritated when she did not hear or gave the wrong answers.

'Stupid fool!' he would mutter.

Well, thought Henrietta, the Queen must endure him, but I need not.

When she presented herself at the Queen's bedchamber next morning she asked leave to speak to her.

Caroline looked at her sharply, no doubt guessing what was in her mind, for it was something the Queen continually feared, and said that she would speak to her after breakfast if there was time; if not, after her walk with the King.

'I trust you are well, Lady Suffolk?' she said anxiously.

'I am well, Your Majesty. And Your Majesty . . .?'

The Queen looked fierce. 'I am *very* well thank you, Lady Suffolk.'

The Queen was dressed and went into breakfast where she was joined by the Princesses Amelia and Caroline.

She ordered chocolate and fruit and cream and prepared to enjoy them, while the Princesses talked of their sister. How was she liking Holland? How was she faring with her husband?

'Did you know, Mamma,' said Amelia, 'that she calls him Pepin?'

'It is a pet name I suppose,' put in Caroline.

'If one put a chain about his neck, people would think he was a monkey and monkeys are often kept as pets.'

'Emily, my dear, your tongue is too sharp,' said the Queen. 'I think it charming that she should call him Pepin. It shows a pleasant intimacy.'

Amelia shuddered and her mother looked at her reproach-fully.

'Nothing would have made me marry him,' said Amelia.

'I should have been horrified if I had to,' admitted Caroline, 'but if he was the only one available I suppose, like Anne, I should have taken him.'

'That is enough of this talk,' said the Queen. 'Oh, here is William. William, my dear, you look pale this morning.'

'I had to be bled twice, Mamma.'

'Oh, my God, why?'

'I fell from my horse. It was nothing much but they bled me . . . and then they bled me again.'

'My dear boy, shouldn't you be resting after the bleeding?'

'Yes, Mamma, but Papa would ask for me and you know how he hates any of us to be ill.'

The Queen was dismayed. But it was true of course. If William had not appeared the King would have asked where he was and then gone to see him; he would have been displeased and pointed out that illness was all part of the imagination and he did not expect a son of his to give in just because he had fallen from his horse.

'William, when Papa and I have gone for our walk, you must go back to bed. Stay there until this evening when you will come to my apartments for my *soirée*. But I will leave early and you must do the same.'

Henrietta was hovering, hoping for a chance to speak to the Queen before the King arrived, but Caroline was determined to prevent this.

She kept up the conversation with her family, and precisely at his usual time the King appeared ready for walking.

He was in rather an ill humour for Caroline was still drinking her chocolate. He pointed out that this was not the first time he had found her still at breakfast when he arrived; and she was drinking far too much chocolate and he was not surprised that she was getting so fat that she couldn't keep up with him and came panting behind him like a wheezy old sow.

Caroline left her chocolate and declared that she was ready. She was glad that he did not notice William's pallor and that neither Amelia nor Caroline was doing anything to irritate him.

But he did notice that one of the chairs had been moved and he began to talk about the incompetence of servants and how they could never leave well alone and that it was useless for him to expect law and order in his palaces unless he saw that it was enforced himself.

One of the guards had had dirty buttons on his tunic this morning.

'I reprimanded him,' he said. 'Most severely.'

'Poor guard! He will doubtless go and jump in the river,' said Amelia, who could never control her tongue.

'I do not think he will regard his offence as seriously as that,' said the King. 'I blame his superior officer. It is his duty to see that no man comes on parade in such a condition.'

The King caught sight of Henrietta and frowned. What was she doing waiting on the Queen at this hour? It was not her usual practice.

'Why is Lady Suffolk here?' he demanded of the Queen.

'She is waiting for a word with me.'

'She's become an old fool,' said the King, slightly lowering his voice, but in such a way that it was still audible throughout the apartment.

'I see Your Majesty is ready for our walk.'

'Ready.' He looked at his watch. 'I have been ready five minutes ago. In two minutes time we should be in the gardens.'

The Queen followed him to the door.

'I wonder you won't let me get rid of that deaf old woman,' he said.

Ever since Anne's marriage Frederick had been growing more and more incensed; and there were plenty to help add to his resentment.

Bolingbroke was urging him to rebel and George Bubb Dodington was helping the Prince with his many debts. But Frederick was growing a little weary of Dodington, and Lord Chesterfield was now seeking his favours. This was a cause for some alarm, for Chesterfield was more to be feared than Bubb Dodington.

Chesterfield was a witty writer and an extremely ambitious man. He was at the time quarrelling with Walpole and had been dismissed from his office of Lord Steward. The Queen disliked him because he had been a friend of Henrietta Howard's and had behaved as though the way to the King's favour lay through her instead of through the Queen; an attitude which Caroline always found hard to forgive.

Now he had irritated the King by marrying Petronilla Melusina von Schulemburg, the daughter of the Duchess of Kendal and George I. The late King had created her Countess of Walsingham in her own right, and as her mother had amassed a large fortune she was very rich, although forty years old. Chesterfield had married her purely for her money, and the couple made no attempt to set up house together but lived next door to each other, Petronilla with her mother and Chesterfield with his mistress, Lady Fanny Shirley.

Being out of favour with the King as well as with the Queen, Chesterfield turned his attention to the Prince of Wales.

All Frederick wanted, he insisted, was his rights. He wanted an income commensurate with his position; and he wanted a bride. He was no longer a youth. How dared his parents keep him in this ridiculous position!

The Queen raged against her son to her daughters. He was so easily led. He was a fool; he was a liar; she wished that he had never been born.

Amelia listened to this and thought: the quarrel grows fiercer. But one day Frederick is going to be King of England and Caroline and I will be dependent on his bounty; a pleasant state of affairs that will be, for how will he feel about his sisters who have to be supported although they had never been very good friends of his?

Amelia went to call on her brother. He looked at her with suspicion which she quickly tried to disperse.

'I want you to know that I'm on your side,' she said.

'What!' demanded Frederick.

'I think the King treats you badly. We all know how mean he is. He loathes spending money on us. He likes to spend it on show for himself, of course. Naturally you should have the same income at least that our father had when he was Prince of Wales.'

'Who sent you to talk to me?'

'No one. Do you think they would send *me*? They want to keep you away from court. *I* want you to come there and ... stand up for yourself. There would be plenty to support you.'

'The friends who support me don't support Walpole ... so should I be welcome?'

'You must be clever, Frederick. You must hide your rancour. You must get what you want through soft words not angry ones. Look at our mother. She always agrees with the King and gets him to do exactly what she wants.'

'I tell you this,' said Frederick. 'I will never come to my mother's drawing room because there is always one at her side whom I hate beyond all men.'

'Who?'

'Lord Fanny, of course.'

'Oh ... Lord Hervey.'

'I loathe that man. I don't trust him. He deceived me once. He would deceive me again. No, I'll never come to my mother's drawing room while she keeps him at her side like a tame pet.'

'He is her pet ... but scarcely tame. Don't talk to our sister Caroline in that way. She adores him. She's in love with him, you know.'

'The folly of women!'

'Yes, it is a little foolish. What hope is there for her, poor Caroline!'

'Oh, to the devil with Lord Fanny and the whole court. I have other things to do.'

'Visit Miss Vane?' asked Amelia slyly.

'Well, her drawing room is more amusing than my mother's.'

They parted – Amelia to go back to her apartments and Frederick to the house he had found for Miss Vane in Soho Square.

Lord Hervey met the Princess Amelia when she was returning from her brother. His large, languid eyes fluttered as he looked at her.

I believe, thought Amelia, that he sees everything. He is a spy watching all so that he can write down what he sees and gloat over it afterwards.

'How was His Highness?' he asked.

'My Lord Hervey is God,' said Amelia, 'all-seeing. And surely all-knowing. In which case is there any need to ask?'

'No need at all,' he replied. 'For His Highness is in his usual state of bucolic appreciation of his own dazzling personality.'

'Absolutely right, of course.'

'And grateful to his kind sister, I hope.'

'You hope nothing of the sort, my lord. For you know Fred would never be grateful to anyone . . . except perhaps Miss Vane who has given him such a fine sturdy proof of his manhood. Or is it *his* manhood?'

'I do not think Her Majesty would wish you to discuss such matters.'

'I hope she would be as tolerant of me as of you, my lord. I could hope for no greater leniency.'

Hervey liked Amelia least of all the Princesses and he knew that his dislike was returned.

'Her Majesty is gracious.'

'I am sure she will lose none of her graciousness towards you when I tell her that one of the reasons why Frederick refuses to come to her drawing rooms – and causes such gossip by staying away – is because you, my lord, are constantly in attendance on the Queen.'

'I am sure I have never done anything more deserving of Her Majesty's gratitude.'

Amelia could think of no retort to that, so swept past him.

Henrietta suddenly had her wish.

It happened in an unexpected way. Lord Chesterfield had asked the Queen if she would speak to the King on his behalf. It was such a small favour he asked that it slipped Caroline's memory.

Chesterfield, who had always believed that a man's mistress must carry more weight with him than his wife, being on very good terms with Henrietta, asked her if she had the opportunity to mention the matter to the King.

This Henrietta did and thought no more of it.

It was shortly after the favour had been granted when

Caroline, seeing Chesterfield at one of her drawing rooms, remembered his request and called him to her.

'I am sorry, my lord,' she said, 'that I failed to mention your little matter to His Majesty. Rest assured that I shall do so at the first opportunity.'

'Your Majesty is gracious,' replied Chesterfield, 'but there is now no need as Lady Suffolk has already put my request to the King.'

The King had come up as they were speaking and when he heard that remark his eyes bulged in the familiar fashion. He said nothing, but he was angry, for he hated it to be thought that his mistress interfered in any manner whatsoever with court matters.

He was cool to Chesterfield who hastily retired, and when Henrietta appeared, he ignored her.

He continued to ignore her and made unpleasant comments about her; and so uncomfortable was she that she begged leave to spend a little time in Bath for her health's sake.

When Henrietta returned from Bath she made up her mind that she would speak to the Queen without delay and begged a private audience.

'Your Majesty,' she cried, 'I have come to ask your leave to retire.'

'Retire!' cried Caroline. 'My dear Lady Suffolk, why should you wish to do that?'

'The King is irritated with me. He no longer wishes me to be here and, Madam, to tell the truth I no longer wish to stay!'

'This is nonsense. The King is not irritated with you. As for myself, have I ever shown that I am?'

'No, Your Majesty. If you had treated me in the same way as His Majesty has, I would never have dared appear in your presence again.'

'You are very heated, Lady Suffolk. You should be calm and think clearly about this. Have you asked yourself how different your life would be if you left court?'

'Yes, Madam; and it is what I wish. I have served Your Majesties to the best of my ability for twenty years and now it is as though I have committed some crime in His Majesty's eyes.'

'Oh, fie, Lady Suffolk. You commit a crime! This is non-sense.'

'The King could not behave so to me if I had not done something to displease him.'

'Have a little patience and the King will treat you as he does the other ladies. You know the King leaves domestic matters in my hands and if you will wait a while I can assure you that you will be treated no differently from the other ladies.'

'Madam, I do not see how I can be forgiven for an offence I have not committed.'

'Fie again, Lady Suffolk, you talk like someone from a romance. Now you are too warm and not very respectful. You will be sorry for this, I know. But I shall not give you permission to go, and if you leave it will be without my consent.'

'Madam, I *must* go.'

'Well, Lady Suffolk, will you refuse me this? Stay a week longer, and we will talk of it again when you are less . . . warm.'

Henrietta left the Queen in dismay. It was clear that Caroline was going to do everything in her power to make her stay.

When the week was over Henrietta told the Queen that she could not stay on as her position was far too uncomfortable.

'You are the best servant in the world,' said the Queen, 'and it will grieve me to lose you.'

'But Your Majesty has so many good servants,' replied Henrietta. 'And I know that Mrs Clayton will see that I am not missed.'

Henrietta vaguely noticed that at the mention of Charlotte Clayton's name a shadow passed across the Queen's face and she felt then, as she had felt so many times before, that there was some secret bond between them. But already her thoughts were far away at Marble Hill.

I shall go, she was thinking. Nothing on earth will prevent me now.

'Is your mind then made up?' asked the Queen.

'Yes, Your Majesty.'

Caroline was sad. She knew that this was more than the loss

of a good servant. She would miss Henrietta, but what right had any person to command another to a life they did not wish for?

He is getting old, she thought. He will have done with mistresses. It will not matter. What has she been to him? A habit, nothing more. There will be little flirtations. Let him enjoy them. There is nothing to fear.

'If you must go, my dear,' she said sadly, 'then my blessing goes with you.'

'I must, Your Majesty. And I thank you for your goodness.' She knelt and kissed the Queen's hand.

And that very day Henrietta Howard left court and went to stay at the house of her brother, Lord Hobart, in his house in St James's Square until she could make her preparations to leave for Marble Hill.

Court scandals

The whole court was talking about Carlton House in Pall Mall which the Prince of Wales had bought from Lord Chesterfield. The cost was six thousand pounds, which of course the Prince could not pay, so he borrowed the money from his Treasurer, giving his promise to repay it within a certain time.

The point was, of course, that when the time came he could not find the money so he had to borrow it from Dodington.

There was nothing unusual in this but for the fact that Frederick who, in the more refined company of Chesterfield had begun to tire of Dodington, boasted that he had wheedled the money out of Dodington who would never, very likely, see it again, as though in deceiving his onetime friend he had done something very clever.

'A very odious young gentleman,' commented Lord Hervey to Sir Robert Walpole when the latter came to the Palace to spend his usual session with the Queen.

To which Sir Robert replied, 'You see into what honest and just hands the care and government of this country is likely one day to be committed!'

Lord Hervey agreed with him and asked himself how he

could ever have looked upon that odious young gentleman as a friend.

His increased rancour towards the Prince made him think of Miss Vane and wonder how that *ménage* was faring. Thus when he occasionally saw the young woman he would look her way and she would look at him.

Her beauty had not diminished; in fact being the Prince's acknowledged mistress had given her a new poise which was very becoming.

Lord Hervey noticed that she no longer gave him cold looks, but was warm, even inviting; and the prospect of what this could lead to was irresistible.

He had heard that she often took a walk in St James's Park for her health's sake and he contrived to be walking there at the same time.

They saw each other, but as Anne had a companion with her, did not speak. But on the next day Anne sent her companion back to her house for a glove which she said she had left behind and this gave her the opportunity to speak to Lord Hervey.

'What a handsome woman!' he said as he approached her.

'What a handsome man!' she retorted.

'But I thought,' Anne remarked with a laugh, 'that they hated each other.'

'You know they could never do that.'

'It was jealousy,' said Anne.

Hervey agreed, adding: 'But we must waste no more time.'

'I shall be joined by my companion soon. She has gone back for my glove. She'll be here at any moment. She must not see us together. I no longer trust anyone and if it should get to Fred's ears . . .'

'There is a coffee house,' said Hervey, 'behind Buckingham House. Let us meet there tomorrow afternoon and make . . . plans.'

It was more than plans they made in the coffee house.

They were both intrigued by the adventure. Anne admitted that she had always preferred Lord Hervey to any of her other lovers. He did not explain that his desire to revenge himself on the Prince of Wales was part of her attraction for him; in any case she was a very personable young woman; and her years with the Prince of Wales, being courted, meeting his friends, men of far greater intellect than his, had had their effect on her.

But she was ready for adventure, too. She had never meant to settle down, which was more or less what she had done since the birth of little FitzFrederick, and living in an establishment set up for her by the Prince of Wales had meant that she could not easily take other lovers.

It was amusing to arrive at the coffee house adequately disguised and mount to one of the rooms which the coffee house keeper kept for occasions such as these, to lock the door and laugh together at the success of their adventure.

And when they had made love she would tell him all the latest exploits of the Prince of Wales – how he was growing more and more tired of Bubb Dodington; how Bolingbroke was constantly with him, advising him this way and that; and how Lord Chesterfield was beginning to take the place which Dodington once had held, only of course the Prince could never despise him as he had poor Bubb. And the amusing thing was that it was Bubb who had introduced him to Mr Lyttleton who was becoming such a close friend and who was working hand in glove with Lord Chesterfield.

'Poor Bubb!' said Anne. 'I don't think *he* is going to last much longer.'

Then she would try to remember everything the Prince had said and done because her lover found that all so interesting; and as she was more devoted to Lord Hervey than to any lover she had ever had she wanted to keep him; therefore it was pleasant to have not only her considerable charms to offer but information which amused him so.

Every time they left the coffee house they made arrangements to meet again.

As they walked in the gardens the King talked to the Queen about the war in Europe.

This was the war of the Polish Succession. Louis XV had a Polish wife and he wanted to secure the throne for her father, Stanislaus Leczinski; Russia, Austria, and the German Princes backed the claims of the Saxon Elector, Augustus III, and when Louis had put his father-in-law on the throne the Russians had driven him from it and made Augustus King. The French, therefore, always with new territorial claims in view, instead of declaring war on Russia which was too far away, turned on Austria as the best way of helping Stanislaus Leczinski. But the real aim of the French was to oust the Habsburgs and secure French supremacy in Europe.

The Emperor naturally looked to his two allies, Holland and England.

The Princess Anne's new husband went off to fight and the King was eager to do the same; and this was the theme of his conversation as he walked in the gardens with the Queen.

'We must tell the fat man (his name for Walpole) that I am determined to go to war.'

'Walpole is against England's going into the war.'

'Then he must change his mind. It is England's duty to be in this war. Why should I stand by and see other generals win the laurels which by rights belong to me !'

'We must persuade him,' said the Queen. 'We must make him see that it is our wish.'

'Send for him! Send for him as soon as we return to the Palace.'

'Shall we return now?'

The King hesitated and looked at his watch. Not even for the sake of the war would he interrupt a habit.

'Fifteen minutes more,' he said.

Caroline sighed inwardly. Her legs ached. They were becoming more and more swollen and the pain was increasing. She was beginning to dread these walks; she was terrified that she would betray the fact that they were too much for her.

'We shall soon have Anne back with us,' she said.

It was an unfortunate remark because it reminded the King that Anne's husband, the Prince of Orange, had gone to the wars and that was why she would be able to pay a visit to her parents so soon after her marriage.

'That baboon! *He* can go to war. He can win distinction in battle while I . . .'

'We will talk to the fat man,' said the Queen.

He glowered at her, venting on her the anger he felt towards a fate which denied him battle honours.

'And who are you to laugh at the fat man? We should call you the fat woman. The way you stuff away at your chocolate is the cause.'

She was silent, hoping no one had heard, for he had raised his voice and their attendants always kept a respectful though not too remote distance as they walked.

Why did she not retort : and you, you silly little man, have scarcely a thought in your head that doesn't spring from your own vanity.

Then she fell to wondering why it was that in spite of all his faults she was fond of him and could not imagine her life without him; and she knew that in spite of the way in which she constantly irritated him he admired and loved her more than any other person on Earth. If anyone else had attempted to criticize her he would have fallen into a passion of rage. She was his, entirely his, and to him only belonged the right to abuse.

She sighed and gave her mind up to the persuasion she would use with Walpole, for this was one of the rare occasions when she and the King were on one side against the Prime Minister.

Walpole faced them in the King's closet. He was as determined as they were. England was not going to war. Usually he could rely on the Queen, but this time she was against him.

Germans! thought Walpole. Both of them, and in an issue like this it comes out. But England is not going to be sacrificed for the sake of Germany for a hundred Kings and Queens.

'Your Majesties, the English people want peace. They have no heart for this fight.'

The King's eyes bulged with fury. 'We have our duty to think of.'

'I know Your Majesty will agree with me that our first duty is to the people of this country.'

'It is the people of this country I think of.'

'Then Your Majesty will rejoice in the prosperity we have brought to them and join with me in admitting that this prosperity is entirely due to peace.'

'And when the French are in command of Europe what peace then?'

'Your Majesty, countries rarely prosper from wars. This will be no easy conquest. And in the unlikely event of Louis's and Fleury's conquering Europe, France will be exhausted by the struggle and we so strong because of our exemption from it that we will be in command.'

'We have our duty,' said the King. 'The Queen and I cannot hold up our heads if we desert our allies.'

'Your Majesties will hold up your heads very proudly among the English if you keep them out of war.'

The King began one of his harangues, not very logical, not very lucid, thought Walpole. What a German he is! His heart is in Germany. And he's a fool – a conceited fool who wants to plunge this country into war so that he can parade as a brilliant soldier, so that he can come home and wear the crown of laurels. But it shall not be. This is my country as well as his and I am going to keep it at peace.

And the Queen? He was disappointed in the Queen. She was a German at heart too. She could not conceive that the German Empire should be at war and she not with it. She had once seemed so loyal to England; she had really loved her new country. But she was ill. Walpole noticed the physical deterioration. There were times when she could scarcely stand for fatigue and she continued to, smiling, pretending, because in this royal family there was something shameful about confessing to physical defects.

Mrs Clayton had some hold over her. Not that Mrs Clayton would ever dare threaten the Queen. It was as though she kept a secret and her reward for doing so was to be on very specially intimate terms.

Strange that she should support the King in this. Was it love of Germany, the effect of fatigue, or the knowledge that the King was so set on going to war that he would never be deterred from this desire and she had no intention of attempting something which she knew could only end in defeat?

Was she losing her physical hold on him? In spite of his infidelities he was still an uxorious husband. He thought

Caroline beautiful; he spent his allotted time with her; her hold on him, Walpole had always known, was partly physical. If that side of their relationship ceased, immediately the bond would slacken. George was that sort of man.

What an anxiety for the Queen!

He brought his mind back to George's torrent of words, but he was not going to be moved by them. He would lose his favour with them both rather than see England forced into a war which could do her no good and could be brought to no satisfactory conclusion. He thought Louis a fool to have put his father-in-law on the Polish throne for sentimental reasons, for that was what it amounted to. Cardinal Fleury, the real ruler of France, must have deplored that action, but at the same time was using the situation to make a fresh bid to satisfy French territorial claims.

Foolish Louis! He, Walpole, would see that George should not be as foolish.

George was glaring at him, eyes bulging, wig askew, cheeks purple; but Walpole lowered his eyes and said coolly: 'If England takes part in this fight for a Polish crown, the Crown of England will as surely come to be fought for as that of Poland. And now may I have Your Majesties' leave to retire?'

'You have!' shouted the King. 'And go ... and don't come back until you have some sense.'

In the coffee house behind Buckingham House, Hervey waited for Anne Vane. He was eager. He had rarely enjoyed an adventure so much; not only had he an extremely pretty and experienced mistress but he was at the same time cuckolding his great enemy the Prince of Wales; he was also dabbling in intrigue because in all affairs at court, however ineffectual he was as a man, the Prince was a figurehead and therefore of importance.

Walpole was delighted with the information he could bring to him; and it was amusing and stimulating for Lord Hervey to be the close friend and informant of the Prime Minister.

Anne came breathlessly and a little distraught.

'My dearest,' said Hervey, 'what is wrong?'

His heart leaped with excitement. Had the Prince discovered their liaison? He almost hoped he had because it would be so amusing.

'It's Fred.'

'Naturally.'

'He wants me to take a house in Wimbledon.'

'He has discovered . . .'

She laughed. 'Not he. There'd be real trouble if he had. He's worried about FitzFrederick's health and he thinks the air of London bad for him.'

'He's not tiring of you?'

'No. Never! But he really is fond of FitzFred. He's continually finding similarities in him to himself.'

'I hope they are not obvious to others . . . for poor little Fitz's sake.'

'No. He just imagines. But what about my going to Wimbledon?'

'We'll find a way.'

'I shall have to come up . . . at least once a week. You'll have to come to my house there. We'll have to give up this coffee house.'

Hervey was not displeased. This gave a new impetus to the adventure.

They embraced and afterwards talked of Frederick.

'He wants to go to the wars.'

'Like Papa to fight for Germany.'

'He fancies himself as a soldier.'

'They all do . . . these Germans. It's the military instinct. And Fred is angry because he is not allowed to go.'

'They're on at him all the time. Lyttleton and Chesterfield with Bolingbroke in the background. He ought to have this . . . He ought to have that. Poor Bubb is going to be dropped soon. I don't know how he'll take it. The Opposition is going to agitate for war . . . just to try to get Walpole out.'

'They won't. But it's amusing to see them try.'

'Let's talk about Wimbledon and what we shall do when I'm there.'

They arranged that Anne should come up to London one

day a week to her town house. There she would keep only one servant while she was in Wimbledon, and she would see that this servant was out when Hervey arranged to call.

This seemed very suitable, and after making their plans, Hervey went straight to see Walpole to tell him the effect the King's clamouring for war was having on the Prince of Wales and his enemies in the Opposition.

He found Walpole in a state of great irritation.

'I have just been given this paper,' he told Hervey. 'Look at it. In French! You can help me translate. It's written by Haltorf.'

'Ha!' cried Hervey. 'One guesses where Philip von Haltorf's sympathies lie!'

'Be fair to the man. He is a German, as well as minister in London for Hanoverian affairs.'

'And so determined to sacrifice England for Hanover.'

'As we are determined that England shall make no sacrifices for the Germans.'

Hervey scrutinized the paper.

'I see he is most disturbed by the growing power of France and the House of Bourbon. He recalls the wars of Queen Anne's reign. He does not understand why the country which went to war then so readily should be so chary of doing so now. If England does not interfere, France will dominate England.'

'I shall answer each paragraph separately.'

'The King will be very peevish.'

'My lord, England shall not go to war to please a peevish boy.'

'Not when Sir Robert Walpole – and in his humble way Lord Hervey – are there to prevent it.'

Walpole grasped his hand warmly and Hervey responded with real affection.

The King continued to fume and the Queen, to Walpole's disappointment, remained sturdily beside her husband in this matter. 'The first time I have known her judgement to fail,' Walpole commented to Hervey. George's temper grew worse and everyone who came near him suffered for it, the Queen most of all in spite of the fact that she supported him in his desire.

Walpole remained firm. England was not going to war under his leadership; and even the King had to admit that if the matter were put to the country, the people would be behind Walpole.

In spite of Hervey's agreeing with Walpole, the Queen liked him none the less. In fact he was growing more and more friendly with her; and this meant that he was on more intimate terms with the King.

Caroline had asked the King to give him an extra thousand pounds a year.

'The creature is worth it,' she said. 'He is so diverting.'

The King grunted that people at the court should serve their Majesties for the honour of it, but he agreed that Hervey should have the money.

As a result Hervey grew bolder and bolder. He would joke with the Queen in the frankest way; and although she often reproved him for his lack of respect, she always did so jokingly and did not wish to change his manner towards her.

Whenever she rode out he must be beside her chaise.

'Divert my attention, I pray you,' she would say, 'from these tiresome people who so like to hunt little animals to the death.'

And he would remember the latest scandal and tell it so maliciously that she would indeed be diverted and find the hunt a pleasure instead of a bore.

She would call him 'child' now and then; and refer to him as her 'pupil' and her 'charge'. All this in the utmost affection; and she would even allow him to laugh at the Prince of Wales. Although she pretended to be shocked and would reprove him with mock sternness, he knew that she liked this conversation better than that about anyone else.

So during those months as the antagonism between the Prince of Wales and his parents grew stronger, so did the Queen's affection for Lord Hervey.

Once when Charlotte Clayton came in and found the Queen and Lord Hervey deep in bantering conversation, Caroline said : 'If I were not so old I should be talked of for this creature.'

Charlotte Clayton smiled benignly. Hervey had made sure that he kept in her good graces for Walpole had told him that it was his belief that Mrs Clayton had some hold over the Queen and therefore carried influence with her.

The Queen was delighted because her daughter Anne was coming to England for a visit. This was a great pleasure, for Caroline had only discovered how sadly she would miss her daughter when she had left; and often she would wake up in the night thinking of Anne with that grotesque creature beside her.

And now Anne was coming home because the Prince of Orange was away from Holland fighting.

When the King heard, he was half pleased, half angry. Of all his children, strangely enough he preferred Anne, although that did not mean he had a great affection for her because he cared little for any of his children. But he was sentimental enough to imagine he was pleased to have her home again. Then he began raging because Orange was fighting and he wasn't.

'That baboon!' he said. 'A soldier.' He glanced in a mirror. Did he see himself as he really was? wondered Caroline. Or did some tall and handsome hero look back at him from the glass? 'And here am I fiddle-faddling at this court when I should be there.' Then another thought struck him. 'I suppose Orange will pay for her journey.'

The Queen soothed him as she so well knew how to do. 'I am sure Anne will be so pleased that you are not at the wars,' she said. 'Otherwise she would miss the pleasure of seeing you.'

He grunted, believing the Queen was right in that.

But he continued to grumble about the *'gros homme'* – his name for Walpole, who had been so high-handed over this matter and was having his way, too, in keeping England out of the war.

'A king's not a king in this place,' said George, kicking at a stool. 'Now at Hanover . . .'

'Ah, yes!' sighed the Queen.

She too was thinking of the *'gros homme'*. He had opposed her over this and she was beginning to wonder whether he did not guide her as she guided the King. But it was the first real difference of opinion they had had; and she must remember that she was after all a German and that it was natural to feel this pull towards one's own roots. It was the same with Walpole. He was English; to him Hanover was a remote Electorate and he was determined to see that it was never allowed to be an encumbrance to England.

The King left her, and she was glad that he had gone before Walpole called for his usual session with her.

As she received him in her closet, she thought he looked less robust than usual; and when a man with his port-wine complexion looked a little pale he somehow contrived to look more ill than a man whose pallor was constant.

This disagreement has upset him, thought the Queen.

Walpole thought the Queen looked extremely fatigued and he was overcome with a sudden fear. Was she concealing an illness? It suddenly struck him that a knowledge of some disability might be the reason for Charlotte Clayton's hold on her.

He bowed and looked at her almost tenderly. But he could not resist saying what he had come to say.

'I have just heard, Madam,' he said, 'that fifty thousand were slain this year in Europe. And not one of them an Englishman!'

'It is sad that fifty thousand have been slain,' said the Queen. 'But a matter of rejoicing for this country that not one of them is an Englishman. It brings satisfaction to know they owe their safety to those under whose care and protection they are, and to be able to say that while the rest of Europe has suffered England remains in its full and unimpaired vigour.'

'You think only of England, Sir Robert.'

'Ah, Madam, whatever motives of partiality sway me, ought they not naturally with double weight to bias you who have so much more at stake?'

She smiled at him affectionately.

'I see, Madam,' he said, 'that you are inclined to agree with me, and that gives me great pleasure.'

Walpole commented to Lord Hervey afterwards that although the Queen's good sense told her he was right, she was inclined to cling to her own opinions.

Walpole shrugged his shoulders. 'And if she cannot convince herself of what in her heart she knows to be right, what chance have I of doing so?'

But as Hervey pointed out it was the government that decided the policy of the country, not the monarch. Absolute monarchy had gone out with the Stuarts.

Anne arrived surprisingly ebullient.

She imparted the news to her mother with the greatest satisfaction. 'I am to have a child, Mother.'

'My dearest daughter!' Caroline embraced her, and checked her own misgivings. What if Anne should give birth to a monster resembling its father!

'I hope for a son, naturally,' said Anne.

'Your husband must be delighted.'

'It is no more than Pepin expects.'

Pepin! she spoke his name affectionately. How could she be so satisfied with her fate!

But there was no doubt that she was delighted to be back in England and she expressed no anxiety because Pepin was at the wars.

It seemed, thought Caroline, that all Anne cared about was her position; she had no reason to be very proud of it, but at least she had a husband who was a Prince and she was pregnant and might well give birth to a Prince. What an ambitious mother she would make!

Her new status clearly delighted her as much as it infuriated Frederick. Lord Hervey discovered how angry he was through Anne Vane who said that he had become really bitter since his sister Anne had returned. Frederick would not be content to remain unmarried and deprived of his rightful allowance much longer. There was going to be trouble with Frederick.

Amelia told Anne to her face that she could not understand how she could possibly become pregnant by such a creature as the Prince of Orange.

'In the usual way,' retorted Anne tartly. 'I often think of you, my poor sister, and what will become of you if ever Frederick comes to the throne.'

Caroline tried to make peace between the sisters, but Anne snubbed her and said she was even more sorry for her than she was for Amelia.

In spite of differences with her sisters Anne was enjoying

her visit. She spent a great deal of time with her mother and they talked of the problems of being married to a ruler of a state; and Caroline, in any case, was delighted to have her daughter with her.

The King was pleased too. He made Anne walk with him, and he grew very sentimental about her and told her about the days when she had been a baby in Hanover.

'Before we came to this place,' he said darkly.

'In the days when you were less important than you are now, Papa.' Anne had a sharp tongue and had no intention of sparing anyone except Pepin.

'Less important! Why I tell you this: In Hanover a ruler is a ruler. Here a King does what a fat man tells him to.'

'The world takes more account of a king than an elector, though,' Anne replied.

And he would have grown peevish if he had not schooled himself to believe he was a sentimental parent.

When they had parted Anne met Lord Hervey on his way to her mother's apartment.

'You are in more constant attendance on my mother than the King,' she commented.

'It is Her Majesty's wish that I divert her.'

'As I am sure you do. Poor Mamma! I am glad that she has a little diversion. The company of some people must be very oppressive. I am glad that Lady Suffolk has been dismissed.'

'Some of us, who are devoted to the Queen, fear that another might take her place who might be more troublesome and more powerful.'

'Oh, I wish with all my heart that he would find someone else, then Mamma would be a little relieved of seeing him constantly in her rooms.'

Lord Hervey made no comment, but he thought that the Princess Anne was as outspoken as he was, the difference being, of course, that he was only frank where he knew how his frankness would be received.

The King was taking a new interest in his young daughters, Mary and Louisa. Mary was now ten and Louisa nine.

'An interesting age,' said the King; and he had begun to

make a practice of visiting their nursery. The strange thing was that he contrived to do this when the children were not there, and thus he was ensured a private *tête-à-tête* with their governess.

Lady Deloraine was a very pretty and very frivolous widow, whose husband Henry Scott, Earl of Deloraine, had died a few years before. She was coquettish, indiscreet, and rather silly; but her extremely feminine charms had attracted the King when, having lost Lady Suffolk, he thought it was necessary to his prestige as a man to look round and find a new mistress.

Lady Deloraine had opened her eyes very wide as he entered the nurseries, had swept a deep curtsy and been very respectful, although at the same time implying by the fluttering of her eye-lashes and the little giggle with which she punctuated her speech every now and then that she was aware of the King's motive.

George lapsed into English when he addressed her, which was a language he used rarely now. If people did not understand French or German, he often said, they must not expect to understand him. It was all part of the growing dislike of the country of which he was king.

'Vell,' he said, 'you are von pretty voman.'

'Your Majesty is gracious.'

He took her ear and pinched it very gently, at which she sprang back as though in dismay.

'And vere are your charges?'

'They are walking, Your Majesty, in the gardens. If you would wish me to have them sent for . . .'

'No . . . no . . . You shall tell me about them. You are the governess. Ve vill sit down and you vill tell.'

So they sat side by side and the King put his arm about her. She had a good body, he thought; not too thin. He did not like them thin. He liked a good ample figure like his dear wife's.

'I fear I am not very learned, Your Majesty.'

'Oh, for shame and you a governess!'

She pretended to look downcast and he patted her hand. 'I have no respect for all this learning. Boets! Vat are they? Scribble scribble. It is all very vell for people like little Mr Pope. He has no other things to do. But I always felt learning vas something below me. Not for a man . . . like going to var or . . . making love.'

Lady Deloraine squealed with horror.

The King laughed and looked at his watch.

'Come,' he said, 've have the time.'

So he rose and gave her his hand; and squealing with pretended horror and assuring His Majesty that she was a very virtuous woman, she allowed herself to be led into one of the bedchambers.

The Queen was very sad when her daughter departed. Lord Hervey called to find her in the long drawing room with her daughter Caroline.

'What, Madam,' he said, 'drowning your sorrows in chocolate! Ah well, parting is such *sweet* sorrow, the poet tells us and you, having some respect for boets . . . er . . . poets . . . believe the truth of this.'

The Queen's face brightened at the sight of her favourite.

'Come here, you wicked infant,' she said, 'and make me laugh, because I am truly sad to think of my dear Anne going back to that creature of hers.'

'Oh, Mamma, he is her husband.'

Lord Hervey turned his eye to the Princess Caroline and basked for a few seconds in her adoration.

'The Princess Caroline has the best heart in the world,' he said.

'I think we are all sorry for poor Anne.'

'Which happily is more than she is for herself. The Princess Anne pities her sisters.'

'How I wish the dear child were with me. It is so sad when one's daughters are taken from one. I am glad I have dear Caroline.'

Caroline took her mother's hand and kissed it. She looked forward to these meetings for three as much as the other two. She wanted to be the constant companion of the Queen and her adored Hervey; and since she knew that he being married and she a Princess, nothing could come of her devotion, she believed it was preferable that her mother share their interviews.

Lord Hervey declined the chocolate they offered him.

'It would be too rich for my digestion, Your Majesty.'

'Are you still living on nothing?'

'I cling to my diet. It is the only way of keeping me on my feet.'

'Oh, then you certainly must. What should we do if you failed to visit us.'

'For Your Majesty's sake I would live on husks for the rest of my life.'

'Does he not say charming things, Caroline?' asked the Queen.

'I think Lord Hervey knows,' said the Princess gravely, 'that he is the most charming man in the world.'

'The best heart in the world. The most charming man in the world. What a *worldly* pair you are! And how much travelled to be able to make such comparisons. I would content myself by saying of the court . . . of England . . . but for you it must be the world.'

This pleasant raillery was interrupted by the arrival of the King.

He scowled to see the chocolate, but he was clearly too disturbed to give it the attention he would otherwise have done.

'Anne is back in England,' he said.

The Queen had grown pale and risen from her chair; the Princess Caroline gave a startled exclamation and Hervey, head bowed, was alert.

'Yes,' said the King, speaking rapidly in French. 'She has come back. I have had notice of this.'

'But why . . .?' asked the Queen.

'She had taken off and the sea was rough, so she says, and she feared for her life and that of the child, so she ordered the captain to return to England. She is at Harwich now . . . abed. And says she cannot stir for fear of a miscarriage.'

'We must have her brought here . . . or we must go to her,' began the Queen; but the King interrupted angrily : 'She talked of lying-in in England. It is what she wishes. Orange wishes her to go to Holland, of course.'

'It is only natural that he should wish the Prince of Orange to be born in Orange, Your Majesty,' said Hervey.

The King looked at Hervey and grunted. Then he nodded. 'Natural,' he said. 'Natural, of course. She'll have to go back.'

'But if she is ill . . .' began the Queen; the King silenced her with a scowl.

'She can't lie in here,' said the King. 'It wouldn't be right and . . . think of the expense! We have had enough with her marriage. She shall rest awhile and then . . . back to Holland for the birth of the baby.'

A great deal of correspondence was going on between Harwich and London.

The Princess Anne remained in her bed at Harwich and wrote to her parents that she must stay in England. She must lie in there. It was imperative for her own safety and that of her child.

The Queen was distraught and the King growing more and more angry every day; but the Princess of Orange was using all her powers of persuasion to remain while the Prince of Orange, realizing that as a matter of honour his son should not be born in England, insisted that his wife return to Calais where he would meet her and take good care that she suffered no ill effects from the journey.

'She must go without delay,' said the King.

The Queen wanted to remonstrate with him but dared not. Lady Deloraine was his mistress and she was not a very important woman, but Walpole had pointed out that although she was a silly, empty-headed creature, fools were often very easy to handle by scheming men, and the fact that the King had now a more or less settled mistress would make them watchful. The Queen must not lose her hold on the King.

Therefore what could the Queen do but side with her husband, particularly as she knew from reports that Anne's malady was largely due to a desire to stay in England, and not go back to Holland.

Poor Anne! She had her husband and her title; and soon she would have her child; that was all she needed. She did not want to have to go to a strange land and live with a monster when there were her own dear family in England. Not that Anne had ever held her family very dear. But, reasoned the Queen, familiarity was always dear, particularly when it was about to be lost.

If only Anne could have stayed for the confinement she would have been happy.

'She must go,' thundered the King. 'Her place is with her husband.'

The people took sides and of course were on Anne's. She wanted to stay in England naturally enough, said the English. She did not want to go back to that deformed husband of hers. Well, who could blame her?

The lampoonists had a new theme.

'Got dam the boets,' said George, and took action. The Princess Anne was to return to Holland, but she was not to come to London. He was not going to have the people lining the streets and cheering her. She was to take the nearest route from Harwich to Dover.

A letter came back from the Princess with the plaintive comments that her advisers had told her that the roads between Harwich and Dover were impassable by coach at this time of the year and that if she went to Dover the only route would be by way of London.

The King was furious, but was assured by *his* advisers that what the Princess said was true and if she was to go to Dover she must come by way of London.

'Well then,' said the King, 'she may come and go over the bridge, but she shall not lie in in St James's, nor shall she stay in London, but just pass through.'

'Does Your Majesty mean,' asked the Queen, 'that none of us are to *see* her?'

'It is what I mean, Madam,' he said, growing irascible.

'It seems . . . hard . . .'

'You are criticizing my conduct of this affair?'

'Of course not.'

'I am glad of that,' he cried, 'for I would have you know, Madam, that you would do better to stuff your chocolate and grow as fat as a pig . . . though I own this is bad for you . . . than interfere with what I decide shall be done.'

His face purple he strode from the apartment and the Queen, her face tinged with pink, her downcast eyes filled with tears, was silent.

And so the Princess of Orange passed over London Bridge and through London without seeing any of her family, and as the journey had been kept a secret there was none to cheer her as she passed along. At Dover she embarked in the vessel which was waiting to carry her to Calais; and there Pepin was waiting for her, looking even more hideous than she remembered him because of the sourness of his expression.

They made a somewhat sullen journey through Flanders to Holland.

In his lodgings in St James's Lord Hervey was waiting for the arrival of his mistress.

He had not yet tired of her, for she was amusing and of course her greatest charm in his eyes was her relationship to the Prince of Wales. He needed such a fillip to rouse his desire for a woman.

For I do believe, he said, studying his reflection in the mirror in his bedchamber, I have a greater preference for members of my own sex. Dear Stephen!

They were still the best of friends, but since his deeper friendship with the Queen, his platonic but extremely enjoyable flirtation with the Princess Caroline, and his intrigue with Anne Vane, he had little time for further outlets. Stephen must understand this.

Oh dear, he thought, it is a very feminine entourage at the moment!

He was looking pale. He pulled down his lids and looked at his eyes. Not as clear as they might be! Was he taking too much rich food? His figure was as elegant as ever. He would hate to be like *le gros homme*. What a figure! And the man's legs were very swollen. Weighed down with all that weight doubtless. But he had his love affairs. The one with the Skerrett woman was quite notorious.

Well, each to his taste, and now my little Vane you are overdue and I long to hear the latest exploits of His Royal Highness.

He had taken to receiving her here in his own apartments because he did not care for her house when all the servants were away – and of course they must be away for her to receive him there.

A man needed a little refreshment after the exertions of lovemaking. A dish of tea, a little fruit, neither very harmful for the figure, and so reviving!—

He smiled to think of Anne opening the door of her house for him and ushering them in. What risks they ran – at least she did. If this liaison were discovered he would merely be laughed at and perhaps admired in some quarters. He could not be more disliked by the Prince of Wales than he was at present. But she, poor girl, would be ruined. If Frederick discarded her what could she hope for? Some other man perhaps to set her up? But no one, of course, could give her the standing which the Prince of Wales could. Yes, she faced ruin for the sake of receiving him. A pleasant thought, for it was gratifying to have such devoted friends.

His wife, Molly, was away on the Continent with some friends and she would be there for some months. Well, if she knew that he were entertaining the little Vane she would only shrug her shoulders and laugh. She had never expected fidelity from him. She was faithful, but not out of love for her husband; simply because love-making – marital or extra-marital – had no charm for her.

He couldn't have made a more successful marriage.

And here was his mistress, be-cloaked and be-hatted, to hide herself so that no one would see the Prince's mistress entering the lodgings of that scandalous fellow, Lord Hervey.

'My dear Anne!'

'My dear lord, I thought I should never get here.'

'Don't tell me His Royal Highness made difficulties?'

'He stayed longer than I believed he would, and so delayed me.'

'He is coming back tonight?'

'No. I have the evening free.'

'Then let us make the most of the time at our disposal. I have had a little supper prepared before I dismissed my servants.'

'Supper for two?' she asked. 'I hope so, for although you eat like a bird, I eat like an ox.'

'I prefer the lion and the lamb because they lie down together.'

Anne laughed and said she hoped he didn't say such things to the Queen . . . or the Princess Caroline.

'You would be surprised if you heard what I said to them.'

'Everyone is surprised.'

They sat down at the table and he told her that his wife would not be back for several months and as there was no danger of her coming here he did not see why they should not make his lodgings their meeting place.

'It's comfortable . . . as far as I can see,' she said.

'Well, let us sup.'

'I'm ready.'

Over supper they talked of the latest development in the estrangement between the Prince and Bubb Dodington.

'Of course, when he bought Carlton House with money *borrowed* from Bubb he told his dear friend that he wanted it because it was next to his house in Pall Mall and he gave Bubb a key to the door in the wall which separated their gardens. "Call any time you like, dear Bubb. Don't stand on ceremony in the house you have bought!" For bought it he had. Bubb will never see his money, you can be sure. In fact Fred boasts of it and laughs every time he comes into the house. But those days are over. No more free and easy for Mr Bubb! Do you know what Fred has done?'

'I can't wait to hear.'

'He's had the door bricked up. Not secretly. He had more workmen than he needed hammering away there. He didn't want anyone to have any doubt what it was all about. Poor Mrs Behan . . . really Mrs Bubb, you know.'

'Interesting situation,' commented Hervey. 'The wife parading as the mistress. Now the other way round . . .'

'Oh, there's some other woman in it who'd get money from him if she knew he was married to someone else.'

'So he is a romantic after all, our poor Bubb. And two women love him!'

'Love his money you mean.'

'Well, they are only following the royal example. But the Prince is not even faithful to poor Bubb's money!'

'Bubb has Mrs B. She'll look after him. He'll never face court after this. I think she'll make him retire to the country.'

'The best place for him. There is a great deal to be said for the country.'

'There are some who think that'll soon be my lot.'

'What's this?' There was real alarm in Hervey's voice.

'Several of my friends are pointing out to me that Fred is seen very often in the company of Lady Archibald Hamilton.'

'That woman! She's all of five-and-thirty. She's been married for years! Imagine it! Years of lying beside a man old enough to be her father!'

'But not too old to give her ten children!'

'And you are afraid of a mother of ten – five-and-thirty years old at that!'

'It's not I who am afraid. It's my friends who are afraid for me.'

'Hamilton,' mused Hervey. 'He's so quiet I can hardly remember what he looks like. He's a Lord of the Admiralty, I believe.'

'That's so. Lord Archibald Hamilton, Scottish and complacent.'

'Would he be complaisant too?'

'No one ever seems to have seen him put out.'

'A born cuckold. Beware. Some men choose their mistresses for their husbands.'

'Not my Fred. He'd never be wise enough.'

So they chatted over the meal, and when they had finished, retired to the bedroom.

They made love and as they lay talking Anne suddenly cried out in pain.

Hervey sat up in alarm. 'What ails you?'

'The colic,' she said. 'I've been having it more frequently lately. I'll be all right in a moment.'

'Lie still,' he said, and she lay back and closed her eyes.

She looked very ill and was suddenly seized with convulsions. Hervey remembered what she had told him of these fits to which she was subject, but he had never seen her in one before. She had once said that a physician had told her that she could die during one of her fits.

'Anne,' cried Hervey, 'for God's sake . . .tell me what I can get you?'

She did not answer and he stood by the bed in dismay, looking down at her writhing body.

She is going to die, he thought. Here in my bed she is going to die. What can I do? The Prince's mistress found dead in my bed! This will be the end of everything. Even the Queen and the Princess Caroline could not get me out of this trouble.

'Anne!' he cried frantically. 'Anne.'

But she did not hear him. Fortunately a hypochondriac such as he was had plenty of pills and cordials to hand; and as the collecting of medicine was a hobby of his, and the discussion of varied diseases one he found extremely fascinating, he was not at so much of a loss as most men would have been in the circumstances.

He hurried to his medicine chest and brought out gold powder which he forced down her throat. But she continued in convulsions. He then took a bottle of cordial and gave her some of that, without effect.

She was moaning softly and he was growing more and more terrified every moment.

He went back to his medicine. What can save her? he asked himself frantically. And was it wise after having given her the gold powder and the cordials, to give her more?

'Tell me what I can do?' he cried. 'Tell me what you want?'

Her writhing ceased and she was suddenly very still.

In terror he took her wrist. Her pulse was feeble but he could feel it. Thank God she was still alive!

He called her name again and again, but she was in a deep faint.

What could he do? He daren't call a doctor who might recognize her. It was so widely known that she was the Prince's mistress. The story would be all over the town by morning.

He bent over her. 'Anne,' he cried urgently. 'You must rouse yourself. I must get you out of here.'

But still she did not answer.

He sat on the bed watching her. He saw the pleasant position he had made for himself at court lost for ever. What would the Queen say when she heard? It was not that she would be shocked, but how could she keep close to her a man who had been involved in such a scandal?

'Anne!' His voice rose on a note of shrill joy, for she had opened her eyes. 'Oh, Anne . . . thank God you're alive.'

'I . . . feel so weak,' she said.

'I know . . . I know . . . but we must get you out of here.'

'Get a hot napkin and put it on my stomach. I'm shivering.'

It was true. He could hear her teeth chattering.

He hurried away and found napkins which he warmed; he brought them to her but she started to twitch again and he called out in his agony of fear.

'What do you need?' he cried. 'What can I get?'

'Have you gold powder?'

He brought it and she swallowed it.

'That's . . . a little better,' she said.

'You must get up. You must get dressed. We must somehow get you back to your house.'

But she shook her head and closed her eyes.

'Come, Anne,' he said. 'You must try to rouse yourself. You must not be found here. It will be the end of you . . . the end of us both . . . if you are.'

But she did not seem to take in what he said.

He managed to lift her out of the bed; he sat her in a chair and began to dress her. She was limp and unable to help him, but after a great deal of fumbling he had her dressed. She swayed as he made her stand, but he was feeling better now. He managed to get her out of the house and half carry her some little distance away.

Good luck was with him, for he found a sedan and setting her in it paid the chairmen handsomely to take her back to her house.

'The lady has been taken ill,' he said.

The chairmen replied that they would see that she arrived safely.

Hervey went back to his bedroom, threw himself on the bed, and discovered that he himself was on the verge of collapse.

The King's birthday, 10 November, must be celebrated at St James's and a round of festivities began.

Caroline, whose health had been growing steadily worse over the last months, felt the strain badly, yet she dared not complain to the King.

Hervey was constantly at her side. He had quickly recovered from the shock of what had happened in his apartments when he saw Anne Vane going about her everyday concerns as though nothing had happened. They never spoke to each other publicly, keeping up the pretence that they were enemies, all of which added to the piquancy of their affair. She came again to his lodgings and told him that she had had such attacks before – colics, she called them. She recovered, and after a day's rest was perfectly well.

From then on the fear that she might die in his bed was an added fillip to his feelings for her and they went on meeting as frequently as ever.

In spite of his cynical attitude to the world, Hervey had a certain feeling for the Queen; and when he saw her looking so ill he ventured to remonstrate with her while he asked himself whether he was really concerned for her health or the effect her illness or death might have on his fortunes. His great virtue, he assured himself, was his determination to be frank with himself.

'These birthday celebrations fatigue you greatly, Madam,' he told her.

'They will soon be over.'

'Should you not explain to His Majesty that you need to rest?'

'My lord, what are you thinking of? You know His Majesty's attitude to illness. He hates it, and there are some things which he hates so much that the only way he can tolerate them is by pretending they don't exist.'

'That, Madam, is a state of mind which cannot exist permanently.'

'You love your illnesses, my lord.'

'I respect them. That is why I am constantly at your side instead of languishing in my bed.'

'I have been twice blooded recently.'

'All the more reason why you should rest, Madam.'

'Pray don't scold. I have known the King when he has been ill, get up from his bed, dress for a levée, conduct it, and when it is over return to bed, hiding from all but his most intimate servants the fact that he was ill.'

'It is not Your Majesty's custom to follow His Majesty's follies.'

'Hush, you young idiot.'

'A most devoted, and at this moment, anxious idiot, Madam.'

'Oh, come, come. You indulge me!'

'Would I might do that.'

'You please me enough with your tongue, my lord.'

'Then I will make further use of my privilege and say that no member of your family, Madam, will ever admit to being ill ... nor acknowledge illness in others.'

'If that is all our subjects will have to complain of us we shall be fortunate.'

'I complain now, Madam, most bitterly.'

'But you, my child, love illness, you pamper it, you study it, you revel in it. We merely spurn it and drive it away.'

'We shall see, Madam, whose method is wiser.'

'I hope not, my lord. I hope not for a long time.'

Sir Robert Walpole, himself suffering from the flying gout, was loath to attend any of the birthday celebrations; he was longing for the quiet of Norfolk where Maria and their daughter would be with him.

Twice a year he holidayed there and he was beginning to think that those two holidays were the best times of his year. Why did he go on fighting a cruel Opposition, a foolish King, and a Queen whom he respected but of late had seemed to be against him?

He allotted himself twenty days in November – twenty days of peace with Maria in his cherished Houghton among his treasures. All his treasures, he told himself with a rare sentimentality.

He looked back on a hard time. It had been particularly difficult keeping England out of war and the elections had not gone very well for him. He was still in power but with a reduced majority.

He must, he supposed, put in an appearance at the King's celebrations otherwise there would be complaints against *le gros homme*. One had to placate the little man all the time.

He dressed with reluctance and presented himself at the Queen's drawing room.

As he made his way to her side he was shocked by her appearance.

She's a sick woman, he thought. Why does she not admit it? Doesn't little George *see*? Of course not! When did he ever see what he didn't want to?

'Madam,' he said, as he kissed her hand, 'I have come to pay my respects and to tell you I shall shortly be leaving for Houghton.'

'My poor Sir Robert, you are in need of a holiday.'

She swayed a little.

'Madam . . . you are not well.'

'I was blooded twice recently. It takes a little time to recover.'

She is going to faint, he thought.

He caught Lord Hervey's eye and he knew that Hervey understood. 'Your Majesty should be resting,' said Walpole. 'Perhaps Lord Hervey would ask His Majesty if he would retire so that the Queen can go to her bed and rest a while.'

The Queen was about to protest, but Hervey did not wait. He went to the King and surprisingly George must, too, have been aware of his wife's wan looks for he made no protests. For once ignoring sacred time he retired to his apartments, leaving the Queen free to do the same.

In the Queen's closet, Sir Robert paced up and down, talking gravely.

'Madam,' he said, 'your life is of such consequence to your husband, your children, and to your country that to neglect it is the greatest immorality you can be capable of.'

'Sir Robert, my dear friend, you flatter me.'

'It is no flattery, Madam. I would be frank. This country is in your hands. The King's fondness for you and the regard he has for your judgement are the only reins by which it is possible to restrain the natural violences of his temper or to guide him to where we wish him to go. We know that he does not care for the company of men, but cares greatly for that of women.'

'You think he may have a mistress who will seek to influence him?'

'That is possible. She might govern him. But I was thinking that if you do not take care of your health you may not be with us and he might marry again. What then? What if the Prince were inflamed against his father more than he is already? Oh, I see a thousand dangers which would come to this realm if you were not in the position you now hold.'

The Queen smiled sadly. 'Your partiality to me, Sir Robert,

makes you see many more advantages in having me, and appre-
hend many greater dangers from losing me, than are indeed the
effects of the one or would be the consequences of the other.'

'But you agree there are dangers?'

'The King would marry again if I died, I am sure. Indeed I
have advised him to do so. As for his government, he has such an
opinion of your abilities that were I removed everything would
go on as it does now. You have saved us from many errors, and
this very year have forced us into safety whether we would or
no, against our opinion and against our inclination. I own this.
The King sees it; and you have gained his favour by your obstin-
ate but wise contradiction, more than any minister could have
done by the most servile compliance.'

Sir Robert kissed her hand for he believed it was noble of her
to confess her fault; but it was what he would have expected of
a woman of her intelligence.

'I need you, Madam,' he said. 'I believe that without your help
I should not be able to persuade the King into any measure he
did not like. So, therefore, I beg of you take care of your health.
I think I will not go to Houghton.'

'But why not, my dear Sir Robert! You need to guard your
health even as I do.'

'I am so concerned for you.'

'But this is nonsense. Go you shall. I order you.'

'Then if you will allow Lord Hervey to send me accounts of
your health . . .'

'I shall command him to do so.'

'In that case, Madam. I take my leave.'

When he had gone, Caroline lay on her bed, and there were
tears in her eyes when she reflected on the friendship of her dear
gros homme.

When Walpole left the Queen, he went straight to Hervey's
lodgings to tell him of the interview and how he wished him to
keep a watch on the Queen's health.

This Hervey said he would do; and he added his fears to Walpole's.

Then Walpole, as was his custom, proceeded to tell Hervey
all that had been said.

Hervey suddenly clapped his hand to his mouth and said: 'A fearful thought has struck me. The King may have heard every word you said!'

Walpole grew pale. 'This will be the end for us both!' he declared.

'I may be wrong,' said Hervey. 'But I must tell you that I went to look for the Princess Caroline shortly after you joined the Queen. You know she always leaves her mother when you arrive to talk of state affairs.'

Walpole nodded.

'One of her pages told me that she had left her mother when you went in and joined her father who was with the Princesses Amelia, Mary, and Louisa. He went through into the Queen's bedroom with them; and you know that is the room next to the Queen's closet in which you were talking to the Queen.'

'He could have heard every word!'

'If he listened.'

'Certainly he would listen. I remember once how he deliberately hid himself in a closet and left the door open so that he could hear what passed between myself and the Queen.'

'Then ...'

'I can only repeat. This will be the end of us both.'

'He will have been forced to see himself as you and the Queen see him – not the all-important king from whom all wisdom flows. This is disaster.'

'You must find out if it is true. Can you?'

'I am sure I can.'

'Then for God's sake do and let me know before I leave for Norfolk. If he has heard what we said then I may as well stay there. As for the Queen ...'

'Leave it to me. I will discover.'

So a very discomfited Walpole left; and it was not a bad thing, reflected Lord Hervey, for all men to see how easily, when they are at the height of power, they can fall to ruin.

Walpole would be feeling now as Hervey had when he had thought Anne Vane was going to die in his bed.

He was almost certain that the King had not overheard, for he had a shrewd idea where he would have gone after he had a few words with his daughters.

Still it was good to know that the great Walpole regarded him as such an invaluable friend; it was very gratifying to have him waiting eagerly for the note which would reach him early next morning.

He went to the page to whom he had spoken before and asked where the King had gone when the Princess Caroline had joined him and his sisters.

The page smiled.

'He went to the nurseries, my lord.'

'I'll swear he spent a long time discussing his children's education with Lady Deloraine,' said Hervey lightly.

At which the page gave a veiled snigger.

Scandal quickly went the rounds, thought Hervey.

He then went direct to Walpole's house in Chelsea because it was always so much more pleasant to deliver welcome news in person and Walpole would remember how his good friend did not wait until the morning.

He was greeted eagerly.

'All is well!' cried Hervey, 'He was *not* in the Queen's closet, and instead of hearing your truths he was talking love and devotion with his daughters' governess.'

They laughed together, like old friends. The bond between them was stronger than ever.

And when Hervey was next with the Queen she spoke to him of her anxieties over Walpole.

'He seemed to me so anxious. He is worried about his position, I believe. These last elections shook him. I feel that some of the spirit has gone out of him.'

Lord Hervey loved to enlighten people, particularly those in positions of power such as the Queen or Walpole, so he whispered confidentially that Walpole's troubles were more personal than political.

'Oh?' said the Queen. 'Does this in any way concern that woman he so dotes on?'

'She is ill, Madam. And could be dangerously so. This is one of the reasons why Sir Robert is so *distrait* at this time.'

'Poor Sir Robert! But I am surprised that a man of his talents should feel so deeply towards such a woman.'

'Your Majesty has heard gossip of this woman?'

'Well, I heard that he paid so much for her and that she makes demands upon him.'

'I have heard that he paid £6,000 "entrance money"!'

'You are an *enfant terrible*, my child.'

'Would Your Majesty care to terminate this rather shocking conversation?'

'I have lived too long at court to be easily shocked by the morals of those about me. Pray go on.'

'Maria Skerrett lodged with her stepmother next door to Lady Mary Wortley Montague, and that's how Walpole met her. He was immediately attracted, but then before he met her he was flitting from woman to woman like a gay old ram in a field of sheep.'

The Queen laughed.

'And, so the story goes, the transaction was made and a year later young Maria was born. Then our minister acquired the Old Richmond Lodge and made a home of it for them all. And every weekend, there he went to enjoy the sweets of domesticity. He was a changed man since he met Maria.'

'I am glad he has amusement for his leisure hours. She must be very clever to have him believe she cares for him.'

'Perhaps, Madam, she does.'

'What, that man with his gross body, that enormous stomach, and his swollen legs!'

Poor Caroline! thought Hervey. She is envious of this devotion between her minister and his mistress. She is beginning to find the strain of placating George unbearable.

'Well, I hope she is soon better and that care is lifted from his shoulders,' said Caroline briskly.

They began to talk of other things and he sought to amuse her with some of the verses he had written about the court personalities.

He was very grateful to be on such terms with the two most important people in the country, to have such a power over both of them.

To work thus in the shadows was a role which became him well.

The Prince and his mistress

The King had been thinking of Hanover for some time. He talked of it continually and whenever he did so his voice would grow soft and his eyes become glazed with tenderness. Finally he announced his intention of paying a visit to his foreign dominions.

Walpole, returned from Houghton, whither he had taken Maria to recuperate after her illness, had now recovered from his melancholy since Maria was well again. He called on the King who received him testily in his private closet, expecting that he had come to protest about the proposed visit to Hanover. He was right.

'Your Majesty,' began Walpole, 'a visit to Hanover will at this time be very unpopular with the country.'

'If there is no visit that will be very unpopular with me,' retorted the King.

'At this time, when there are disturbances on the Continent . . .'

'In which we are not involved as you so wished,' put in George.

'In which, sir, we are most happily not involved. It is not a good moment for the visit. If it could be postponed . . .'

'It has been postponed too long. There will be no more postponements.'

'Parliament is about to rise,' said Walpole. 'There will be business to attend to. To send dispatches from my home in Chelsea
to St James's or Kensington is an easy matter. To send them from
London to Hanover . . .'

'They'll survive the journey.'

'The King of Prussia is Your Majesty's enemy. He would seek
every chance of discomfiting you. Who knows, with affairs as
they now stand, he might decide to drive you out of Hanover.'

'Let him try! Nothing would please me more than to show
him the stuff I'm made of.'

'Your Majesty would agree that for you to be involved in combat with Prussia would not be to England's advantage.'

'Enough!' said the King.

'Your Majesty, I must point out to you . . .'

'Pooh and stuff!' shouted the King. 'You think to get the better of me, but you shall not!'

There was nothing Walpole could do but retire.

He went to the Queen.

Could she persuade the King to see reason?

Caroline looked at him steadily and he saw that this was
another occasion when she was not on his side.

'He continues to talk of Hanover,' she said. 'He will go on
fretting and fuming until he has what he wants.'

'Madam, the situation is dangerous. He will be with his German advisers. They might persuade him to enter the war.'

'He could not do it without the consent of Parliament.'

'The Opposition would support him merely to discomfit me.'

'If you decide there shall be no war, there would be no war.
That was what happened, was it not?'

'I have reduced my majority, Madam, and increased my enemies. I should prefer the King to stay in England.'

The Queen did not speak. How ill she looks! thought Walpole. Oh, God, why will she not admit it? There is something
wrong. Is she hiding it? What does Charlotte Clayton know?
Could he ask her? The woman had always hated him so it was
hardly likely she would tell him.

He understood suddenly. The Queen wanted the King to go

because she needed a few months rest from his eternal tantrums, from his husbandly attentions, from his ill-temper. The Queen needed to be free.

Walpole had never doubted the importance of the Queen. He respected her mind and her judgement. It was rarely that they disagreed; and over this matter of war she had admitted she was wrong. The fact that she could admit this enhanced her value in his eyes.

He needed the Queen, and the Queen needed a respite from the King.

Walpole made up his mind. He would put no more obstacles in the way of the King's going to Hanover.

The King left for Hanover and in a few days the Queen seemed to have recovered a little in health. She now rested for a part of the day; she curtailed her walks; she was more relaxed. When Walpole visited her he knew that he had been right to run the risk of what mischief George could fall into in Hanover for the sake of giving the Queen this respite.

Caroline was contented. She kept her daughter, her namesake, at her side as her constant companion, and on the other was, of course, Lord Hervey. How she doted on that man! She could scarcely bear him out of her sight. Walpole was not disturbed, for Hervey was his man too. Hervey was really the son she would have liked. The relationship was of that nature, for they were a perfect trinity – Caroline the mother, Caroline the daughter, and Hervey, so beloved of them both.

The Prince of Wales was growing more and more angry at this friendship between his mother and his great enemy, but who cared for the Prince of Wales? And really young Frederick was a fool. What would happen to the country when he became King, Walpole could not imagine. Fortunately for Walpole it would be some other long-suffering minister's unenviable task to control him. Our conceited little man seems considerably preferable, he thought.

Amelia went on her own way – probably having a love affair with Grafton. Who could be sure? In any case Amelia would know how to take care of herself. William was arrogant, passion-

ately interested in soldiering, like all these Hanoverians, but a
bright boy. A pity he had not been the eldest. The children, Mary
and Louisa, were still in the nursery and the only reason their
names were mentioned outside the immediate family was because they had a pretty governess who had caught the eye of the
King.

We can go on very pleasantly like this, thought Walpole. Let
His Majesty find diversion in Hanover.

The Queen was certainly diverting herself. One day in the
great drawing room at Kensington she, with Lord Hervey and
Princess Caroline, was discussing art, and Lord Hervey looking
at the pictures adorning the walls gave his candid opinion of
them.

'They are very bad,' he said. 'I cannot understand how Your
Majesty can endure them.'

'I've never liked them,' the Queen admitted.

'That fat Venus is quite revolting.'

The Queen admitted that she was. 'There are some excellent
Van Dycks in this Palace,' she said, 'where they are not shown to
advantage.'

'Perhaps Your Majesty would like them brought into this
drawing room and these . . . horrors . . . taken away.'

'I think it would be amusing to make the change.'

'Do let us do it, Mamma,' cried the Princess Caroline, who
always thought everything Lord Hervey suggested was absolutely
right. 'Shall I order it to be done?'

'Pray do, my dear,' said the Queen.

The next day when the trio assembled in the great drawing
room they agreed that the aspect was decidedly improved. One of
the Van Dyck pictures was that of Charles I's children which the
Queen said she liked particularly. The children were so charming and it was so sad to remember what happened to their
father.

Being rested, she felt better, and she decided to put into action
a plan which she had had in her mind for a long time. The King,
as she explained to Hervey, hated spending money except on
show for what he considered his own state.

'Henrietta Howard never had very much, poor soul, although

she was his mistress all those years – a position in which normally a woman might have made a fortune to comfort her old age.'

'Poor Henrietta. I hear George Berkeley is courting her.'

'How is it you hear all the news, *mon enfant?*'

'I feel it my duty to gather it for the sole purpose of diverting Your Majesty.'

'Well, I have a diversion for you. You are going to help me plan Merlin's Cave.'

He had heard of this project which she had long cherished. It was to be a combined library and waxwork show in Richmond Park. Secretly he believed she wanted to give employment to a poet, a certain Stephen Duck. He was the son of a peasant in Wiltshire and worked as a thresher on a farm. But he had written some poems which had come to the Queen's notice and, because they had been written by this humble man, she was much impressed and sought to help him. To mention poetry to the King was to ask for snorts of derision, so the only way to award such a man was to do so in George's absence.

Stephen Duck was to be the Librarian in this small thatched building with its romantic Gothic windows; and, among lifesize waxwork figures which Caroline had added to the place, were effigies of Merlin and his secretary, Queen Elizabeth and Elizabeth of York, wife of Henry VII. There were several busts of philosophers and metaphysicians whose works had interested Caroline when she lived at the court of the Queen of Prussia and which she had had little chance of studying since her marriage.

The building of Merlin's Cave provided a great deal of interest during those days and the people flocked into Richmond Park to see and admire it.

Both the Queen and Walpole had hoped that the King would find Hanover diverting so that he would not make his visit too short.

They did not guess how diverting this would be. The first indication of this came from the King himself. As usual whenever he was absent from the Queen, he made a habit of writing regularly to her. These were no mere notes, but epistles which ran to forty or even sixty pages. His passion for detail had always been strong; in these letters he gave it full expression. Caroline knew how he passed every minute of his day. He would describe the food, the weather, the behaviour of his servants. So it was only natural that he should tell her of his excitement over a lady he had met in Hanover.

'My dear Caroline, she is young and beautiful. She is of the first fashion and I shall not rest until I have made her my mistress. I think of nothing but this charming creature. How different from these English women! Her name is Amelia Sophia de Walmoden and she is married to a Hanoverian Baron, but I do not expect much opposition from him. This, of course, makes no difference to my love for you, my dear Caroline, and I know that you will wish me every success when I tell you how greatly I desire to be the lover of this beautiful enchanting creature . . .'

When Caroline read this she let the letter flutter to the table in dismay and anger. Oh, my God, she thought, was there ever such a man! Why is it that other men keep their amours secret from their wives and this husband of mine seems to imagine that I have pleasure in sharing them!

Even so at that stage she was not unduly alarmed. He was writing and telling her how his courtship progressed step by step. She was too delicious a creature it seemed to be unduly hurried, but his dear Caroline, knowing the man he was, would guess at his impatience. Perhaps she, being of the same sex as his delightful enchantress, would be able to help him understand the dear creature. Did she think he should feign slightly less interest? Or should he declare himself wholeheartedly?

Caroline showed the letters to Walpole who read them with shocked amusement.

'At least, Your Majesty,' he said, 'we get our information at the fountain head. If this is a passing affair no harm done, but I should not like him to become too enamoured of one particular woman.'

Later he returned to say that he had discovered that Madame de Walmoden was related to Ermengarda Schulemburg and the Countess von Platen. The Platens had supplied many mistresses to the royal house of Hanover including Ermengarda Schulemburg; therefore the lady might be of a clinging disposition. Walpole thought the situation should be carefully watched.

'And your advice as to how I should answer this letter?'

'I am sure Your Majesty has already made up your mind that the only way to deal with this matter is to sympathize. In that way we shall be made aware of every detail of the affair as it progresses.'

It was a painful way. Each week the letters were growing longer and longer and more and more space was devoted to his affair with Madame de Walmoden.

It was not progressing quite as speedily as he, the ardent lover, could wish. Perhaps his methods were not as acceptable to the dear creature as they might be. The Queen should show this to *le gros homme* whose affairs with women had been so numerous that he must be most experienced. Ask his advice. Ask what he would do in similar circumstances. The King would be eager to hear.

When Walpole saw the letter he asked if this was a new departure of the King's, for the Queen seemed dismayed by these revelations.

'He has always talked of his love affairs with women . . . most intimately. He believes that I am so devoted to his interests, and that means his pleasure, that I can only rejoice in whatever way he achieves it. When he has been away on other occasions he has written of his brief adventures but never in quite the same way, never so exuberantly. And of course he talked freely of the women he made love to here at home. But I sense something different about this.'

'That's what I feared,' said Walpole.

Lord Hervey came in while they were talking together and would have left with an apology, but the Queen called him to her and told him what they were discussing.

She showed him the letter; and after that she showed him all the King's letters, so he too was fully aware of the growing importance of the Walmoden affair.

'I know you will rejoice, my dear wife, that Madame de Walmoden has now become my mistress. What joy! I was not in the least disappointed.'

There followed a description of the event and the peculiar charms of his mistress.

He would like, he wrote, to keep her with him day and night, but that was not possible in view of his duties as Elector and King. But Caroline would remember well the gardens of the Leine Schloss. Well, he had given his dearest mistress apartments there so that she could have a charming view. He, of course, had to spend a great deal of time at Herrenhausen, but Caroline could be assured that he spent as much time with dear Madame de Walmoden as possible. He loved his dear wife none the less because he had this joy in his mistress; and he knew that his dear Caroline must be very happy at this time to know of his satisfaction.

Surely, thought Caroline, such a letter could never before have been written by a husband to his wife!

How firm was the hold of this woman on him?

It was comforting to read the footnote at the end of the letter.

He had heard news of the Princess of Modena, a young woman of immense sexual dexterity who was very free with her person. The Prince of Modena was, as Caroline knew, to pay a visit to England at the end of the year. He wanted her to insist that the Prince bring his wife with him. 'She is a daughter of the Regent of France, the Duc d'Orléans, and I have a great inclination to pay my addresses to her; and this is a pleasure which I know you will want to procure for me when you know how much I wish it.'

Caroline laughed. It was seeing these sentiments written down which made him so ridiculous. He was the man with whom she had lived over all these years, but seen from a distance one had the clearer view. For him with his arrogance, his utter selfishness, his blind conceit she had subdued her desire for learning; she had pretended to follow him, to think no thought that he did not think first.

But how different it had really been! It was she who had led him.

And this silly little man had not the remotest idea of the true figure he cut.

In her reply Caroline gave no indication of the rancour she felt; Walpole was right when he said she must encourage him to give absolute frankness.

She wrote long letters to him, for since he wrote them to her he expected them in return. She told him all the court gossip she could think of and when she heard that Henrietta Howard had married George Berkeley, gave him the news. This was not considered a very good match, for Berkeley was old and neither handsome nor rich; but he had long admired Henrietta and Caroline guessed that the marriage would be a successful one for Berkeley was devoted to her and Henrietta was looking for a quiet and peaceful happiness.

The King wrote that he was surprised his former mistress had married gouty old George Berkeley and he was not displeased, though he would not wish to confer such presents on his friends, but when his enemies robbed him, he prayed God they would always do it thus.

This was a churlish gesture, thought the Queen, towards Henrietta who had suffered so long from the boredom of his visits and the sharpness of his temper.

But perhaps now, compared with the wonderful Madame de Walmoden, every other woman seemed worthless.

Then came a letter in which was a piece of news which Caroline realized must be acted on without delay.

He had found a bride for Frederick. It was time that young puppy was married. They would have no peace until he was. And in any case he was no longer young and should start getting heirs. While at Herrenhausen the Princess Augusta of Saxe-Gotha had been presented to him. He found her a worthy princess in every way and he had decided that she would make a bride for the Prince of Wales.

When this piece of news was imparted to Walpole he was delighted.

'It will please the people,' he said, 'and it will take away one of the Prince's main grievances. We must not allow this oppor-

tunity to pass by. Your Majesty should write to the King expressing your pleasure. And then we must acquaint His Highness
with the good news.'

The Queen sent for the Prince of Wales.

Oh, my God, she thought, this is my son. How she disliked
the prominent eyes, the heavy jaw, everything that so reminded
her of the King! Frederick's manners in public were excellent,
but in private they were far from good. The fact was that he did
not like his family any more than they liked him.

'I have good news for you, Frederick,' his mother told him.
'Your father has a bride for you.'

Frederick's expression lightened. This was the best news he
could have heard.

'Who is she?' he asked.

'The Princess Augusta of Saxe-Gotha.'

'Young?'

'Very young . . . almost too young. Sixteen.'

'That's not too young,' said the Prince with a grin.

'Then you are pleased?'

'I'm in love with the girl already.'

'I wish you would be serious. Your father reports that she is a
worthy match so I think you should prepare yourself for marriage.'

'Prepare myself. I have had so long to think about it that I am
fully prepared.'

Yes, he was insolent. He was more so during his father's
absences because he so resented his mother's being Regent when
he believed he should be.

'I am referring to the mistress you keep . . . rather ostenta-
tiously.'

'You mean Miss Vane?'

'My God, don't tell me there are others to whom I might
refer.'

'There is only Miss Vane.'

'Well, you must make it known that you are no longer interested in her. She should cease to become your mistress. It will be
most unfair to the Princess Augusta if she arrives to find that

you are prominently displaying a mistress.'

'It seems to be a common thing prominently to display one's mistress . . . even though married.'

He was referring to the Walmoden scandal. How did these matters become common knowledge, however much one tried to keep them secret? Officials whispering to their wives? Wives whispering it to servants . . .?

'Nevertheless,' said the Queen, 'as a compliment to a new wife you should not be keeping a mistress . . . openly. So, I beg of you, dismiss Miss Vane.'

Frederick nodded slowly and said it would be his first duty.

Caroline was surprised at his docility. It could only mean one thing. He was tired of Anne Vane.

On his way from the Queen's apartments the Prince met, as if by accident, Lady Archibald Hamilton. She had heard rumours that the Prince was to have a bride and wanted to discover whether or not they were true.

He quickly assured her that it was so, and that his mother had sent for him to tell him that he must rid himself of Anne Vane.

'That is quite true,' said Lady Archibald. 'That affair has been a disgrace because everyone has known that she wasn't true to you.'

The Prince flinched. Like his father he hated references to the possibility of his having been duped. Lady Archibald hurried on: 'Oh, she is a clever one. At least there were many others before . . .'

'Ah, before,' agreed the Prince. 'Well, I shall say my last farewell to her now.'

Lady Archibald said that with a woman like Anne Vane there would always be rumours; she did not think the Prince would be really safe while Anne was in the country. She ought to go abroad for a few years and then everything would be *discreet*.

The Prince smiled at his mistress. Everything was so discreet between them. He didn't think that Lord Archibald had the remotest idea that his wife and the Prince were lovers. He always welcomed the Prince so warmly to his house; and although

certain wags had commented that the Prince's nose seemed inseparable from Lady Archibald Hamilton's ear that was about
the extent of the gossip, for owing to Lady Archibald's discretion
no one had been able to prove that the affair had gone farther
than nose and ear.

Well, this was the opportunity to be rid of a mistress of whom
he had grown tired.

So quickly did the Prince act that Anne Vane had not heard the
rumours and she was surprised when Lord Baltimore, whom the
Prince had chosen as his envoy, called upon her at the house she
had acquired in Grosvenor Street.

Anne thought he was a new admirer and prepared to receive
him coquettishly, when he quickly disillusioned her.

'I come from the Prince of Wales,' he told her.

'For what reason?' she asked quickly.

'He has decided that you and he must end your friendship
because His Highness is shortly to be married.'

'I see. Why does he not come and tell me this himself?'

Lord Baltimore ignored the question. 'His Highness is of the
opinion that to avoid scandal you should leave the country for a
while. He suggests that you settle in France or Holland for two
or three years. Then you would be free to return.'

'France!' echoed Anne. 'Holland!'

'Precisely. Or if you do not fancy France or Holland you will
be free to choose any place . . . as long as it is out of England.'

'I'll see him in hell first!' cried Anne.

Lord Baltimore looked astonished and Anne hurried on. 'You
can get out. You can tell him that anything he has to say to me
he can say himself . . . You can tell him . . .'

Lord Baltimore held up a hand. 'You have not heard all,' he
told her. 'His Highness will continue to give you £1,600 for life
if you obey. If you do not, you will not receive one penny.'

'And . . . his son?'

'The Prince will take care of his education here in England.'

'So I am to be separated from my son?'

'Those are the Prince's terms. It is for you to accept or reject
them. But pray consider what rejection would mean. All those

who have been your friends when you enjoyed the Prince's
favour would perhaps change their feelings towards you when
you were poor and of no consequence . . . which you will most
certainly be if you fail to agree to His Highness's conditions.'

She did not speak. In a few moments her life was collapsing
about her. She knew that the Prince was fickle; she would not
have been surprised to hear of his unfaithfulness, but that he
should send another man to tell her he was giving her up hurt
her pride and robbed her of her dignity.

She controlled herself sufficiently to say that she could not
reply to the Prince yet. She would think of what Lord Baltimore
had said; and Lord Baltimore hurriedly took his leave.

As soon as he had gone Anne sent a message to Lord Hervey.
She must see him without delay.

As soon as Lord Hervey reached the house in Grosvenor Street
Anne threw her arms about him and told him what had happened.

He listened carefully, weighing up how best he could embar-
rass the Prince.

'It is not that I care for that young fool,' said Anne. 'His protection was worth having . . . nothing else. I'll be glad to be rid of
him, but if I go out of England how am I going to see you?'

Hervey considered this. He enjoyed their meetings, though
when she was no longer the Prince's mistress she would not be
able to give him the accounts of that young man's follies; all the
same he was by no means tired of her.

He told her that he did not see why she should be banished
from England. She must write to the Prince and tell him that she
refused to go.

'I write! But you know I am useless with a pen.' A mischievous look had come into her eyes. 'Not like you, my lord. A
pen in your hand is a sword . . . or whatever you want it to be.'

It was true. Hervey could scorn, wheedle, plead, and make
love with words.

He sat down and wrote a letter in the name of Anne. In this
he reminded the Prince of all they had been to each other. She
regretted that he was to marry, but she had been prepared for
this; what she was not prepared for was banishment. Her child

was the only consolation she had left and she could not leave him. Nothing but death would make her leave the country in which her child was. The letter hinted at the blame which would attach itself to him when it were known how he had treated her.

When she read the letter Anne chortled with delight. She wanted to send it to the Prince immediately, but Hervey would not allow this. She must copy it out in her own handwriting before she sent it.

He suggested that she sit down and do it while he watched her and forced her to obey it. Once this was done Hervey took the precaution of destroying the original.

'Now,' he said, 'we must not be hasty. Before you send this letter to the Prince you must show it to your brother and ask him whether he thinks it is advisable to send it, for if he did not and blamed you for it he might disown you and that could be disastrous since it would give the Prince the support he needs to act in this dastardly way.'

Anne looked at him with admiration.

'I will obey you in all things,' she told him; and while she went to her brother's house he returned to his lodgings in St James's to think about the matter.

The Queen was breakfasting with her family and Lord Hervey was in attendance when the Prince of Wales called. He was in a passion of rage and never had he looked more like his father.

He threw the letter on to the breakfast table, for since his father had gone to Hanover his manners inside the family circle had grown worse. He was very angry with his father for refusing him the Regency and with his mother for having it, and as his friends continually pointed out the injustice of this he could never forget it.

And now in addition to that he had received a letter the like of which he declared could never have been addressed to a Prince before.

'Read that, Madam, and tell me if you think it was written by Mistress Anne Vane.'

The Queen read the letter and Amelia and Caroline stood on either side and looked over her shoulder reading it with her.

'You should be able to tell far better than we whether she wrote it,' said Amelia. 'We were never on such terms of intimacy with the creature as you were.'

'She is certainly erudite,' said the Queen. 'Look at this, my lord, and see if you don't agree.'

Hervey took the letter and read it.

'She has a way with her pen,' he admitted.

'What nonsense!' cried the Prince. 'The woman never wrote that letter. Some scoundrel wrote it for her.'

'Has Your Highness any idea which scoundrel?' asked Hervey. 'There must be so many in Your Highness's circle.'

The Prince was too incensed to feel the barb. 'No,' he cried, 'but I am going to find out.'

'Will she not tell you?' asked the Queen. 'She must be proud of a friend who would do so much for her.'

'She swears she wrote it herself. She is showing it to all her friends and boasting about her cleverness.'

'How difficult it is to cast off a mistress!' sighed the Queen. 'I pray you will not allow too large a scandal to be created over this woman. The people would not like it, nor would your bride.'

'You can depend upon me to settle this matter to *my* satisfaction!' cried the Prince.

And not glancing at Lord Hervey whom he detested, he flung out of the room, cursing his father for not allowing him to be Regent, Miss Vane for daring to send him such a letter, and Hervey for being in continual attendance on his mother.

Poor Frederick always seemed to get the worst of any bargain, and even in this one Anne Vane outwitted him. So piteously did she tell her story that the whole court was humming with it. She could starve in England, she declared, if she would not go abroad and be parted from her child.

This was a dastardly way to behave, said Anne's brother and Lord Hervey and others. The woman had been his mistress; he no longer desired her and he was about to marry; but he must remember his obligations.

Frederick floundered ineffectually. He denied that he had sent such a message; then he recapitulated and said he had written to Miss Vane because a friend of hers had intimated that the settlement he offered would be agreeable to her.

Everyone was talking about the affair of Miss Vane, and the Prince was in such a position that he could only declare that she should continue in her house in Grosvenor Street and that he would pay her £1,600 as long as she lived.

Hervey walked to her house and was let in by Anne herself and smuggled up to her bedchamber that her servants might not see him.

She was exhilarated.

'I've never been so comfortably placed in my life,' she said. 'All this and no encumbrances. I wish him joy of his Augusta. Poor girl, I pity her!'

They laughed over the affair and she told him that she had had some anxious moments, for after all it was dangerous to do battle with a Prince; but she had such good friends and she would always be grateful to them. However, the affair had brought on her fits of colic and her doctors had suggested she go to Bath for a few weeks.

'I shall leave little Fitz with my brother and his family while I go,' she said. 'They'll be happy to have him.'

'Don't stay away too long,' Lord Hervey instructed.

She passionately assured him that she would not and that very soon they would resume their exciting adventures.

This they did not do, however, for Anne had not been long in Bath when her little son died of a convulsion fit. When she received this news Anne had an attack of what she called the colic. It was rather more severe than the previous ones and her doctor ordered her to keep to her bed for a few days.

In a week she was dead.

The Prince of Wales was overcome with grief at the loss of the little boy whom he claimed to be his son.

'I should not have thought him capable of such emotion,' said the Queen.

The King's temper

Meanwhile the King was finding it more and more difficult to delay his departure from Hanover, for with each day Madame de Walmoden seemed to grow more irresistible.

There were despatches from Walpole. His presence was needed in England. His Majesty had not forgotten his birthday and that his subjects would take it ill if he was not in London on that day, which was one of universal celebration.

He knew it – yet he delayed. But the time came when he could delay no longer if he were to be in England in time for the birthday. He had already given himself the minimum of time to reach home, not accounting for any delays which could so easily occur on the way.

Madame de Walmoden declared that she did not know what she would do without him. He meant everything to her. He was the most handsome, charming, intelligent man she had ever met and if he were the humblest servant in his own household she would still love him.

George basked in this admiration and believed it. His mistress was so convincing. She had also told him that she was pregnant and she could not bear that he should not be there when their child was born.

'I will soon be here again,' he promised.

'Do you mean that?' she asked tearfully. 'Will you swear?'

'I swear,' he declared solemnly.

'I must have a date to look forward to.'

He sighed. November ... December ... January ...

She shivered. 'You must not attempt to cross the sea during such months. I should die of fear.'

He kissed her and assured her that that fat old man in London would try to put a chain on him and certainly not let him off it so soon. 'But ... by May ... the end of May, then I shall come. No matter what they say, I shall come in May.'

'Seven whole months!' she sighed.

'My dearest, they do not want me to come once a year. They are going to do everything they can to prevent me in May.'

She did not press the matter but she constantly talked of the 29th of May.

The night before he left Hanover there was a banquet over which he presided with a great deal of melancholy which the Hanoverians found very flattering, although they knew that the reason that he was so sad was because he must part from his mistress. Still, she was a Hanoverian – one of them; and the King made it clear twenty times a day that he loved their country and hated the one of which he was King.

Madame de Walmoden toasted him with tears in her eyes.

'The 29th of May!' she cried, and everyone present took up the cry.

'The 29th of May!' responded George.

After a night of passionate love and protestations of fidelity on both sides, the King left Hanover next morning, realizing that if he were to make the journey in time for his birthday he must travel fast.

Caroline was returning to the Palace after morning chapel when a messenger hurried to her to tell her that the King was on his way to Kensington and would be there very shortly.

She hastily summoned the court and went to meet him.

As George alighted from his coach he managed to suppress the pain he felt. He was wretched, uncomfortable, and unhappy. It had been a trying journey for he had made it in less than five days by riding far through the night and scarcely stopping at all for rest and food. As a consequence this had brought on an attack of haemorrhoids from which he suffered intermittently; he was tired, and in pain, and moreover he was angry because he had left his mistress and wouldn't see her for a long time. As he grew farther and farther from Hanover and nearer to England he realized that there were going to be lifted eyebrows and, worse still, remonstrances when he suggested returning to Hanover 'so soon', as they would say.

All this did not make a very happy homecoming.

And here he was at Kensington. Too grand, he thought. Too ostentatious compared with dear Herrenhausen. And Caroline. She was fat. Doubtless she had been guzzling chocolate more freely than ever since he had been away. His dearest Amelia Sophia managed to have exactly the right amount of warm, soft flesh without being fat.

But this was his dear wife and he loved her. She was his comfort and he would never forget that. She was smiling and so happy because he was home.

She bent and kissed his hand and with a gesture of tenderness he took her arm and they went into the Palace together.

He wondered how he managed to keep his temper while all the ceremonies went on. There were as many ceremonies in Hanover – but somehow they seemed more reasonable; in any case he was in pain and he wanted to go to bed and he hated being ill because he always felt that was a slur on his manhood.

At last he was alone with the Queen.

She was anxious, but one did not suggest that the King might be ill.

She said that it must have been a tiring journey.

He told her exactly how long it had taken between each stage and grew quite animated doing this. He doubted the journey had ever been done so quickly.

'It must have meant long hours sitting in the coach,' she said. He looked at her sharply. So she guessed.

He said gruffly: 'I had better see one of the physicians. Have him brought here without fuss. Let no one know that I have sent for him.'

The Queen nodded. This distressing complaint! She sympathized. He hated her to know of his humiliating illness; and she was determined to keep the knowledge of hers from everyone – except of course Charlotte Clayton. And *she* would never have known if she had not guessed.

'I will see that the physician comes with as little fuss as possible. I will tell Hervey to arrange it.'

The King grunted his satisfaction and lay on the bed. She took his hand and was alarmed to find how feverish he was. How foolish of him to exhaust himself with such a journey unnecessarily. He could have taken ten days – had he given himself time.

Well, dear Lord Hervey would see that everything was conducted with the utmost secrecy.

She was right. The physician came and treated the King; but when he suggested that His Majesty should take to his bed for a few days until the fever subsided the King told him not to be a fool and that he would take orders from no one.

He rested until the next morning, then he was up at precisely the same time that he rose every morning. No matter what pain he suffered, how much fever he had, no one at court was going to know it. But there was an outward sign of his disorders which he made no effort to suppress. His temper flared up at the slightest thing; not only that, he seemed to look for trouble, as though abusing everyone around him soothed the pain he was suffering.

A pity he hadn't remained in Hanover with his darling mistress, said the court. That was where he wanted to be and Heaven knew no one wanted the disgruntled little man here.

The Queen was in the drawing room with her daughters, and of course Lord Hervey was in attendance, when the King came in. He looked at his watch testily as though to ask what they were all doing in this particular place at this particular hour.

The Queen looked at him nervously. He had always been of

a violent temper, but it had never flared up quite so frequently – and for such trifles – as it had since his return from Hanover. She could tell that he was in pain, although the fever had subsided.

'Gossip, gossip, gossip!' he said. 'That's all that seems to go on in this court. I can tell you it is different in Hanover.'

He scowled at them all and kicked a footstool out of his way; the effort clearly gave him a stab of pain which made him glare at the stool. But that inanimate object could not soothe his irritation, so he turned to the Queen.

'Your Majesty breakfasted well?' she asked tentatively.

'Breakfasted well! When, Madam, did I ever breakfast well in this country? Tell me this: is there an Englishman living who knows how to cook? Or an English woman for that matter? The English are the worst cooks in the world.'

Lord Hervey tried to soothe matters by saying that he would send his own cook to His Majesty's kitchens for he was sure that the man could not fail to please.

'I beg of you do no such thing,' snapped the King. 'There is no man in England who can cook to my satisfaction. There is no servant, sir, who knows his duty. Look at those chairs! I will not have them placed near the window thus. I have said so a hundred times. The English servants have no sense.'

The Princess Caroline hurriedly changed the position of the chairs. The King watched her with derision.

'No Englishwoman knows how to walk across a room. They should take a lesson from the people of Hanover. And you're getting fat like your mother. That gown is too drab. It makes you look sallow. My God, the women of England should go to Hanover and learn how to dress.'

'Your Majesty is fortunate to possess such a paradise among your dominions,' murmured Hervey.

The Queen was startled at the hint of sarcasm, but the King missed it; his eyes became slightly glazed with fond memories. The Queen was relieved for a moment and then it immediately occurred to her that he had never been quite like this before; he was more under the influence of that Walmoden woman than she had realized.

The King came out of his reverie and noticed the pictures. He stared as though he could not believe his eyes.

'What has happened to the pictures?' he asked.

Everyone stared blankly at the walls.

'Have you all turned silly?' he shouted. 'These are not my pictures.'

The Queen said: 'We thought a change would be pleasant. We decided to put these Van Dycks here instead of the old ones.'

'I don't find the change pleasant.'

'These are very excellent pictures,' ventured the Queen. 'The others were of no great value.'

'I do not find them excellent and I want the old pictures back here . . . at once, do you understand.' He looked at Hervey and said: 'See to it . . .'

Hervey was startled, for some of the old pictures had been so worthless that he and the Queen had decided they were no good for anything and had given them away; others the Queen had said should be sent to Windsor.

Hervey murmured that some of the pictures had gone to Windsor and that it would not be easy to get them back quickly. 'Would Your Majesty allow the two Van Dycks to remain . . . for a while? I am sure Your Majesty will agree that they are very fine.'

The King's eyes looked red as they did when he was angry.

'I'll swear that you have been giving your fine advice to the Queen when she was pulling my house to pieces and spoiling all my furniture. I suppose I should be grateful that she has left the walls standing. Keep those two Van Dycks if you like, but take away those nasty little children hanging over the door. I will not have them, I tell you, I will not have them. And do this quickly. I want to see it done before I leave for London tomorrow, for I know if I do not see a thing done with my own eyes it will not be done.'

'Your Majesty cannot mean that he wants the fat Venus put back over the door.'

'And why cannot I mean that, pray? I tell you, my lord, that is exactly what I do want . . . and what I mean to have. Oh, I have not such nice taste as your lordship. I happen to like my fat

Venus better than anything you have given me. See that my orders are carried out.'

'At Your Majesty's service now ... as always,' said Lord Hervey.

The King turned to the Queen.

'It is time that we walked.'

She rose immediately and he carried her off to the gardens to scold her for pulling down his house in his absence, for daring to suggest he hadn't her fine taste, for stuffing so much chocolate that she looked like a pig, for planting too many flowers in the garden; in fact he must give way to his anger that Kensington was not Herrenhausen and Caroline not Amelia Sophia de Walmoden.

Sir Robert came to the Queen's closet to talk to her very privately.

There was no use hiding from the truth, he said; he was a man who must speak the truth and he knew that the Queen respected frankness. In fact it was the only way in which they could be of use to each other. The Queen assured him that she was of this opinion.

'There is no doubt,' said Sir Robert, 'that in Madame de Walmoden we have a danger which we have never had to face before.'

'I believe,' replied the Queen, 'that in time he will forget her.'

Sir Robert cleared his throat. 'And how has he been with ... Your Majesty since his return?'

The Queen hesitated and Sir Robert went on, 'I understand. Previously the King has always been your devoted admirer. Now there is a threat in this younger woman. She is three-and-twenty and Your Majesty is three-and-fifty. You cannot compete against youth, Madam.'

Caroline was startled, but she was accustomed not only to the minister's frankness but his crudeness of expression.

'Before,' he went on, 'the King has been enamoured of your person and such feelings are of great use when it is necessary to revert to the art of persuasion. I am sure that your success with the King has been due to the effect you have had on him in the boudoir. Let us face the fact. Your Majesty can no longer hope to exert the same influence in that respect. You must now rely entirely on your intellect.'

The Queen clearly disliked this conversation. She steeled herself to remember that Walpole was only concerned with the good of their alliance and that they should not fail to carry the King with them in spite of her loosening physical hold on him.

'He always declared that however many mistresses he has makes no difference to his feelings for me.'

'That was in the past, Madam. That was when he desired you along with the others and you had the additional value of being his wife – which, to his reasoning, is a fillip rather than an obstruction to passion. But now we have Madame de Walmoden.'

'And you think that he is so enamoured of her that it has completely changed his outlook?'

Walpole nodded grimly. Had not something similar happened to him? There had been no greater rake in London than Sir Robert Walpole until he met Maria Skerrett; and now he was so enamoured of her that he was almost ready to throw up politics for her sake. At least he did not care if the whole world knew what she meant to him. And if that could happen to an old cynic like Sir Robert Walpole, how much more easily could it catch a sentimental man like George II?

'We must try to turn his thoughts from her,' said Walpole. 'After all, we have an advantage in the fact that she is miles away and he cannot visit her. At least without our knowing. And we must do all in our power to prevent little trips to Hanover. That should not be difficult. I can move Parliament to put obstructions in his way. But ... he is dissatisfied and will continue to think of this woman unless we can divert his thoughts. Has he visited Lady Deloraine?'

'He has not mentioned that he has.'

'But he has been in the habit of giving Your Majesty details of his affairs, and if he had, it is to be presumed that he would compare Lady Deloraine with Madame de Walmoden and want to discuss the differences with Your Majesty.'

'He has not mentioned her and I believe that he has been feeling too ill since his return. He goes about his ordinary business, but he suffers great pain although he does not show it.'

'Except in his temper, Madam, which, though never of the best, has deteriorated since his return. How much this is due to his disability and how much to his loss of this woman we shall doubtless discover in due course. But I am not entirely pleased with Lady Deloraine. She is a fool, though I am ready to admit one of the prettiest women at court; but fools can be used by clever men. His Majesty was at one time rather pleased with Lady Tankerville who has now gone to the country. It might be that we should get her out of the country and set her to play quadrille every night in the King's company.'

'He plays now with the Princesses.'

'Madam, it is not possible that the King longs to pass his time in the company of his own daughters when he has tasted the sweets of spending it with other people's. It is better that the King should have a mistress chosen by us than by himself, and although Lady Tankerville is a fool, she is at least a safe fool.'

'I will consider this,' said the Queen.

'I know that Your Majesty appreciates absolute candour,' replied Walpole.

She did of course; but she found the interview embarrassing and it added nothing to her comfort.

When the King arrived at St James's it was to find London almost empty.

'For this,' he cried to the Queen when he came to her apartments to see her before the levée, 'I have been forced to come to London. I must celebrate my birthday. The people expect it. And then the people do me the honour of leaving London. The English are the most ill-mannered people in the world!'

Caroline sighed. If he continued to condemn the English in this way he was going to become even more unpopular than he already was.

'You should be ready by now,' he declared. 'Your women are clumsy fools.'

Caroline saw Mrs Purcell, her hairdresser, wince. She would have to placate her in some way later. Why didn't the King realize that people were noticing how much more ill-tempered he had become, how much more irascible since his return from Hanover; and they all knew the reason for it.

The next thing would be the spate of lampoons.

She wanted to explain to him; but when had one ever been allowed to explain to George?

His temper did not improve when his subjects assembled in his drawing room to pay their respects, and he noticed that they were not wearing their best clothes. He had seen many of the coats before and as he never made a mistake about such details, he knew he was right.

An empty town! An ill-dressed company! A fine way to greet the King!

He asked the Duke of Grafton why he thought so many had come in their second-best coats on such an occasion.

'Your Majesty,' answered Grafton, 'we hope soon to be attending the marriage of the Prince of Wales. Everyone is saving his best for that occasion.'

The King's eyes narrowed. 'I see,' he said, 'that the marriage of the Prince of Wales is of more importance than the King's birthday.'

Grafton looked astonished, for believing himself more royal than George, he had never hesitated to show his feelings. Naturally the wedding of the Prince of Wales would be the most important event since the coronation.

'And I suppose,' went on the King, 'that you will be going to the country in a few days' time?'

'I have always gone to the country at this time of the year, sir. It is the best time for hunting.'

'A pretty occupation for a man of your age to spend all his time tormenting a poor fox that is generally a better beast than those who pursue it.'

'The farmers will tell you, sir, that the fox does great damage to the crops.'

'The fox hurts no other animal and those brutes who hurt him do it only for the pleasure they take in hurting.'

'I must tell Your Majesty that I hunt for my health.'

'Why not walk or merely ride for your health? And if there is any pleasure in the hunt I'm sure you know nothing of it, for with your great bulk of twenty stone no horse, I am sure, can carry you within hearing, much less within sight, of your hounds. No. Sir Robert Walpole must leave London at this time to recuperate his health. And that I understand. His mind needs relaxation and his body exercise. And he has his private business. It is natural enough that he should take a month in the country to see to these matters.' The King raised his voice and his face took on a deeper tinge of scarlet. 'But why other puppies and fools have to run out of town to do their silly business now, when they have had all the summer to do it, I cannot imagine. I have come back . . . against my inclination . . . to find the court empty and every young fool and every old fool running to the country. And I might have stayed in Hanover.'

It always came back to Hanover.

Life, thought Caroline, was becoming almost unbearable. The King's continual irritation was hard to bear, more so now than it would have been earlier, for she was more and more unable to ignore her illness.

There had been one or two occasions when she had almost fainted at a levée and it was only due to Charlotte Clayton and Lord Hervey that she had managed to hide this. Charlotte had now become Lady Sundon, for her husband had been raised to the Irish peerage as Baron Sundon of Ardagh; and this fact had given Charlotte even more prestige in the Queen's bedchamber.

Charlotte was very angry at the King's behaviour and didn't hesitate to say so.

'It is bad enough,' she said, 'to have these wantons in England, but when they lure the King from his duties to his country and exert their influence from across the seas I don't know what things are coming to!'

It distressed Charlotte to see the Queen so saddened, for in the privacy of the bedchamber the Queen could not always hide her sorrow.

Charlotte often felt that she could have slapped the little man for his lack of consideration; she would have liked to pack him off to Hanover where he could have vented his ill humour on That Woman. But of course he would have been all sweetness to her; for the very reason that he was so bad-tempered was that he was separated from her.

'Your Majesty should stay in bed for the rest of the day,' Charlotte said one afternoon when the Queen was preparing to rise from the after-dinner nap.

'Impossible,' said the Queen. 'His Majesty will be coming in less than an hour to walk with me.'

'Your Majesty is unfit.'

'I am well.'

'Not well enough, Madam. I know . . .'

The Queen silenced her with a look. She knew. Yes, she knew! Oh, my God, why did she ever discover! thought Caroline. If this were known it would be the end. He would never return to her. It would be his excuse. And gradually he would slip away, for there was never a man more held by his emotions. The woman who shared his bed could share his confidence.

A curse on encroaching age, on female ailments, on all that could come to a woman.

How peaceful it had been when he was away in Hanover – and how dangerous it had proved!

Far from resting in bed, she must rise earlier, for it took longer to dress.

Her feet were so swollen that they would not fit into her boots.

Lady Sundon was looking at them in dismay which turned to a sort of triumph. 'Now Your Majesty will be forced to rest. I will send to the King and say that you are unwell.'

'I forbid you to,' said the Queen shortly.

'Your Majesty, you cannot . . .'

'Bring me a bowl of cold water . . . as cold as it can be.'

'*Cold* water, Your Majesty.'

'That is what I said, Lady Sundon.'

Charlotte dared not disobey when the Queen spoke in that voice, so she retired and in a short time returned with the required bowl of water.

The Queen signed for her to put it on to the floor and when she had done so plunged her bare feet into it.

'Your Majesty!' cried Lady Sundon in alarm.

But the Queen, wincing a little, managed to smile at her.

After some minutes' immersion in the ice-cold water the Queen was able to put on her boots, and by the time the King called she was ready for their walk.

He looked a little disgruntled to find her on time because he had hoped to scold her for being late; however, he would soon find something of which to complain.

Lady Sundon looked after them as they left the apartment. She was very worried about the Queen's health.

Caroline tried to fight off the feelings of fatigue – and, more trying still, the nagging pain.

It had worsened, there was no doubt of that; but she would not admit it. Far stronger than any discomfort was the urgent desire that no one should know.

So she smiled and pretended she was well and meekly accepted the King's perpetual scolding.

But there were times when it was almost impossible to go on doing this.

One of these occasions occurred one morning when the King had been particularly unkind. She had borne all his complaints patiently, and only the slight flush in her cheeks and the rather nervous movement of her hands betrayed her emotion.

Lord Hervey was in attendance with the Princesses and, as the King was about to leave for his own apartments, she could not hold the words which rose to her lips.

'As Sir Robert Walpole has always been a particular friend of mine,' she said, 'and as he seems to be the only person at court who is in Your Majesty's good graces, I think I shall ask him to speak to Your Majesty on my behalf in the hope that he can persuade you to soften your treatment of me.'

The King stopped and stared at her. The whites of his eyes seemed to turn red.

'I do not know what you mean by these complaints,' he said.

The Queen merely smiled, which made the King grow more angry; but even he was aware of the worsening of his temper since his return from Hanover; and his anger took the form of self-pity.

'I am ill,' he said, 'and I believe nobody is in the same good humour sick as well. And if I were well, do you think I should not feel and show some uneasiness for having left a place where I was pleased and happy all day long and being come to one where I am incessantly crossed and plagued?'

The Queen was suddenly stung to a retort which astonished all those who heard it.

'If Your Majesty was so happy at Hanover why did you not stay there? I see no reason that made your coming to England necessary. You might have continued there without coming to torment yourself and us, since your pleasure did not call you. I am sure your business did not, for we could have done that just as well without you, and you could have pleased yourself without us.'

The King was so astonished at this outburst that he could think of no retort.

He was trembling with rage as he stalked out of the room.

Later Lord Hervey discussed the incident with the Queen.

'Your Majesty has endured so much that it was time you said what you did.'

'I fear I have shocked him deeply.'

'Madam, is it not time that he was shocked deeply?'

'I think he is a little repentant. He is much quieter. And he has promised me some fine horses for my coach. He says they are some of the finest he has ever seen.'

'He must have brought them from Hanover.'

'He did.'

'Where,' went on Lord Hervey, 'horses like everything else in that paradise are much finer than they are in this poor island.'

The Queen laughed. 'I hope you do not let him hear you talk thus.'

'He would think I was showing good sense . . . for once. But, Madam, why has he given you these horses? Firstly to show you how much finer Hanover horses are than English ones; and secondly that you may have the expense of feeding them.'

'You are wicked, *mon enfant*. But what I should do without you to make me laugh in these trying times I do not know.'

Princess Augusta

The Prince's bride

The Prince of Wales was the only member of the court and royal family who escaped the King's bad temper. George's attitude to his son had not changed since his return from Hanover because he had ignored him before he went away and continued to ignore him.

Frederick was delighted that he was to marry. He had always believed that marriage would give him the status he needed, and as he was nearly thirty it seemed ridiculous that a man in his position should be denied a wife.

He was becoming more and more truculent. In the old days he had been a mild young man, intent only on pleasure; but his relationship with Bolingbroke and Chesterfield had changed that.

Bolingbroke had now left England. He had given up the fight. He had hoped for a time to oust Walpole from his position and take his place, but it had become increasingly obvious that this was something he could not do. Lady Suffolk had been his friend and had kept him informed of certain happenings at court, and now she had retired another avenue had been cut off.

Bolingbroke had always spent a great deal of time with writers; he had enjoyed their company and patronized many of them by allowing them to earn a living writing for him. Now he believed that there was nothing in England for him, so he decided to retire to France where he owned Chanteloup, a beautiful *château* in Touraine. Here he said he would devote himself to literature, for his part on the stage of English politics was over and the man who remained on the stage after that deserved to be hissed off.

So to France he had gone, and the Prince felt his loss, but he decided that he was able to manage his own affairs; and now that he was to have a wife he would do what Bolingbroke had told him he should : demand that he be paid an income commensurate not only with his title of Prince of Wales, but with his status as a husband.

He was delighted at the prospect of a young bride. He greatly admired Lady Archibald Hamilton, who was a very different mistress from Anne Vane; but he felt that if he had a pretty young girl as a wife and a handsome, clever woman as a mistress he would be very well served.

He had been very willing to promise Lady Archibald Hamilton a place in his wife's entourage. She should be a lady of the bedchamber, he told her, and there be able to guide the Princess in all that she should know.

Lady Archibald expressed herself willing to take on this responsibility; and she was clearly delighted that the Prince should offer it.

Caroline, hearing of the arrangement, asked her son to come and see her, and when he came she immediately brought up the subject.

'You cannot allow your mistress to be one of your wife's bedchamber women. It will not be fair to the Princess Augusta.'

'It will be ideal for her,' retorted the Prince. 'Lady Archibald Hamilton will be a . . .'

'A mother to her?' asked the Queen slyly.

'She will be a good friend to her.'

'I doubt whether your wife will want the friendship of your mistress.'

'She is to be one of the ladies-in-waiting. I have arranged it.'

'I do not think the King will allow it.'

'This is my wife's household.'

'This is the King's court.'

'And if I appoint her, what do you propose to do about it?'

'The King could dismiss her. He could even retire the lady from court.'

The Prince was startled. He had powerful enemies, Chesterfield had told him that. Walpole was his enemy and Walpole had great power. One never knew what that man would do if he and the King and Queen put their heads together.

'You think to use me as you will,' he mumbled.

'I wish you would speak up,' said the Queen.

'There is the matter of my allowance,' he began.

She looked astonished and replied: 'I thought we were discussing your wife's household. But let me tell you this: If the King is displeased with that you will never get an increased allowance.'

The Prince bit his lip in rage.

'I have promised Lady Archibald Hamilton . . .'

The Queen interrupted, 'Your wife will have four main ladies-in-waiting. I suggest that the three appointments which have been put forward and which do not include the lady in question be granted; let the other remain open and when the Princess arrives, if you can persuade her that Lady Archibald Hamilton is the best possible choice then let the lady have the post. But I am sure you will agree that in such circumstances it is your wife who should decide.'

The Prince hesitated. This was a way out. He would have to explain to Lady Archibald who would readily understand; and when Augusta came – young Augusta who was only a girl – he would quickly make her do what he wanted her to. The position was safe for his mistress.

'Then that matter is settled,' said the Queen; and he did not deny it, for at that moment the King came into the Queen's drawing room and gave the Prince his now familiar stare which Lord Hervey had said made one feel the Prince was a ghost invisible to the King.

'Why are you not wearing your cloak?' said the King to the Queen. 'We shall be two minutes late for our walk.'

Sir Robert came to see the Queen and he was very grave.

'I have just made an alarming discovery,' he said. 'The King has promised to return to Hanover in May.'

'You mean he has promised Madame de Walmoden.'

'That is so. She has given birth to a boy which she will assure the King is his.'

'And you have reason to doubt that it is his?'

'Two reasons and many grave doubts.'

'I know the lady has a husband.'

'And His Majesty is not her only lover, although of course she deludes him into thinking he is.'

'I fear he is easily deluded.'

'As we have found to our advantage in the past, Madam. But we are not in the past now, and we have the future to consider.'

'What do you propose?'

'To use every means at my disposal to prevent the King's going to Hanover.'

'And if he is determined?'

Sir Robert lifted his shoulders. 'Who can say?'

'He went before, when you and Parliament wished him to stay.'

'But you wished him to go and so were against us on that occasion.'

'There are often times when I wish he had stayed there.'

'Oh, he will continue to be trying while this passion for that far-off lady obsesses him.'

'Is there no way of breaking that spell?'

'Lady Deloraine is a very pretty woman and he does show interest.'

'But I still think he yearns for Hanover.'

'We must stop his going, for the longer he stays away from her the more likely he is to forget her.'

'He could not leave when the Prince will shortly be married.'

'No. If we can arrange that marriage for June he will certainly not go in May.'

'There seems to be some fixed idea in his mind that he must go in May.'

'Then we will have the Prince's marriage after May.' Sir Robert smiled slyly and Caroline wondered if he had instructed Lord Delaware, who had been sent to Saxe-Gotha to negotiate for the Princess Augusta, not to hurry the matter.

The King was growing angry. The beginning of April and still negotiations hung fire! His temper grew sharper than ever, and everyone felt the brunt of it, but more especially the Queen.

If Lady Suffolk had still retained her old position it would have eased matters, for he would have been spending with her that evening session which he now spent with the Queen. Lucky Lady Suffolk, peaceful in the country with old George Berkeley who, although he might not be handsome or rich, was devoted to her and determined to make her retirement happy. How she would have suffered if she had been at the court at this time! As much as I do, thought the Queen. But she is not here, lucky woman, and I must bear the full brunt.

He would join her in her drawing room at nine o'clock exactly when her children were with her; and she always managed to have her Chamberlain in attendance, for what she would have done without dear Lord Hervey at this time she could not say.

She would sit knotting – anything to employ her fingers – waiting for the time to pass while George would sit scowling as he contemplated his dislike of all things English, or smiling now and then as his thoughts flitted to Hanover and the delectable Madame de Walmoden. His silences were preferable to his outbursts, but alas, they were not usually of very long duration. And after half an hour or so he would usually leave them to retire to his own apartments to write to Madame de Walmoden. Caroline imagined those letters; he would tell her every detail. He was a great letter-writer as she always knew from those times when he was away from her.

She was tired because that day she had been visiting the house of one of the noblemen of the court. She knew how these visits were appreciated not only by the mistress and master of the house, but by the servants to whom she was always gracious.

She looked upon them as a duty, and an extremely enjoyable one.

While the King sat smiling dreamily into the past, she mentioned to Lord Hervey that she was visiting again tomorrow, and she would need money as she had given away all she had to the servants at the house she visited on this day.

'They were so delighted,' she said, 'when I complimented them on my excellent dinner; and it was a great pleasure to see the new pictures they have. Their picture gallery is one of the finest I have seen. I told them that you would doubtless be very interested. You will shortly receive an invitation.'

Lord Hervey replied that he had heard of that collection and he was waiting for the opportunity to inspect it.

The King did not appear to be listening and the Queen said with a laugh, 'I have just been looking at the *Craftsman*. Did you see, my lord, that they have attacked me for making Merlin's Cave? They must be short of scandal to turn their attention to that.'

The King came out of his pleasant reverie and seemed angry to find himself in a less rosy world.

'I am very glad to hear it,' he said. 'You deserve to be abused for such childish, silly stuff. It's the first time I've ever known that scoundrelly *Craftsman* right.'

There was silence; the Princess Caroline looked as though she were about to burst into tears, the Princess Amelia merely scornful, while the Duke of Cumberland stared at the tips of his shoes in embarrassment.

'I mean it,' shouted the King. 'What a silly idea! Wax figures? What next. And books ... ! Who wants books? I'm surprised Walpole advanced the money for such folly.'

'The people enjoy it, sir,' said Lord Hervey, who always made a point of coming to the Queen's rescue, particularly as he realized that the King did not object to this. It was a strange thing, but through all his criticism of the Queen, George's fondness for her was apparent. His snubbing her came from his familiarity; and when she was looking tired he grew more angry than ever, perhaps because secretly in his heart he was worried on account of her health. Much as he longed to be in Hanover with his mistress, he wanted to think of Caroline, his wife, in her place waiting for him, never changing towards him no matter how badly he behaved. And Lord Hervey with his peculiar perception was aware of this; and although his own motives were mixed and were born of a genuine affection for the Queen he was always conscious that in protecting her in her skirmishes with the King he did no harm to himself.

'A lot of fools playing childish silly games with a lot of silly waxworks ... and books. Books!' He spat out the word as though it described objects of the utmost contempt. The Queen went on knotting quickly. There were tears in her eyes, which was unusual, but she felt tired and ill and the pain was nagging and she thought: I'm so tired of this. Let him go back to Hanover ... anywhere, but out of my life.

The King saw her lowered head and construed this as indifference, so he went on: 'And giving money to servants when you visit. What silly, childish games!'

The Queen murmured quietly but defiantly that it had always been the custom to reward servants when one visited their employers' houses. 'Is that not so, my lord?' she asked Lord Hervey.

'It is true, Your Majesty,' said Lord Hervey. 'It has always been the custom for the King or the Queen to distribute such largesse. It is expected and would be noticed with great disfavour if it were not done.'

'Then the Queen should stay at home as I do. You don't see me running into every puppy's house to see his chairs and stools. I stay at home. Nor is it for you, Madam, to be running your nose everywhere and trotting about the town to every fellow that will give you some bread and butter, like an old girl that loves to go abroad no matter whether it be proper or not.'

Continuing to knot, the Queen made no answer, but her fingers faltered and the thread became tangled and her efforts to untangle it were fruitless. She held it nearer the candle and in doing so snuffed out one of them.

'Why must you be so awkward?' demanded the King. 'Why can't you sit quietly as I do? Why must you always be doing that silly, childish stuff ...'

He rose suddenly and stumped out of the room. It was ten

minutes before his usual time to retire. A bad sign when he began breaking habits.

Caroline knew where he had gone.

It was to his own apartments to write a long sixty-page letter to Madame de Walmoden, telling how he longed to be in Hanover and that he would soon be there in spite of them all.

'Sir,' said Walpole, 'you cannot go to Hanover until after the marriage of the Prince of Wales.'

'Well, where is this bride of his? Why is her coming postponed?'

'In a matter of this sort negotiations always take a little time, Your Majesty.'

'A little time! I tell you I have made up my mind to go to Hanover in May and nothing . . . *nothing* is going to stop me.'

'But the Prince of Wales's marriage, sir . . .'

'I don't care about the Prince of Wales's marriage. He can go without a marriage. He can have a marriage without me. But I am going to Hanover in May. And you may try to stop me, but you won't succeed.'

Walpole saw that the King was a man bemused. There was no point in delaying tactics. In fact they must be hurried on, for clearly the King would become more unpopular than ever if he could not attend his son's marriage because he had gone off to visit his mistress.

On 25 April, the Princess Augusta of Saxe-Gotha arrived at Greenwich. She was seventeen, very shy, and could not speak a word of English.

The royal family behaved towards her as they had to the Prince of Orange, and ignored her coming. The Prince of Wales, however, went to Greenwich to meet her.

When she saw Frederick she was delighted, for he exerted all his charm. He was very pleased, first because he had wanted a wife for so long and secondly because she was so young and clearly in awe of him. It was so rarely that anyone was in awe of Frederick that he appreciated this very much.

The young girl had stayed the night in Greenwich Palace and here she first saw Frederick.

He took her hands and kissed her warmly. His German was fluent and she told him that she was delighted because she was a little frightened to be among all these foreigners; but Frederick did not seem like a foreigner: when he spoke he seemed as German as she was.

Frederick said he would teach her to be English and she need have no fear of anything while he was there to protect her.

Her eyes were wide with admiration and it was very clear to all the observers that the young couple were pleased with each other.

He was not tall, but his expression was charming and he only looked sullen when he was not smiling – and he had many smiles for her; his eyes were a startling blue and his complexion fresh. She thought him very handsome, although he was smaller than she was.

She had the charm of youth, and although she was tall and slender she moved rather awkwardly, never having been taught deportment; but this *gaucherie* pleased Frederick. He did not want a poised and too beautiful young bride.

That was a very happy meeting and Frederick told her that the royal coach would take them to Lambeth and then they would sail down to Whitehall by barge which would give her an opportunity of seeing the city of London.

She clasped her hands and said that she thought what she had seen of England was wonderful, so different from everything at home. All the people were so sumptuously dressed, and she was going to enjoy so much learning to know England and to understand the English, but just at first she was a little frightened.

There was nothing to fear, said Frederick. She would have the Prince of Wales to protect her.

The King was waiting in the drawing room at St James's Palace to greet his prospective daughter-in-law.

He was slightly mollified because it was only April and she was here; he would be able to leave for Hanover without upsetting people by not staying for his son's wedding.

The Queen stood beside him – a little drawn, though smiling perhaps too affably, too joyously. Lord Hervey was close to her and so was Lady Sundon, both watchful, both guessing how weary the Queen was, and Lady Sundon knowing of the pain and its cause.

The King's good temper was rapidly disappearing, because the Prince and Princess were late.

He looked at his watch. They should have been here half an hour ago!

He said: 'The King and the court have been waiting for half an hour and still the Prince has not brought his bride.'

'The river is crowded today, Your Majesty,' volunteered the Duke of Grafton. 'No doubt their barge is being impeded.'

'Time is time, Grafton, craft or no craft, and I do not like impudent puppies who keep me waiting.'

It seemed as though the bride would be greeted with scowls and reproaches as the time went on, and still the couple did not arrive.

Each minute increased the King's anger, and when news was brought that the barge had reached Whitehall and the Princess was being carried across St James's Park in a sedan, he was almost on the point of retiring to his own apartments.

They could hear the cheers of the people as the Prince and his bride in their sedans came nearer. The King remained, grimly silent; and he did not speak until the Prince led in his bride.

It was not without grace that Frederick presented his shy bride to his parents.

And because she had the charm of youth and because she was so much in awe of him, the King's anger disappeared.

Augusta dropped the deepest curtsy the King and Queen had ever seen and remained kneeling until George said in a soft and kindly voice: 'You may rise, my dear. Let us look at you. Why, I think the Prince is most fortunate. Welcome to England, my dear.'

Augusta blushed and looked very pleased; so that in spite of the fact that she had arrived an hour late, this was forgotten and the first meeting was a success.

There was no point in waiting for the wedding. Indeed in the King's opinion, there was every need that the ceremony should take place without delay, for once it was over he would start making preparations to leave for Hanover and no one was going to stop him.

The Princess looked very attractive in her gown of crimson velvet with its rows of ermine, wearing a crown with one bar, set with diamonds. She was led in the procession to the chapel by her young brother-in-law-to-be, William, Duke of Cumberland; the Duke of Grafton and Lord Hervey were in attendance with the ladies of her household; and the Bishop of London performed the ceremony.

Afterwards at supper, the Prince of Wales sat on the King's right hand with his brother William, and on the Queen's left hand sat the Princess of Wales and her sisters-in-law, the four Princesses.

The Queen spoke very kindly to the bride and found her so modest that she could not help liking her, but, as she said afterwards to Lord Hervey, she feared she was a little stupid and that her mother was to be blamed for not giving her a better education. 'Nevertheless,' she added, 'I daresay she will suit Fred the better for that.'

Then of course there followed that ceremony of undressing the bride, which was done by the four Princesses, and she was put to bed to await the coming of the Prince who eventually appeared in a cloth-of-silver nightgown and a nightcap of fine lace.

Ministers and courtiers walked through the bedchamber to see the young couple in bed; and in spite of her awkwardness and shyness in company, the Princess of Wales seemed not in the least disturbed, for already her husband seemed to have inspired her with confidence.

The King, in his wedding clothes of gold brocade, embroidered with large flowers in silver and pale colours, cut short the ceremony, and taking the Queen's hand, gave the signal to retire and leave the young couple alone.

As they walked out the King commented on the costumes of Lord Hervey and the Duke of Grafton; he had noted the diamond buttons and was calculating that they must have cost somewhere in the region of three to five hundred pounds.

The Queen replied that it was fitting they should on such an occasion. 'As long as,' she added, 'they do not outdo Your Majesty in their splendour, which it is clear they did not.'

In her own yellow silk trimmed with pearls and diamonds, with diamonds at her throat and on her hands, Caroline herself was a glittering figure and the King looked at her with approval. Her gown was low-cut, revealing that bosom which he had once called the most beautiful in the world.

But his satisfaction was short-lived.

'No Englishman knows how to dress,' he said. 'I suppose it is because no English tailor knows how to make a suit.'

'You are comparing them with their Hanoverian counterparts,' the Queen could not resist saying, and she added quickly to change the subject. 'Perhaps now that he is married, Frederick will give us less trouble. She seems a pleasant creature, though dull, and I think she should suit him well.'

'They have dressed themselves up for this wedding as they never did for my birthday,' grumbled the King.

But he was not seriously angry. He was thinking : the wedding is over. I shall be in Hanover for May as I promised.

The Duchess of Marlborough laughed at the marriage. 'A Princess of where, pray? Saxe-Gotha? What *is* Saxe-Gotha? Young Fred will regret the day he didn't get Lady Di.'

And she jeered at the preparations and said that she had heard the bride was a nice little thing but stupid.

'He'll have his regrets before long !'

But Frederick was not regretting. Nor was his bride. They were greeted by cheering crowds wherever they went. The people liked them. Just wait, thought Frederick, until we have a son. Then the people will be all for the Prince of Wales. They're tired of bad-tempered George, anyway.

He would get his hundred thousand a year. He was going to ask for it as soon as it was possible to do so. He would get his privileges. When the King went off to his mistress he, the Prince of Wales, would be the Regent.

Everything was going to be different now. And it was all due to his dear little Augusta who adored him and wanted to do everything to please him.

When he said to her that he knew just the lady to fill the vacant post among her ladies-in-waiting, she listened eagerly.

'It's Lady Archibald Hamilton,' he said. 'I will present her to you.'

'Please do,' cried Augusta. 'Is she young?'

'You would not call her so . . . She is twice your age.'

Augusta clapped her hands with pleasure. 'I was afraid she might be young and beautiful,' she said.

There were some things she had learned, evidently, thought Frederick.

And when Lady Archibald Hamilton was presented to her, Augusta thought her, although a little stern, a very gracious lady.

'Lady Archibald Hamilton hopes for a post in your household,' said Frederick. 'I hope you will agree with me that no one could be more suitable.'

And of course Augusta agreed with her husband.

The King's absence

In the middle of May the King left England for Hanover. The Prince was sulking because once more he had been passed over and the Queen was made Regent.

In his own apartments he raged against his parents and the Princess Augusta listened, nodding her head, looking angry when he did, smiling when he did, agreeing with every word.

The King had not seen his son before his departure, but had sent a messenger to him with a letter which told him that wherever the Queen resided during his absence there would be apartments for the Prince and Princess of Wales.

'Well,' retorted the Prince, 'the apartments may be there but we shan't be in them.'

'No, we shan't,' agreed the Princess.

'I hate them . . . both of them,' declared the Prince.

And the Princess nodded as though he had said something even more clever than his usual utterances.

'And I'll show them.'

She nodded eagerly.

'They're going to be sorry for the way they've treated me.'

'Very sorry.'

'They can't imagine I shall endure these humiliations for ever, or if they do they're bigger fools than I take them for. We are not going to live under the same roof as the Queen Regent ... and we are going to do everything to annoy her. Do you know, Augusta, I think I hate my mother more than my father. He after all is just a fool. She's the one who has made him what he is. She left me when I was only seven ... left me all alone in Hanover and it wasn't till I was in my twenties that I saw her again. There's a mother for you!'

It did not occur to Augusta to wonder in what circumstances the Queen had behaved as she had. Frederick said she had been cruelly neglectful, so in Augusta's opinion she had.

'But I'll be revenged on them. You wait! I'll ask for my hundred thousand. After all it's my due. And when I've got that it will be only a beginning. You'll see, Augusta, the sort of man you've married.'

Augusta laughed gleefully. She was sure she had married the most handsome, the bravest and the best man in the world.

It was no wonder that the Prince of Wales was pleased with his marriage.

Augusta was amused and impressed by the way in which her clever husband outwitted his mother.

She, the wicked Queen, had sent to them from Richmond saying that she intended staying there a while and, in accordance with the King's orders, she thought that the Prince and Princess should join her there.

Augusta listened wide-eyed to what her husband had to say.

'We're not going,' he said. 'We'll write and tell her that you're indisposed.'

Augusta thought this a clever idea; but the Queen, it seemed, was clever too for she wrote to her son and said that since his wife was indisposed she would call and visit her on her sick bed.

This threw Augusta into a panic, but her husband assured her that he had a plan. She would keep to her bed and the room would be so darkened that the Queen would not see her properly so it would not be difficult to feign illness. All she had to do was lie back and look wan.

When the Queen arrived and the Prince came with the Queen to her bedroom, the Princess of Wales was lying in her bed, her eyes closed.

The Queen took a seat beside the bed and asked how she felt.

'Very weak, Your Majesty,' said Augusta, but even to herself her voice sounded high-pitched and false. She was not, she feared, a very good actress.

The Queen inquired about her symptoms in such detail that the Princess became very muddled, but the Queen was kind and said that she would not stay long as she could see that her presence was a little exhausting to one in the Princess's state. On the other hand she had every confidence that very soon her daughter-in-law would be completely recovered.

With that she took her leave, telling herself that one could not blame the Princess whatsoever; she would be a pleasant creature without that odious husband of hers.

She implied to her son as she took her leave that he had not deceived her one bit, and asked him why he had not attended the council which had assembled to see her break the seals of the King's commission which made her Regent.

'My apologies, Madam,' retorted the Prince insolently. 'But I mistook the hour.'

She curtly left him, thinking: we shall have trouble with him. His marriage has not helped us at all.

But at Richmond she summoned her family because she needed the comfort they always gave her – William, her particular favourite, and Caroline, her more constant companion. Caroline she took just a little for granted perhaps, but on William she doted.

Even the King liked his son. William was bright, quick-witted, which was a pleasure to his mother; and his preoccupation with military affairs gave him something in common with his father.

It was a pity, thought Caroline, that Frederick had ever been born.

The less rigorous routine immediately had its effect on the

Queen's health. Lady Sundon was pleased that there were no more of those cold foot-baths which she was sure were the worst possible thing for the Queen's health. If Caroline's legs and feet were too swollen for walking, then she merely pleaded a pressure of business and rested in her bedchamber.

It was a great relief to escape from the King's temper.

He was writing to her every day, long letters describing every detail of his days, and these were largely taken up with Madame de Walmoden.

It had been a wonderful reunion. She was an enchanting creature. He described her body in detail so that Caroline would be delighted to know how happy he was. They had a fine boy now – a very pretty fellow. He wished Caroline could see him.

She showed the letters to Walpole who nodded gravely but did stress the one good point that the King was still as frank as ever and it was an asset to know the exact state of his enslavement.

Then came the letter which set the Queen laughing and yet at the same time made her sad, for it was rather melancholy to have the follies of one's husband so blatantly brought home to one.

The King was in a quandary and he wanted his dear wife's opinion on this matter.

She knew of course that he had given his dear Madame de Walmoden apartments in the Leine Schloss and she would remember the gardens which ran down to the river. Well, one night a gardener had seen a ladder propped against the wall of the Schloss and this was immediately under Madame de Walmoden's window. The gardener was a zealous man who was certain that a thief was trying to steal Madame de Walmoden's jewels; so, cautiously leaving the ladder where it was, he called together some of his fellow gardeners and posting one at the foot of the ladder he and the others made a search of the gardens and – sure enough – they found a man hiding in the bushes. Thinking they had discovered a low fellow bent on robbery, they called the guard and in spite of his protestations the man was arrested. Now comes the awkward part of the story because the man was no low fellow after all, but a diplomat who had come to Hanover on the Emperor's business and was a very high official. His name was Schulemburg and he was, of course, a connection of the Duchess of Kendal. On showing his credentials, he was immediately released, but not before the story was being talked of all over the court.

His dear Madame de Walmoden was most distressed. As Caroline could imagine one so beautiful and enchanting and honoured, of course, through her liaison with the King, was bound to have enemies. She had assured him that the whole thing was a plot contrived by her great enemy, Madame d'Elitz. Caroline would remember Madame d'Elitz, as one of the ladies with whom he had had a little affair of gallantry before he had the great good fortune to discover his peerless Madame de Walmoden. Poor Madame d'Elitz could have been jealous. He would understand that. But there was a great deal of gossip and he could see that so many people did not really believe Madame de Walmoden's story.

Now he trusted his dear wife's judgement, as she knew well, and he would like to have *her* opinion of this little affair.

'Show this letter to *le gros homme*,' he finished, 'for my dear Caroline, he is more experienced in these affairs than you are, and less prejudiced than I myself am in this one.'

Caroline summoned Walpole and showed him this letter. He laughed over it.

'I think, Madam,' he said, 'that this is a step in the right direction. This could well be the beginning of the end.'

But although the King continued to write pages about the affair it soon became clear that his infatuation had not diminished in one small degree; and the fact that he was eager to believe in the innocence of Madame de Walmoden over the ladder affair showed how deeply he was involved with her.

Trouble was in the air. Caroline knew that the Prince was fermenting it. The story of the ladder had leaked out and was seized joyfully by the lampoon writers. The King had never been so unpopular, and this reflected on the government. All over the country there was unrest. In the West of England there were riots among farmers over the importation of corn; and the Spitalfields weavers declared they would no longer tolerate the

Irish workers in their midst who were ready to work for a lower wage than they were. There was fighting among the English and Irish and the Queen ordered that soldiers be called out to quell this. The act enraged the Spitalfields workers who declared that more consideration was given to foreigners than the English since they had foreigners on the throne. They even forgot their own grievances to ask what the Germans were doing here and demanding that they be sent back to Hanover.

'Long live James III, the true King of England!' was a cry which was heard frequently in the streets that summer.

But it was the Prince of Wales who caused the Queen the most anxiety. Trouble was brewing there. His hatred of her had increased since his marriage and she knew it was due to the fact that she had been Regent while he had been passed over. It was alarming to contemplate that he hated her even more fiercely than he hated his father.

She found that she was wishing he was dead. How much less trouble there would be if he were! William would make such a fine Prince of Wales and in time King – and how happily they could dispense with Frederick!

He was teaching his wife to cause trouble, too, although one could not blame her. Poor little thing, she hadn't a mind of her own.

She was obviously instructed to do the things she did, such as arriving late at church and as the only way she could reach her seat when she entered by the main door was by passing along the pew in which the Queen sat, this was very uncomfortable for the Queen, in view of her portly figure – uncomfortable and undignified; yet on every occasion the Princess did this.

She had given orders that no one must enter by the main door if they arrived late which was a direct command to the Princess of Wales.

Frederick had retorted that his wife could not possibly enter by any door but the main one, so he ordered the poor child not to go to church at all if she could not be there before the Queen.

So distressing, so unnecessary; but a sad indication of the deterioration of the relationship between them.

However what struck at the heart of the people more than

anything else was the government's attempt to stop the terrible effect gin drinking was having on the population. Gin was so cheap that it was available to the very poorest and it had become a habit to drink away miseries in the gin palaces which had sprung up all over the country.

One tavern in Southwark had attached a cynical but inviting notice on its door which was taken up by others and was a reminder to the public how cheap gin had become.

> *Drunk for a penny,*
> *Dead drunk for twopence.*
> *Clean straw for nothing.*

The prospect of being deprived of this 'solace' so enraged the people that they determined they would rebel against it; and the ballad-makers were busy turning out laments to the demise of Madam Gin while the taverns put out mourning signs. There was even a mock procession when the Gin Act was passed which paraded with torches through the streets of London and of course became very intoxicated . . . on gin, rioted and caused a great deal of damage.

It soon became clear that nothing could stop the sale of gin and that the result of the Act was merely to set in motion a number of illegal methods of passing it to the consumer. It was sold over many a counter with a wink, in bottles labelled 'Ladies Delight', 'Take 2 or 3 spoonfuls 4 to 5 times a day as the fit takes you', 'Make Shift', 'Cuckold's Comfort' – for whatever happened the English must have their jokes.

At the same time, they were enraged at this attempt to stop what they called 'the pleasures of the poor' and they would talk about it in the taverns over their gin sold by another name and ask themselves why German George should be having his pleasure in Hanover while they were deprived of theirs in London.

The Spitalfields controversy was nothing compared with the anger of an enraged population deprived of its gin, and the government realized that action would have to be taken to modify the Act during the next session of Parliament.

All these troubles were blamed on the royal family and a

rather ugly incident occurred one day when Caroline was riding by coach from St James's to Kensington. Outside a tavern from which hung a huge sign 'In Mourning for Mother Gin' a crowd was standing and as the royal coach approached they recognized it. People stood across the road barring the way so that the coach was forced to stop.

The Queen put her head out of the window and asked what was wrong.

An ugly face was thrust close to hers while a pair of bleary drunken eyes glared at her. Fists were shaken.

'You took our comfort away from us,' they shouted. 'You ride in your coaches but you take our comfort from us.'

'This is a matter for the Parliament,' began the Queen.

But they shouted : 'Where is the King? In Hanover with his whore. Is he allowed to drink gin there, think you?'

'The King will not be drinking gin.'

'No time,' shouted someone. 'Too busy with his whore.'

The cry was taken up and Caroline sat mortified, more disturbed because of the manner in which this scandal had seeped out, than the fact that she herself might be in danger.

'No gin, no King !' someone shouted.

It was an implication that if they were deprived of their gin the King could stay in Hanover for ever.

'Be patient,' cried Caroline. 'Next session you will have them back again.'

'Which?' shouted a voice close to her.

'Both !' she answered.

'You can keep George, but give us our gin.'

'Next session,' she answered, and the coachman, seeing his chance, whipped up the horses and they galloped on to Kensington. It had been an unpleasant experience.

But the internal family strife still remained her greatest anxiety. Even her daughter, Caroline, usually of a mild temper, was beginning to hate her brother. There was great enmity between Amelia and Frederick, because at one time Amelia had thought she might work with her brother. He had soon discovered she was no true friend to him and this had made them dislike each other more than the others did. William of course disliked Frederick with the great passion of a younger brother who knows that but for his elder brother, he would be heir to the crown. It was hard for the ambitious young man William was becoming to take second place to a brother whom his parents wished they had never had, and whom they all wished dead a hundred times a day.

'Fred is our thorn in the flesh,' said the Queen.

Breakfasts were very peaceful occasions now that the King could not descend on them and reprove them for taking too much chocolate. And oh, the comfort of a dish of chocolate! sighed the Queen.

Of course she was anxious about Amelia who was flirting openly with the Dukes of Grafton and Newcastle. She believed that affair with Grafton was quite serious and she was afraid to inquire too closely into it. Amelia was no longer a young girl; she was very much the eldest daughter now that Anne was in Holland, and determined to receive the homage due to her. She was very proud and haughty and this did not endear her to the public, nor to her immediate circle; and her preoccupation with hunting and animals made her appear rather masculine. Caroline was her comfort. Dear Caroline, who was so virtuous and truthful and could be relied upon; but even she was a cause for anxiety, for lately she had been complaining of rheumatic pains and the doctors could do little for them. Caroline was her comfort and William her pride. As for the two little girls, they were young yet, but already showing signs of their personalities. Mary was meek, rather like Caroline, but Louisa, the youngest, was vivacious and impulsive, traits which might well have to be watched as time passed.

The peace of this breakfast was, however, shattered by Caroline of all people, when she announced that she really was most ashamed of her silly little sister-in-law.

'Mamma, what do you think she does? She walks in Kensington Gardens with a page holding up her train! A train, Mamma, in the informality of the gardens! And that is not all. Two gentleman ushers and her chamberlain have to lead the way, and her maids of honour have to walk behind.'

'But this is . . . ridiculous. Why does she do it?'

'Because, Mamma, the silly girl is not accustomed to being the Princess of Wales.'

'Fred will have to learn how easily people can be laughed at in this country.'

'Fred, Mamma, will never learn anything, I fear. He has put Lady Archibald Hamilton among her ladies and the poor little simpleton does not know why.'

'Do not blame her for her simplicity, Caroline,' said the Queen. 'Remember she knows nothing but what Fred teaches her; and after all it is no bad thing to be a docile wife.'

'Let her go on being a docile wife and doing what Fred tells her. That is the quickest way to upset the people.'

The Queen was thoughtful. 'I wonder who allowed her to walk out in that way. Perhaps Lady Archibald Hamilton takes a pleasure in making a fool of her. Caroline, tell her that she should not walk in the gardens like a queen at her coronation. Explain that it would be better if she walked informally as we all do.'

Caroline said rather tartly for her that she would take an early opportunity of telling her sister-in-law what a fool she was making of herself.

Poor Caroline, thought the Queen. I suppose her pains are bad today; she suffers even as I do. And of course, even though her pains came from a less humiliating cause the custom in the royal family was to keep silent about one's ailments.

And here was Lord Hervey come to cheer them. The Princess Caroline's face lit up with pleasure and she looked a different girl from the one who had talked so slightingly of her young sister-in-law.

The most serious disaster of that unhappy summer occurred in Edinburgh. Scotland had always stood behind the Stuarts and had never accepted the Hanoverian rules, so that it was regarded in the South as a spot where trouble could quickly flare up. And it seemed it was about to do so.

The trouble began absurdly when two smugglers named Wilson and Robertson were arrested and put into the Tolbooth to await execution, the penalty for smuggling. This was an unpopular punishment for taxation was never popular and it was believed that if a man was clever enough to outwit the tax men what he gained was a just reward. These two prisoners, however, attempted to escape and their method was to file off their chains and cut through one bar of their window. This they managed, and Wilson who was older than Robertson and considerably fatter, insisted on going first. He did, but he became jammed in the window and and thus not only did he prevent his own escape but that of Robertson also.

The people of Edinburgh were intrigued with the story and all sympathy was on the side of the prisoners. The day of their execution was fixed and, in accordance with the custom, they were taken to church the Sunday before. Wilson, smitten with remorse because his selfishness had prevented the escape of his fellow prisoner, attacked the guards in church and shouted to Robertson to escape, which he did. This exploit delighted the people who did all they could to help Robertson, but Wilson remained and the Captain of the guard, John Porteous, declared that such a dangerous man should be hanged without delay and the sentence should be carried out the next day.

Wilson was duly hanged, but crowds turned out to see the execution and several tried to get the body from the gibbet to give it a decent burial. John Porteous, who was hated by the mob, ordered the soldiers to fire on the crowd and several people were killed.

Porteous managed to reach the guardhouse but so unpopular was he that because of public insistence he was arrested and sentenced to death. He appealed to the Queen who reprieved him.

It was this reprieve which enraged the people of Edinburgh. What right had the German woman in London to interfere in a purely Scottish affair?

They would not have it. 'Let the usurper go back to Hanover!' they shouted. 'And long live James III.'

They stormed the jail where Porteous was celebrating with his friends because of the reprieve. The friends managed to escape but Porteous, afraid to be seen by the mob, hid himself in the chimney. There he was discovered, dragged out of the prison and hanged in sight of the mob.

'So much for Germans!' cried the people of Edinburgh. 'Let them keep their rule for the English. Scotland rules herself.'

When this news was brought to Caroline she was angry. This was a direct flouting of her order; it would have happened if the King had given the reprieve, but it would be said that she had failed, and the Prince of Wales would make much of the failure.

In her anger she began to consider taking punitive measures; but she was quick to realize the tone of the Scottish peers who defended their fellow countrymen in the Lords.

Walpole discussed the matter with her and advised against action. A nominal gesture, perhaps. A fine of two thousand pounds on the city of Edinburgh.

Caroline saw the point of this; and when a young girl walked to London from Edinburgh to see her to beg for a reprieve for her sister who had been condemned to death because of the suspected murder of her illegitimate child, the Queen saw the girl and granted a pardon which the sister triumphantly took back to Edinburgh with an account of the Queen's mercy.

But the Edinburgh affair, while it lasted, had threatened to be an even bigger disaster than the Spitalfields riots or the resistance to the Gin Act; and this was the most troubled of her Regencies.

And as these affairs seemed to settle themselves she was conscious of the real brooding shadow which threatened her peace now and in the future: Frederick.

Frederick did everything he possibly could to upset his mother and show his contempt for her Regency. He would talk openly of the scandal of the Gin Act and the state of Spitalfields workers; he sided with the Scots in the Porteous controversy; he spread the scandal about Madame de Walmoden and the ladder affair; he was constantly reminding his companions of his father's dislike for England, of his long stay in Hanover. It was clear that he was trying to make a royal court just as, Caroline reflected bitterly, she and his father had done when they had quarrelled with his grandfather.

There was one thing above all others which aroused the Prince's fury and that was the knowledge that his parents so deeply regretted his birth, that they wished him dead so that William might be the Prince of Wales. Everywhere the Queen went, William was with her. He was treated as though he were the Prince of Wales.

'Let them give him all honours,' said the Prince to his wife, 'it makes no difference. *I* am the Prince of Wales and nothing can alter that. You wait till we have a son. That will be an end to Master William's hopes for ever.'

'We will have a son,' cried Augusta.

'Many of them,' replied Frederick, 'just to make sure of it.'

The Queen was certain that the Prince would never have a child; she did not think him capable of begetting one. The rumour was that he was impotent and that wise people were paying court to William because he was certainly going to be the next king.

Then the Prince began treating the Princess with that very special care which indicated that she was already pregnant. Nothing official was said about this but the Princess, acting on her husband's orders, played up to the story.

The Queen was anxious and there were endless discussions between her, the Princess Caroline, and Lord Hervey.

The Queen was tormented by the thought of Frederick's having a child, and one day she summoned Lord Hervey to her and told him that she wanted to speak to him very privately.

When they were alone she said: 'The Prince is putting it about that the Princess is pregnant. I do not believe this to be possible. I believe that the marriage has never been consummated.'

'Why should Your Majesty believe this?' asked Hervey, always curious to discover such secrets which were just the kind which appealed to his nature.

'Because I know something of my son. And I believe you know a great deal, too. You know, do you not, that little FitzFrederick was not Frederick's son. He was yours. Oh, come along now, my lord, put aside all affectation and answer me, for I am very anxious to be satisfied.'

'Madam, it is difficult to know who was the father of Miss Vane's son.'

'Perhaps she knew.'

'She did not always speak the truth.'

'No, I'll warrant she told you FitzFrederick was yours, and Frederick he was his. Frederick pretended to believe her. He was so proud of having fathered that boy. A little too proud perhaps. What did Miss Vane tell you of the Prince?'

Hervey hesitated and the Queen said impatiently, 'Pray do not be coy. You and I have talked of such matters often enough.'

'She would describe the Prince as being inexperienced and ignorant, but she did not say he was impotent.'

'It is very important to me to know,' said the Queen. 'If I thought he were impotent I should be very easy in my mind, for then the way would be clear ahead for William. Could you ask Lady Dudley? She was his mistress and as she has been to bed with half the men in town she would know whether Fred is like others or not.'

'There is one way to find out all Lady Dudley knows of course, but I do not think my curiosity is strong enough to make me risk my nose to satisfy it.'

'I know of his great desire to have children and I believe him capable of anything to get the Princess with child. He was so anxious to be thought the father of Miss Vane's child – over-anxious – and although you have perjured yourself by assuring me it was not so, yet I am sure that had he asked you to get a child for him . . . Pray, hold your tongue. I do not want to listen to any more lies on this subject.'

'I was not going to comment on that,' said Lord Hervey, boldly interrupting her. 'But suppose it were true. There is a difference between asking a man to lie with one's mistress and asking him to lie with one's wife. The Princess would have to be in the secret in order to reach a satisfactory conclusion.'

'I am sure if you undertook it you could contrive it, though I don't know how you could bring it about without her knowledge.'

Such a possibility delighted the devious imagination of Hervey. 'If the Prince had consummated his marriage it would be

possible,' he said. 'But if he hadn't, that would be very difficult
. . . nay, impossible.'

'Now suppose you were both willing, how could you, without her knowledge, go to bed with her in his place?'

'It would be simple.'

'My God, tell me how.'

'Well, for a month before the time I would advise the Prince
to go to bed several hours after his wife and to pretend to get up
several times during the night and then to scent himself with
some powerful scent. He would have to accustom her to his
silences in bed and then the man who would be the same size as
the Prince would go into her in his place.'

The Queen laughed. 'You are ingenious, Lord Hervey, and I
love you mightily, but if I thought you would get a little Hervey
by the Princess of Saxe-Gotha to disinherit my dear William, I
could not bear it, nor do I know what I should be capable of
doing.'

'Your Majesty need have no fear. I am the last man with
whom the Prince would enter into such a compact. And my dear
great good Queen, you must cease to fear on this score. The
Prince would never make such a request to any man.'

'I think he is capable of it,' replied the Queen. 'He would hate
to be thought impotent and I think he would go to any lengths
to foist a child on us.'

'No man would enter into such a bargain, Your Majesty. The
risks would be too great. No sum of money would be large
enough to compensate a man for taking such a risk, for who
knows, with such a secret he might easily be found too dangerous
to be allowed to live.'

'He would have the honour of being the father of a King.'

'In secret, Madam. Vanity has little to feed on in private. It is
only in public that it shines. Suppose I had the honour to be born
Your Majesty's son.'

'I wish to God you had,' said the Queen with vehement
affection.

'Your Majesty is very kind, but if it were so and I believed any
man other than the King was my father I should never act as

though I believed it. But, Madam, this is a little play we are making. It may be that the Prince is impotent, in which case the way is clear for His Highness of Cumberland. But if he is not, then the Princess Augusta, even if she is not now with child, may well be one day – and we must make the best of it.'

'You are right,' said the Queen; 'but I fret on this point; and I pray you, if you should hear any rumour as to the Prince's capabilities or the true state of the Princess, tell me without delay.'

'My dear Majesty may rely on me now as ever.'

'I know, I know,' said the Queen. 'You are my comfort in this troublous realm.'

When the King wrote that he would not be back for his birthday, Walpole was seriously disturbed.

He came to see the Queen immediately.

'This is the first time he has failed to come home for his birthday,' he said. 'He knows the seriousness of this. There will be comment and he does not care. This is significant.'

The Queen agreed that it was.

'It means, of course, that he will not leave Madame de Walmoden.'

'Then . . .' The Queen spoke almost sharply. 'He must stay with her.'

'Madam, if he does he will not stay King of England.'

'Then what . . .'

'There is murmuring in the streets already. He was never so unpopular as he is now. More and more people are looking to the Prince. I tell you this can be disastrous . . . not only for the King, but for the House of Hanover.'

'I know it,' said the Queen.

'There is a way out.'

'Pray what?' asked Caroline.

'You must invite Madame de Walmoden to the court.'

'Invite her . . . here?'

'It is the only way. Here she will be to the King what Lady Suffolk was. It is the only way.'

'I refuse,' cried the Queen.

'Your Majesty should consider the alternative. I would feel more comfort from knowing that woman was under our own roof than keeping the King in Hanover.'

'I will not have that woman here.'

'Doubtless Your Majesty will wish to consider this matter. We will talk of it later.'

When Walpole had gone the Queen went to her apartments and refused to see anyone.

This is too much, she told herself. I won't endure it. It's bad enough to read about her . . . but to hear him talk day after day of her charms, of her reactions to his passion . . . Oh, my God, I won't have it.

She was surprised to find that there were tears on her cheeks. It is too much, she thought. Frederick, the riots, the unpopularity, Augusta's pregnancy, real or trumped up, and this nagging pain, this awful foreboding which envelopes me.

She covered her face with her hands and suddenly she was aware that she was not alone. She dropped her hands. Lady Sundon was standing watching her.

'I . . . did not send for you.'

'I sensed Your Majesty needed me. May I help you to bed.'

The Queen felt suddenly defeated. There was no point in pretence now. Lady Sundon *knew*.

'Come, come,' she said, dropping ceremony and talking as though the Queen were a beloved but wilful child. 'You should be in bed. Allow me to help Your Majesty.'

'Oh, Sundon,' said Caroline, 'I'm so . . . tired.'

'I know, Madam. And . . . the pain has been bad today.'

'You knew.'

Lady Sundon went to her knees and kissed the hands. 'I always know, Madam. My heart bleeds.'

'Oh, get up, Sundon.' She laughed. 'It's folly to lie to you. You know, don't you?'

'Yes, Your Majesty. I know.'

'He knows . . . Sundon. He knows too.'

'His Majesty?'

'Yes. He suspected long ago when it first started after Louisa's birth. I told him it would pass. It often happens. He believed me. He wanted to believe me. He always wants to believe we are all well, Sundon.'

'Yes, Your Majesty.'

'And he never spoke of it again and I pretended that it was not there. Oh ... but the pain, Sundon.'

'I know, Your Majesty.'

'And then when he came home from Hanover he was aware of it. He mentioned it and I was angry ... So rarely am I angry with him that I alarmed him. I said he was tired of me, that he made this the excuse ...'

'Oh, Madam, *Madam*.'

'He swore he wasn't, that he never would be. But he is, of course, Sundon. He is. Why am I telling you this? Why ... why ... when I have kept silent all these years? You have known. The secret has been there, Sundon, all these years.'

'But safe, Madam, I have never breathed a word ... never betrayed by a look.'

'I know it.'

'Nor will I ever without your permission.'

'My dear, good friend.'

'But I am afraid. The time has come when you should tell the doctors.'

'Tell the doctors! Never. It has been our secret ... and so shall it remain. I should never have told you if you had not guessed. And thank you ... for keeping silent.'

'Your Majesty, I would serve you with my life but I know there should be no more of this secret.'

'There will always be this secret. Remember that, Lady Sundon.'

'As Your Majesty wishes.'

'Oh, what has come over me tonight. I am behaving like a fool. I talk too much of other things because I am wounded ... deeply wounded. The King will not be home for his birthday.'

'Oh, no, Madam!'

'Yes, it is so. He cannot tear himself away from Madame de Walmoden.'

'Oh, Madam.'

'So, Sir Robert Walpole thinks we should ask her here. The King will not live without her and it seems the House of Hanover cannot live as rulers of England without the King. It is all very simple, Lady Sundon.'

'But Your Majesty will never receive that woman here.'

'So I tell Sir Robert.'

'I should think so! What next! How dare that man! He is so coarse and crude himself that he expects everyone else to be the same.'

'He tells me that I shall change my mind.'

'Your Majesty will not.'

The Queen looked sadly at Lady Sundon.

'Help me to bed,' she said. 'I am utterly weary.'

When the King received the Queen's letter inviting Madame de Walmoden to England, he was delighted.

> You know well my passions, my dear Caroline [he wrote]. You know my weaknesses and that I hide nothing in my heart from you. How I wish that I could be more like you for I so admire you. How I wish that I could be good and virtuous like you but you know my passions and my weaknesses . . .'

My God, thought the Queen, so I do.

He went on to tell her how enchanted she would be with Madame de Walmoden's beauty. She would quickly understand why he took such pleasure in this lady and she herself would be happy contemplating *his* happiness. He wanted her to have the lodging Lady Suffolk used to have. 'That would be most convenient for me to visit her, my dear Caroline.'

Caroline showed Walpole the draft of the letter she had written to Madame de Walmoden.

He was delighted with it.

'A masterpiece,' he said.

'A humiliating masterpiece,' retorted Caroline.

It was impossible to keep secret the knowledge that Madame de

Walmoden was coming to England. The Prince's friends soon discovered it and decided to make the most of it.

It was discussed through the court and the city.

When is the King coming back?

Soon now. He has permission to bring the Walmoden with him. He was staying away until that permission was given. Now the Queen and Walpole are letting the little boy have his own way.

The people in the streets were less polite.

One morning the Princess Caroline, her cheeks flushed with rage, brought a paper into the room where her mother was having breakfast.

'It was attached to the palace gates,' she said.

The Queen read:

'Lost or strayed out of this house a man who has left a wife and six children on the parish; who ever will give any tidings of him to the churchwarden of St James's parish, so that he may be got again, shall receive four shillings and sixpence reward. N.B. This reward will not be increased, nobody judging him to deserve a crown.'

The Queen flushed slightly and went on drinking her chocolate.

The Prince of Wales riding in his carriage through the city with the Princess saw the crowd gathered round an old horse with a dilapidated saddle on its back.

He stopped his coach and asked if there had been an accident.

When he was recognized he was cheered, for the people wanted to show him that anyone who was an enemy of the King was their friend.

Then he saw the notice attached to the horse.

'Let nobody stop me, I am the King's Hanoverian Equipage going to fetch His Majesty and his whore to England.'

The Prince read this in a loud voice and laughed heartily at which the people cheered him more than ever; and they followed him back to St James's shouting, 'God Bless the Prince of Wales and let his father stay in Hanover.'

Caroline was disturbed by these public demonstrations of disapproval.

'What will happen when the King sets foot in England with that woman?' she demanded. 'There'll be a revolution.'

'Have no fear,' smiled Walpole. 'She'll never come.'

'But you suggested I should ask her.'

'Ask her by all means, but I have a strong feeling that she will not come. My brother has always been of the opinion that she would not come.'

Walpole was smiling. It had been a wise move to send his brother, Horace, to Hanover with the King. He was sure then of hearing all he should know.

'She's no fool, this Walmoden. She realizes that her position as the Lady of Hanover to be visited as a special treat puts her in a far happier position than she would be in if she lived in this country. My brother tells her of the life poor Lady Suffolk led. She wants none of that. No, she will find excuses when the time comes. Your Majesty will never have to receive Madame de Walmoden in England.'

'I hope you are right,' said the Queen. 'I admit to profound relief. And if she will not come, what of the King. Will he decide to stay with her?'

'That is something he cannot do. He will have to return very soon.'

The King continued to postpone his departure; but Madame de Walmoden, as Walpole had said, found excuses for not coming to England. She assured him of her fidelity; he must promise to return to her soon; but she could not come to England. She felt that it would jeopardize the King's position if she did. That, she declared, was her sole reason.

In vain did the King plead. She was determined. She would not imperil his crown; rather would she grieve for him in Hanover and hope and pray that he would soon return to her.

The King gave a farewell ball and then another and another. December had come and he was still in Hanover.

The Queen wrote to him that she had alarming news of Anne, the Princess of Orange, who was preparing for her confinement which threatened to be a difficult one. Perhaps he would call at the Hague on the way back. He would still have time before the weather became too bad.

But the King could not bear to leave Hanover and he gave another farewell supper. By that time it was 7 December and he dared not delay any longer, for in a few weeks the weather could grow so bad that he might not be able to leave until the spring.

The Queen waited for his coming, for she had now heard that he had definitely left Hanover, and once he had she knew he would travel with all speed.

The weather turned stormy and the wind howled through the Palace. News came from the coast towns of storm damage; but there was no news of the King.

Caroline was alarmed. If he had put to sea he might well be drowned, for how could any ship survive in the storms which were sweeping the seas?

The King's name was on every lip throughout the country. Where was he? Why was there no news of him? He must be drowned . . . drowned coming from his whore, said the people, with all his sins on him.

The Prince of Wales showed no regret, but he gave himself airs; he was receiving more attention than he had ever received before. The general opinion was that he was in fact no longer Prince of Wales but King of England.

The Princess Amelia went about tight-lipped. If Frederick were King there would be changes. The Princess Caroline frankly declared her horror. This was the worst thing that could possibly happen to them. Fred would have no respect for any of them. He would humiliate them in every way he could think of . . . particularly Mamma. William was making secret plans, wondering how he could discredit Fred and take the throne from him.

And the Queen waited for news and thought of him, the little man who had lived so close to her for so many years, who had snubbed her and bullied her and had declared always that he loved her. What would she do without him? Did she love him? How could she love one who humiliated her as he did, who so recently had planned to subject her to the greatest humiliation of all, who told her the intimate details of his love affairs because he believed she loved him so much that she was delighted to hear them? He was obtuse; he had no love for the things of the mind which once had been so precious to her; he was a silly little man, a bad-tempered, vain, little man – and yet to lose him would be like losing part of herself.

The Prince of Wales came to see the Queen.

He could not hide his delight, so she knew he brought bad news.

'I have a letter which I think you should see, Madam,' he said. 'It is from a friend at Harwich who a few days after that when we believe the King must have set sail, heard distress signals fired at sea. There can be no doubt that these came from some ships of the King's fleet.'

'There must have been many ships at sea on that day,' said the Queen, reading the letter.

'Not many, Madam. I am convinced that this was one of the King's fleet and that we must reconcile ourselves to his loss.'

'I do not think – in that unhappy event – you will have much difficulty,' said Caroline coldly; and she turned away indicating that the interview was at an end.

But by the end of that day a messenger arrived with a letter from the King.

The messenger had been several days at sea in a fearful storm, but the King wanted the Queen to know that he had not set sail as arranged and was awaiting a good wind at Helvoetsluys.

The Prince's discomfiture was as obvious as the Queen's delight. But the position was very quickly in reverse, for no sooner had the King set sail than a storm came up more violently than ever and now there could be no doubt that the King was drowned.

But yet again came the news that although the King had set sail his Captain had prevailed on him to go back to land when the storm threatened and the King had reluctantly allowed himself to be persuaded.

Thus he still lived though the sea parted them.

So overjoyed was the Queen when she heard this news that she wrote to him and told him how she had suffered through her fears that she had lost him. The King, always responding to sentiment, wrote a long letter to her – a passionate love letter, for the first time omitting any mention of Madame de Walmoden. She was the perfect wife; for her he had love which was all her own and could never be shared by any other person. She was his perfect Venus; and the reason he had allowed the Captain to overrule him was because he could not risk the chance of never seeing her again.

When Caroline read the letter she wept with joy. It was the kind of letter he had written in the days of their courtship, for he had always loved to pour out his sentiments on paper.

She could not resist showing it to Walpole who had told her so bluntly that she could no longer hope to appeal to the King's senses.

Walpole smiled cynically. He knew his King, and he was not surprised that the dramatic circumstances had produced such an epistle. Still he was ready to concede that it was a good sign that the King could still write so to his wife.

Now there was the King waiting for a fair wind at Helvoetsluys and the nation was caught up in the drama, as it so liked to be.

'How is the wind with the King?' was the catch-phrase of the day.

And the answer was: 'Like the nation, against him.'

In time the wind turned favourable and the King immediately set sail.

It was mid-January before he reached England and more than eight months since he had left.

The Queen, with all the family, was waiting to welcome him in the courtyard as his coach trundled into the Palace.

Even the Prince of Wales was there, but there were only cold

looks for him. The King had eyes for no one but the Queen, and
with tears in his eyes he embraced her affectionately, that all
might see in what love and devotion he held her.

Accouchement at midnight

'The King is dying!'

This was the theme of conversation in the Prince's apartments. The change in Frederick was being noticed and many people who had followed the King's habit and ignored him, now found him worthy of their attentions.

It would not be long, it was said, before the Prince of Wales was King.

George had returned from Hanover this time in a very different mood from last. The irritable temper flared up now and then, it was true, but it was mingled with moods of subdued affection towards his wife. Whenever he mentioned her, tears filled his eyes and he said again and again that she was the best wife in the world.

He did not mention Madame de Walmoden and Walpole wondered whether that little affair had come to an end; but according to his brother, Horace, the King's farewells to his mistress had been as touching as ever and he had sworn to return to her; and when it was considered that he had delayed leaving her so long that he had not had time to see his daughter who was, it had been thought, at the point of death, it was strange that he should have forgotten his mistress.

The fact was that the King was ill. The trying journey had had its effects on him and he suffered as well from all the depressing ailments which attacked him intermittently.

In fact when it was believed he was with the Queen he was actually keeping to his bed. He would get up, dress for a levée, and come back to bed, so anxious was he to keep the state of his health from his subjects.

Walpole asked the Queen to tell him the truth about the King's condition, and she replied that the journey had been too much even for him and he was merely feeling the consequences of it; but the minister was not entirely convinced; and as he believed the King to be suffering from some malady about which he had forced his doctors to be silent, he was forming all sorts of conjectures.

The King saw that the Queen was anxious and wanted to know why.

She told him that Walpole was suspicious and thought he was suffering from some fatal complaint.

When he heard this George got from his bed and insisted on dressing.

'You should not do this,' cried the Queen. 'You know you need to rest.'

'You know who is putting these rumours about. It's that young puppy. He thinks he is King already. I will show him.'

The King appeared that evening and played quadrille. Lady Deloraine sat beside him and the King paid her marked attention.

'He looks very wan,' said the Prince's friends. 'And what a lot of weight he has lost.'

But George had made up his mind. He was going on with the old routine; and night after night found him at commerce and quadrille, and he was quite clearly showing a very purposeful interest in Lady Deloraine.

He seemed to recover from that night and grow gradually better. He was soon his old self, giving vent to outbursts of temper, flaying everyone within sight with his tongue if they angered him, and visiting Lady Deloraine.

The Prince was disappointed. He had really thought that the King was in decline and that he himself would be crowned within the next year.

He was sulky. It was unfair. First he had been led to believe his father was drowned; then that he was dying; and now here he was as perky as ever – and as maddening.

He deplored the fact that Bolingbroke had deserted him to go and write in France. He had powerful friends in England though. There was Pulteney of course, and Carteret, and men like young Pitt and Lyttleton, and of course Chesterfield.

He summoned them to his apartments to talk seriously of what could be done.

'I'm Prince of Wales. I am nearly thirty. I am married . . . perhaps soon to become father to the heir to the crown . . . and I am treated like a child. I tell you, gentlemen, I shall not endure this much longer.'

Pulteney had realized that it was concerning this matter that the Prince had called them together. In fact it was continually on the Prince's mind. He wanted the £100,000 a year which his father had had when he was Prince of Wales, and since that amount had been taken into consideration when compiling the Civil List, this did not seem unreasonable. He wanted a dowry for Augusta – and if the Opposition made sure, through their writers, that the people knew how the Prince had been cheated of these things by his father, they would all be in favour of the Prince.

The King had been at the height of his unpopularity when he was in Hanover with Madame de Walmoden, and although he had regained a little regard by running the risk of drowning, he was still heartily disliked by his people.

Pulteney saw that the Opposition could bring discomfort to Walpole's ministry by bringing up this matter of the Prince's allowances and at the same time win the Prince's approval. As it was not at all unlikely that the Prince would be King, possibly in the near future, only good could come of it, for once the King died the Queen's power would die with him. It was quite clear how the Prince regarded his mother.

Pulteney therefore declared that with the support of his friends he would bring up in Parliament the question of the Prince's allowances.

When Walpole brought the news to the King and Queen they were furious.

'We could,' said Walpole, 'suffer defeat on this.'

'The young puppy!' bellowed the King.

'These disputes will kill me,' murmured the Queen.

Walpole lifted his shoulders. 'We must face the facts,' he said. 'The Prince has a case.'

'You are the Parliament,' shouted the King. 'You have insisted on having your way in some things . . . and now on this you say you'll be defeated.'

'I have a very small majority now, Your Majesty will remember. Perhaps we could compromise. If Your Majesty would offer the Prince £50,000 a year and give the Princess a dowry . . . and offer this *before* the motion comes on in the House . . . he might accept it. It would be better than what he is now demanding and what may well be assigned to him.'

The King swore he wouldn't and cursed the Prince, Walpole, and the government. They were all a lot of boobies.

But the Queen prevailed upon him to write to the Prince as Walpole had suggested – an effort which misfired, for the Prince was certain of success.

Walpole was his brilliant self in the House. He told of the King's wish to live on good terms with his son, of his offer which had been rejected; and he stressed that this was more than a dispute between a father and son; this was trouble in the royal house, something which could affect the nation. So did he sway the House that the Prince's claims were rejected.

Walpole himself went to the Palace to tell the King and Queen of their victory.

George was delighted.

'You are a man of spirit,' he told Walpole. 'What the Queen and I should do without you, I do not know. As for that young puppy, I'm going to tell him to get out of my house. I'll not have him in St James's. He can leave with his wife at once.'

'Your Majesty,' cautioned Walpole, 'that would be a most unpopular move. It would be remembered how the King, your father, behaved to you – and you know what unpopularity that brought him.'

'This is different. I was ready to be a good son, whereas this young puppy . . .'

'I wish he had never been born,' said the Queen.

Walpole sighed. 'Your Majesty should now make good your promise and without delay make arrangements for the Prince to receive the £50,000 you promised him.'

'I see no reason why . . .'

'Your Majesty, there is every reason . . .'

'I see none. I see none.'

Walpole left the King in disgust and dismay; he knew that he had to be brought round to his point of view.

The Prince was not entirely downcast to have lost the support of the Commons, for his friends, led by Chesterfield, promised to bring up the matter in the House of Lords; this they did, and although here they were defeated again, it was by a small majority and it became clear that public opinion was on the side of the Prince.

Walpole enlisted the support of his ministers to force the King to keep to his bargain and make the allowance he had promised.

The King was furious. 'The motion has been defeated by the Parliament,' he insisted.

'But only, Your Majesty, because of your promise to meet the Prince half way.'

'Half way! Half way!' cried the King. 'That is it, this government is too half-hearted.'

The Queen, who to Walpole's surprise was not on his side, added her voice to the King's and murmured that if the Whigs could be so little depended on, it might be time to see what the Tories could do.

This shook Walpole, because his majority in the house was so small and he knew that it would take very little to bring him to defeat, and that would mean the defeat of the Whigs, and a Tory ministry.

Moreover he knew that Lady Sundon's influence with the Queen was growing stronger, and Lady Sundon had always been his enemy.

Lord Hervey, Heaven knew, was deep in her confidence, but Walpole believed Lady Sundon had some hold over the Queen which even Hervey knew nothing about.

It was an anxious time. And of course soon they would be hearing that the King wanted to go to Hanover, for although he did not mention Madame de Walmoden, he was still writing to her; and Walpole had reason to believe that he was as much enthralled as ever by that woman.

In fact the Queen had no intention of breaking her alliance with Walpole. She respected and admired him too much; but she thought there was no harm done in letting him believe that unless he supported her and the King with all his power she was dissatisfied with him.

'There is one good thing which has come out of this trouble with the Prince,' said Walpole to her one day.

'I can see nothing good in anything the Prince does,' replied Caroline.

'He is restive; he is ready to take strong action should the opportunity be offered to him.'

'What opportunity?'

'If the King should go to Hanover. I foresee fatal consequences if the King left the country at this time.'

This was a matter in which the Queen and her minister were in complete agreement.

Oddly enough, strong as was the desire to be with his mistress, the King saw the point of this too.

The Queen was in her apartments when a letter was brought to her from the Prince. The sight of his handwriting always displeased her and hastily she read its contents, wondering what fresh trouble this might mean.

As she read she was saying to herself: 'I don't believe it. It's a lie.'

She threw the letter on to the table. The Princess Augusta was pregnant. There was no doubt about this, wrote the Prince, and he hastened to tell his mother the joyful news.

Joyful news indeed! He had his income; he had his wife; and now they were going to produce a child.

She went to the King and said she must speak to him alone.

Then she showed him the letter; his eyes blazed with anger.

'It is a lie. He is incapable of getting children. He is an insolent, lying puppy!'

'Do you think this is a plot to foist a spurious child on us?'

'It is such a plan,' declared the King.

'It could well be. I have thought the Prince to be impotent. FitzFrederick was Hervey's. "Why," I said to Hervey, when Molly Lepel's young William was presented to me . . . "that could be FitzFrederick's twin." '

'It's a plot . . . and it shall not succeed. I will command that he and the Princess live under our roof and we will see the progress of this pregnancy.'

'And I shall be present when the child is born,' declared the Queen. 'I shall not allow William to be done out of his rights.'

The Prince knew what was said of him and jeered at his parents. They wanted to pass him over in favour of that insufferable brother of his. Well, thank God the English people were behind him and he was not surprised at that, for he had always loved England. He was not like his father running off to Hanover at every possible moment and declaring his dislike of everything English. The Prince could not understand why the English tolerated such a King.

He disagreed with everything the King said and did. Augusta, the meek little wife, supported her husband. He was the best husband in the world, she declared; and when the time came – and every right-thinking man and woman in England prayed that time would not be long in coming – he would make the best King in the world.

'My child shall be born in St James's Palace,' declared the Prince. 'The Princess and I have made up our minds about that.'

'The child shall be born where I am at that time,' declared the

King, 'and as it will be summer that will be at Hampton Court.'

'I say St James's Palace,' said the Prince.

'I say Hampton Court,' retorted the King.

The Queen's comment was: 'Wherever it is I shall be there. I am going to see the entry of this child into the world.'

The court was at Hampton for the summer and the Prince and Princess were obliged to have their apartments there.

On those occasions when the Prince had to be in the company of his father, the King behaved as though he didn't see his son; and the Prince declared again and again that he resented his parents' attitude; and as for his mother's being present at the birth, he was determined she was not going to be and he was as insistent that the child would be born at St James's as they were it should be born at Hampton.

'In this,' he said to Augusta, 'they see a symbol. Heirs to the throne should be born at St James's and they want to pretend even at this late date that our child will never ascend the throne and that it will go to that dreadful William – on whom they dote.'

'You are right, Frederick,' said Augusta.

'And I am going to outwit them.'

'How?'

'You will see. Leave everything to me.'

'Oh, yes, Frederick.'

'All you have to do is as I say. By September I shall have you installed in St James's, never fear.'

The Prince was with his friends on the last day of July when one of the Princess's women came hurrying into the room in a state of agitation.

'Your Highness,' she said, 'please come at once to the Princess.'

Frederick hurried to his wife's apartments to find her sitting on the bed looking frightened.

'My pains have started,' she said. 'What shall I do?'

'It can't be . . . it's two months too early.'

'But Frederick, I'm sure . . .' She broke off to cry out.

One of the women said: 'The pains are coming fairly frequently, Your Highness. That means that the baby will soon be born.'

'Not here,' cried Frederick. 'Not here at Hampton.'

'There is no help for it, Your Highness.'

'But there is,' cried Frederick. 'Have the coach made ready. We are leaving without delay for St James's.'

The Princess's pains were increasing with every minute.

Lady Archibald Hamilton said : 'Your Highness cannot move her now. It is too late.'

Frederick's jaw set in a sullen manner. 'The child will be born at St James's,' he said.

For the first time the Princess seemed as though she would go against her husband's wishes. 'Frederick, please let me stay here. I can't move . . .'

But Frederick thrust aside all hindrance, and commanded that the Princess be carried down to the waiting coach as quietly as possible and as quickly.

He was determined that she should give birth to her child in St James's Palace.

The Princess shrieked as the coach rattled along at great speed.

'We must reach St James's,' cried the Prince.

'Oh, Frederick, I am dying . . .' moaned the Princess.

'Have courage ! It'll all be over soon.'

It seemed to Augusta that they would never reach the Palace. She would die before they did. She should be in her bed at Hampton with her ladies about to minister to her. This was wrong . . . to be rattling along in this coach over the cobbles and each jolt an agony.

'We are here . . . !' cried the Prince. 'Praise God we are here ! Now carry the Princess upstairs. Put her to bed at once.' His voice had a triumphant ring. 'Her child will be born at St James's.'

There were no sheets to be had, but Lady Archibald Hamilton found a pair of tablecloths and with this made some sort of bed. There were no towels, no hot water . . . nothing of what was required for a comfortable accouchement.

But the child was born – a seven months' baby – a fragile little girl.

It had, so the Queen thought, been an ordinary evening at Hampton. She and Amelia had been playing quadrille. Lord Hervey and the Princess Caroline had been playing cribbage, a habit of theirs now, and one to which the Queen knew Caroline looked forward with more pleasure than Lord Hervey did. The King was paying marked attention to Lady Deloraine and was playing commerce with her and the maids of honour. It was the sort of evening exactly like so many others.

She and the King retired at the usual time and were asleep when they were awakened by a knocking at the door.

The King rose up, startled. The Queen left the bed knowing that something startling must have happened for them to be aroused in this way.

'Is the Palace on fire?' cried the Queen.

'No, Your Majesty, but there is a messenger from the Prince.'

It was Lady Sundon, startled out of her sleep, scarcely believing what she heard could be possible.

'I have just been told that the Prince of Wales has sent to let Your Majesties know that the Princess is in labour.'

'I will come to her at once,' said the Queen. 'Fetch me my robe.'

'Your Majesty will need your coach,' said Lady Sundon. 'The Prince and Princess are at St James's.'

'Are you mad? You're dreaming.'

'No, Madam. The Princess's pains started, so I hear, and the Prince insisted that they leave by coach at once for St James's.'

The King had appeared, the red of his face seeming to be reflected in his eyes.

'What's all this? What's all this?'

Lady Sundon repeated what she had told the Queen.

'The puppy!' cried the King. 'The insolent puppy!' Then he turned on the Queen. 'This is your fault. You're supposed to be so clever. Now they've outwitted you! We shall have a false child put on us, depend upon it. Fine care you have shown for your son William, haven't you? He will be mightily obliged to you. And you deserve anything he can say to you.'

The Queen did not answer him. She turned to Lady Sundon, 'Help me dress. I must be at St James's if possible when the child is born.'

The King did not accompany her but stumped angrily back to bed while the Queen made the night journey to St James's.

There the Prince met her and coldly kissed her hand.

'The child is born,' he said. 'A girl.'

A girl. That made the Queen feel better.

She went to the Princess's bedroom where Augusta lay exhausted. Caroline kissed her and said she was afraid she had suffered a great deal.

'It was nothing,' said Augusta, smiling.

'Where is the child?'

Lady Archibald Hamilton brought it wrapped up in an old red coat and a few napkins. She apologized to the Queen, explaining this was all she could find.

The Queen took the baby and kissed her.

'Poor child,' she said, 'you have come into a troublesome world. It is a miracle that no harm has come to the Princess. What a pair of fools! And I'm surprised at you, my Lady Archibald. You have had ten children, you should have explained what danger the Princess was in.'

Lady Archibald Hamilton turned to the Prince and said: 'You see, sir!' in such a tone that the Queen was satisfied that she had at least attempted to stop the venture.

The Queen went back to Hampton where her daughters Amelia and Caroline were already up waiting to hear the news.

'I have seen the fools,' she said. 'He is a scoundrel and she, poor thing, has no mind. If she were to spit into my face I should just wipe it off and not hold it against her.'

'And the child, Mamma?'

'A poor ugly little she-mouse. If instead of her there had been a brave, large, fat jolly boy, I should have been suspicious. As it is, I must accept the fact that this son of mine is an arrogant fool, but at least he is not an impotent one.'

Shortly after the birth of the Prince's daughter, Lady Walpole died. She and Sir Robert had meant little to each other for years and Sir Robert's immediate thought was that now he would be able to marry Maria.

At the same time he was expected to show some sorrow and the Queen summoned him that she might express her sympathy. This he accepted perfunctorily, but the Queen's desire to know exactly how Lady Walpole had died aroused his interest.

What had been her symptoms? Was she not young to die?

'Death,' said Sir Robert, 'can strike any of us at any time.'

'That I know well,' she said, 'but she was a woman who fancied her comforts.'

'She lived . . . well,' commented Walpole.

'She had had her children. I wondered whether her death was due to . . .' The Queen paused and her manner became almost furtive. 'Some women,' she went on, 'often suffer injuries in childbirth from which they never recover. I have heard of internal ruptures which can be dangerous. I wondered whether this had happened to Lady Walpole.'

'I know of no such thing.'

'You do not think that perhaps she kept it a secret?'

'Why should she?'

'Oh . . . it might be something of which a woman did not care to speak.'

Walpole said: 'It was nothing of that.'

And he knew then that he had discovered the Queen's secret. This was the knowledge she shared with Lady Sundon; and she would tell no one, receive no treatment, because she thought it was too humiliating. Or was she afraid that through it she would lose the King's affection?

It was folly. If the Queen did suffer in this way she should consult the physicians; he believed there was an operation that could be performed.

He went home to discuss with Maria this depressing matter and the exhilarating project of their coming marriage which, for the time, because it would follow so quickly on the death of his wife, they must keep their secret.

Two secrets, he thought. One so morbid, one so joyous; and

neither need be secret. Nor would they be long! Soon everyone would know that he and Maria were married. And the Queen? If she did not look after her health the news of her disability would soon become common knowledge.

The secret betrayed

It was a misty November morning when the Queen decided that she would go to inspect the new library she was having built in the stable yard of St James's.

The King, strangely enough, had raised no objection, and Walpole had somehow found the money from the treasury to enable this project to become a reality. She had been wise, Caroline told herself, to have started the library after the King had returned chastened from Hanover.

Now she was watching it grow with real pleasure and she and her daughter Caroline came every day to inspect it.

It was pleasant, she said to Caroline, to have something that was a comfort to contemplate.

Caroline agreed; they were both thinking of Fred who, since the birth of his daughter, had behaved so badly, particularly to the Queen whom he seemed to dislike more than he did his father. If he had a chance of slighting her, he would seize it and the situation between them all had become so bad that the King had exiled Frederick, his wife and his child from St James's, declaring he would not have him under the same roof.

This was exactly what Frederick and the Opposition wanted. He had taken up residence at Kew and started a new court there. The Opposition was behind him, seeing in him the King who would very soon be on the throne. The young Tories believed that once the King was dead, that would be the end of Walpole and the Whigs; they would have their chance. Therefore the Prince's court was to be feared, and neither the King nor the Queen knew when the next trouble would appear.

So, as Caroline said, it was very comforting to inspect the growing library.

But while she stood there, the smiles on her face became fixed and the Princess Caroline, herself something of an invalid for her rheumatic pains were showing signs of returning now that damp cold weather was back, noticed that something was wrong.

'Mamma,' she said, 'are you well?'

'I think,' said the Queen, leaning heavily on her daughter, 'I should go back to my apartments.'

'It is an attack of colic,' said the Queen, looking at Lady Sundon as though daring her to suggest otherwise.

'I have sent for Dr Tesier, Mamma,' said the Princess.

'I will lie down until he comes. I shall feel better then.'

Dr Tesier arrived and asked the Queen many questions.

'It is my tiresome colic back again. The same as before, you remember, doctor?'

He did remember. It was a most unpleasant complaint while it lasted and after a bout of it the Queen often felt in better health.

'Take a little Daffy's Elixir, Madam,' he said. 'It cured you before. It will do so again.'

Lady Sundon brought the Elixir. When she had taken it, the Queen said she would rest a while.

The King came bursting into the bedchamber.

'What's this?' he said. 'What's this?'

'Her Majesty was taken ill at the library.'

'A waste of money! Who wants libraries!' Then he saw the Queen's pale face and a look of fear came to his face. 'You're a fool,' he shouted, 'to tire yourself with these stupid things. Making libraries for a lot of boobies to gape at. No wonder you feel faint.'

The Queen knew that his abuse in a way measured his devotion for her. He attacked her because he was frightened.

So, she thought, I must look ill.

'We shall cancel the drawing room,' he said.

'No,' insisted the Queen. 'I shall be well in an hour or so. If I sleep now I shall be fully recovered. It has been so before.'

The King was immediately cheered.

'Stupid libraries for a lot of boobies!' he muttered as he left her.

In the drawing room Lord Hervey approached the Queen's table.

'My God, Madam,' he said, 'are you ill?'

'I have had a touch of my old enemy, the colic. I was at the library this morning when it started, so I came back and went to bed.'

'You are still in pain, Madam. What did you take?'

'Daffy's Elixir. Dr Tesier recommended it.'

'Madam, you should not be here. For God's sake, go to your room.'

'You are very vehement, my lord.'

'I fear for you, Madam.'

The Queen did not meet his eyes. She tried to smile at someone who was approaching. Oh, God, she thought, let this pass. Let the King dismiss these people and let me get to my bed.

Lord Hervey stayed by her side.

God bless him, thought the Queen. He is a cynical man, worldly, perhaps a little wicked, but I love and bless him.

She was watching the King, eagerly waiting for him to retire. And now . . . he was doing so and at last she was free.

Oh, the comfort of bed!

Lady Sundon was efficiently helping her to it.

'Rest, Sundon. I need rest. Oh, my God, I feel so ill.'

'Yes, Madam. I think I should send for the doctors.'

The Queen was very ill. There was no denying it. Many remedies had been tried; she had been given snake root and brandy, more Daffy's Elixir, mint-water, and usquebaugh; she had been given clysters, and blooded, and nothing eased her.

The King was frantic with anxiety, cursing the Queen, the doctors, and all those who came near him.

'She'll be better soon,' he insisted. 'It's a colic . . . nothing more. She's had colics before.'

She seemed a little quieter and the Princess Caroline sat by her bed with Lord Hervey, for although she wandered a little in her mind she seemed comforted to have them there.

She spoke suddenly to them and said: 'I have an ill which no one knows of.' And then she closed her eyes and seemed to sleep.

After that she seemed a little better and expressed her anxiety about the Princess Caroline, who was herself ill and should not be sitting up; whereupon Lord Hervey said that he would keep watch by her bedside, and if there was any change in her condition he himself would tell the Princess Caroline without any disguise exactly how the Queen was.

Only then would the Princess leave her mother's bedside.

The King said he would sit in the Queen's bedroom with Lord Hervey and Sir Hans Sloane was sent for and, with Dr Hulse, ordered purging and blooding. Princess Amelia lay on a couch in the Queen's bedroom; and once or twice during the night Lord Hervey went to report to the Princess Caroline what was happening in the sick room.

In the morning the Queen seemed a little better.

As the days passed people began to believe that the Queen was dying.

The Prince of Wales came from Kew to Carlton House.

When the King heard this he shouted: 'If the puppy should, in one of his impertinent affected airs of duty and affection, dare to come to St James's he shall be told I wonder at his impudence. I am in no humour to bear with his impertinence and I shall tell him to get out of my house.'

But soon the Prince was letting it be known that he had come to Carlton House so that he might be near his mother, and this again set the King in a fury.

'This is one of his scoundrel's tricks,' he cried. 'I always hated the rascal and now I hate him more than ever. He wants to come here and insult his dying mother, but he shall not come here and act his silly parts, the false, lying, cowardly, nauseous puppy. And suppose the Queen loved him as much as she hates him, she is not in a condition to bear the emotion.'

The King went to the Queen and sat down by her bed, scowling at her. Get well, that scowl seemed to say. How can I live without you?

She smiled at him and said she was surprised that the Prince had not sent to ask after her. 'Sooner or later,' she said, 'I shall be plagued by some message because he will think it will look well to ask after me. No doubt he hopes I'll be fool enough to let him come and give him the pleasure of seeing my last breath go out of my body, by which means he will have the joy of knowing I was dead five minutes sooner than he would in Pall Mall.'

'You need not fear he will come here,' said the King. 'I have taken steps to prevent that.'

'He is a sad wretch, and if I should grow worse and be weak enough in my ravings to ask for him, I beg of you understand that I am raving. Promise me now that you will not let him come to me.'

'I promise,' said the King.

The King bent over the Queen's bed.

'Caroline!' he whispered.

She opened her eyes and looked at him.

'I'm afraid your illness comes from a thing I have given you my promise never to speak of. I can no longer keep that secret.'

Caroline started out of her languor.

'You must. You must.'

'I cannot. My dearest, I must tell the doctors. They must act. It may not be too late.'

'I beg of you . . .'

There were tears on his cheeks. 'I cannot, my dear. I must not. It is a chance. Do you not see that I will take any chance —'

'Please . . . please . . .'

But he had turned away. She saw him talking to the doctors. She saw the doctors approaching the bed; and she turned her face to the wall and wept.

An operation had been performed on the Queen, but the doctors feared they were too late to save her life. Now there could be no doubt that the Queen was dying.

The King was stricken with grief, roaring his rage one moment, breaking down and weeping the next.

The Queen was in great pain, and now that her secret was known she showed no desire to live. She seemed as though she was eagerly awaiting death.

The King would not leave her. He slept on her bed, giving her restless nights and enduring them himself.

'I must be near her. She will be happier to know that I am near.'

He told everyone how good the Queen was, how there had never been another woman in his life whom he cared for as he cared for her.

He would sit by her bed and remind her of how he had come to court her. 'I loved you then . . . I love you now. You cannot leave me, Caroline. What shall I do without you?'

Then he would grow angry because she was restless.

'You should sleep,' he would shout at her. 'How can you expect to rest when you won't lie still a moment?'

Then he would go back to the days of their youth.

Did she remember when she had first come to Hanover . . . the first days of their marriage? Monsieur de Busch . . . the ardent young man who had come in disguise to court her . . . and he turned out to be the Prince of Hanover, later to be King of England. Did she remember those days at Herrenhausen, at the Leine Schloss?

He would see her as she was then, young and very handsome . . . and this poor woman in the bed was what she had become.

'Don't lie there staring before you like a calf waiting to have its throat cut!' he called out angrily.

Then he was tender again and he would berate the women for not being quiet enough in the sick chamber.

And the Queen continued to cling to life.

Sir Robert Walpole came to her; he had been in the country and had ridden up with all speed when he heard the news.

He was weeping as he knelt by her bed and kissed her hand.

'My good Sir Robert, we have been friends.'

'We are friends ... Madam, friends always.'

'I have not much time left, Sir Robert.'

'I beg of Your Majesty, conserve your strength.'

'Ah, you see me in a different situation. I have nothing to say to you, good Sir Robert, but to recommend the King, my children, and the kingdom to your care.'

'You must recover your health, Madame. We need you ... the country needs you.'

She smiled and said: 'May God bless you.'

She lingered on in pain and often delirious. The King was constantly at her side, forcing food into her mouth because the doctors had said she needed her strength to be built up. She was pleased to have him there, though; for she knew in those days that in spite of all she had suffered through him, in spite of the fact that she had seen so clearly all his conceits and vanities, his follies and his tantrums, yet she loved him, and he was in her thoughts more than anyone else.

She had been ill for eleven days and she knew that her end was rapidly approaching.

She wanted her family about her. She wanted to tell Caroline to take care of her little sisters; she wanted to take her last farewell from Amelia and her beloved William; and then she wanted the last moment of her life to be the King's.

At the last she put her hand in his and said: 'Farewell, my beloved King and husband. Farewell.'

Then she took the ruby ring from her finger and gave it to him. It was the one he had put on her hand at the time of the coronation.

'This is the last thing I have to give you. Naked I came to you; naked I go from you. I had everything I possessed from you and to you everything I have, I return.'

The tears were falling down the King's cheeks. He tried to speak, but he was too overcome by grief.

'Do not grieve too long for me,' she said. 'When I am gone you should marry again.'

'No,' cried the King. 'Never. I shall have mistresses.'

And her dying face was twisted suddenly in a smile as she said, 'That would not stop you.'

Then the King began to weep again and to tell her that he had never loved as he loved her. That he would never know happiness again when she was lost to him.

She rallied and sank, but the end was in sight.

The King was at her bedside when she died. Frantically he kissed her face and hands as though by doing so he could persuade her to return. Then he sent for a picture of her and shut himself in his room with it and stayed there for two hours.

After that he came out and said : 'Take the picture away. There was never a woman worthy to buckle her shoe.'

Sergeanne Golon

Angélique Book One 40p
The Marquise of the Angels

Only the dazzling and incredible world of Louis XIV could have produced the passionate Angélique. Married to the sinister Joffrey, Comte de Peyrac, and installed as Queen in his voluptuous Court of Love, Angélique enters a life of brutal terror and sublime ecstasy – an ecstasy soon to be shattered by her husband's enemies.

Joffrey is taken by the Inquisition and sentenced to death for witchcraft – and Angélique swears to kill the men responsible . . .

Angélique Book Two 40p
The Road to Versailles

Seventeenth century Paris – for the emerald-eyed Angélique a city of wild love and vicious hate. Penniless and alone, sworn to kill the men responsible for her husband's death, Angélique plunges into the squalid underworld – to the nightmare Court of Miracles, home of the deformed and the degraded – a world of violence and lust. Spurred by revenge and ambition, Angélique begins the slow climb back to Versailles, the glittering court of the Sun King himself . . .

Angélique and the King 40p

Angélique challenges the luxurious and licentious world of Versailles to win her rightful place at the glittering court of Louis XIV.

But the path to royal favour is beset with treachery, intrigue, kidnapping and attempted poisonings.

Trapped in the struggle for power between the Sun King's two famous mistresses, the bewitching beauty from the Paris underworld becomes the one woman the elegant, libertine King desires but cannot win . . .

Angélique in Revolt 40p

Emerald-eyed, marble-breasted, with an unquenchable sensuality that makes her beauty irresistible, Angélique flees the silken prison of Louis XIV to become the most hunted woman in his kingdom.

Harried and driven by the King's brutal and licentious cavalry through the forests and marshlands of France, she seeks refuge in the arms of the brave warrior-leader of the rebellious Huguenots.

Must she succumb to the King's insatiable lust or die a traitor's death . . . ?

Angélique and the Sultan 40p

The tempestuous Angélique had known many lovers. But always in her ecstasies of passion, she had been haunted by the memory of her first love, Joffrey de Peyrac.

Now Angélique flees France to risk the perils of Barbary.

In this savage world she learns the horrors of a pirate galley, the degradation of the slave market, the tortures of the seraglio, before being chosen as the beautiful plaything of a lust-crazed Sultan . . .

Angélique in Love 75p

Half-angel, half-devil and wholly woman, Angélique finds herself on board a pirate ship bound for the New World.

An eventful voyage brings murder, lust, storms, mutiny, icebergs and hot-blooded excitement. It also reveals the true identity of the implacable buccaneer captain.

What does the future hold for this emerald-eyed beauty – a happiness she does not believe possible, or a life irretrievably ruined?

The Temptation of Angélique Book One 30p
The Jesuit Trap

Spring comes to the wilderness of New France, and Angélique, as lovely and as sensual as Eve, glories in the torment and delight of passion . . .

Tricked into separation, Angélique finds herself friendless on a frontier ripe for war – a target for Indian attack, Jesuit anger and pirate lust.

Face-to-face with Gold Beard, the Herculean freebooter, Angélique looks again on Destiny . . .

The Temptation of Angélique Book Two 30p
Gold Beard's Downfall

Angélique had lain naked in Gold Beard's arms, responding to his caresses, yet remaining faithful to Joffrey de Peyrac.

Now as savage Indians gather for war, she is humiliated, spurned by the one man she loves, scorned by those whose life she had once saved, a prey to Jesuit hatred.

Her heart torn by conflicting emotions, Angélique watches Joffrey set sail to destroy the blond corsair – Colin Paturel, her desert lover from the past . . .

Angélique and the Demon 75p

Now mistress of the settlement of Gouldsboro, Canada, Angélique feels at peace at last.

But when the man she loves leaves on a mission, Angélique becomes prey to evil forces and unknown strangers – a demon intent on the destruction of her life and her love . . .

Unwilling hostess to the strange but beautiful Duchesse de Maudribourg, Angélique combats poison, intrigue and death – finally to grapple with the unmasked Demon, face to face . . .